Not good!

A Circle of Friends

Jill Ferrell works for the Chandler corporation in San Francisco, which has recently been taken over by Randall Enterprises. The very attractive **Scott Randall** is taking a personal interest in Chandler—and in Jill. Their interest in each other is mutual. But it's not until Jill faces a family crisis that she truly recognizes their relationship for what it is….

Kris Gilroy is a young black woman from Piney Woods, Georgia. She's recently left the protective enclosure of her family and small community. Through her friendship with Jill, Kris meets **Tom Harris** and they quickly, perhaps unexpectedly, fall in love. Kris hides her relationship with Tom, a white man, from her family, who will definitely *not* approve.

David Bernstein, a state senator running for Congress, is one of Tom's public relations clients and a good friend. Dave is married to the wealthy **Claire**, Scott Randall's sister. At Dave's insistence, Claire refrains from using her personal fortune to support her husband's political campaign—or even pay their family's bills.

All friends. And like friends and colleagues everywhere, they influence each other in many different ways.

Like couples everywhere, they learn that husbands and wives need to be equal partners, in love and in life.

Dear Reader,

What a wide, wonderful world would be open to us if our hearts reached out to embrace all people with no barriers against color, creed or class. Such barriers (as I touch upon in my MIRA novel *No Crystal Stair*) were greatly lessened in this country during the civil rights struggle. In this present novel, my characters grasp with *Heart and Soul* the privilege to work, play, live and love in unions that transcend all prejudices. As Kris, my black heroine, declares, "I'm not a category! I'm *me*."

I hope you have as much fun reading about people who refuse to be categorized as I had writing about them.

Eva Rutland

Heart and Soul
Eva Rutland

HARLEQUIN®

TORONTO • NEW YORK • LONDON
AMSTERDAM • PARIS • SYDNEY • HAMBURG
STOCKHOLM • ATHENS • TOKYO • MILAN • MADRID
PRAGUE • WARSAW • BUDAPEST • AUCKLAND

ISBN 0-373-71255-3

HEART AND SOUL

Copyright © 2005 by Eva Rutland.

This edition published by arrangement with Harlequin Books S.A.

® and TM are trademarks of the publisher. Trademarks indicated with
® are registered in the United States Patent and Trademark Office, the
Canadian Trade Marks Office and in other countries.

www.eHarlequin.com

Printed in U.S.A.

To Judy Omer for her vivid descriptions
of the beautiful Alaskan seacoast, details about
the family fish cannery and, most of all, for the
many inspiring pep talks. Thank you, Judy.

ACKNOWLEDGMENT

A wealth of gratitude to Judith Ryan, whose wisdom
and invaluable assistance enabled me to finish this novel
on time with ease and joy. Thank you, Judith.

Books by Eva Rutland

HARLEQUIN SUPERROMANCE
769—A CHILD'S CHRISTMAS

MIRA
NO CRYSTAL STAIR

HARLEQUIN ROMANCE
2897—TO LOVE THEM ALL
2944—AT FIRST SIGHT
3064—NO ACCOUNTING FOR LOVE
3240—ALWAYS CHRISTMAS
3283—FOREIGN AFFAIR
3412—PRIVATE DANCER
3439—MARRIAGE BAIT
3490—THE WEDDING TRAP
3518—THE MILLION-DOLLAR MARRIAGE
3550—HER OWN PRINCE CHARMING
3621—ALMOST A WIFE

HARLEQUIN REGENCY ROMANCE
MATCHED PAIR
THE VICAR'S DAUGHTER
ENTERPRISING LADY
THE WILLFUL LADY
GRETNA BRIDE

CHAPTER ONE *

KRIS GILROY SAT in the family pew at Bethany Baptist Church and kept her eyes closed, refusing to see the coffin, or the body within. But she couldn't stop the tears that rained down her face.

Josie Lee Turner's sweet soprano rose, soft and clear, in the haunting melody of the old spiritual, "Swing low, sweet chariot." Suddenly it seemed that Aunt Freda herself was singing, her own lilting voice painting a picture that flashed beneath Kris's closed eyelids. A beautiful golden chariot swinging from the heavens, angels bending earthward, arms open in welcome... "Coming for to carry me home."

Kris's heart filled with a surge of pure joy. What was there to cry about? Aunt Freda was on her way to heaven. Probably, Kris thought, hardly able to restrain a giggle, straight into the arms of Gus Whitlock and the heaven he'd given her for a brief time on earth.

That had been years ago, long before Kris was born, but the scandal had never died, and even as a child, Kris had heard whispers of her great-aunt Freda's shocking behavior.

Kris's grandpa, Freda's brother, had been in the pulpit then. It had shaken the black community of Piney Woods, Georgia, when the minister's sister left town with some no-account guitar player she hardly knew. Seemed he was with a band that had played for a dance in Macon. He'd stopped off in Piney Woods to visit a cousin. A week later, he took off, and Alfreda Gilroy went with him.

Of course, this had been during the war years, when most anybody might do most anything.

But not Miss Alfreda Gilroy! Not that spinster lady living quietly with her parents on their farm, giving piano lessons and taking in a little sewing, hardly leaving the old place except to attend church where she played the organ and conducted the choir. No one would've expected her to pull such a harebrained stunt, least of all her pa. He was furious, and who could blame him? They might call it an elopement, but gossip had it that the guitar bum hadn't even bothered to marry her! Old man Gilroy had answered her farewell note with a thundering decree that she was never to show her face again.

She never did. Freda hadn't returned to Piney Woods until her father died and even then only for a few short visits.

Strange that Freda had requested she be buried in Piney Woods, with services at Bethany Baptist Church, held by her nephew who'd succeeded to the pulpit when his father died. Maybe, Kris thought, because Papa so resembled Grandpa, Freda's beloved brother, who'd been her unfailing support. Though her departure had left his church without an organist, he had faced his congregation the next morning with a smile. "You know my sister as well as I do," he said, "Freda throws herself heart and soul into whatever she undertakes. This time it's love and I'm glad for her." To critics of her behavior, his only comment had been "Love is a joy, not a sin."

Now Kris did look into the coffin, at the mobile face that still retained a trace of its youthful beauty. *Joy.* That was why Alfreda Gilroy had abandoned family, friends and the only home she'd ever known, to follow Gus Whitlock, guitar player. *Just as I'd follow Tom Harris to the ends of the earth.*

The comparison frightened Kris. True, she'd met Tom Harris *after* she'd left Piney Woods, but had it not been for Freda, she would never have met him. Wouldn't even have been in San Francisco if that letter hadn't come.

Dear Lord, had it been over a year ago? Early June, the beginning of vacation from musty school rooms, chalk and children. She'd been enjoying her freedom, sitting at the picnic table in the backyard, completely absorbed in dabbling, as her father put it, with her paints.

Papa had come out, waving the letter from a woman named Sara Spinella, a friend and neighbor in Freda's San Francisco apartment complex. She wrote that Freda had had two heart attacks, the second one requiring a two-day stint in the hospital. She didn't want Freda to know she'd written, but she was concerned about her, and thought someone in her family should know she was ill.

Papa, who'd always had a fondness for his aunt Freda, even if she wasn't "quite right in the head," was shocked. "Of course we should know," he said. "Somebody should go out to see her right away, and it has to be you, Christina. I have that conference coming up, and since you're on vacation…"

So help her, she'd been glad. Glad of the chance to get away from the church and the choir, the Baptist Young People's Union, Sunday school, the Ladies' Aid Society—and Ed Simmons. Papa considered Ed the answer to any woman's prayer. *Especially mine.* She'd been so glad to get away from this little boxed-up community, where everybody knew what everybody else was doing.

But I did think of you, Aunt Freda. I did! It was a silent cry from her heart to the woman in the coffin. Kris had also had a fondness for her aunt. As a teenager during Freda's short visits, she'd been fascinated by her fashionable aunt, her fancy clothes, alluring perfumes and exciting tales.

Dear wonderful, exotic Aunt Freda! When that letter came, Kris had been eager to go.

Dear Lord, forgive me! Forgive me, Aunt Freda. I didn't want you to be sick, but Papa wouldn't have let me go if you hadn't needed me.

I was the one in need.

But she was thinking of Freda the day she climbed to the

fifth-floor apartment on Elm Street in San Francisco. How could Aunt Freda possibly manage all these stairs in her condition? She must be very dependent on that woman who wrote or her other neighbors.

Kris remembered how she'd pushed the buzzer, quite ready to assume her nursing duties.

No response. Loud music from somewhere inside had drowned out the sound of the buzzer. She recognized the song. It was all about accentuating the positive. She'd once been told the lyrics were written by a man after he'd just left his psychiatrist. True or not, it was darn good advice, Kris thought, the lines running through her mind as she knocked, automatically keeping time with the jazzy rendition.

Suddenly she paused, hearing another sound. Someone was…tap-dancing? What on earth was going on? With Aunt Freda sick… She pounded on the door. Finally the music stopped and she heard footsteps clumping across the floor.

The door opened. Kris stared at the woman in shorts, horn-rimmed glasses on her nose and a pair of outlandish purple tap shoes on her feet.

She couldn't believe it. "Aunt Freda! That was you…tap-dancing?"

"Easier than climbing these San Francisco hills. It's exercise, like my doctor—" Freda broke off to enfold her in a warm embrace. "Christina, child! Why didn't you let me know you were coming? I could've had someone meet you at the airport or… Well, how did you get here? Never mind. I'm that glad to see you. Come on in, let me take your bag, and tell me what you're doing in San Francisco."

"Just wanted to see your city," Kris stammered. Mrs. Spinella had said not to mention that she'd written. "Thought I'd surprise you."

"Bless you! What a *nice* surprise!"

Freda bustled about getting Kris settled in the spare room, talking nonstop about what there was to see in San Francisco.

"We'll cover the town," she promised. "I'll make sure you see it all."

The shiny tap shoes seemed to blink with every step, as if inviting Kris to join the dance.

And what a dance! Several days of plays, musicals and a whirlwind tour, from art galleries to shopping malls.

"There's still the zoo," Freda said at the end of week. "And we'll have to visit the Japanese tea garden."

"But I'm worried," Kris had told her mother when she finally escaped from the apartment and called home from her cell phone. "She hasn't said one word about being ill, Mom. Not one. Just takes me gallivanting all over town. But I've seen her pause repeatedly on the stairs trying to catch her breath. And I can tell when she's overtaxed. She slips a pill into her mouth but she won't even admit that she's tired. I don't know what to do! She's in denial or she's trying to fool me. She almost did. When I got here, she was tap-dancing for Pete's sake! Can you believe it? And now she's busy treating me like royalty and escorting me all over the place. She's not up to it, Mama. I can tell. She gets so short of breath she scares me."

"You've got to do something about that, Christina. She'll kill herself trying to entertain you. Can't you act like you're the one tired or sick?"

Hard for Kris, who was never sick or even tired!

It was Mrs. Spinella who had the answer. "The only way to make her slow down is to slow down yourself," she had whispered to Kris. "Or get too busy to go anywhere with her."

It was with this thought in mind that Kris bought art supplies. "You have such interesting neighbors," she told Freda. "I think I'd like to take some time out and sketch a few portraits."

Two days later, Jerry, from the second floor, stood in Freda's kitchen and whistled as he gazed at his handsome likeness. "Hey, this is damn good! You ought to go into business."

"Great idea." Kris held out her hand. "That'll be fifty dollars, sir."

"Bad start. I'm practically broke." Jerry rubbed his nose, his eyes still on the sketch. "But you've got real talent, girl. Tell you what. I'll set you up in business."

"Ha, ha! Big time-financier, huh? I thought you were broke."

"Doesn't take much for a spot at the flea market. I'll stake you for a month. No interest. You can pay me back when the cash starts rolling in."

Kris laughed. "That is, *if* anything rolls in."

"Wanta bet on it? Hey, I oughta take a cut of the profits. But I'm a good guy and I like you, Kris." He sat down and began to scribble on a pad. "Now, all you'll need are two chairs and an easel. Oh, and art supplies. How're you fixed?"

Kris stared at him. Was he joking about what Papa called her "doodling?" "It's nice to have a little hobby, honey," her father had said. "Keeps you out of mischief."

But Jerry wasn't joking and Mrs. Spinella approved the idea. "If you're occupied, dear, Freda might rest."

A week later, Kris had found herself installed in a little booth at San Francisco's flea market. She quickly settled into a kind of routine. Kris spent half her days in her little booth, astonished that—as Jerry had predicted—people were actually buying her sketches. The rest of her time was spent at the apartment, lugging in groceries, doing the household chores and entertaining Freda with tales from the flea market.

It worked. Freda, relieved of tour duty, succumbed to the rest she needed, and even confessed that those stairs were about to do her in.

It worked for Kris, too. She was having fun doing what she most enjoyed. Still, she had no idea that Jerry's idea would change her whole life.

Tom. Just the thought of Tom sent shivers of delight spinning through her. If she hadn't been in the flea market she would never have met Jill, who'd introduced her to Tom.

In fact, Jill had introduced her to more than Tom. Kris remembered the day the attractive, well-dressed woman had stopped at her booth. Kris had felt like a paint-spattered country bumpkin and was surprised that the woman began to talk with her. Even more surprised when the woman suggested she apply for a job at Chandler Associates, a company Kris had never heard of. "Tell Mr. Gibson in Human Resources that I sent you," she said, handing Kris her card.

After the woman had left, Kris stared at the embossed card. Jill Ferrell, Deputy Administrative Officer, Chandler Associates.

Well, why not? If she had a regular paying job, she'd never have to go back to teaching, back to Piney Woods. It'd be a miracle if she got a position at this Chandler outfit. But...why not try? She looked at the card again. If she brought it with her...

She was right. She was hired on the spot.

What she hadn't known was how much she'd love the job. It was an advertising company where she could put her sketching and creative ideas to work. Papa was always talking about God moving in a mysterious way, his wonders to perform. *Thank you, God,* she'd whispered, *for taking me out of Piney Woods and teaching, and sending me to Freda, San Francisco and this marvelous opportunity to do what I want to do.*

She ought to thank Ms. Ferrell, too, she'd realized. When she phoned to do so, Jill had invited her to lunch. Thinking she should return the favor, Kris had invited Jill to share Freda's pot roast. Strange, Kris thought now, how the country bumpkin and the sleek executive had clicked. Or maybe it was Freda with whom Jill had clicked. "I like that gal," Freda had said. "She's a dynamo. She knows you gotta run to keep up with life."

Whatever the reason, she and Jill had become close friends. She was with Jill when she first saw the tall lanky man with the crooked grin and laughing blue eyes. A man she could love. She'd known it, right there in the coffee shop, even before Jill introduced them.

"Watch this guy," Jill had said. "He's one of those danger-ous love-'em-and-leave-'em types."

Kris couldn't heed the warning any more than she could have stopped breathing. Tom's blue eyes had beckoned and she'd followed. Out of the coffee shop, through San Francis-co's crowded streets and parks…eventually to his bed. Just like Freda, without commitment, promises or legal ties.

And he was not a love-'em-and-leave-'em type. *We've been together almost every minute since that day in the coffee shop.* He'd be with her now, if she'd let him come.

Maybe I should have. He loved Aunt Freda, too. But… Oh, in San Francisco it doesn't matter that he's white and I'm black. But Piney Woods, Georgia, is a long way from San Fran-cisco.

A soft stirring in the congregation awakened Kris to her sur-roundings. Dear Lord! She'd been daydreaming. Back in San Francisco. She hadn't heard one word of Papa's bereavement sermon. He'd just finished and now invited those who wished to speak of Freda.

Kris watched as people rose, one by one, describing anec-dotes and incidents from Freda's life here in Piney Woods.

Strange, Kris reflected. In the months she'd spent with her in San Francisco, Aunt Freda had seldom talked about Piney Woods. It was as if her real life had begun the day she left with Gus Whitlock.

Her stories had always focused on the years she'd spent with the Basin Blues Boys, the songs she'd sung, the towns they played. They'd never made it big, and, according to Freda, had gone through some pretty rough times. Kris smiled. Freda al-ways had them laughing about the bad as well as the good. Never once had she sounded bitter, or even mentioned when or why Gus, the guitar player, had abandoned her.

She'd even laughed as she talked about her years alone in San Francisco—stories about the rich society dames who fre-quented the exclusive salon where she worked as a seamstress, and the crazy happenings at the Candlelight Bar on the weekends she filled in when the pianist was too drunk. As if it had all been fun. Aunt Freda made everything sound like fun.

You were a gift, Aunt Freda. You and San Francisco. New people. New places. The freedom and time to be me. Tom.

I didn't want you to die, Aunt Freda. I didn't.

"Don't cry, honey." Kris felt her mother's hand close over hers. "Freda's at peace now. At rest from all the trouble and turmoil of her life. From all the misery."

Misery? Kris stared at her mother, seeing Aunt Freda, fingers banging the keys of her old upright, head thrown back as she belted it out, "I've had my fun, if I don't get well no more."

AFTER ALFREDA GILROY'S service, the congregation gathered at the Gilroy farm. The old farmhouse that had sheltered three generations of Gilroys had been Kris's home for twenty-five of her twenty-six years. The people she'd known all her life—former students, old friends and, of course, Ed Simmons—reached out to embrace her and welcome her back. As if she, like Freda, had come home to stay.

The house hadn't changed, Kris observed as she gazed around the kitchen the next morning. Everything was as she'd left it more than a year ago. The old-fashioned free-standing gas range, its nickel-plated surface shining, the clock ticking above the built-in cabinets, Mama's geraniums spilling from the glazed pot on the windowsill. Warm and familiar. Embracing….and closing her in.

Even what she was doing now was familiar. As usual after a large gathering, Kris was helping her mother and Miss Lizzie sort and distribute the dishes and utensils piled on the big wooden table. The hard part—washing up, putting away folding chairs and tables—had been done the night before, courtesy of the Baptist Young People's Union.

"Mama's the perfect well-organized minister's wife," Kris thought as she studied her mother. Anna Gilroy stood erect, her small frame trim and neat in a crisp dress. Although she'd been up until after midnight, she looked as fresh as the breeze that drifted through the open window. "Whose is this?" she asked, puzzling over the big casserole bowl she held.

"Rosella Tinsley's," Miss Lizzie said. Miss Lizzie had come to the house to help her mother, from eight to two, five days a week, for as long as Kris could remember.

Anna Gilroy frowned doubtfully. "It could be the one Maude brought with her string beans. Are you sure it's Rosella's?"

"Sure am. Didn't you see her, holdin' it up and talking 'bout how she brung her corn pudding 'cause Freda always loved it so?" Miss Lizzie laughed. "Like she thought Freda was gonna be here to eat it."

Kris laughed with them. But it *had* felt as if Freda had come alive among the old friends who'd gathered after her burial to commemorate and remember her.

"You two carry on," Anna Gilroy said. "I'm going down and put these linens in the washer. Maybe you'll have time to iron them before you leave, Lizzie."

"Yes'm," Lizzie answered, but she was looking at Kris. "Don't put that up there, Christina. I keep them odd pieces over here."

"Oh." Kris turned to hand her the bowl.

Miss Lizzie took it, but stood, just staring at Kris. "Lord, child, I can't get over it. You look different. Citified."

Kris hoped so. Smart and sleek like Jill Ferrell.

"And all your long white folks' hair! Gone! What were you thinking?"

"That it wasn't citified. And it's Indian hair, not white. Cherokee, from Papa's great-grandpa."

"Sure didn't come from us. In my view, the Lord didn't do us right about hair. Got to straighten, braid or cut it off, and now some of us gone to twisting it all kinds of curious ways. All *you* had to do was let yours hang!"

"Let it hang like when I was a kid, or pin it up in an old lady's bun!"

Lizzie sighed. "That's always the way. Them what's got it don't 'preciate it."

Kris preened. "Don't you like my haircut?"

"Oh, Christina!"

Kris winced at the sound of that long drawn-out *Christeena,* glad she'd also shortened her name. With a more "citified" spelling, too.

Lizzie shook her head. "You don't look like you no more."

Kris gave the old lady a hug. "Don't worry, Miss Lizzie. I'm still me."

"Maybe so, sugar pie, but you sure look different. And what does Mr. Ed Simmons think about it?"

"I don't know and I don't care."

"Umph! Guess you heard he's been courtin' Luella Jenkins."

"I don't care about that, either!" Kris snapped. Small towns! Everybody watching who's seeing whom. Worse...who they *think* is seeing whom! She was glad to hear her mother returning.

"Good. You're finished in here," Anna said. "Lizzie, we'd better get to the bedrooms. Christina, honey, why don't you go out and talk to your father? He hasn't had a minute with you since you got here. You'll find him either in his den or on the porch."

"All right." The perfect wife again, making things smooth for her husband. *And difficult for me,* Kris thought, as she dutifully left to face the inevitable.

During one of the many renovations, the porch had been widened and expanded so it encircled half the house. The section by the apple tree had become a pleasant extension of Allan Gilroy's den, and that was where Kris found him. Working on his sermon, she guessed, since he was scribbling on a legal pad beside an open Bible, and a couple of other books lay on the wrought-iron table. Kris knew there was a computer in his den, but she wondered if he ever used it.

She bent to kiss his cheek. "I see you're busy."

"Never too busy for you, honey." Allen Gilroy stood to enfold his daughter in his arms. "We missed you, Christina. But I'm proud of you. You've been a real trooper. I know it was hard for you."

"Don't say that, Papa! It wasn't hard."

"That's my Christina! Making the best of any situation."

"But it was—" Her voice caught on a sob. She shouldn't say *fun*. "I loved Aunt Freda."

"We all loved her." He rocked her in his arms. "And you were with her when she needed you."

"I know."

"She's at peace now," he said, just as her mother had. "She wouldn't want you to cry."

"No." She'd never seen Freda cry. Not once.

"She'd want you to be happy, and just keep on keeping on." He sounded so much like Aunt Freda that Kris smiled.

"So sit here and let's plan." He pulled out a chair for her. "I've already talked to several members of the school board. Your job is waiting for you."

"Papa, I…" Kris felt heavy as she sank into the chair. "I don't think I want to continue teaching."

"Christina! You're a born teacher."

"No, I'm not. I—"

"Don't tell me that. I saw Hattie Jackson's child throw her arms around you last night. And Hattie herself told me her daughter had never been interested in books until she was in your class. You do that for all your students."

Kris felt a rush of guilt. She did love the kids. Was she being selfish?

"You have to use your God-given talent, honey, or you lose it."

Talent. But teaching was more of a duty. Another restriction.

What about joy? Like painting and…okay, the excitement and challenge of her job in San Francisco.

"Another thing, Christina. You belong right here, giving to your people. Do you know why I came back to Piney Woods?"

"Of course I know." Her father, who had received his doctorate from one of the most prestigious theological institutions in the country, had received many brilliant offers. But he'd elected to remain in Piney Woods among *his* people. Not that it was a hardship for him; he was well supported by the income from the land he'd inherited and now leased. Even the pecan orchard and the vineyard he kept, both of which were managed by a hired man, brought in a tidy profit. She knew he gave much of his money back to the community—gave *more* than money. He had a compassionate concern for anyone in need.

She touched his hand. "You're a loving, caring person, Papa."

"So are you, Christina."

"No, I'm not."

"Nonsense. You dropped everything and went to Freda when she needed you."

Because that's where I wanted to be. But she didn't say it. Papa wouldn't understand how stifled she felt in this community. *He* didn't feel stifled, she thought with a surge of anger. All right, he did give his personal attention to each person who needed it, as well as careful attention to his church and civic duties. But he certainly wasn't stifled. Almost every month, he was off to some board or council meeting in New York, Boston or wherever. He even went to London last year for some international something or other. While Mama tended his flock, seldom accompanying him.

And I'd be like Mama, living in his shadow. Until San Francisco, Kris had hardly been farther than Faith, the Women's Christian College near Macon, which had been even more stifling than Piney Woods.

Her father seemed unaware of her silence. He chuckled. "I don't think you'd be teaching long. Not the way Ed Simmons was hanging on your every word last night."

"Oh, Papa, don't you start. Ed and I are just friends."

"I suspect he's got more than friendship in mind, honey. And Ed's doing quite well in his law office in Macon."

"Good for him."

"'Course he's here once, sometimes twice a week, looking after his mom and their place. Just a good country boy, despite his success. I like Ed."

She knew what else he'd like—for her to marry Ed and live in Ed's shadow, as Mama did in his.

Forget it! She wasn't in any hurry to get married. Not even to Tom.

Not that Papa would sanction a marriage to Tom any more than he'd sanction their current relationship. Tom wasn't one of "his people.'"

And not that Tom had marriage in mind. He liked his freedom as much as she liked hers. His greatest appeal was his easygoing carefree attitude.

Just thinking about Tom sent a shiver of excitement down her spine. She wondered if he was thinking of her.

"Guess you do need a little R and R, honey. I'm just glad to have you back."

"But I'm not back! There are…things I have to settle in San Francisco. Aunt Freda's stuff. I just left, you know—with her body."

"Yes, I know. But…" He looked puzzled. "Can't be much to settle. Freda, bless her soul, always put up a good front. But…I got the impression that she lived a rather hand-to-mouth existence."

If he only knew! But he was right. There wouldn't be much to settle. "Well, I have to see about a few things in her apartment." She couldn't bring herself to say that she planned to take it over herself.

"Once that's done, you can come back here where you belong. Then we'll sit down and decide what's best for you."

"And there's my job," she hurried to add. "I have to give notice, allow time for them to find a replacement." She felt guilty. Papa had often said evasion was just another way of lying. "I can't just leave." That much was true. She couldn't bring herself to leave the job she loved. Besides, her soap ad had been a big hit! She couldn't wait to tell Jill.

"Well…" Reverend Gilroy rustled his papers. She could see him weighing his teachings about being responsible against wanting her to come home immediately. "I suppose you have to clear things up. But don't stay more than two weeks."

She left it at that. She wasn't up to battling over what was best for her. Easier to tell him in a letter that she wasn't coming home.

CHAPTER TWO

WHY HADN'T SHE joined the fleeing horde?

Jill Ferrell sat at her desk in the executive suite of Chandler Associates and scolded herself. She couldn't expect to retain her exalted post as deputy to the Chief Executive Officer now that the Chief himself was gone. She hadn't been privy to the negotiations, but she bet her bottom dollar that his prompt resignation was instigated by the Randall takeover. Randall Enterprises was relatively new, but already known for shedding deadwood when it acquired a new company.

Deadwood. Chandler Enterprises wasn't there yet, but...

Surely Randall couldn't have bought Chandler just to shed it for tax purposes, could they? A common ploy.

She sighed. Her boss—former boss—was the last of four good old boys to head the company during the past seven years. Not one of the chosen had managed to stem the firm's downward spiral. She knew that her post as deputy CEO was due to the last downsizing fiasco, when so many old retainers had grabbed the golden handshake. Or as she liked to call it, the hunk of cheese given to rats deserting a sinking ship.

Why had she hung on?

She wasn't eligible for the golden hunk, but she had her MBA, her five years' experience and a few good contacts. That should be enough to land her a position with more potential. Maybe she was...

Stupid! Stupid to be sentimental about a job. She was still seeing Chandler as the dynamo it could be. Unbelievable that an advertising company could go into a slump in today's market. She hadn't yet earned her MBA when she was hired five years ago. But even then in her lowly position in the mail room, she'd spotted the problem. Just plain bad management. Too many new acquisitions, companies they'd usually picked up when they were on a downward slide. Those acquisitions had kept them out of the red, but barely. Why not try to invigorate the advertising company itself? They could offer a hefty retirement package for old retainers and bring in new people with fresh, innovative ideas. She sighed. Chandler was rife with incompetence. From the board room to the basement! If—

A buzz sounded and her secretary spoke through the intercom. "Mr. Randall from Wilmington, Delaware, on line four, Ms. Ferrell. Will you…?"

"I'll take it." *As if I have a choice.* "Jill Ferrell," she said crisply as she lifted the phone.

"Good morning, Ms. Ferrell. Scott Randall here."

Her breath caught. She pressed the phone closer, lulled by the soft, husky drawl.

"I'd appreciate it if you could schedule some time on Monday."

"Monday?" Time for what? she wondered, as she jerked to attention.

"Short notice, I know. I apologize. But it's crucial that we move quickly."

"Certainly, Mr. Randall." What had he said? "One moment, please." She managed to sound alert and professional as she picked up her Palm Pilot. "Just let me note the details. Monday at…" She paused on an expectant note.

"Nine? If that's convenient."

"Certainly, Mr. Randall." Must be the usual—get the team in to meet the new coach. "I'll notify the board members and—"

"Oh, no! We're not quite ready for that." A low throaty laugh. "Let's take a look at the forest before we deal with the trees."

She was surprised. "Then it'll be just…?"

"Just the two of us."

"Of course." She replaced the phone, his "Thank you, Ms. Ferrell" still lingering like a melody in her ear.

She shook herself, feeling like an idiot. How could she be so mesmerized by a voice! It was that southern intonation, seldom heard on the West Coast.

Well, whatever it was, she'd been so affected she still wasn't sure what she'd arranged. "Let's take a look at the forest before we deal with the trees." Did that mean he wanted to scan the whole operation with her before...

Nonsense! He'd said "Just the two of us." Okay, he was probably bringing the new head honcho, politely easing her out before introducing him to the staff.

Him. Of course it would be a man. Hadn't she watched one incompetent man after another come and go for five years?

Okay, granted, a woman could be just as incompetent. But men were always in charge! At least in this company.

Just like it had been at home. In spite of herself, the old bitterness surfaced. The executive suite of Chandler's headquarters in San Francisco might be thousands of miles from the small Alaskan fishing village of her childhood. But had anything changed?

She looked down at her smart leather pumps, buried in the plush carpet.

Saw, instead, her old rubber knee boots as she stood on the slippery dock in front of her father's cannery. Breathed in the heavy pungent mixture of salty sea water, fish and diesel oil emanating from the fishing boats. Heard the squawking of seagulls reverberating through the air and the raucous haggling of the men. Saw the dominant figure of her handsome father, his white cords work-stained, his worn white cap at a jaunty angle, his heavy boots stomping the dock in a commanding swagger as he cursed and wrangled with the fishermen.

To a child, it had been an exciting daily drama. The angry

shouts or loud laughter of heavy trading, the big wooden boxes loaded with the day's catch hoisted by pulleys and placed on the roller transporting them the hundred feet from the dock to the cooker.

Just as it must have been when her father's father had built the nondescript building and hung the lopsided sign, Ferrell's Cannery.

The first thing she would've done was straighten that sign. Well…after she'd remodeled, painted inside and out, installed a new cooker… As she grew older, she couldn't contain the visions of improvement dancing in her mind. She itched to take over. She had suggested, argued, pleaded.

To no avail. She was that useless thing…a woman. In her father's world, she was fit only to bear children and serve her man.

She would not. She had no intention of marrying some local fisherman and, like her mother, serving, adoring and bowing under his domination for the rest of her life! She was out of there before she was eighteen, making her way through college with scholarships and hard work, on to a career of her own. She'd returned home only twice, a year after college to nurse her mother during the months of her fatal illness, and two years ago for Dad's funeral.

She questioned now, as she had then, how Jake, her brother, would manage. As the man of the family, he'd inherited the small plant. Like his father, Jake was addicted to wine and women. But unlike Dad, she thought, he wasn't prone to keep an eye on business. Jake would rather be out on a fishing boat or gambling or…

Darn! She'd better get her mind off the cannery and back on business. Business continued as usual between one change and the next. All the employees did their jobs while holding their breath, wondering if they'd still have a job under the new head.

She wondered about that herself.

She chuckled. Maybe she should be sending out résumés.

She'd likely be out of a job as soon as Randall brought in their next good old boy who would then appoint his own good old boy assistant.

She knew them well. From the strictly-business demons to the goof-offs with sticky hands; lust in their eyes and more sex than business on their minds. And always, of course, the ones who liked to mix a little pleasure with business.

She could handle the good old boys. She was just damn tired of doing it.

AT SEVEN O'CLOCK Monday morning, Scott Randall smeared his face with shaving cream and grinned at his reflection in the mirror.

He might never be known as a great entrepreneur, but he was getting on with what he wanted done.

He'd outbid Crown and three other corporations. Snatched Chandler right out from under their unsuspecting noses.

Not that he wanted the almost-defunct advertising company. His target was KLICK, the camera company. But it was an all-or-nothing sale, and he'd had to buy the whole conglomerate.

He couldn't complain. He now had KLICK, with its accompanying patents and old records. That was all he needed. Once he dumped the deadwood and set Talbert Sims and his team to work on the new camera software…

His cell phone rang and he grabbed it with his left hand. "Randall here."

"Scott! Where are you?" His sister sounded anxious.

"Right here, honey. I was going to call you." He picked up his razor and began to shave. He was to be at Chandler's by nine.

"Where are you?" she again demanded.

"At the Ritz. I—"

"The Ritz? Are you in San Francisco?"

"Yes."

"How could you! I fixed dinner and waited up for you last night. You said you'd be in yesterday and I thought—"

"Oh, Claire, I'm sorry. I didn't get in until after midnight."

"As if that matters! Well, I've got the spare room fixed up for you. So check out and come over here and—"

"I'd better stay where I am, Claire." He winced as he nicked himself, but managed to finish shaving while he talked. "I love you and the kids, and I'll sure be around. But you're rather far out. I'm here to work, so I need to stick pretty close."

"It's dumb not to stay with us if you're working in San Francisco. I never get a chance to sit down and really talk with you anymore."

"We'll talk." He was back in the bedroom now, dressing with the phone in one hand. "I'll come over this evening." Damn. He'd hoped to arrange a dinner meeting with that woman—what was her name? Fenton? No...Ferrell.

"Get here early, Scott. David and the kids are as anxious to see you as I am. And David will be leaving right after dinner, going back to Sacramento."

"I'll be there."

"Early! Promise?"

"Early. Gotta go now, sis." He shut off the phone, but couldn't shut off—what? Something in Claire's voice nagged at him. Something lacking. He hadn't heard her usual all's-right-with-the-world lilt.

Oh, hell, she was probably just mad at him for not staying out there. He'd get to the house early with all that junk he'd brought for the kids.

As he straightened his tie, his mind switched back to the company he'd acquired. Chandler had picked up a lot of heavy baggage during the past few years. Racing with the stock market. A bad tactic. That could really throw a company off track. He knew the market; he'd started working part-time in his father's brokerage when he was a sophomore in high school, and had headed the firm when his father died.

His dad was the cleverest broker he'd ever known. Even toward the end, when he worked at home and could hardly lift his head from the pillow, he could gauge the market, knowing instinctively when to buy, when to sell. They'd made millions just shuffling paper.

But he'd watched companies get lost in the shuffle. Lots of good products got lost, too.

He glanced at his watch, picked up his jacket and left for his appointment.

THIS WAS SCOTT'S FIRST visit to Chandler headquarters. He entered an old but imposing building and boarded the elevator for the penthouse suite. As soon as he entered the reception room, a slender, attractive woman wearing a chocolate-brown suit came forward to greet him. She held out a hand and looked up at him, a smile radiating in gold-flecked hazel eyes. "Good morning, Mr. Randall. I've looked forward to meeting you. I'm Jill Ferrell."

"Ms. Ferrell," he echoed, taking her hand. "I've been looking forward to this meeting, too." His informers had said she was the employee most knowledgeable about the whole operation.

Snap judgments were his specialty. A few casual questions and he'd know all he needed to know about her.

"I think we'll be more comfortable in here," she said, as she led him to an area evidently reserved for private VIP conferences.

No sign of the company's defunct financial status here, he thought, gazing at an informal arrangement of comfortable sofas and chairs, flowers in crystal vases and other elegant amenities. It looked more appropriate to a social gathering than business.

"Coffee?" she asked.

"Thank you." His eyes fastened on her as she gave directions to the receptionist. Her movements were quick and decisive. In an instant, she was seated before him, her pose expectant. "You said you wanted to view the forest?"

"Forest?"

She smiled. "A general overall status of the company, I assume?"

"Well, yes. Chandler's picked up quite a few companies in the past few years." He hadn't examined them as closely as he should have, his only interest being in KLICK. Someone experienced had to be placed in charge of disposing of the excess baggage and readying KLICK for its new project. "I'd like your opinion on a few aspects." He couldn't say he'd come to size her up. "I have a few questions, if you don't mind."

"Of course not. I'm happy to—" She paused to pour the coffee the receptionist placed on the table. "Cream? Sugar?"

"Black." He was anxious to get to business.

Evidently she was, too. "I'm at your service, sir. Fire away."

He fired the pertinent questions at her—including a number that concerned KLICK—and was pleased by her quick perception and intelligent opinions. He watched her closely, appraising every answer, pressing her for details. He fastened his eyes on her, as she made quick taps on the Palm Pilot in her hand and instantly came up with the precise information requested. That tiny computer could pack in more information than a team of economists could gather in a year.

"You should own one," someone had suggested.

"Not as long as he has people," David had countered.

Scott grinned. His smart-ass brother-in-law was, as usual, right on target. Scott preferred to concentrate on the big picture and depend on other people to handle the details.

People like the bright and alert Ms. Jill Ferrell. He continued to watch her as he asked more questions, happy to have found just the person he needed. A few more sessions with her and they'd have the ball rolling.

When he checked his watch, he couldn't believe how much

time had passed. If he was to keep his next appointment… He stood and again grasped her hand. "Thank you for your time, Ms. Ferrell. You've been most helpful. We'll talk again soon."

CHAPTER THREE

ALONE ONCE AGAIN, she stood quite still, gazing at one of the sofa pillows that had fallen onto the floor. Wondering…

Okay, maybe he *wasn't* coming on to her. But the way he kept staring, as if he was sizing her up…

She gave the pillow a vicious kick. She wasn't stupid. She'd watched him watching her. She knew that look. The same appraising look her father had fastened on each new conquest.

I'm not a conquest, Mr. Randall!

Yet there was nothing she liked better than a business discussion with a competent knowledgeable person. She liked to focus on the status of the company, and on its potential, tossing ideas back and forth.

Like you did this morning?

Well, yes! She laughed as the thought struck. Replacing the pillow, she stood for a moment, recalling the words that had flown between them. It had been…stimulating. Their minds had connected and—

No, they hadn't exactly connected. He'd zeroed in on certain aspects that puzzled her. Products lost in the stock-market paper shuffle.

Walking to her office, she reflected that Scott Randall might've been heir to a brokerage, but she was a stock market buff. You had to follow the product as well as the rating.

Anyway, the session had been interesting. She'd like to delve further, sound him out about his ideas. What did he—

"Jill!" Candy Atkins burst into the office, closed the door and rushed toward Jill, her eyes alight with interest. "Was that *him?*"

"Who?"

"That gorgeous guy who just walked out."

"Oh."

"Is he really who Nora said he is?" she asked, referring to Jill's assistant.

"He is if she said he's Scott Randall."

"I didn't believe her."

"No reason for her to lie."

"Oh, I know. I know. But he's *the* Scott Randall? Like in Randall Enterprises?"

"The same." Jill moved around her desk to sit behind it.

"Wow! I had no idea. Why hasn't he made the tabloids? One of those eligible bachelor columns. He is single, isn't he? Single, young and rich! Not to mention handsome! God, I'd like to get my fingers into that thick, wavy black hair. Mmm. His mouth— Did you notice that wicked curve when he smiles? And those eyes. They're almost black and they look right at you." Candy's hands moved in a rapid series of exuberant descriptive gestures.

Jill laughed. "I see you got a good look."

"He bumped into me and—"

"Uh-huh. If I know you, Candy, you did the bumping."

Candy chuckled delightedly. "Well, when an opportunity presents itself, I seize it. And as to who bumped into whom… *He* apologized. He said, 'Oh, pardon me, ma'am' in that slow sweet drawl." She closed her eyes in an expression of ecstasy.

Jill gazed at Candy, hearing it again. That slow and intimate meant-just-for-you drawl. Low and melodious, drawing you closer. Was that why she'd thought he was interested in *her?*

It's just the way he talks, she told herself. *To everyone.*

"And all the while I didn't know I was face to face with Mr. Enterprise himself. The very man who took us over, lock, stock and barrel. And he just walks quietly in, all by himself. Is he

coming back? To bring in the head man or something? Jill!
Come on. Give!"

"What?" Jill had barely heard a word Candy said.

"When will he be back? More to the point, *is* he coming
back? To bring in the head man or…" Candy leaned across the
desk. "To meet with us…you know, the managers."

"He didn't…" Jill hesitated, shocked that she didn't know.
Why hadn't she asked more questions? The next head man—
who and when? "He was indefinite about future plans," she
said. He did say he was coming back, she thought. But not
when, why, or with whom. "Anyway, what's up, Candy?" she
asked, changing the subject.

"This." Candy waved the papers in her hand. "Maybe it was
fate that I chose just this moment. Surely I'll have another
chance to…well, get acquainted. Surely he'll want to meet with
the managers."

"Possibly," Jill said, knowing that Candy would indeed
seize every opportunity. And might very well become better
acquainted with Scott Randall, she thought, surveying the mass
of red hair, the seductive green eyes and voluptuous figure.
"Let's take a look."

"A couple of ads we've been working on for a new client I
just brought in," Candy said.

"Good," Jill said. Clients were few and far between these
days. She wasn't sure whether it was poor salesmanship or
poor work. Probably both. As marketing manager, Candy Atkins was in charge of the salespeople who brought in the clients, as well as the art department whose teams created the
desired work. Too big a job for a lamebrain like Candy. But her
looks and—charm, Jill guessed you could call it—had made her
quite a favorite with the former chief executive. Jill wondered
if she'd have the same pull with whoever Randall brought in.

"I think this is going to be a real hit," Candy gloated, spreading the papers on Jill's desk.

Jill hoped so. It took creative ideas to hold on to clients.

She sat at her desk to study the sketches. Her eyes widened. One, captioned WHITE AS SNOW, depicted graphics of a heavy snowstorm that dissolved into stark white linens to depict the effectiveness of a new laundry product with bleach. The other, showing a mountain of suds in the shape of soft billowing pillows snuggling against delicate lacy lingerie and fluffy sweaters, was an ad designed for Soft Suds.

"Fantastic," Jill said—as she'd said the first time the proposed ad had been presented to her. Three months before. By Kris Gilroy.

"I wanted to check it out with you first, Jill," Kris had said. "It's just the germ of an idea, and a few tentative sketches. But I'm so new at this. Do you think this would work? Will they like it?"

"They'll love it," Jill had answered, congratulating herself. She'd done the right thing when she got Kris a job in Art. Of course, Candy wouldn't know that she'd seen the sketches before, and she wasn't about to tell her.

"An excellent concept. Very catchy," she said now. "Your idea?"

"Well, yes." Candy brushed a bit of lint from her skirt. "As you know, mine is the final say. But we always work as a team. I talk with the client first to determine his needs. Then I meet with the art people and make a few suggestions. This time I think they came up with exactly what I asked for."

"I see," Jill said. She saw that Kris's sudsy gem had billowed through units and supervisors all the way up to the head of the department. So each brilliant idea became teamwork, to be presented as the handiwork of the brilliant coach. Just one of Candy's personal promotion techniques.

Obviously disturbed by Jill's silence, Candy hurried on. "The point is, do you like these ideas?"

"Of course. They're terrific."

"So is it approved? I'd like to get it set up for television before presenting it to Mr. Jasper at Soap."

"Well…" Jill hesitated. Business might be going on as usual, but who had the go-ahead say on any Chandler project? And why hadn't Mr. Crucial-To-Move-Quickly Randall brought him in or made that clear or— "Look, Candy, why don't you put this on hold for a while. At least until the staff meeting with Mr. Randall." Surely the great man would stick around long enough to tell them who was in charge.

Candy seemed to have the same reaction. "Yes. I see what you mean. I'll do that." She picked up the material, her face bright with expectancy. Already picturing herself showing it to the great man himself, Jill thought. She looked as eager and excited as Kris had the day she'd come to Jill's office with the "germ" of an idea. Too bad Kris wasn't getting the credit. She was buried so deep among the employees that Candy probably didn't even know she existed, much less that the concept was hers.

Well, Kris, it's true that "Full many a flower is born to blush unseen."

She shivered. That line was from Gray's "Elegy Written in a Country Churchyard." Kris might be, right this minute, standing in a country churchyard. Adhering to her aunt's wish that she be buried in her old hometown in Georgia.

The pang of sorrow returned. She had liked Kris's aunt Freda. Enjoyed the times spent with her, the music, talks and meals shared in Freda's small apartment. They had known Freda's heart wouldn't last much longer. But they never talked about it. Mostly they just listened as Freda reminisced about the old days. Or sang, in a quavery contralto voice that wasn't quite gone, some of her old blues songs. Always ending with a triumphant cackle of laughter.

"And we're not going to cry now," Kris had said when Freda's heart gave out. "She remembered the fun, and so will we."

Yes, Kris had her aunt's flair for fun, and maybe that was why they'd become such good friends. It wasn't customary for a lowly fourth-floor employee to socialize with a penthouse executive.

An unlikely friendship, in any case. If she hadn't wandered into the flea market that day hoping to spot an abandoned antique…

If Kris hadn't been at her stand…

Even so, Jill had almost missed her. She'd hardly glanced at the disheveled teenager in cutoffs and paint-spattered T-shirt.

If she hadn't bumped into that woman with the sketch…

"Sorry, I didn't see you. I was just… Look!" The woman, more exuberant than apologetic, held up the charcoal sketch for which she'd just paid twelve dollars. "Look at this! I'm going to have it framed. Isn't it exactly like me?"

"It is," Jill said. A remarkable likeness. The kid had talent. She turned to look at Kris who was now at her easel sketching a heavyset man seated before her.

Jill watched as a few quick dabs from palette to canvas (water color this time) produced a caricature of the man, the exaggerated features still retaining a remarkable likeness.

"It's for a roast at my club," the satisfied man explained, pointing to the quip beneath.

Clever quip, Jill thought. Clever kid. She could sure perk up the advertising department. If she was older…

When she lingered to watch, and later to talk, she discovered that the "kid" was a twenty-six-year-old woman.

"This is just a hobby," Kris said, going on to say that she was a schoolteacher from Georgia. On vacation. "Well, kind of a vacation. I have an aunt who's alone out here, and not too well."

"So how did you get into this?" Jill asked, gesturing at the easel.

"A friend's suggestion. But I'd seen those artists with sidewalk studios smack in the middle of the city. Why couldn't I join the fun?" She laughed. "I love San Francisco!"

"So do I," Jill said, laughing with her. There were lots of things they both liked. Yoga, chamber music and every play that came to town. It was great to have a friend to accompany you when you didn't have a date.

And it was a cinch to get Kris hired in the art department. In any department, for that matter. Minority employees were a plus in securing government contracts.

She must ask Tom when Kris was due back. *If* she was coming back.

Well, she had to, if only to clear out her aunt's apartment. But Jill knew that Kris's parents, who appeared to have a great deal of influence over her, didn't like her being so far from home. Or, rather, from *them.*

And now, with the death of her aunt Freda, Kris wouldn't have the excuse to remain.

But Tom was here. Jill grinned. She was beginning to suspect that Kris loved Tom Harris even more than she loved San Francisco.

They did make a striking couple. Tom was so good-looking—very blond, very blue-eyed white movie-star type. And Kris with those dimples and that heavenly smooth chocolate-brown skin. How had she ever thought of Kris as a grubby teenager? Even for a few minutes? With that smart haircut and the right clothes, in *anything,* for that matter, Kris was a strikingly beautiful woman. And the way she fastened those big eyes on Tom…

Oh, yes, Kris will be back! I'll bet my bottom dollar that Kris isn't about to leave that man, or this city.

She frowned, wondering about that. Maybe Kris was a bit too trusting.

CHAPTER FOUR

JILL WAS STILL fuming about her encounter with Scott Randall when, at the end of the working day, she changed into shorts for her usual run at Crissy Field.

Her energy was at its highest peak, undiminished by the pace she steadily increased in an effort to calm down.

The more she ran, the madder she got. At herself. Instead of running herself crazy on the darn beach, she ought to be sitting at a table with Mr. Big Shot, sipping wine and nailing down answers! *Who's in charge?* That was the main question. Once they knew that, everything else would fall into place.

She wasn't mad at herself, she decided. She was mad at *him*. Strolling in like a casual visitor, drinking coffee and engaging in inconsequential small talk. Okay, a few bits and pieces about Chandler's. *But mostly about me. My experience, my background, how I felt about this or that. Like he was more interested in me than in the company. No wonder I got the wrong impression and thought the dinner invitation was a come-on.*

If I got the wrong impression!

Anyway…where was the fanfare? The awaited announcement from the board that Mr. Well-Respected-So-and-So, along with a long list of his exalted accomplishments and experience, will be assuming the presidency, with a definite date, time and other particulars established. Then a big to-do at a special meeting to introduce the boss to the managers. A lot of scurrying around as titles, positions and office space got shifted.

Okay, so there'd be some bitching about who got the biggest office and who got windows. And yes, she'd probably still be mad when the next good ol' boy was fanfared in! But at least she'd know who was in charge.

Scott Randall understood the procedure. Ought to, anyway. He wasn't all that new at the takeover game. Chandler wasn't his first.

Oh, well, it wasn't her concern.

Yes, it was! The president had cut out and she was a sitting duck.

A lame duck. With absolutely no authority.

The problem was that there was nobody with authority.

The hell with it! She slowed to a walk, skipped the stretching and headed for her car. A shower would cool her down.

She was on the way to her apartment when she remembered her date; dinner at that new supper club with Frank Cassels. She called to cancel.

Frank was annoyed. "This is a hell of a last-minute thing."

"I know and I'm sorry. But something's come up." She couldn't say she wasn't in the mood and would be bad company.

"Do you know how hard it is to get reservations? I hate to cancel."

"And that's why you're already checking your little black book." The city was full of attractive women and Frank kept an extensive list.

He laughed. "I'd rather enjoy a stimulating conversation with you. Even," he added, "if that's all I'm going to get."

"Ha!" she scoffed. "Tell you what—I'll make it up. How about Wednesday night around seven?"

"Depends. What do you have in mind?"

"Dinner at my place?"

"Bingo! Chili?"

"Whatever the house is pushing." Which would depend on her mood.

"I'll take it."

"Enjoy this evening." With whomever, she thought. Frank never lacked for female companionship.

Neither did she lack for male company. Usually short-term. Most, after one or two dates, moved on, desiring more than "stimulating conversation."

When it comes to my life, I call the shots! That statement, often repeated to herself, rang in her mind as she rounded the last hill and turned into the garage across from her apartment. She couldn't be casual about relationships. Best to stick with the one or two willing-to-be-a-buddy guys, like Frank.

She unhooked the hanger holding her office attire and picked up her shoes, feeling a glow of satisfaction as she walked across to her apartment. Her beautiful apartment on Nob Hill, across from Grace Cathedral and a few doors from the famous Fairmont Hotel. She loved Huntington Park around the corner, the fabulous view, the nearby supper club and quaint eateries.

Very posh and very expensive. Two hundred dollars a month for parking space alone.

Frank said she was stupid. There were cheaper places to live.

She knew that. She had lived in some.

But San Francisco had cast its spell.

From her first glimpse, she'd wanted to live on Nob Hill. In one of those high-in-the-sky apartments, complete with costly antique furnishings, the right pictures and clever knickknacks.

She wanted to be here, and she wanted to belong. At eighteen, in worn jeans and scuffed loafers, she had stood in midtown San Francisco, her eyes on the elegant people who stepped out of cabs, off on some important mission, or floated in and out of the grand hotels. She'd wanted to be one of them—like that woman with the shiny leather briefcase... Or that one, with the soft cashmere coat dress molding to her figure and stylish high-heeled boots on her feet.

Jill knew dreams wouldn't get her there.

She planned. Even on her first job as a waitress at a posh restaurant, she stashed her tips. Surprisingly the tips grew to quite a pile. Then Kathy, another waitress, had a setback. Her boyfriend walked out on her just when she got laid-off for missing work because her baby was sick. She needed the money more than Jill.

So the stash was gone, but the habit remained. Jill saved some small portion of her earnings at her several odd jobs while attending tuition-free City College. At the end of that two-year stint, she had a scholarship to state college, and was employed as a sales clerk at Saks Fifth Avenue. At Saks she learned about fashion, and at State, she studied finance. By the time she started working at Chandler's and entered the MBA program for the fully employed, she looked chic and polished in the designer outfits she'd picked up for a song. She wasn't as financially sound as she intended to be, but her stock portfolio and bank account were steadily growing. At present, the income from her stocks sometimes exceeded her salary.

I can afford me, job or no job, she told herself, as she cleared up from her solitary meal of soup and salad. So why was she worrying about what might happen at Chandler's? She dismissed the company and its new owner from her mind and retreated to the smaller bedroom. It held little more than her desk and a small pull-out sofa, but it was a colorful and charming combination office and guest room. If she ever had a guest. Most of her friends lived in the city.

She switched on the computer and brought up her stock portfolio. Her investments, like everything in Jill's life, were organized and carefully divided into categories—a third in mutual funds, one third in old reliable stocks, the other third for gambling. From the first, although she'd started with almost nothing, Jill had been good at gambling.

I'm still good at it, she thought, as she sat down and began to trade. At the end of an hour, she shut off her computer. She was getting richer.

But where was the glow? The rush of excitement, the sense of accomplishment she'd felt in the old days when she'd made only a few dollars?

Maybe once you had everything you needed, you lost interest in money.

Something was missing. She felt empty. Depressed. And she wasn't that kind of person.

Maybe she should've gone out with Frank, she told herself as she got into bed and switched on the television. Stupid unfunny comedy. She blacked it out with the remote and picked up a novel. Didn't hold her interest. Stupid heroine couldn't see past her nose and whined about everything.

Jill put the novel aside and turned off the bedroom lamp. Tossed and turned.

What was wrong with her?

She lay on her back, stared into the dark, and let the rage return.

Chandler was a good company. At least it had been. But with mismanagement…

And now, with no management at all!

Mr. Big Shot Randall wasn't being fair to Chandler and the people who worked there. She meant to tell him so. First thing in the morning, she'd phone him.

Wherever he was. Even a small-talk, do-nothing big shot must have a secretary who knew how to reach him, even if she didn't know anything else!

SCOTT RANDALL WAS seated on his private plane when she reached him. He was at breakfast with his male secretary while they went over the day's business.

The secretary placed his hand over the mouthpiece. "Ms. Ferrell from Chandler?"

Scott took the cell phone, surprised. Pleased. Had he only

imagined her animosity? "Good morning, Ms. Ferrell! I'm glad you called. I planned to see you today, but—"

"Good. That's why I'm calling. You'll be in today? At what time?"

"Not today. There's a pressing matter in Washington that needs my immediate attention. Perhaps…" He took a sip of coffee, speculating. Could he possibly get back by—

"There are pressing matters here that need your immediate attention!"

He choked. The animosity was not imagined. He dabbed at the sputtered coffee, and cleared his throat. "I'm sorry, Ms. Ferrell. But this trip is absolutely necessary."

"Mr. Randall, there are situations here that need settling. Immediately. Surely your trip can be delayed until—" She broke off. He could almost see her. Blinking, trying to subdue the flashing fury in those brilliant hazel eyes. "Really, Mr. Randall, you must realize that—" Another abrupt pause. "I'd appreciate it if you could postpone your trip and come here instead."

He heard the attempt at an apology she didn't want to make. "That's not possible. I'm already en route."

"You're…en route?" Now it was she who sputtered.

He glanced downward through the clouds. "Over Nebraska, I think."

"You can't be!"

He smiled, enjoying the sparring. "Maybe not Nebraska. Could be—"

"I mean you can't *do* this. You can't go off and leave a business—a whole company just hanging!"

"Hanging?"

"Even when a company changes hands, Mr. Randall, business goes on. Or it should!"

"Right." That was the way he handled it. Business as usual until he looked things over and decided—

"And to achieve a smooth, business-as-usual operation, someone has to be in charge. Someone who can approve procedures, okay projects, sign requisitions, decide, direct, appoint!"

"All right." Damn. He forgot that weasel of a president, Wilcox, had absconded before he could fire him. "Okay, so who should that be?"

"You're asking *me?* I think the correct procedure is to elect, appoint, or however you do it, a CEO or whatever title you—"

"Forget all that." He tried to think. Who was next in line? His investigators had said... "You, Ms. Ferrell. You're in charge."

The anger had turned to shock. "I beg your pardon. Did you say—"

"That you're it, Ms. Ferrell. Take over. Decide, direct, appoint. The buck stops with you."

JILL STARED at the phone. Stunned. He'd said...

He *couldn't* have said...

No. He was Randall Enterprises. He could say.

Well, it had to be certified in writing. Or something.

He didn't know a thing about protocol, no matter how many companies he'd bought.

Her buzzer sounded. "It's Mr. Stewart, Ms. Ferrell."

The last person she wanted to see. George Stewart had made no bones about his resentment at her appointment as deputy CEO. Over *him,* who'd been her boss when she was promoted from gopher to a lowly clerk in Finance. "Tell him...okay." No point in stalling.

Everything about George Stewart was correct: the polished Gucci loafers, the custom tailored suit that concealed the paunch, his precisely knotted tie. He was a short man, but his erect stance was commanding. "Good morning, Jill." As always, his cheery greeting was just a bit condescending.

"Morning, George. How are you?"

"Under quite a bit of pressure." He glanced at the closed

door to the president's office, vacant since the ex-president's departure. "Nora says Randall was here yesterday."

"Yes."

"So what's what?"

"Pardon?"

"Who's in charge?"

"No one yet." Scott Randall might be crazy, but she wasn't! "Still up for grabs, huh?" He actually seemed…relieved? Eager? Of course. George was, or thought he was, in line for the exalted executive position.

"Nothing's settled yet," she said. It sure wasn't settled by a casual remark over the telephone.

George tugged at one ear in a thoughtful gesture. "I'd better check with Randall."

"All right." Seemed everyone wanted to check with the great man.

"Let me know as soon as he's available."

"Certainly." As if she had any idea!

"These are urgent." George tapped the requisitions in his hand. "I'm concerned. We can't dispense money without a final okay."

"Just leave them," she said. "I'll keep them on hold."

"No." George shook his head. "This is my area. I'll just hang on to these until I see Randall," he said, and departed.

That was all right with her. Never mind that buck-stops-with-you business. She wasn't about to sign any okay to dispense *one* buck, not to mention millions. Not without certified, notarized authority to do so.

SCOTT RANDALL WAS no fool. And this wasn't the first corporation he'd acquired. Best to allow the new company to function on its own for a while. Just appoint a good insider as administrator. Within the hour, every official at Chandler headquarters had received, via e-mail, an official notice announcing Jillian Ferrell's appointment as Chief Executive Officer, in charge of all operations, national and international, of Chandler, Inc.

Jill, feeling a little numb, stared at the document on her computer.

There was nothing numb about Nora who stared over Jill's shoulder. "Hot diggity dog! You're it, Jill! Howdy do, ma'am! *Ms.* Head Honcho!" she sang, and swung Jill into a whirling dance.

Jill tried to keep pace, tried to catch her breath. "Wait!"

"Wait, nothing! We aren't stuck with another good ol' boy! It's you, honey! Says so in black and white."

Jill still found it difficult to take in.

Nora Cullen didn't. By day's end, Jill found herself installed behind the big desk in the chief's office, name plate proudly announcing her right to be there.

"No doubt now about who's in charge," Nora said, observing her handiwork. "And not a good ol' boy in sight."

Jill laughed with her, but, strangely, none of that seemed to matter.

It was the challenge. This was an opportunity to pull Chandler out of the doldrums, and she was bursting with ideas. First, they had to get Chandler on a secure financial footing. The last string of good ol' boys had tried to do that by picking up other companies, some of which were holding their own, while others— She had to think about that. Maybe...

Wait! She shut her eyes, willed her reeling mind to stop. She had to get everything in order. There were a dozen routine matters on hold. First things first.

She went at it with zeal. She prioritized data and began the process of consulting with the various managers and analyzing their reports.

But nothing went smoothly. At almost every encounter, she was hampered by some setback or petty problem. By the end of the first week, she was exhausted.

How did she get so bogged down by the simple routine? It

wasn't as if she was doing anything new. Hadn't she always dealt with each matter before giving it to Wilcox for his final okay and complacent signature? How had that same work become so complicated?

Position, of course. She was the boss now. And chosen from the crew, many of whom might consider themselves more competent than she.

She stayed late on Friday to catch up, but couldn't get the damn status thing off her mind. It was chiefly because of the managers with whom she dealt, particularly those who doubted her capabilities. Or rather, considered themselves more capable. Like George, she thought with a wry smile. He was no longer openly condescending, but he did have a tendency to argue, or at least question. "Are you sure about this?" he'd say, or "This looks out of proportion to me. Doesn't seem ready for a go-ahead."

Jill tapped her pen against her chin. In fact, sometimes George was right. Which sure didn't boost her confidence!

Of course, no one dared to be as audacious as Candy Atkins. "Good going, kid! That was fast! Didn't know you and Scott Randall were an item!"

But who listens to Candy's retro crap? She's still back in the get-the-man game.

Oh, to hell with the petty jealousy! It goes with the territory.

You wanted this job, Jill Ferrell. Quit crying and get to work!

Her hand tightened on her pen and she looked down at the documents on her desk and rubbed her eyes. The figures were beginning to blur.

"Oh, 'scuse me, Ms. Ferrell. I thought you'd gone."

"Good evening, Sadie. No, I'm still here. Sorry." The apology was overdue. It wasn't the first time she'd stayed late and upset the cleaning routine.

"Oh, that's all right." Sadie pointed at the overflowing

wastebasket. "Why don't I just clean around you? Get some of this trash out of your way?"

"I'd appreciate that. Just don't touch the mess on this desk, all right?"

The cleaner moved around her, collecting trash, dusting, vacuuming, chatting as she did so. "Isn't this—what d'you call it? Thank God it's Friday?"

Jill smiled. "I believe you're right."

"Everybody else is gone! Off to enjoy the weekend. And you still here. Working your head off. Don't seem right to me."

"Don't seem right to me, either." Jill sighed. She had neither time nor energy for runs in the park. And she'd had to break her Wednesday dinner date with Frank. She sure didn't have time to cook!

"Well, it looks better in here," Sadie said as she gathered up her cleaning equipment.

"It does indeed. Thank you, Sadie."

"Pity I can't say the same for you," Sadie said.

"Oh?" Jill drew the word out.

"Now don't go getting your dander up. You look frazzled is all I meant."

"Okay, Sadie. I got the message."

"You're working too hard, Ms. Ferrell."

"Tell me about it."

"Don't seem fair to me," Sadie mumbled as she wheeled out her load. She stopped, glanced back at Jill. "You need some help, child."

Jill stared at the closed door. Out of the mouth of…the cleaning lady?

Well, someone had to tell her! Maybe she wasn't CEO quality—trying to do everything herself and forgetting a key priority. Delegate!

No wonder Wilcox didn't get bogged down by routine. Hadn't *she* cleared the decks? She'd been his buffer.

She looked at her vacant office…thinking.

ON MONDAY, Jill stood in her old office with Nora Cullen.

Nora regarded her warily. "You're putting Mr. Stewart in *here?*"

Darn. She'd forgotten that Nora, who'd been her personal everything, had an ego, too.

"Yes, he'll be my deputy. I'm promoting you, too. And as my executive assistant, I'll need you in the office next to me."

"Oh, my." Nora brightened. "I see. Oh, thank you, Jill!"

Jill only nodded, her mind on organization. "What do you think of Beth Morgan as your replacement on the front desk? And tell Stewart I need to speak with him right away."

Nora wasn't one to keep her opinions to herself. "Are you sure about George Stewart, Jill?"

Jill smiled. "Equal employment, Nora. We ought to have at least one good ol' boy up here."

"Maybe. But George Stewart? I hate to say this, but he's about the least charming man I know. He's got no people skills."

He's got numbers skills, though. "I can handle George," Jill said confidently. She could handle just about anyone. She had plenty of people skills—her time as a waitress hadn't been for nothing.

CHAPTER FIVE

TOM SPOTTED KRIS immediately. He loved her walk, the slow seductive sway of low-slung hips.

She saw him. Smiled. He loved that smile. Full lips curving around tiny, even teeth, so starkly white against her deep brown skin. The dimples in her cheeks danced when she smiled. He rushed to meet her and, in one swift movement, took her bag and gathered her in his arms. He loved the yielding softness of her, the taste of her mouth, the fresh, tangy tantalizing scent of her perfume.

"I missed you," he said.

"Me, too." She smiled up at him. Arms encircling each other, they skirted the crowd and made their way through the terminal and parking lot to his car.

"How did everything go?" he asked.

"Just as she would've wanted. Like...well, like everybody was welcoming her back home. No. Like she'd never been away. It's funny, but I kept thinking I'd tell Aunt Freda about that later and we'd laugh and—" Kris's voice broke. "Then I'd remember."

His arm tightened around her. "I should've been with you."

"You were. Honestly. Every minute. It was as if you were with me, a part of me all the time." Even as she said it, she wondered how it would've been had he really been there. Papa was perceptive. He would've discerned that she and Tom were pretty close. He would be shocked out of his wits if he knew *how* close.

She wouldn't think about that. "Oh, Tom, your flowers were absolutely beautiful. Azaleas. You knew how she loved them. And, yes," Kris said, laughing, "that was something else I found myself starting to say to her."

"Your place or mine?" Tom asked when they were settled in his car. His place, he thought. Where she'd first come to his bed. Astounding him with an eager trusting innocence he'd never experienced before. From its beginning, theirs was a pulsating, passionate sexual union. But he'd missed more than the sex. He'd missed *her*—a warm, overwhelming companionship. Which was something else he'd never experienced with anyone else. It was more potent, maybe, than passion.

"My place," she said.

"But…" Freda's apartment. But *his* place was their private sanctuary. How to say it? Two weeks without her had been agony. Now… He didn't want their union spoiled by sad memories. He wanted to make love, talk, laugh, and—

"My place!" she repeated with such enthusiasm that he was momentarily distracted. He loved her enthusiasm. She sparkled with it. About everything—music, poetry, politics. Sex.

"Can you possibly imagine what it means to me?" she said. "My own place. I'm twenty-six years old and this is the first time in my life that I've had a place of my own. Where I can do whatever I want to do. And nothing I *don't* want to do! I can scatter my things around, eat breakfast in bed or—" she giggled "—make love with the man I love."

He grinned. "Okay, your place. As long as you're thinking what I'm thinking," he said, gently caressing her thigh.

"Always." She lifted his hand to her lips, sending an ecstatic shiver through him. He loved that way she had of kissing his hand…as if he held all that she wanted from life.

Later, they lay in her bed completely sated, their bodies entwined. They did talk about Freda, but even that was fun. The memories held no sadness for Kris. For either of them.

"The feeling that I can really talk to her is even stronger

here," Kris said. "Can't you just see her laughing? Celebrating with us."

"Well…" He didn't have Kris's imagination, but he did remember Freda's laugh. And any time with Kris was a celebration.

"I never would have met you if—"

He covered her mouth with his, and pulled her closer. "Don't say it. We were destined to meet."

She caressed his cheek. "Maybe. But Freda made it happen." She sat up, eyes bright. "And now I have a job and I can stay here. My supervisor really likes my ideas for the soap commercial."

"Not surprising. They're damn good."

"Anyway, I had the whole thing finished before I left. He was really great about giving me the time to go home. Two whole weeks! And I like my job. I like the challenge of promoting an idea."

He smiled. "You like everything! But I must admit, you're born for the ad business."

"And think of this, Tom!" She spread her hands. "A place to live. Where else in San Francisco could I find a place this nice for one hundred and fifty dollars a month? I'm going to—"

Tom stared at her. "One hundred and fifty dollars!" he broke in. "That can't be right."

"That's what Aunt Freda paid. Because of some arrangement with the landlord," she added. "I'll move into her room and set up my easel in here."

He was about to say something else when a knock sounded on the door. Kris grabbed her robe and went to answer. He heard her talking to Mrs. Spinella from downstairs before he dozed off.

It was almost dark when he awakened to her urging. "Get up, lazy bones. Mrs. Spinella brought us a casserole."

"Come back to bed."

"No. I've got it in the oven."

There was a little skirmish before he captured her, and it was some time before they showered and dressed.

"Lucky the casserole didn't burn," Kris said as she took it from the oven.

He was looking at the roses decorating the table. "Where did these come from?"

"Jerry and Clarence, the guys in number two. They brought them along with my mail. Wasn't that sweet?"

"Yeah," he said, vastly relieved. Those two had eyes only for each other. He was always surprised and somewhat disturbed by a sudden burst of possessive jealousy when some guy even looked at Kris. Funny. He wasn't the possessive kind. *Easy come, easy go* had always been his motto.

Before they were seated, there was another knock. Les Wimbush, the young minister from Freda's pray-to-whom-it-may-concern church, held out a bottle of wine. Kris invited him to stay and share it with them, but he said that May Webster had come over, and she'd brought dinner. The minister was no threat, either, Tom thought. There was always a May or some other devoted follower awaiting his command. Tom grinned. Kris wasn't the "awaiting" type.

"What are you smiling about?" Kris asked.

"About how everybody loved your aunt," he lied.

"Because she loved them," Kris said. "Everybody but the landlady. Aunt Freda positively hated Carol Sampson."

That reminded him. There was something he was going to say. What was it?

"She always told me Carol had no couth."

"No what?"

"Just an old folks' expression. No class or dignity, which fits Carol to a T. Aunt Freda said she was a floozy who latched on to Mr. Manuel, the former owner, even before Mrs. Manuel died, and moved in as soon as she was gone."

"Just moved in?"

"Yes. She used to work in his office. He was in real estate and she just brought the paperwork here. Freda said the old man was quite feeble by then, and Carol soon had their union legalized and took over everything he had. Which, Aunt Freda said, was what she'd wanted in the first place."

"Smart lady, huh?"

Kris laughed at his sardonic tone. "Smart, I grant you. But, according to Freda, she's no lady." She pushed back her plate and stood. "Well, I cooked, so you can clean."

"Sticking something in the oven isn't cooking."

"Whatever works. You ate it, didn't you? Besides, I've got to go through this mountain of mail Jerry kept for me. Mostly junk, it seems," she said, pushing aside dishes to make room for the papers.

She was halfway through the "junk" when Tom heard her scream. "Look at this!"

"Dammit, Kris. You made me drop this plate. Why the hell didn't Freda have a dishwasher?" he grumbled.

"Oh, shut up about dishwashers. Tom! Look at this."

"Okay, okay." He turned from the sink, wiped his hands and took the paper she held out.

"The nerve of her!" Kris cried. "Aunt Freda was right. She's got no couth. No sorry-about-your-aunt or we-need-to-talk-over-something stuff. This is so impersonal! *Look* at it."

He was looking. The document stated that said lease on Apartment 5B at 1400 Elm Street held by Alfreda Gilroy was terminated by decease of lessee. There would be an allowance of one month for the premises to be vacated. The apartment would be available for rent by the first of the following month. Lease available on yearly basis. Rent set at $1800 per month, first, last and security to be paid in advance.

"Can you *believe* this?" she cried.

He could. That was what had been nagging at him. Freda must have moved in here thirty years ago. Even so, by this time, her rent should've gone up. Way up!

Kris's eyes flashed. "I'm going downstairs right now and tell Carol a thing or two."

"Won't do any good, sweetheart."

"Why not? This can't be legal. No way could rent zoom like that! Not from a hundred and fifty to eighteen hundred dollars a month!"

"All this space and in this area? Eighteen hundred's the norm. I can't believe Freda got it for a measly hundred and fifty."

"Well, she did. I saw the checks. Anyway, she couldn't have paid more. Her social security check was just a little over five hundred, and that was all she had to live on!"

He'd never once thought about what Freda did or didn't have. He scanned the document again. "I don't know what kind of lease Freda had, hon, but I've never heard of one like this—even with rent controls. People are holding on to any lease like mad. This guy I know has a place on Nob Hill where his sister lived before him and his cousin before her, all under the same lease their uncle signed years ago. Or else Pete sure couldn't afford to live there now."

Kris's eyes brightened. "And that's what I'm doing. I'm taking over Aunt Freda's lease."

Tom shook his head. "It doesn't work like that. Freda's dead, Kris, and so is the lease. Pete's uncle is still alive and still holding that lease, even though he allows Pete to live there."

"Oh. It's Freda's lease, not mine." She sighed. "Even so, this isn't Nob Hill. Carol can't set such exorbitant rates."

"You'd be surprised. Check the classifieds."

"Oh, I intend to." She paused and looked around. "But this place is so perfect. On the top floor with all that light. I'll talk to Carol in the morning. Maybe we can reach some sort of compromise."

He knew the circumstances better than she. Long after she was asleep, he lay awake, worried. She'd never be able to afford a decent place in the city. And the places she could afford… Well, he didn't like to think of her living there. In fact, he wouldn't have it! He had to laugh at himself. There'd been other women, and…yes, he guessed he had cared. But never had he felt a need to protect them. Not the way he felt about this woman who lay curled against him—so innocent, so vulnerable, so trusting. He buried his face in the softness of her sweet-smelling hair and pulled her closer.

There was nothing for it. She'd have to move in with him—and his mostly absent uncle. She wouldn't like it. In the middle of a mammoth building. There wasn't much light. And no place to put her easel. Bob's room was sacrosanct, even if he was never there. Come to think of it, though, he might be back soon—if the Giants won the playoffs, and it looked like they might.

Tom hoped they would; he wanted Bob to meet Kris. Over coffee the next morning he suggested that Kris move into his place.

"What about your uncle? Didn't you say it's his apartment?"

"Well, yes. But I pay the rent when he's away, which is most of the time. Bob's too busy covering every major sports event from Australia to Timbuktu."

"He must come home sometimes," Kris said as she refilled their cups. "He might blow a fuse if he found a woman cozily installed in your bachelor quarters."

Hardly, Tom thought, since Bob was frequently accompanied by a female. Kris's naiveté never failed to surprise him.

"Bob? He wouldn't give a damn," he said. His uncle had never given a damn about what Tom did or with whom. Not since Tom had landed on him at fourteen, uninvited and unexpected. That was the night Angela had… No, he recalled his mother hadn't kicked him out. He'd run away after his run-in with her latest heavy-handed bedmate.

"Well, I'd give a damn," Kris said. "I'd be embarrassed if he walked in and confronted me, a perfect stranger."

Tom looked at Kris, but he thought about Bob. He'd been a virtual stranger himself, facing Bob that night. The man might be his dead father's older brother, but Tom had only seen him twice before, both times as errand boy when Angela begged a handout. He had stared at Bob out of his one good eye, as scared of him as he was of sleeping in the streets.

"Best to stay out of a scrape you can't win," the man advised, the first of his wisecracking advice. "And we'd better put something on that eye." He didn't say much else, and Tom worried that he might be thrown back on the street. Even now he remembered his surprise and overwhelming relief when he heard Bob say, "You can bunk here, but you're on your own, kid. I'm no baby-sitter."

Tom felt Kris's lips touch his cheek. "What are you dreaming about?"

"Nothing." He didn't like to talk about the bad times. "I'm thinking about you."

"Well, stop thinking. Your coffee's getting cold. And I can take care of myself."

"The hell you can. And Bob wouldn't—"

She touched his hand. "This isn't about you or your uncle. It's about me. For the first time in my life, I can be independent. Nobody telling me what to do or where to go."

"As if I'd stop you! Hell, Kris."

"That's exactly what you're doing. You don't want me to talk to Carol or look for another place or—"

"All right. Talk to Carol! Look for a place. You'll see."

"Thank you. I will." She wrapped her arms around his neck and kissed him on the mouth. "But right now…" She glanced at the clock on the wall. "I've got to get going. And didn't you mention a meeting at nine?"

"Yeah!" Tom jerked his mind from Kris and the past. "I've got this meeting with David Bernstein."

But Kris and the past still haunted him as he dropped her at Chandler, and drove to his place to park the car. Except that, as she'd reminded him, it wasn't his place. Thirty years old and he didn't have his own home. Never had. Before his uncle Bob, he'd been with his mother—moving from one crummy apartment to another, or worse, to a room in some rooming house or crowded commune. Angela, as his mother made him call her—and no wonder, since his birth certificate listed her as eighteen at the time—was a true flower child. No wonder about that, either. She'd been reared in an orphanage, relatives unknown, and her husband was killed in Vietnam two months before Tom was born.

Must have been tough, he thought as he strode through the streets toward Bernstein's office. He liked the exercise. Pressed by time or distance, he'd take a cab to his meetings. Less trouble and expense than parking.

He couldn't stop thinking about Angela this morning. Funny how his mother popped up in his mind now and then, although he'd never really known her. He'd spent more time with baby-sitters, both day and night, since she worked mostly at night as a cocktail waitress and slept during the day. He was ten, maybe eleven, when she cut out the sitters. By that time, she must've been well into the stuff that eventually killed her.

"Bad stuff. Stay away from it," Bob had said in his succinct way.

Dead from an overdose was the verdict when his mother was found, alone in her apartment. Tom had seen her only once since the night he'd left her, two years before. Maybe if he'd stayed…

Grief, weighted by a strange feeling of guilt, had been only partially lifted by the excitement of his first plane ride. The day was bright with only a scattering of clouds, and the little plane bobbed crazily as he scattered Angela's ashes over the deep blue ocean. He remembered the ashes, blowing free in the wind.

"As free as your mom is now," Bob had said.

Tom didn't know why that made him feel better but, like almost anything Bob said, it did.

Just as he'd claimed, Bob was no baby-sitter. Not a big

sports commentator, either, as he was now. A young struggling reporter, trying to survive on his own; sure didn't have much money or time to fool with him. But he took him in. Said he knew how it was to be out on your own before you were ready.

"Like your father and me," Bob had added.

But it didn't sound that way to Tom. True, they'd been raised by a single parent, their mother having died with the birth of Tom's father. But theirs was a stable parent with a regular nine-to-five job. And they hadn't had to move from one crummy place to another. "Sounds cool to me," Tom had said. "Always living in the same house, right across the street from the high school where your pop was a teacher, and guys coming over to shoot balls at the hoop over the garage door." If he'd had anything like that…

"That changed when I was nineteen, and I sure as hell wasn't ready," Bob said. "I was at San Francisco State on a football scholarship, having a great time." Bob sighed. "Then Pop had that fatal stroke, and everything went to pieces. I didn't have Pop's smarts. Didn't know what to do with Carl, your father, who was seventeen. I brought him with me, and I guess the change from our small town to the big city was too much for him. If I'd kept him away from Angela and the wrong high school crowd… Or got him into college before he got drafted…" Bob had a faraway look in his eyes. As if seeing what might have been, regretting what had been.

He tried to make up for it with me. Tom skirted through traffic, momentarily at a standstill. True, Bob had left him mostly on his own, but a casual word or two, dropped every now and then, sure kept Tom out of trouble. Being a certified coward might've helped, too. He grinned, thinking of the day Ray Gonzales had accosted him in the temporary safety of the high school gym. How was he to know that the blonde who'd been coming on to him was Ray's steady? He'd been scared out of his wits when the husky leader of the Mexican gang hissed, "I'm laying for you, honky! Gonna whip your white ass!"

"Gotta catch me first!" he'd shot back. "And I ain't no track star for nothing." He'd tried to keep the quaver from his voice, but he sure as hell meant it. Thank God that amused Gonzales. They'd never reached the buddy stage, but did achieve a friendly how-you-doing nod.

Yep, Bob's advice to stay out of a fight you can't win had paid off, just as his "You ain't built for body work. Best use your brain" had pushed him through college.

He owed Bob. Owed David, too, he thought as he boarded the elevator for Bernstein's office. His senior year in college, he'd been one of the student volunteers working on Bernstein's campaign for supervisor. That had landed him a job on David's staff, mostly as a gopher between Bernstein's law office and his supervisor's office in City Hall. Not much money but terrific training in the political life. Tom was hired as campaign manager when Bernstein ran for State Assembly and as his chief aide when he took the seat.

Tom had hesitated when he was solicited by Ron Baker, the prestigious lobbyist, to join his firm. It was David who'd urged him to accept. "Get out of here," he'd said. "You're the best negotiator I know. Lobbying is your thing."

David was right. Tom's expertise gained him so many clients that a few months ago he'd left, with Baker's blessing, to start his own firm.

Yep, he owed Bernstein, Tom reminded himself as the elevator slid to a stop. He knew the term in the Assembly was coming to an end and Bernstein was planning to run for the Senate. If there was any way he could help him, he would.

"David, you've got the contacts!" he was saying ten minutes later. "You need a lobbyist like you need a hole in the head."

"You can't tell me what I need."

"I can tell you what you can't afford."

"Oh, I see!" David's brows shot up. "You're telling me you're such a big wheeler-dealer now that I can't afford you?"

"Well, I don't come cheap." Tom grinned as he added, "Face it, buddy. You're not rich, and I don't see much money pouring in from the commercial big shots, given your penchant for the needy and other unpopular causes."

"I choose my own causes and I pay my own way and what's more—"

"Shut up and listen!" Tom demanded. "You don't need me. And, if you work it right, you won't need much money." He sat at Bernstein's desk, picked up a pad and began to make notes. "Talk to James Conover. Hold on!" he said when David began to object, "I know he's a right-winger, but he's heavy on the Christian right—pretty consistent with your do-good agenda. And get Asa Lockhart to run things. He's on the loose now, and he's good with the leftists. Now the fund-raising—"

"Wait!" Bernstein held up a hand. "There you go, Tom. As usual, giving away your expertise before you remember to charge for it."

"All I'm saying is—"

"And *I'm* saying you need a financial consultant. You're a patsy, but damned if I'll take advantage. Let's set your price before you tell me who to hire, how to plan and whom to draw on for funds."

Tom laughed. "Okay. But now that I've told you…"

"Yeah, who to get and why. But I need you to do it. You've got a knack like nobody else for bringing together diverse people with different objectives."

Something else he'd learned from Bob. "Everybody wants something," he said. "Find out what it is and work from that angle."

But what Bernstein wanted was Tom, and Tom finally took him on. He liked David, he liked his politics, and he got a kick out of telling people the best way to plan and accomplish what they wanted to do.

He didn't like the fact that stiff-necked David insisted on

paying him. He brooded over this as he entered a coffee shop for a late and solitary lunch. If he could raise enough funding, he figured, that might compensate.

CHAPTER SIX

NO WONDER poor Freda had dragged her sick self up these steps until she had to be carried out of here, Kris thought, as she mounted the stairs to the fifth-floor apartment. Where else could she have lived on her stipend from social security? And Freda was lucky, Kris realized now, that Mr. Manuel, her former landlord, had looked after her.

Tom had said there was no use mentioning Freda's lease, but Kris had done so anyway.

Overweight, overpainted, still trying to look sexy, Carol had grinned. "What your aunt had, sugar, was a love lease."

"Love lease?"

"That's what she'd probably call it, anyway. She was after him, tooth and nail! Dinner'd, pie'd, and cake'd him up the ying yang after his old lady died. But I soon moved in and put a stop to that!"

Kris thought of Freda in her jazzy purple tap shoes. Of course, measured in Carol's eyes... Carol wouldn't know about Piney Woods customs. You cared for a friend.

No matter. But she asked about the lease. She just wanted to know.

"Pity for the old bag. He knew she couldn't keep living here on her pittance," Carol said, revealing that Mr. Manuel had left notarized papers and a clause in his will stating that Alfreda Gilroy's rent was to remain as it was until the day she died.

Kris, weighted by anxiety, now dragged up the steps she'd skipped up lightly and happily only a few weeks before. There was neither pity nor love between Carol and her. No compromising with the strictly-business Carol, who had declared in smug screw-you terms that Kris must vacate by the end of the month. Less than three weeks away.

Where could she go? Every fairly decent place... Heck, even the not-so-decent places were out of her reach.

"Stay here," Tom had said. "You like this apartment."

"Are you crazy? Eighteen hundred? I can't afford it."

"I can."

"No!" she'd almost screamed.

"What's wrong with that? I'm here most of the time anyway."

"It would be your place. Not mine."

"So?"

"I told you. I want a place of my own. One *I* can afford."

"Why?"

"Oh, I don't know! I..." She hesitated. "I guess I just like being independent," she said, not for the first time. *Prepared* was what she meant. Jill had said it only once, the day she introduced them. But Kris remembered every word. *Watch this guy. He's the dangerous love-'em-and-leave-'em type.* Okay, she hadn't heeded the warning. She loved...was close, very close, to Tom. But when— *if* he moved on, she wouldn't have to move out. "I just want a place of my own," she said again.

She wasn't having any luck. She hated to leave the city, but tomorrow she'd try across the bay. An easy commute by BART. Of course, Jerry said rents were going up in Oakland and other nearby areas, as well. In any case, she intended to see for herself. She might just find the perfect place.

The thought lifted her spirits. She *would* find the right place, make it hers. Good thing she had Freda's furniture.

Oh, dear, that was something else. Moving costs.

Having reached the top landing, Kris entered the apartment and looked around. How did they get that old piano up the stairs in the first place? More to the point, how would she get it down? She laughed. Why was she getting sentimental over that clumsy awkward thing that sure wouldn't fit any place but here? If she couldn't sell it, and she probably couldn't, she'd leave it behind. As for the rest, she'd have to hire a professional mover. Better start checking on costs.

Well, she'd think about that when she found a place. With first, last and moving costs, she might have to ask Papa for a loan.

How could she do that? She hadn't even drummed up the courage to tell him she planned to stay in San Francisco. All she'd told him was that she'd been requested to stay on a bit longer at Chandler. A lie. And now that she had to leave Freda's place… What was the famous line? "Once you practice to deceive…"

Anyway, she couldn't put off her weekly call home another day. She dropped her bag and resolutely picked up the phone.

"Christina!" Miss Lizzie's throaty laughter rippled in her ear. "Felt in my bones this was you. Your ma's been waitin' all week for your call. And now when she and the Reverend are both at the Lodge Hall, here you come."

"Mama, too?" Kris felt guilty that she was relieved neither of her parents were home. They always asked questions that were hard to answer. "What's going on at the Lodge?"

"Oh, you ain't heard! Well, missy, this is gonna interest you. Big meeting. Some folks, 'specially your pa, are gonna talk about putting Ed Simmons up for Congress come the next election. Old Man Granger from across the river's finally steppin' down and they think Ed's ripe to take over."

"What a great idea. I think—"

"You like that? You'd like being Mrs. Congressman Simmons, huh? Up there in Washington with all them high falutin'—"

"Will you stop that, Miss Lizzie! Where Ed Simmons goes has nothing to do with me. How's everything at home? Did Mama get the new sofa for the living room?"

"Oh, yeah, she's tickled. I'll let her tell you 'bout it when she gets home. 'Spect she'll call you right back. Leelee, put that down! Lord, that child…"

"Oh, your granddaughter's with you? Let me talk to her."

"Yeah, she's here. Been here all day. Her ma had to work. Leelee's in first grade now and don't like it worth a hoot. Plays sick. Ain't hardly got a sniffle today but she claims she sick." Come here, Leelee. Christina wants to talk to you."

"Christina! You coming home?" a happy voice chortled.

"Not today, but soon. And I'll want you to read me a story. Have you learned how to read?"

"Not yet."

"I'll bet you will, if you go to school every day and do what your teacher tells you. Who's your teacher?"

"Miss Thomas. I don't like her. She don't laugh and play like you do."

"That's because she has to work so hard, trying to teach all the little boys and girls in your class. I'll bet if you smile at her and help her all you can, she'll be so glad. You're a smart girl, Leelee…." Kris chatted on, and in a short time had the little girl promising to go to school every day and pay attention and tell Billy Smart to behave.

Miss Lizzie laughed when she took the phone. "Lord, Christina, you always did have a way with her. I'll be glad when you get back here. Will it be soon?"

"When I can. Tell Ed good luck. It's been nice talking with you, Miss Lizzie. Ask Mama to call."

Kris put the phone down and sighed. Freda's stuff had to be out at the end of the month, and she'd been a real packrat.

She sighed again. So much to be done. What with spending nights checking the classifieds and looking at apartments during any daylight hours she could spare from work, she'd hardly given a thought to sorting and packing. It would take some doing to separate the wheat from the chaff, and she'd better start now. She munched on a sandwich and drank a hot cup of tea to fortify herself.

Clothing. Freda had been a seamstress with an excellent sense of style. Most of her outfits would be perfect for underprivileged trainees applying for their first jobs. She'd donate them to the appropriate organization. Freda would like that.

Papers. Tonight she'd clear out the rolltop desk. Mostly old bills and cancelled checks, she surmised, since Freda never threw anything away.

But when Kris opened a drawer, the first thing that confronted her was an envelope addressed to "My beloved niece, Christina Gilroy."

Kris stared at it, feeling her eyes fill with tears. Freda, who'd never talked of dying, had chosen this way to say goodbye. How kind. Kris wished she'd been as thoughtful, had remembered to tell Freda how much it had meant to be here with her.

Slowly, almost reluctantly, she opened the envelope.

Her eyes widened as she began to read. There was nothing about death or dying or anything sad. This was her light-hearted, joyful Aunt Freda, talking as if she were still alive and well.

My dearest darling delightful Christina,
Thank you for being here. It's been so wonderful to be part of your youthful enthusiasm and everlasting joy. The music and poetry sessions, the artwork making a mess of my kitchen, and your excited babbling about everything going on in this crazy city—it all awakens my old brain and gives me a new lease on life. It's been such a joy to share the adventures of my own youth with you and your friends, Jill and Tom.

  Never could I repay you, Christina. There's no way to repay joy. Certainly not with money or things, and I don't have much of either. But whatever is left goes to you. Can you believe that dizzy, impractical Alfreda Gilroy actually made a legal will? Consult my attorney, Richard Brown, 822 Market Street, Suite 402. I wanted everything clear, although there's not much beyond the attached insurance policy, which I took out when I started work at Finer Fashions. Have fun with it. Buy some paints and mess up your own kitchen.

Christina, you're a breath of fresh air, making my last days on this earth very happy. I love you,
Aunt Freda

TOM HEARD HER singing before he reached the top. One of those old spirituals. Kris was always humming or singing softly. But now her voice rang out quite loud. "Go tell it on the mountain! Over the hills and everywhere!"

He grinned as he opened the door and heard the next line, louder and definitely her own. *"Go tell it on the mountain that I'm staying right here!"*

She swung him into a dance as she sang the verse. Same tune, different words: "Tell it to Carol Sampson, the greedy scheming bitch! Tell her not to mess with Christina, that lucky gal is rich. Ha, ha, ha, hallelujah! Go tell it on the mountain, over the hills and everywhere! Go tell—"

"So tell me!" He laughed as he lifted her from the floor, bringing the dance to a stop. "What are we celebrating?"

"Tom, look!" She wriggled out of his arms, ran to the desk, and held up the paper. "This policy Aunt Freda left. Twenty thousand dollars! I don't have to move anywhere."

He sat with her on the sofa, reading it carefully. He could almost see the old lady grinning at them. "This is great, Kris."

"Isn't it! It's such a relief. I can stay right here."

He hesitated. But it had to be said. "For a year, maybe."

She stared at him, as if allowing his words to sink in. "Well," she finally said. "Okay, but by that time…"

"By that time you'd be right back where you are now."

Her face fell. "You're spoiling everything! I thought—"

"Hear me out. What you said this morning got me thinking.

It's time I had my own place, too. Could be a place with plenty of light and big enough for both of us."

"But I told you—"

"All right. Your place. I'll move in with you."

Her mouth dropped open. "Of course! Why didn't we think of that before? This apartment is—"

"Not here." He smiled. "You don't want to make the bitch richer, do you?"

"Well, no, but—"

"Make yourself rich. Your aunt gave you the stake, Kris. Invest it in your own place."

"With twenty thousand dollars? That wouldn't even make the down payment and my salary isn't—"

"I was thinking of us buying it together. It can be yours, in your name. We're always together anyway and…" He talked rapidly, trying to convince her. As he'd convinced himself this morning. He had a stake, which he'd been saving until he could acquire his own office. He already had an office, courtesy of one of his clients. TW Technology had eagerly offered him space in their building when he left Baker, and he was still there. And since he had a long-term contract with TW…

"I don't know," Kris was saying

"Well, think about it." One step at a time, he told himself. It might take a while to convince her, once she realized he'd have to supply much more than her twenty, and probably rely on his line of credit. *If* she found out. That wouldn't be a problem if she left the business details to him.

"I'm not sure that's a good idea," she said slowly.

"Will you at least go with me to look? See what's available?"

"Oh, sure, but—"

"Great." He smiled. *Once she sees those new condos on Ocean Heights…*

CHAPTER SEVEN

JILL, ALWAYS AN EARLY RISER, prided herself on being in ahead of the staff. Even before the efficient Nora, with Jill's schedule in hand. This was her quiet time to research and plan.

So far, she was pleased. Within a month she'd achieved a smoothly running operation at Chandler. And she'd done it with full cooperation from each member of the staff.

She was doing it!

Moreover, she was enjoying the challenge. She envisioned a brighter future for Chandler and welcomed the opportunity to pave the way.

Confess! You like being in charge of Chandler's business as much as you like being in charge of yourself.

More. It was definitely more fun than sitting alone at her computer, juggling figures and building up her own bank account.

Now came the hard part. Pulling Chandler out of the red. Which was why she'd arrived even earlier than usual this morning for a meeting with George Stewart.

She was just putting her bag away when he rushed in. "Hi, Jill. Been waiting for you. Here's your coffee."

"Thanks," she said, so surprised she almost dropped the mug.

The condescending George Stewart actually serving *her!* And, just as she'd predicted, he'd been her strongest support from the minute she brought him in. "Thanks for...well, for all your help, George. We couldn't have made it without you."

"I doubt that!" he said as he pulled up a chair. "You've got a soft-as-velvet manner, but underneath you're tough as nails."

Compliment or criticism? she wondered. Anyway, this wasn't about her. It was Chandler that was on the brink. "George, I've got to have the facts."

"Oh? What's up?"

"What's down is more to the point."

He grinned. "Like Haskin's Hardware?"

"Exactly. I'm not sure why we picked up those four companies anyway. Diversification," she said, frowning. "A big mistake."

"Maybe so, maybe no. Haskin's in the red, but Pack and Post might be keeping us afloat, and KLICK is holding its own."

"Just barely. That's what I need. Present financial standing, as well as a future prognosis of all four acquisitions. Precise, in a nutshell, and ASAP." Before she approached Randall, in other words. Chandler, a subsidiary of Randall Enterprises, couldn't dump a subsidiary of its own without Randall's approval.

"I'll get Carson on it right away. When are you seeing Scott Randall?"

"Soon!" she snapped. "Sorry," she apologized to the startled George. "Something else on my mind." She didn't want him to think her irritation was aimed at him. It was Randall she hadn't seen or heard from, nor did she know when she would.

"That's it?" George asked. At her nod, he departed, assuring her he'd have the data pronto.

It would all be a waste of time unless she could get ahold of the elusive Randall. He sure had a strange way of running a business. How could they possibly devise a constructive mutual agenda without conferring?

Well, she'd have to call him again, she decided and was about to lift the phone when her buzzer sounded. "Kris Gilroy, Ms. Ferrell."

"Kris!" she cried, "I'm so glad you called. I've been thinking about you, but I've been so damned busy I—"

"I know. I heard the scoop, which is why I haven't bothered you. Congratulations, Ms. President!"

"Oh, I think the closest I've come is Ms. CEO, Kris."

"Whatever. I know you're swamped and the only reason I'm calling is to ask if you'd like to have Aunt Freda's rolltop desk."

"Oh, Kris, you're leaving?"

"No. Just moving."

"You found a place?"

"Tom did. Oh, you're a little behind, Jill. You've been so busy at work and I— Oh, things have moved so fast I haven't had time to tell you. There was this letter from Aunt Freda. The sweetest letter. It almost made me cry. And laugh. She left me some money, Jill. Her insurance, twenty thousand dollars. Can you believe it? And then Tom... Oh, I'll tell you all about it when I see you. The thing is, I'm moving into a condo. With Tom!" Kris cried, a happy note in her voice.

It's as if she's hanging a halo around his name, Jill thought. She felt a tickle of apprehension. "When did you decide this?"

"Yesterday. Tom found it. Jill, it's absolutely fabulous! You've got to see it. Honestly, the most fantastic thing happened. Oh, I'll tell you all about it later. Right now, I've got to get Freda's things out and I wanted to ask—"

"Of course I want the desk. You know I love it. Look, why don't I meet you after work and—"

"Great! In the lobby. I'd like you to see the condo. And I'll be able to tell you what's happening."

Jill rang off, wondering. Was Kris doing the right thing? Kris had stars in her eyes. *Like I had right after college when I shacked up with Kevin. The stars were gone in one short year, and we were glad to get rid of each other.* No hurt. No regrets. *But Kris isn't like me.* She was the forever-after type. An innocent country girl who'd taken on the veneer of a carefree anything-goes city gal. Jill wasn't surprised by this move. She knew Kris would follow Tom, through hell or high water.

What did surprise her was Tom. He wasn't the shacking-up type. She tried to remember. Had she ever seen him in a long-term relationship with any woman?

No, his was usually a short spin with whoever took his fancy at the moment. And, with his good looks, he had to fight off the Tiffanys and Tanyas and Terris.

How long had he been seeing Kris? Has it been four months? No. Not quite three months since that morning at Starbucks.

I should never have gotten those two together.

Wait a minute—she didn't! She'd been having coffee with Kris when Tom came striding in. He marched straight to their table, his eyes on Kris, and the way she looked at him… *It was like I wasn't even there. Can't be my fault that she fell like a ton of bricks, can it?*

Maybe I should tell her…

Tell her what?

That dating and living with were two different things.

Anyway, how could she say anything that would dim the jubilation with which Kris showed off the condo later that day?

"Isn't this *fantastic?*" Kris asked as she directed Jill to their place.

"More than fantastic," Jill replied, overwhelmed. The condo was one of several that bordered the private Ocean Heights Country Club, with its tennis courts, eighteen-hole golf course and other facilities. "Will you have membership privileges?" she asked as they passed the club.

"It's optional," Kris answered. "We joined. Tom's a golfer, you know."

This was no little shack-up den, Jill realized as they entered the condo. Tom must really be in the money.

Kris only seemed interested in the fact that it was a private place she and Tom would share. Never one to keep still, she danced about, waving her hands as she talked. "We're so lucky that there are two bedrooms in the loft. We'll have the master and the other bedroom will be my studio! It's not a hobby anymore. I'm taking my painting seriously. And this spot—looking out, high above the ocean with all that sunlight streaming in!" She giggled. "I told Tom he could have the Jacuzzi. It's just by his office. But I'll have the light. Isn't this perfect!"

Perfect and very expensive, Jill thought. Fireplaces in both the living room and the master bedroom, and that fancy Jacuzzi off the den. Kris said they were buying it together, a strictly business equal-share arrangement, but Jill wondered about the *equal* part. Tom must've added a bundle to Kris's twenty thousand.

Still, Jill could only exclaim and admire. Yes, she agreed, the patio was large enough for some potted plants and one of those small wrought-iron tables with matching chairs, and she knew just where to look. Yes, she could see that Tom would want his own desk in the den that was to be his office. She was glad to take the rolltop desk and the lovely little chair that went with it. How much?

"How dare you ask!" Kris exclaimed. "Aunt Freda would want you to have it."

So she thanked Kris, and made arrangements to have the pieces delivered. They were valuable antiques. If Kris ever needed ready cash…

She shook her head, skeptical about Kris plunging headlong into this situation. Wholeheartedly and enthusiastically, no what-ifs diminishing the joy.

Oh, for goodness' sake, she'd better get her mind off Kris and on to her own business. She'd gotten ahold of Randall, and he said he'd be there at nine the next morning. Good. Just in time for their staff meeting. He'd get an overall view of the present status, and that would be a good base from which to introduce her proposals.

SCOTT RANDALL STIRRED restlessly, hoping the damned meeting wouldn't last long. He'd scheduled this time for a session with Jill Ferrell. He'd acknowledged her introduction with a few quick words, urging them to move on with business. However, no one except him seemed in a hurry, and it looked as if they planned to cover aspects of company business that interested him not at all.

Scott tried to relax. Yep, he'd made a wise choice, he decided as he watched Jill chair the meeting. Interesting.

The tilt of her chin in concentration or question, the way her delicately arched brows drew together as she considered something.

She had taken off the jacket of her tailored black suit; the plain white blouse with the wide cuffs and gold cuff links had a masculine cut. But the softness of the material, her habit of pushing back the sleeves and throwing up one small well-manicured hand to bring a stop to a heated debate, was so commanding and yet so touchingly feminine that...

Damn! Why was he watching her?

Listening with only half an ear.

And he didn't like the half he was hearing. What was all this about hardware?

His fault. He hadn't pointed out yet that his only interest was KLICK.

Well, what did he expect? He knew that Chandler had picked up these extraneous companies, focusing on profit, on the stock rating. Product often got lost in the process.

The build-a-better-mouse-trap approach made more sense to him, and when he'd sold the brokerage firm and started Randall Enterprises, he'd determined that his focus would always be on the product. The product that interested him now was a magic camera that, if developed, could have medical applications and save lives. Sims had been working on this, and said that someone at KLICK had been working toward the same objective. When this person died, the project was dropped. Scott didn't know anything about cameras. But when Talbert Sims said certain patents held by KLICK contained components he'd need, Scott didn't hesitate.

Not quite right, he thought, smiling. He did hesitate for a moment when his researchers filed some rather questionable reports about Sims. But… Hell, nobody was perfect. Sims was a genius and already credited with a slew of remarkable inventions. The value of this camera was worth a gamble. So he bought the company.

Scott's mouth twisted. Sims might be an inventor with a phenomenal vision, as his researchers had reported, but he was also an astute businessman. It had cost Scott a bundle to bring him in and a bigger bundle for his patents. Not to mention the time he'd spent in Washington between Talbert and the patent office.

Which was why he hadn't been here to get things going in the direction he'd planned. That was his policy with any company he purchased. It was even more crucial in this case.

Well, he was here now. He'd set everything in motion. One of KLICK's warehouses in Silicon Valley could be converted into a working lab. Sims, a stickler for the proper working environment, would have to select the right spot. There'd be plenty of space available once they dumped the extraneous companies.

About time, he muttered to himself as he watched Jill bring the meeting to a close. He started toward her, but was blocked by several members of the staff who converged upon him. Most of their greetings were the usual "Glad to have this opportunity to meet with you and so excited to be part of Randall Enterprises." Except for a gorgeous female with a mound of red hair who wondered if she might have a moment to get his opinion on some damn soap promotion.

"Later, perhaps," he said to her. He responded cordially to all the salutations, adding, as he tried to extricate himself, "I see that Ms. Ferrell is waiting."

Jill was indeed waiting, a veritable picture of polite and complacent patience.

Inside she fumed. The *real* head honcho had finally surfaced. She watched the managers gather around him—to present themselves, of course.

And this was your *show-off time, huh?*

She almost laughed out loud. That was exactly what she'd planned. Use this arena to show off the status *she* had achieved, which would serve as the base for *her* plans to change and improve. Just like Candy Atkins, she thought, thoroughly ashamed.

"I'm glad you were here for the staff meeting," she told him when they finally walked toward her office. "It was an excellent opportunity for you to meet our management team, to see what we're doing and what we're planning."

"Yes," he agreed. But he seemed distracted and was looking at her in that odd way. What was he thinking?

He was thinking he was hungry, and would have to be back at the hotel for a telephone conference at two. The time he'd planned to spend with her had been taken by that damn meeting, which only proved he should've gotten here sooner. "Could we have our discussion over lunch?" he asked.

"Of course. The executive dining room is—"

"Not here." He'd had his fill of executives. "The Ritz."

"The Ritz?" Her eyebrows lifted.

"Where I'm staying."

"Oh."

"I have a two o'clock telephone conference there, and in case our talk is extended…" He gave her a quick glance. "Is that a problem?"

"Oh, no. Not at all." So what *was* the problem? she wondered. Why did she find herself shying away from this man in anything other than a strictly business setting?

As they emerged from the building, a chauffeured car drew to the curb. He touched her arm to lead her to it, and she felt a strange quiver shoot through her.

Good Lord, I'm the problem. A simple touch, or the sound of that drawl...

She was being ridiculous, she told herself, settling back as the car moved into traffic. He was just a man. A man like her father, with the same winning smile. It was a good thing her dad didn't have that voice, though. He'd have had even more affairs than he did!

Steadying herself, she tried to focus on what Randall was saying.

"This talk is overdue. It's time for us to discuss our future plans."

Past time, and she was ready. "Yes. I've been waiting—that is, I need to consult with you about several matters."

"Same here. It's important that we not work at cross-purposes."

"There's more than one purpose?"

"Pardon?"

"Other than profit?"

His gaze sharpened. "No. There are simply different aspects."

"And different methods of achieving the same end."

"Certainly."

This was her area. She felt more comfortable and confident. "It's important that we're compatible on the approach. Which is why I've been anxious to meet with you. You're an elusive man, Mr. Randall."

He smiled. "Not elusive. Just involved."

"I understand. I realize you have concerns other than Chandler."

"Chandler is my concern at the moment, and has been for the past month."

So where the hell had he been? Chandler's concerns were based here. And shouldn't *she* have been involved, too?

"The preliminaries are pretty well taken care of," he continued. "Now we need to get started."

Finally. "The situation here is rather complex," she said.

"I know."

"We have problems that...that may take some time to re-solve."

"Which is why I plan to remain here. In residence."

"Here? I mean...you're moving here?"

"Temporarily. That's my policy with any company I pur-chase."

"I see." But she didn't see. Did that mean he'd be moving into the office, too?

He bent toward her. "I always have a definite plan in mind, and I like to be on hand to direct the approach to my ultimate goal."

He *would* be moving in to take charge. No wonder he hadn't been interested this morning, nor would he be interested in her proposals. He was going to direct.

She was only...what? The token. Not the first time a woman or a black had been used to give the impression that the com-pany employed minorities in prominent positions. It was a current practice.

But, as always, back to basics: White male in charge.

Suddenly she was finding it hard to breathe.

CHAPTER EIGHT

BITE YOUR TONGUE, she told herself as the car drew to a stop. *He owns it all.*

He doesn't own me! If she wasn't going to be a participant… If she was just a token CEO…

He can take this job and shove it!

And yet… It pained her to think of deserting. She had plans. She could pull Chandler out of its slump.

She'd pulled herself out, hadn't she? Waitress to…okay, not exactly wealthy, but pretty darn secure in five short years.

She had to chuckle. Comparing herself to Chandler?

Well, why the hell not! The only difference was that she'd have more to work with at Chandler.

"We're pressed for time," Randall said to the hostess as soon as they were seated. "I'd appreciate it if you could hurry things along."

Hurry should be his middle name, she thought. His first visit to the company had been a hurry-in, hurry-out affair. Now he was anxious to hurry out of this meeting, too.

"Have you decided?" he asked.

She looked up to see that a waiter had immediately appeared and both he and Randall were awaiting her order.

"Salad…er, the shrimp salad," she said, wondering if she could choke it down. "Pardon? Oh, yes, white zin." She needed the wine.

Randall bent toward her. "Listen. The very first thing I want you to do is find some space for—"

"That's right! For you."

"Me?"

"The president's office, of course." *If* she decided to stay and that was fast becoming a very big *if;* she didn't intend to be used as a front.

His gaze bore into hers. He picked up his knife. Put it down. "I think we need to get a few things straight," he said. "In the first place, I have no intention of invading your territory."

"My…what?" Was he reading her mind?

"You'll have your hands full with the proposed business changes, which will be completely under your supervision. In the second place, I already have an office. At Randall Enterprises in Wilmington."

"But if you're going to be here…"

"Temporarily. All I need is a small corner for me and my secretary. Until this project gets underway."

"I'll arrange for office space this week," she said. Wondering what project he was talking about and when she'd be informed, she added, "Our problem seems to be time."

"Good point." He glanced at his watch, nodding as the waiter brought their wine. "That meeting took up the whole morning. Doesn't leave me much time to clue you in."

"I arranged that meeting to clue *you* in," she said.

"Oh?" He actually looked puzzled.

"A brief review of company status. An introduction to key personnel, and—"

"Ms. Ferrell," he broke in with a show of impatience. "I was aware of Chandler's status before I bought it. As for key personnel… That's exactly what I want to talk about. Ah, quick service. Thank you," he said, pausing to let the waiter place their entrées before them.

He is hungry, she observed, watching him cut into his steak. "You mentioned key personnel," she prompted.

"Yes. The man who'll be heading this project will be here

tomorrow to look over the situation. He's particularly interested in seeing the KLICK buildings and equipment."

She stared at him, then took a sip of her wine as she waited for some kind of explanation.

"For the project. He'll be heading the *project*," he repeated, emphasizing the last word. "You'll be directing the business end of things."

Still reading her mind. Did he expect her to read his? "I see. Am I to be informed about this project?"

"I don't know." He caught her expression and laughed. "It's a deep secret. I was only included because the guy needed backing. And I'm telling you because you're to arrange working space for him as soon as possible."

Which in your language means yesterday, she thought. This new guy would probably have his own secretary and she'd have to rearrange everything. "Office space for how many?"

"Lab space. And I don't know how many. He's bringing in his own team. It's in the area of research and development."

"Oh." She felt her pulse quicken. Of course. "It has to do with cameras?"

"Yes."

"Good." She bit into a shrimp, relishing the idea. "We need help in that area. We lost a big contract with MGM because we were so far behind in the new projectors for the larger screen."

"This has nothing to do with movie projectors."

"Oh. What does it deal with?"

"Computers. And that's all I'm telling you. Except that Talbert will be here tomorrow to look over the area and select a suitable spot."

"Talbert?"

"Talbert Sims. You've heard of him?"

"Oh, yes." Who hadn't heard of the famous inventor? Cameras and computers... She became excited as it all started to make sense. "You mean Talbert Sims is working on new camera software for computers?"

"I'm not telling you anything except that Talbert's costing me a mint. So I'd like him to start as soon as possible, and a lab is crucial."

"That shouldn't present a problem. A whole floor at the KLICK plant is reserved for research."

His mouth twisted. "I see you know nothing about inventors, Ms. Ferrell. New projects are always developed in great secret with maximum security. He'll probably want a whole building complete with bars, burglar alarms, guards, guard dogs—whatever is needed to keep outsiders from knowing what's going on inside."

"I see. A fortress of sorts." Which Mr. Hurry-up Randall expected in the blink of an eye. "I suppose Mr. Sims has a design in mind for the space?"

"We'll talk with him when he gets here. I had thought that one of the empty warehouses could be converted for his use."

"Empty? All our warehouses are filled to capacity."

"But once we dispense with those holdings… That's another matter I need to discuss with you. These extraneous companies Chandler's picked up. I want them on the market. Immediately." She'd been thinking along those lines herself, but… "*All* of them?"

"Except KLICK, of course. Talbert wants access to the KLICK plant, old work records, that sort of thing."

And what Talbert wants, Talbert gets? She tried to adjust her thinking. Tried to see KLICK as just a cog in Randall Enterprises.

"Something bothering you, Ms. Ferrell?"

"KLICK." She swallowed. "Only a few years ago, you didn't buy a camera. You bought a KLICK. Then the appearance of digital cameras from competing companies had KLICK on the brink of bankruptcy."

"Well, yes, but—"

"But KLICK's making a rapid recovery now with its own digital model."

He smiled. "You're being sentimental, Ms. Ferrell. But you're right. And the recovery will be fantastic when Sims's project gets—"

"I'm *not* being sentimental. I'm being practical."

"Pardon?"

"A moment ago you spoke so callously of dumping what you termed those extraneous companies. I suppose that includes Chandler itself."

"Probably." He glanced at his watch again. "Time's up. We'll talk later. First, I'd like you to meet with Sims. He arrives tomorrow morning. I'll bring him by your office for a brief session, just to acquaint you with some idea of what he wants. Around eleven?"

She nodded agreement, still feeling somewhat at a loss. They hadn't discussed Chandler at all. They'd only talked about some great project that the great Talbert Sims was to direct.

JILL FOUND IT hard to conduct business as usual that afternoon. It was clear that she and Scott Randall were at cross-purposes. She was anxious to see Chandler restored to its former status in the advertising field. At their first meeting, Randall himself had indicated that it was the product that counted, and Chandler's primary product was ads, in print and on TV. With creative minds like Kris Gilroy's, they could be a contender, the way they used to be.

However, Randall's *only* interest seemed to be in KLICK. He saw it as a tool toward developing some magic camera software that Talbert Sims planned to produce.

She and Scott Randall both had excellent goals. Maybe they weren't incompatible. A KLICK camera in a unique computer software would certainly be an economic boost, if nothing else. And with such a famous inventor on staff, there was no telling what else might come forth!

The man was noted for many magical inventions. Phenomenal telescopic gadgets for NASA, a national award for some breakthrough in physics, which, like most of his achievements, she didn't understand.

Something else stirred in her mind, something vague and not complimentary.

In any case, it wasn't her habit to go blindfold into any situation. That night she entered the name *Talbert Sims* into her computer and found him all over the place—newspaper accounts, book reviews, national and international awards, scientists' meetings and discussions, patents, legal disputes and lawsuits. There was no time to delve deeply, but she learned much as she skimmed through the mass of information. The brilliant scientist had a difficult past. He had left—or been forced to leave—NASA for some undisclosed reason, and his laboratory, established five years earlier, had gone bankrupt shortly thereafter. She couldn't tell from reports on the various lawsuits whether Sims was the cheat or the cheated.

However, it seemed, at the very least, that Sims was a difficult man to work with.

Well, Jill decided, all professions had their glory-seekers, and in such a competitive field, there was bound to be some who-did-what squabbling. She determined that she wouldn't be influenced by what she'd read about him.

It took only a few minutes in the man's presence the next day to convince her that he was exactly what all those articles purported—an arrogant, obnoxious, demanding SOB!

He didn't seem to have much regard for her, either. Or maybe he was ticked off by Randall's advice to "Be nice to Ms. Ferrell, Sims. Your lab will be under the auspices of KLICK, and she's the one who'll get things going for you."

Sims gave her a curt nod and immediately turned to Randall. "Shouldn't be any problem. I've brought a few sketches. Here, I'll show you."

It didn't bother Jill that Sims spoke directly to Randall, ignoring her. Of course he'd defer to the generous donor with the deep pockets, rather like a greedy pig at a well-filled trough. He even looked the part—paunchy build, bald head, small squinty eyes.

Don't be nasty, she told herself, and began to listen.

Sims had laid the sketches on the desk. "This is a replica of my old lab, with several improvements," he explained.

Jill wondered about that. Was his old lab, the structure anyway, still in existence? Available? That would save a bundle, even if they had to buy it back.

Randall didn't ask. He was listening in respectful silence as Sims detailed the necessity for a specially constructed lab, special equipment and arrangements for twenty-four-hour surveillance.

She knew she should take her cue from the awed Mr. Randall, who seemed unconcerned about costs and anxious to please the cocky wizard. But she kept thinking about money. And KLICK.

They were on the project itself now. Still very hush-hush as far as she was concerned, but she did gather that it was something phenomenal in the medical field. She also gathered that some scientist at another company was reputed to be working on a similar invention. Someone who'd previously worked with Sims and could have gotten an inkling of the idea, at that time a germ in Sims's mind.

"He's got the concept," Sims was saying. "But he's not too sharp on procedure, and he won't have access to KLICK's old records."

Old records. The little digging she'd done last night had taught her about spin-offs from one scientist's innovative idea to another's great invention. Someone at KLICK at some time must have been developing something that offered the same kind of promise.

Randall turned to Jill. "You understand how important it is to set up this lab as soon as possible?"

"Of course," she said, and looked at Sims. "You spoke of

your old lab, I presume at Sims Electronics in New York. What's its status at present?"

He seemed surprised that she was still there. "Status? What do you mean?"

"Condition and availability."

"Unavailable," he said.

He seemed uncomfortable, and she didn't press the point. She could check it out. "I see," she said. "Then perhaps—"

"Besides," he interrupted, "I prefer a new building. The necessary improvements are extensive as well as necessary."

"I see," she said again. It might cost less to build than convert, after all, if his requirements were so stringent. "Have you considered a site?"

"Site?" He frowned at Randall. "We agreed that I'd work in Silicon Valley."

"We did," Randall answered. "I hadn't explained that to you, Ms. Ferrell. But Dr. Sims wants to work in close proximity to the old KLICK production plant."

"Then perhaps we should consider extending the production plant itself," she said. "We could go above or below."

"Unacceptable," was Sims's stiff reply. "Conversion of any existing structure could not possibly meet my specifications."

"It may be difficult to find a desirable site in the Valley. And the cost would be—"

"I made it perfectly clear that I wished to work in this area."

She smiled, in spite of her annoyance. "I realize that. But we may have to make a few compromises. We can look around and—"

This time Sims did focus on her, and his face was flaming. "Young lady, you should know that my contract with Randall clearly states that I shall have jurisdiction of my lab—personnel, equipment and location!"

She forgot to hold her tongue. "And *you* should know, Dr. Sims, that your lab is—"

"Let's not get ahead of ourselves," Randall's conciliating

drawl cut her off. "This is no time to discuss the details. You haven't even had a chance to settle in, Talbert. Why don't you do that now? My driver will take you to your hotel, and we'll meet for dinner later. I'll be detained here for a while."

Within minutes Jill found herself alone with Randall. He slammed the door and wheeled on her. "What the hell are you trying to do? Run him off before we get started?"

"He won't run."

His eyebrows lifted, whether in anger or amusement she couldn't tell. "You can guarantee that?"

"Absolutely. He's not about to let go of such a well-padded…"

"Sucker?" he supplied.

Now she knew. He was laughing. At her.

"Benefactor," she corrected, remembering that he was the boss. "Mr. Randall, I don't mean to…to…"

"To take my name in vain?" he asked, deliberately goading her, waiting for that irresistible sparkle of defiance in those remarkably readable eyes.

He was disappointed when she backed down. "I'm sorry," she said. "I'm just a bit concerned about your…your—"

"Judgment?" he challenged.

"Procedure."

He restrained a chuckle. She was trying to be diplomatic and finding it difficult.

"I certainly don't mean to question your methods," she said. "But…"

"Go ahead. Question."

Now came the flash of defiance. "You did say you wouldn't invade my territory."

He smiled. He liked a woman who stood her ground. "I did."

"The business is my territory, Mr. Randall."

"Right. You're in complete charge of all business details."

"Then I'd like to suggest that it might be more profitable to retain some of Chandler's holdings."

He shook his head. "You're losing me. I thought we were talking about KLICK."

"We were. And so far, all we've covered are expenditures. A vast amount."

"Toward the production of a phenomenal computer camera that will revolutionize the medical field and save many lives."

"Ah, yes, our eyes are on the product."

He knew where she was heading. "All right, I said it, Ms. Fer—no, Jill!" His mouth twitched. "Easier to argue on familiar ground, wouldn't you say? And I repeat—many a product gets lost in the profit-and-loss game."

"A few, maybe, Mr. Randall, but—"

"Scott."

"All right. Scott. I must point out that—"

"Hold it." He held up a hand. "I think I should explain something to you. I got out of the money market, deciding that I'd focus on product. KLICK is a necessary component in the product Sims plans to develop, and it was my only motive in purchasing Chandler."

"Oh. I see." Her eyes focused on him as if seeing much more. "Didn't you recently purchase HEALTH CARE?"

"Yes." How did she know?

"Like Chandler, HEALTH CARE's stock was still in the black," she said. "But only just. Why did you pay so much for the controlling shares? Especially since it's *losing* money now?"

She wasn't only a smart-ass, she was damned astute. He didn't like to admit that his reason for purchasing HEALTH CARE was purely personal. "Medical care is also a product," he said. "And don't worry, we'll get the company back on track."

She leaned toward him. "Mr. Ran...Scott?"

He grinned, watching the little furrow between her brows. She was gearing up to say something she knew he wouldn't like. "Yes?"

Jill paused, intrigued by that cocky I'm-on-to-you grin. For some crazy reason, it gave her courage. "Dr. Sim's contract is with Randall Enterprises. The laboratory, as I understand it, is to be provided under the auspices of KLICK?"

"Right."

"Having Dr. Sims with us is a bonus. This new computer software that he proposes, or indeed any innovation in cameras that he might develop, would be a plus." She hesitated, not sure how to put it.

"Exactly," he said. "KLICK's products are sadly in need of upgrading, wouldn't you say?"

"True. We do have that new digital camera, although it hasn't made a real impact on the market—yet. But research and new innovations take time and money."

"So?"

"We're not, as Dr. Sims seems to think, a charitable foundation that exists solely for the support of *his* particular research! We're an operating company that's having a hard time just keeping afloat and—"

"You forget that KLICK is now a component of Randall Enterprises."

Jill took a deep breath, hoping she could get her point across to Mr. Bountiful. "However," she began, "you did appoint me CEO and I feel it's my duty to make KLICK an asset rather than a liability. I'd like, if I may, to approach this from a different angle."

"Oh?" His brows went up and she couldn't tell if he was mocking or in a mood to listen.

Well, what did she have to lose? "If you'll allow me a free hand," she said, "I might be able to work toward a happy compromise."

"Oh?"

"Conduct a business. One eye on profit and the other on product, whatever it is. Let's say char—" The word stuck in her throat and she swallowed. "Scientific progress, if you will?"

"An interesting approach, Jill." The smirk in his smile told her that he'd heard what she didn't quite say.

Well, nothing wrong with a little *charity* if one could maintain a good balance, she decided.

"I think so," she said. "I have some ideas I'd hoped to clear with you."

"Ideas concerning what?"

"To ensure that we're not working at cross-purposes."

"Ouch! Unfair, Jill. Hitting me with my own words."

She returned his devilish grin. "Well, there'll be times when we may *seem* to be at cross-purposes. But if we're to maintain a good business—"

"Which is your territory?" He was doing it again. Half listening, watching her.

"Responsibility might be a better word." Her lips parted in a smile that didn't quite erase the frown. "We can't limit business to one territory. It's a factor in each segment of the whole—the making and marketing of each product, the personnel and machinery involved, as well as the financial structure to ensure ongoing production and profit."

She'd said a mouthful this time and he heard it. He opened his hands in full surrender. "As CEO of Chandler, you're that factor, Jill. So—"

The look she flashed him was more defiant than doubtful. "I'm not the whole factor and you know it! But I'd like to have some say in the business end."

"Such as retaining the baggage I'd like to dump?"

"Yes. Some of it, anyway. If it makes business sense."

"Okay, you have a deal."

"You mean it?"

"Absolutely," he promised, and watched the full lips blossom into a real smile. He wondered how it would feel to have those lips pressed to his.

CHAPTER NINE

SCOTT TRIED to keep his promise to Jill, but it was hard. Jill and Talbert Sims were definitely at cross-purposes, her focus on making money and his on spending it. Scott had difficulty refereeing the feud between them. It was one of their bouts that kept him at the office the night he visited his sister several weeks later.

He glanced at his watch as he pulled out of the parking lot. He had already missed dinner. Claire would be hopping mad. Like Mom, she always made her dinners special.

It was easy for Mom, he thought. She'd be sitting and conversing with her guests, the kids upstairs with a nanny, hired help dealing with the dinner details.

It wasn't so easy for Claire. On his first visit, he'd seen her preparing dinner as well as supervising two active kids and a fretting baby at the same time. Claire did say she'd hired help, but Scott wondered how much. He knew Dave was reluctant to spend Claire's money.

Hell, the guy was reluctant to spend any Randall money. He even limited Randall Enterprises campaign contributions.

Anyway, Claire seemed to be doing just fine. The night he'd made it for dinner there were flowers and candles on her perfectly set table, just like on Mom's. Delicious dinner, delightful conversation. The baby had been asleep, the other two well-behaved under their father's authoritative eye.

He remembered David and Claire talking like crazy—*to each other.* It reminded him of the very first time they met. He shouldn't have been surprised. Claire could appear frivolous, but she had a save-the-world heart. And David was full of ideas on how to do it.

Still, it had never occurred to him that Claire would take to David, the nerd, as he was classified by the girls at Yale. Claire hadn't lacked for suitors, and seemed to prefer the good-looking preppy New England type.

Actually, Scott was the one who'd latched on to David. He'd wanted the smartest guy in the whole school in his study group, and it proved to be a good plan. He could allow himself to get distracted during the rollicking years at Yale because David kept him on track.

When he'd brought David home for a visit, Claire had latched on to him and wouldn't let go. Never mind that their parents opposed this hasty union. As did David for that matter. For the very same reason. Claire was rich, and his moderate prospects didn't compare.

But when Claire wants something… And maybe I helped. I like David, and I knew he wasn't interested in Claire's money.

"Hey, do you two ever give me credit for this marvelous union?" he'd asked during that dinner a few weeks ago.

They hadn't even heard him. They were in a deep discussion about a bill that Dave, the do-gooder, was introducing— treatment instead of prison for small-time drug offenders who were addicts.

What had finally shut them up was a loud wail from the upstairs nursery. The baby was awake.

Then there'd been only confusion. Claire tending to the baby and readying the children for bed. David gathering his things for the trip back to Sacramento. And Scott had to take off to prepare for the trip back east. There hadn't been time for the talk he'd promised Claire.

No chance for a private talk tonight, either, he thought as he ran up the front steps. He'd take her out to lunch one day soon.

Dave opened the door and Scott heard the children making a fuss upstairs.

"I'd better run up and see them," he said.

"Better not!" His brother-in-law led him into the den. "You didn't show. Again."

Scott winced. Damn! He'd clean forgotten. He'd promised to take the kids to the water slides, but Jill and Sims had been going at it hot and heavy. "I got held up."

"I understand. Problem is, the kids don't. Claire's having a hell of a time getting them settled. Best to leave her alone."

"Mad, huh?"

"What do you think?" David selected two glasses from the bar.

Scott pushed aside a toy truck and sank onto the sofa. "I think I'm glad you're here." Claire was always in a better mood when her husband was home.

"I live here."

"Ha, ha!" Scott scoffed. As a member of the California Assembly, David was more often in Sacramento.

"At least I'm always in touch," David said. "Which is more than I can say for you. You've been here over a month, and Claire says you might as well have stayed in Delaware."

"Unfortunately she's right."

"Oh?"

Scott took the drink David offered and sighed. "It's been one hell of a month."

"Problems? Love or money?"

Scott snorted.

Dave grinned in response. "Forgot. You're never *in* love or *out* of money. What's left?"

"Women!"

"Oh." David, back at his perch on the bar stool, eyed him reflectively. "In general? Plural? Or one woman in particular?"

"All of those." Scott put down his glass, stood and glared at David. "A while back, I got a spiel from Talbert Sims. You know, the scientist. Really smart guy. And he's working on a project—tremendous stuff! Big medical innovation. Hell, it might've saved my dad if—oh, never mind the details. The point is, Sims needs money."

"Well, he came to the right guy!"

"It's going to be a big breakthrough. But in the wrong hands, it could become a moneymaker rather than a lifesaver. Know what I mean?"

"I know he came to the right guy!" David repeated.

Scott hardly heard. He strode around the room, talking rapidly, as if to himself. "It was tough getting Sims signed on in the first place—patents, contracts, that sort of thing."

"Seems Sims is also into big business," David commented.

"Yeah." Scott nodded, remembering Sims's complaints about his former sponsors. "Granted, he's a difficult guy, but he's been screwed so many times, he wants everything in black and white. I even had to buy KLICK, that old camera company that's on the skids, before he'd sign. The thing is, there's this woman CEO at Chandler, which owns KLICK, who—" Scott paused as a vision of Jill's determined face flashed before him "—who's, well, got a different agenda."

"Aha! The one woman in particular, I presume?"

"Yeah. New female executive type. Tough. Determined to hold onto the subsidiary companies Chandler's picked up that don't have a damn thing to do with this project. KLICK's the only reason I bought the company. Because of the camera software."

"You bought HEALTH CARE."

"That's what she said. But you know, I only bought it—"

"Because your mother's cook's brother was in that nursing home and he wasn't getting the treatment you thought he should get."

"Yeah. David, people are dying in some of those nursing homes!"

"A common occurrence at such residences."

"Oh, you know what I mean. Dying for lack of a little extra care that wasn't written up in the proviso, and just might mean extra money or special treatment. These HMOs have plenty of protective legal jargon."

"Uh-huh. Incidentally, is HEALTH CARE still in the red?"

"It's…well, yes. But I didn't expect a profit right away. Health care is big business now, more's the pity."

"And apparently you sold your business acumen, along with your brokerage. It amazes me, Scott, that your luck still holds."

"What are you saying?"

"I'm saying that thinking with your heart messes with business."

Scott raised his brows. "I can't believe I'm hearing this from a professional do-gooder!"

"Oh, I'm all for taking care of the needy. But business is one thing and charity another." Dave shook his head. "You've got so much charity in your system, I'm amazed your luck still holds. It's a puzzle to me how you can pick up a pile of garbage and sooner or later it comes up roses."

Scott brushed his nails against his chest in a gesture of mock pride. "Must be my business acumen."

"So you say. What I say is that a tough-thinking exec may be just what you need."

"Well, I've got one." Scott found himself smiling, thinking of Jill's "business is my territory" speech. Okay, that didn't bother him. She could dish out advice and he could take it or not. But…

"Hell, now she's going head-to-head with Sims. You gotta watch these strictly-business women who stick to their points like glue."

David laughed. "Now we're on to women in general?"

"Damn right! They're hard to deal with. *Harder.* The higher they land on the ladder, the harder they are. They're determined to prove they can handle anything and everything. Ms. Ferrell is busy handling Sims, who's determined not to be handled, and I'm caught in the middle. Can't afford to lose him."

"So fire *her.*"

Scott gave a start. "Huh?"

"Get rid of her. You don't have to keep her just because she's a woman. Not anymore. Affirmative action is losing out." David frowned. "Not that I approve. It's a good concept although it's often misused. You know, Scott, a large segment of our society, women included, have long been kept out of the mainstream. We owe…"

David had launched one of his lectures, but Scott's mind centered on Jill Ferrell. *Get rid of her?*

The overwhelming feeling of emptiness surprised him. He couldn't imagine not seeing her cheerful smile every morning. The smile was always there, no matter how tense their previous day's parting. Come to think of it, he'd even miss that determined set of her mouth each time she disrupted his day.

"It leaves me trying to balance between what's good and what's plainly a crazy giveaway. See what I mean?" David's voice got louder. "Hey, are you listening?"

"Huh?"

"I'm talking about women in business."

"Oh." Scott grinned. "At least they decorate the office," he said, well aware that it was an outrageous remark. But he liked the way Jill looked, so crisp and definitely feminine in some not quite-strictly-business garb, wafting that fresh and delicately enticing scent, dashing in with her quick purposeful stride.

"Never mind. That kind of sexist talk's going to get you in trouble. Come on back. Claire left dinner for you."

It was a simple meal. Tossed salad Claire had put in the fridge. Meat loaf and mashed potatoes David heated in the microwave. Manna from heaven for Scott, fed up with fancy restaurant fare. David was a lucky man.

"I hope you didn't get the last one, David."

"Last what?"

"Last woman on the home front."

"Thought you were the big-time liberal."

"Oh, don't get me wrong. I want women to be what they want to be. Football players, auto mechanics, corporate execs, whatever. I'm only hoping there's one who'll just want to have a family—and that I'll be able to find her. A woman like Claire, whose life is full with just you and the kids." He was grinning as he said it, but sobered. That woman wouldn't be Jill Ferrell.

David, however, was doubled over with laughter. "So you don't want a football player or an auto mechanic…."

THE LAUGHTER ECHOED all the way upstairs. Claire heard it and was suddenly engulfed by a painful wave of longing. To be downstairs with them, sharing in the talk, the laughter.

The baby on her shoulder whimpered.

"Shh, Joey. Mommy's right here," she whispered, nuzzling him, loving the feel of his soft downy hair against her cheek. This was where she wanted to be, cuddling her baby.

Nanny had cuddled her like this, even when she was older than Joey. Not the au pair girls, though. Mother? She couldn't remember. Actually, Mother had seemed more like an older sister. Just as she seemed now. A dazzling, bewitching, rather distant older sister, more often cruising with her new husband than visiting her grandchildren.

"I'm not bewitching," she told Joey, "but I'm here."

There was another burst of laughter downstairs. She smiled. "Your daddy's a clown. Did you know that? We don't want to listen to those stale old jokes, do we?"

David didn't tell stale jokes. He would be telling the unvarnished truth about something very current. But he could do it with a wry humor that captivated any audience.

He'd captivated her. The very first time Scott brought him to the house. She chuckled. *I'll bet he hadn't been there a whole day before I made up my mind to marry him.*

She sighed. It hadn't been easy. From the beginning, Mother and Dad bitterly opposed the match. Dave had…well, it wasn't so much that he had no money, but no connections, and she'd fallen head over heels for him.

It had been a real blow to her parents, especially her mother. She'd expected Claire to follow her into the high-society charity-ball arena. It had been hard to convince mother that she just wanted David.

Harder still to convince Dave that he wanted her. This time it was money, that she had it and he didn't. Well...not exactly. David felt that if she took care of the children, he should take care of the finances. He had to support his family. And how could he do that when she had so much money?

Of course he didn't express such a stupid old-fashioned idea in precisely those words, but it was what he meant. She would gladly have given him her money or given it away. But of course this, too, would have been a stumbling block because of that cursed pride.

She reached for the glass on the table and took a swallow of wine. She thought with sudden nostalgia of the small apartment they'd shared early in their marriage.

Then, a few years ago, Dave's father had a stroke. He'd made a quick recovery, but the stroke did prompt both parents to take early retirement from their university posts.

"Your grandparents aren't very rich, but they're very smart," she whispered to Joey. "They'd already bought into a retirement facility and they moved there, leaving this house for your daddy and me. Isn't it nice?"

It was nice. An old Victorian house far enough from the Haight Ashbury district to be respectable even then, but it could've been a slum for all she cared. With a rent-free house, David thought he could manage once they had kids, and if she promised not to touch a cent of her money....

"What did I care about that awful old money? I had your dad." And she'd had him every minute at that time, she remembered with deep longing. "I was his secretary in a little two-room law office. His pillow was next to mine each night, and every day was a new and exciting adventure," she told Joey. They'd had long, impassioned debates about politics, and she'd loved it!

"Your dad's where he belongs. He's a real statesman, concerned, caring and competent. I'd be right there with him if you guys hadn't come bing, bing, bing!" she said, laughing. "But not to worry. He has a way of getting things done, with or without me. Yup, your daddy's a smart man. Did you know that?"

Joey's only answer was a sharp cry.

"I know, I know," she said. "Your tooth's coming in, and it hurts. Mommy'll fix it." She applied teething gel, talking soothingly all the while. Settling him back on her shoulder, she rocked and sang a lullaby, occasionally sipping from the nearby glass of wine.

CHAPTER TEN

KRIS STEPPED from the curb into the Jag the minute Tom drove up, leaned over for a quick kiss, fastened her seat belt and smiled. "Nice!"

"Oh?" Tom said as he made a thank-you gesture to the driver who'd paused, allowing him to pull into the stream of traffic. "Nice to be chauffeured to and from work, huh?"

"That, too, since you're the chauffeur. But I was thinking in terms of *everything.*"

"Everything?"

"Everything nice, including my job. I love the work, I love the sketching and the new ideas that keep popping into my mind whenever we start on a new ad. And I love our condo, Tom, especially now that we've got it pretty well furnished. I think those azaleas in the planter off the patio are about to bloom. September! It's my favorite time of year, and for once I'm not stuck in a stuffy schoolroom. I love being here, and I love—" She heard Tom's cell phone ring and broke off. Which was a good thing. Best to stay away from the love-you mush. Jill's warning stuck in her mind. *Watch this guy! He's the love-'em-and-leave-'em type.*

But Jill didn't trust any man! What did she know?

She knows Tom. Knew him long before you did.

So? I'm not interested in forever. I can enjoy now, can't I? Anyway, Tom and I have—

Tom's next words caught her attention. "You've got it all wrong! I didn't cut out on you. Okay, I'm not at the apartment, but I'm still in San Francisco. I've just been too busy to… Oh, never mind. I'll explain later."

Kris's heart skipped a beat. Explain what? That he didn't cut out on whom? A woman?

"That was Bob," Tom said, shutting off the phone. "He's here to cover the play-offs and he's mad as hell at seeing no sign of me at the apartment. I told him not to unpack and to meet me at the office. He can follow us out. I want him to see our place. Okay if he bunks with us?"

She nodded, still reveling in the flood of relief that had swept through her at the sound of his uncle's name. How could one phone call, a few casual words, turn her into a suspicious, jealous bitch? She'd promised herself she'd never—

"Good thing we brought your bed from Freda's," he was saying.

"And a good thing I haven't had time to turn that room into a messy studio," she said, laughing. "My bedroom at home was always a sore spot with both Mom and Miss Lizzie, and Aunt Freda wasn't too keen about my mess in her kitchen."

"Never mind, sweetheart. The condo's your place, and you can be as messy as you please. I'm mess-proof. You should see some of the places I've stayed in."

"Well, our place is clean for Bob. The cleaning lady was here today. I'm glad you made me hire her, Tom. She's—"

"There's Bob! Right on time." Tom circled the parking area, motioning for Bob to follow him out. "This'll be a big surprise."

Bob was more than surprised. "I'm impressed," he said.

Kris knew he was. She'd heard his enthusiastic exclamations as Tom led him on a whirlwind tour. Tom was proud to be showing it off, she thought.

Well, of course he would be. Just as she'd be to show it off to Mom and…

No, she wouldn't. She'd told them that she'd bought "into a little place." But she'd given none of the details, and heaven forbid they ever found out, much less saw her new home.

"This is quite a place," she heard Bob say when the two were settled in the living room. "No wonder you dumped me."

"I didn't dump you." Tom sounded upset, even a bit guilty. "The apartment's still there, along with all your stuff and some of mine. The rent's paid up and I intend to keep it paid up."

"That's a waste. I'm not back here that much."

"Your things are there—golf clubs, computer, lots of personal stuff. It's your home whenever you do come back."

"You can't come home to a place, buddy. Only to people."

There was a long silence before she heard Tom's voice, a bit hoarse, as if he might choke. "You're right. I don't know what I would've done if you hadn't been there the night I walked out on Angela."

"Cut the guilt crap. You didn't walk out on your mom. You were thrown out. And now that you mention it, I'm glad you were. You being around kept me out of many a scrape."

"Oh, shut up. It was the other way around and you know it!"

"Good. I'm delighted you think you owe me. After the play-offs, we'll go over, dump stuff, store the rest and turn in the lease. I'll leave my golf clubs right here at home. Now let's move on. I'd like to follow my nose."

"What's smelling so good?" Bob asked as he and Tom joined her in the kitchen.

"Pot roast," she said, glad she'd prepared and cooked it last night with potatoes, carrots and onion soup, which added to the rich gravy and the appetizing odor. All she had to do was warm it up in the oven. "Hope you're hungry."

"Very. And getting hungrier," he added, touching his nose.

"Need any help?" Tom asked.

"Just the wine. Give me half an hour. Why don't you two relax in the living room while I—"

"We're staying right here with you." Bob's blue eyes, so much like Tom's, focused on her. "Got to get acquainted with the home folk." He seemed puzzled. "Kris… We had such a quick introduction. Gilroy? Did Tom say Gilroy?"

She nodded and opened the oven to slide in the pan of corn muffins. "That's me."

"Hmm. I knew a Gilroy once. God, it was ages ago! When I was a cub reporter at the *Chronicle*. We used to hang out at this bar. A couple played there, put on a great show. The guy, Gus, could whip the hell out of a bass fiddle, and the woman played the piano and sang. Boy, she could turn your heart over. Freda. I think her last name was Gilroy, and damned if you don't look like—" He stopped when Kris clutched his jacket.

"Aunt Freda!" she cried. "You knew her! Did you hear that, Tom?"

Tom smiled. "It's a small world," he said and gave Bob a short account of the connection, and how they'd all been together until just a few months ago. "And yes, Kris does look a little like Freda, doesn't she? Sings a little like her, too."

Bob was shaking his head. "I can't believe Freda's dead. She was so…well, so alive! And so happy, she and this guy."

"Tell me…" Kris still held on to Bob's jacket as if it was a piece of Freda. He'd known her during the happy times, when she and Gus were together. She peppered him with questions, so distracted she almost let the muffins burn.

She was rewarded. He seemed to enjoy talking about Freda and Gus as much as he enjoyed the roast, fresh green beans and crisp salad. "Guess I'll be back more often. Can't remember when I've had a good home-cooked meal like this," he said as he dug in with relish.

Kris hardly touched her dinner. She was too busy asking questions. "What did Freda sing? How did she look? And Gus, what kind of guy was he?"

"Funny!" Bob said. "He'd have us cracking up over his off-the-cuff jokes. The next minute we'd be spellbound when he and Freda'd pull out one of those blues songs and—"

"Would he sing it, too?"

"Both singing, both playing. They were great together. And

the way they'd look at each other... I never thought they'd ever—" He broke off, looking uncomfortable.

"Didn't think they'd ever break up?" Kris prompted. "Why did they?"

"Can't answer that. Things happen. I got into sports reporting, moved around a lot. I came back to the club one night and they were gone. Guess it was about six years later that I spotted Gus in a bar in L.A. He seemed as happy as ever, but he was looking a little seedy."

"Did you ask why they split up?"

"I did ask about Freda. All he said was 'we ain't together no more.' I said that's too bad, that she was a good pianist, a good vocalist. 'Good inside, too,' he said. 'That's why I cut out. She was too good for me.' Made me feel a little sad," Bob finished.

But Kris thought of her sparkling, delightful Aunt Freda. "You shouldn't be sad," she said. "Didn't you say he was as happy as ever? Those two had the kind of happiness that lasts a lifetime, no matter what."

IT WAS A WEEK LATER that Kris loped down the beach, trying to keep pace with Jill. She was panting, but energized by great gulps of fresh salty air.

Jill was right. If you *had* to run, Crissy Field was the place to do it—across long stretches of sandy beach to the rhythmic pounding of ocean waves rolling in from the bay.

If only they could skip the stretching, she thought as they slowed to a walk. The beach wasn't deserted by any stretch of the imagination.

"Everybody's busy with their own things. What makes you think they're looking at you?" Jill asked.

Kris shrugged. She didn't know why she felt as if the kids stopped building sandcastles, the mothers stopped watching the kids and the windsurfers stopped surfing to laugh at her. But doing that stretching right out here in the open...

Jill, bending to touch the ground, grinned. "We're not the only exercise freaks in the city."

Okay, so maybe she didn't look as dumb as she felt. And nobody in San Francisco cared what anybody else did.

Maybe it was the stretching itself that she hated, Kris decided as she did more squats.

"This is torture," she said. "Are you *sure* it's necessary?"

"Absolutely." Jill was lying unashamedly on her back, hands and feet reaching skyward. "My trainer says stretching is a must, both before and after running, to prevent sore muscles and to firm tissue."

"It's not doing much for my pot belly," Kris grunted. "Guess it's competing with my good old southern cooking."

"Which you do for Tom. You're spoiling that man. Better spoil yourself. Tuck that belly in. That's one thing my trainer says. Hold your belly flat when you're exercising, walking or just plain sitting."

"I'm having enough trouble just plain breathing. Not that I'm complaining!" Kris quickly added. "Since I'm getting all this instruction for free. How much do you pay that torture teacher?" Kris tightened her stomach, but almost lost control when she heard the price.

"She's worth every penny," Jill calmly said. "I still fit into all my size fours."

Kris gave an envious sigh and continued her stretching. Would she ever fit into one of those tiny designer outfits like Jill wore?

It seemed forever before they completed their routine and retired to a boardwalk table to rest and drink from their bottles of water.

"Tomorrow I'm bringing my camera," Kris said.

"Oh?"

"Or my painting gear. I want to catch the colors."

"Oh."

"This is absolutely the best time, too. When the sun starts to set. See that spectacular glow that's…well, not quite orange, more reddish, I think. See how it glints on the Golden Gate Bridge and brightens the focus of Sausalito's hills and houses in the distance? If I could catch that I—hey, you're not listening!"

Jill blinked. She'd heard Kris, but hardly a word had penetrated. "Sorry. I was thinking."

"About what?"

"Men!"

"Ah-ha! So is there a special man in your life?"

"Hell, no!"

"Then we're talking about business." Kris chuckled. "Don't think you can escape, Jill. The business world abounds with men."

"You've got that right! And they pack together like bloodhounds." Jill tapped a finger on the table. "Let a good ol' boy pull one magnificent merger and he's a big know-it-all-tycoon who can do no wrong, no matter how many blunders he makes. And there *are* blunders. I've checked his other acquisitions and—"

"Oh! So this deep meditation involves one good ol' boy in particular?"

"He's not even a good ol' boy. Just a lucky son and heir to daddy's brokerage and lots of money to play with. He should've stuck with the stock market, which *registers* profits. Doesn't know a damn thing about *making* profits"

"That's funny. I thought Randall was a big deal."

"Oh, he is." Jill frowned. "And I can't figure out why, the way he throws money around. Maybe it's the people who manage his other acquisitions. This one… Well, he's a hard guy to manage."

"Oh?"

"I'll say. You should see him handing over whatever Mr. Greedy Sims demands. And Sims isn't the only recipient of Randall generosity. I know Randall Enterprises is growing in leaps and bounds, but I don't see how. Scott Randall is more interested in giving than getting!"

"That's it!" Mischief gleamed in Kris's widened eyes. "You have the answer right there!"

"Where?"

"In the Bible. That's exactly what it says. Whatever you give, you get—in good measure, pressed down, shaken together and running over!"

"You and your Bible! This is business."

"It's working, isn't it? You said yourself that Randall Enterprise is thriving. You just don't like the man."

"Well, I…I…" Jill stuttered, thinking about it. "I guess it's his way of doing business that I don't like."

"Sounds like a smart businessman to me. He made you CEO, didn't he? What more do you want?"

"Cooperation. Not standing-over-my-shoulder supervision. And with that arrogant little scientist right beside him, hands out, ready to strip Mr. Moneybags of everything if I don't prevent it!"

"He can't be all that bad. Didn't you say he was thinking of dumping all the companies except KLICK and you talked him out of it? I'm glad Chandler's still in business. And going strong with my Simply Soap ads everywhere, even in Europe." Kris's eyes shone with pleasure. If he hadn't agreed with you—"

"It's the *way* he agrees—as if every dumb little woman has to be handled with care."

"Maybe you're misinterpreting what he says."

"It'd be impossible to misinterpret those 'Thank you, dear' pats on the shoulder every time he gets what he wants— Don't laugh!"

"I can't help it. He sounds like Papa thanking sister somebody for some favor she's done!"

"Believe me, there's nothing fatherly about Scott Randall. Nothing priestly, either," Jill muttered.

"The guy can't win," Kris said, still laughing. "Whether he's going your way or thanking you for going his. All that sweet talk isn't getting him anywhere."

"Oh, Candy Atkins eats it up! But she's still back in the dark ages when the big strong man was—"

"Ms. Atkins? She's the head of my department. She's a gorgeous woman."

"And capitalizes on it. She can be oh-so-helpless," Jill mimicked in a wispy intonation.

"Plays the little woman to the hilt?"

"You've got it. Between you and me, Candy's only asset is her looks. But me—I've got brains and good business sense. And Scott Randall's patronizing drawl is driving me crazy!"

"Drawl?" Kris sat up. "Where's he from?"

"Delaware. No, that's the business. I think the family home, estate, rather, is somewhere in Virginia."

"No wonder he sounds like Papa. He's southern. That explains the drawl, Jill. And the old-fashioned courtesy. It's ingrained in southern gentlemen."

"Bull! It's either condescending or a come-on. Or both."

Kris grinned. "What's wrong with a come-on? The first time Tom looked at me I knew what he wanted. I wanted it, too."

"Sex."

"What's wrong with sex? I've never been this happy in my entire life."

Jill couldn't restrain her start of surprise. This was obviously Kris's first affair, and with her upbringing…

"I know exactly what you're thinking," Kris said. "And, yes, my church and my father would condemn me for living in sin. But I think of what my grandpa said when Aunt Freda ran off with the guitar player. Okay, he used the word love, but I'll put it in my own words. Sex is a joy, not a sin."

Jill smiled. "Did he really say that?"

"He did. And he was a minister, mind you. But I've read the

Bible, too—believe me—cover to cover. And it seems to me that man, not God, put the sin in sex."

"All right. So you've cleared it with God, your grandpa and your father, but—"

"Oh, not with Papa! Good Lord, if he found out I was living with a man, let alone a white man, without benefit of holy matrimony, he'd skin me alive!" She took a swig from her water bottle and shrugged. "But I've cleared it with me. It's just one of the good things I learned from Aunt Freda. Remember that song she used to sing? *Ain't Nobody's Business But My Own?*"

Jill chuckled. "Indeed I do."

"Well, that's how I feel about Tom and me. And it's more than sex, Jill. I've never felt like this about anyone else. Tom's so loving, so full of fun, so straightforward and—"

"Spare me. You're in love," Jill said, and wondered if Tom felt the same way. And if he did, how long would it last? Legal ties do not a commitment make, she reminded herself, thinking of her father. Still… "Do I hear wedding bells?" she asked.

Kris looked surprised. "I hadn't thought about that, and I guess Tom hasn't, either. Anyway, Papa and Mom would… Well, marriage would make it everybody else's business, and I like it the way it is. Just Tom and me. Oh, did I tell you Tom's uncle was here?"

"Bob Harris, the sportscaster?"

"Yeah."

"No, you didn't tell me, but I've met him. How is he?"

"Fine. He stayed with us last weekend. I really like him."

"Hmm." Jill glanced at her skeptically. "He's older, but almost as good-looking as Tom and has just as much charisma."

"And you've got a bias against good-looking men with charisma. Well, I like Bob. He's comfortable to be with. And he's…well, deep. Almost like a philosopher."

Jill blinked. "Bob Harris? A philosopher?"

"Okay, maybe not quite, but…" Kris smiled. "Well, what

he says sometimes. It might be just a short snappy quip, but…
it's deep."

"If you think so."

"Oh, you! Anyway, he's Tom's family. And you know something? He made me feel like I was family, too."

Jill decided it was time to change the focus. "Sounds as charming as Scott Randall with all his smooth talk. Which reminds me of my father, too."

"All men remind you of your father. If he's a man he only wants one thing—sex."

"Yup."

"But, Jill, I don't think Mr. Randall's done anything wrong. So what if he's a little too charming for his own good—or for yours? Anyway, there's more to love than sex. So much more with the right man—compatibility, companionship, caring and just plain fun! But you don't give yourself or the man a chance. A second look, and you think all he's after is your underyonder—as Freda used to call it."

Jill smiled. "You sound like her. But you're right."

Kris shook her head. "Your dad sure did a number on you."

"Not me. On my Mom. Broke her heart a hundred times."

"And broke you—kept you from trusting any man."

"You got that right, too." Jill picked up her empty water bottle. "Coming?"

But Kris had taken her ringing cell phone from her pocket. "At Crissy Field, Tom. With Jill. Wanna pick me up? We could get hamburgers. Okay. And, Tom, bring that small palette, will you? And some tubes of…"

CHAPTER ELEVEN

JILL RETURNED Kris's farewell wave and went on to her car, suddenly feeling...lonely? Was she envious of Kris? Of the boundless joy and enthusiasm that sprang from her close relationship with Tom?

Had she ever felt that way about anyone? Certainly not Kevin, Jill thought as she got into her car. Their long-ago year of living together had been more convenience than love.

But Kris *was* really in love. Jill wondered again about Tom. He was known for short-term stints, one of which had been with Candy Atkins. Had Candy kept in touch? She hoped not. The up-and-coming Tom was becoming quite prosperous, ripe for the plucking, and Candy was an opportunist, as cunning as she was seductive.

Yes, Kris could be hurt. She was young and innocent. Trusting. Too trusting.

Jill considered all that as she maneuvered the car through the evening traffic. Kris's father had also, as she put it, done a number on her. He might be a so-called man of God, but so was that big TV preacher who got into deep trouble over his fling with a teenage parishioner! That guy was still in the pulpit, though, still surrounded by faithful followers who reminded Jill of her mother. Crying and packing to leave Dad one minute, and crawling all over him the next.

Well, I'll never let any man mesmerize me like that. Mr. Honey-voiced Randall could take his charisma and— Oh, why didn't he just stay away and let her run things?

Men! Dad wouldn't let her run the cannery, either. Of course, she'd left the island long before he died, mainly because she knew he'd never let her manage the business. He'd probably thought he was being fair when he left the new house to her, and the old house and the cannery across from it to Jake. It should've been the other way around. Jake had no head for business. Just last week, he'd called asking her for another loan. And he hadn't even begun to pay back the previous two. This time it was for a new cooker, which the inspector said was needed.

That was just plain maintenance. That old cooker should've been replaced long ago.

She couldn't understand where the money went. There'd been no oil spills or other emergencies, and the cannery had always brought in a profit, even when the catch was low.

All Jake had to do was haggle with the fishermen. He liked that. Playing the big boss. Stomping along the dock, just as handsome and virile as Dad, and—

That was it! Women! Jake was like Dad in that regard, too, but more of a soft touch. That must be where the money went. Or was it gambling?

Whatever. She wasn't going to support Jake's habits. Not anymore. She'd told him so in no uncertain terms.

Had she been running the plant…

The old bitterness returned.

And the loneliness. Suddenly she didn't want to be alone in her empty apartment. She was near the office, and decided to park in her reserved slot and walk around the corner to Tobey's for something to eat.

There was no one she knew at the sandwich shop. Well, she wasn't alone, even if she wasn't *with* anyone.

Seated at a corner table, she ordered a BLT.

While waiting to be served, she glanced at the couples around her. They seemed to be having a good time. Together.

Maybe she didn't *have* to be alone, she thought, taking her cell phone from her purse. She'd check her messages. Hearing Frank's voice, she smiled. She'd call him back as soon as she'd listened to her other messages.

The next voice blew everything else out of her mind. "It's Clem, Jill. Clem Dawson. I've been trying to get you. Sorry to leave a message, but…Jill, there was a fire at the cannery and Jake…he's been flown to the burn center at Hale in Seattle." The phone fell limply from her hands as the specter rose before her—flames shooting high, burning bodies tumbling. It was some time before she realized the message had continued and she hadn't heard. She returned to the beginning and listened, shivering as the words penetrated. *Burn center.* That meant…she forced herself to concentrate. "…trouble tracking you down. Sorry. Call me as soon as you can. Same number. 348-6690."

Oh, God! She dialed. The ringing went on. Eight, ten times. She cut it off. Checked to confirm the number and dialed again. No answer.

She carefully laid the phone on the table as everything blurred.

Except the fire. She saw the flames rising, heard the crackle of splintering wood. Saw Jake…

SCOTT RANDALL seldom wore his glasses, but he couldn't read small print without them. And this paperback, the latest horse-racing mystery by that jockey-turned-writer, was definitely in small print.

And…his glasses lay on his desk at the office.

Damn. He'd counted on the mystery to block out the latest Ferrell-Sims controversy.

What the hell! He'd walk over to the office and pick up his glasses. Good exercise. He stuffed the paperback in his jacket pocket. He'd start it while he had a sandwich and coffee at Tobey's.

A few minutes later, he was about to enter the sandwich shop when Jill brushed past him. Running.

Tobey was right behind her. "Wait, Ms. Ferrell. Your—"

Scott grabbed Tobey's arm. "What happened?"

Tobey shrugged. "Don't know. Took off like a bat out of hell. Left her phone on the table."

Scott held out his hand. "I'll take it to her." Seeing her turn into the garage, he sped after her, clutching her phone.

No wonder she got away so fast, he thought when he finally reached her at the car. She was in running shoes and shorts. He'd never seen the sleek Ms. Ferrell looking so disheveled— or so distressed.

"Can't find my key," she exclaimed, fumbling in her purse, heedless of things spilling from it.

"Check your pockets," he advised, retrieving the fallen objects.

"Oh." She found it in a back pocket.

He took it from her. "I'll drive," he said, and was surprised that she didn't protest at all. He replaced the lipstick and other objects, closed her purse and led her to the passenger seat. "What happened?" he asked as he fastened her seat belt.

She looked up as if just now aware of his presence.

"What's wrong?" he urged.

"Jake." In heartrending anguish, she repeated the name again and again. No mistaking her deep love for this unknown Jake. It shook him.

"I should never have left." That was all she said.

He got in the car, trying to figure it out. Something had happened to someone named Jake. A man she'd loved…and left.

But she hasn't forgotten him. He was surprised by a jolt of jealousy.

He was driving out of the garage when he realized that he didn't know the problem, nor where he was going. "Where to?" he asked.

"Seattle."

"Huh?"

"Sorry. I'm not thinking straight." She raised a hand to

brush back a strand of hair. "I need to catch a flight to Seattle. My brother's in a hospital there."

"Your…brother?" His relief was as much a surprise as the jealousy when he'd assumed Jake was her lover.

"Yes. I just got the message. There was a fire at the cannery, and Jake was taken to the burn center. He…he must be badly burned."

"I'm sorry, Jill."

"I'm sorry, too." Her voice caught on a sob. "It's…oh, God, it's my fault."

"Your fault? A fire in Seattle?"

"Alaska. The fire was at Dad's—Jake's cannery in Petersburg, Alaska."

"And you're in San Francisco. You're right about not thinking straight," he chided.

"I know," she said. Her lips trembled. A fire could've started anywhere, but she kept thinking about the dilapidated cooker. She hadn't sent the money. Self-recrimination overwhelmed her, doubling the fear. Her heart thundered against her ribs, and she found it hard to breathe.

He pulled to a stop at a curb. "Are you all right?" Silly question. Obviously not. She'd gone completely pale.

"Lean your head back," he said, adjusting the seat. "Now take a deep breath. Hold it. Let it out. Again…" He was glad to see a bit of color return to her face. "Better?" he asked.

"Sure. I'm okay. Kind of—"

"Discombobulated." The word just popped out, and almost coaxed a half smile from her. "That's what Mandy, our cook, said every time she got flustered. And that's what you are," he added. "Flustered. Rushing ahead before you find out where you are."

"What?"

"Isn't that what you always tell me? Stop and assess where we are before we take on something else."

"Oh, for God's sake! Business is one thing, and this is quite another!"

He was glad to see her angry. He could deal with that. "Now, listen."

"You listen!" she almost screamed. My brother is...is..." She faltered. "I don't...oh, God, I don't *know* how he is. I—"

"That's what I'm trying to tell you," he broke in, somewhat at a loss. He'd never seen the levelheaded Ms. Ferrell so out of control. He reached across to grip her shoulder. "You're imagining the worst. You don't know—"

"I know he's so badly burned they flew him to Seattle."

"Where he's getting the best possible treatment. And you..." He shook her gently. "You're no help if you fly off the handle. Go to Seattle, talk to his doctor, assess the situation—which is probably not as bad as you think."

She nodded. "You're right." She forced herself to speak calmly. "I'll call Agnes in travel and tell her to get me on the earliest flight."

"Don't do that. I'll have Red run you up tonight."

"Red?"

"My pilot."

"Oh." She stared at him, her confused mind trying to grasp what he'd said. He spoke as if his driver was going to drop her across town.

"I'll drive you to your place so you can pack," he said.

At her apartment, he took the key from her shaking hand and opened the door. "I'll park your car. Then I'll get a cab to the hotel. My driver will take us to the airport. We'll be here to pick you up in an hour."

Her head jerked up. "Us?"

"It's just a short detour. I was supposed to leave for Wilmington in the morning."

"Oh," she said again. "It's kind of you to rearrange your plans to—"

He cupped her face with one hand. "You didn't think I'd let you go alone, did you?"

This was ridiculous; she always traveled alone. She opened

her mouth to tell him so. But she couldn't speak past the lump in her throat. And she couldn't deny the comfort of those cool fingers against her burning cheek.

WHAT DID HE HAVE to lose? It was three days before the board meeting in Wilmington. He could easily stay in Seattle for one day, help Jill get settled and pull herself together. She was in no condition to face this ordeal alone.

When he returned for her, however, she seemed calmer. She had packed and changed for the short flight. Casually attired, but stunning, even in jeans. Especially in jeans. They'd arrived at the airport, and the heels of her ankle boots clicked as she walked slightly ahead of him. He noted the enticing sway of her slender hips in the form-fitting designer jeans. Looping an arm around her shoulders, he said, "This way, Jill."

The soft tone, the gentle touch, was strangely consoling. It didn't banish the fear and guilt inside her, but helped her bear it. And it was a relief not to have to endure the waiting and the hectic crowd of a commercial flight, she thought as she was ushered into the private jet.

"This is so kind of you," she said.

He smiled. "Glad to be of service, ma'am," he said, and she was reminded of what Kris had said about her father and southern gentlemen.

He led her into what appeared to be a luxurious living room, seating her in one of four chairs surrounding a small table. She'd forgotten he was rich, she realized abruptly as she sank onto the soft leather cushions. It was easy to forget, because he seemed so...well, not exactly humble, but he sure wasn't ostentatious about his wealth. Or his power, she conceded, remembering their heated one-on-one confrontations at the office. As Kris had said, he *did* listen to her. And he was never overbearing or condescending or—

"Coffee? Tea? Wine? Are you hungry?"

"Oh. No. No, thank you." She'd been so absorbed in thinking about him that, for the moment, everything else, even Jake, had escaped her mind. She was beginning to know Scott Randall, and found that she'd like to know him better.

Even though they reached Seattle early that morning, she was not permitted to see her brother until after consulting with his doctor, who wasn't available until ten. Scott insisted she have some breakfast, then stood by during her consultation with the doctor, who tried to reassure her. "His condition is critical, but he's holding his own."

"What does that mean?"

"It means he has a strong healthy body, and it's rallying. An encouraging sign."

"I want to see him."

The doctor shook his head. "That wouldn't be good for either of you."

Jill stiffened. This doctor who didn't look old enough to have graduated from high school, let alone medical school, was *not* going to keep her from her brother! She argued with him.

She won.

In protective garments to ward off infection, she was admitted to the intensive care unit for three minutes.

Outside the unit, Scott paced the floor. He shouldn't have let her go in alone.

What the hell was this compulsion to be with her?

She wasn't as strong as she thought she was. *That's it,* he told himself. *She needs somebody, somebody who's close.*

That threw him. Who was close to her?

Not you.

No, he couldn't say he was exactly close to the officious Ms. Ferrell, who'd given him nothing but hell during his three months at Chandler.

Attracted, maybe.

He shook his head. No *maybe* about it. Who wouldn't be

attracted to the engaging smile that sparkled in her eyes and lifted the corners of those kissable lips?

Kissable—even when she was crossed. Oh, yes, despite her strictly business stance, Ms. Jillian Ferrell was the most enticingly feminine woman he had ever encountered. The lips, the delicate curves of her slender figure, even the faint elusive scent she wore was so seductive that…

God! This was one hell of a time for it to hit him! How long had he been aching to take her to bed?

JILL FELT SICK. "Oh, Jake…oh, no."

"Sit here, Ms. Ferrell."

Feeling her knees buckle, she sank into the chair the attendant pushed toward her. Her heart turned over as she stared at the mass of raw flesh that was her brother. She saw only patches of skin. Dear God, could he be alive? It took a moment for her to comprehend. Jake was lying on his stomach. Completely naked and uncovered except for a kind of netting suspended above and not touching him. Oh, God! Raw flesh. Only patches of skin across his whole back. How could he stand it?

She couldn't. She hid her face in her hands. Couldn't block out the horror.

Her fault.

Dear God, please. *Please make him well. I'll never let him down again.*

She had to…had to tell him. She uncovered her face and whispered, "I'm sorry, Jake. I'm sorry."

Could he hear her? She wasn't sure. She felt a flutter of hope as she remembered the doctor saying that the front of Jake's body had mercifully escaped the flames. But all she could see was a little of his face, his handsome, always smiling face, now swollen and strained.

If she could just kiss his cheek.

No! She couldn't touch him.

"I'm sorry." She spoke louder, bending close. And caught her breath as a groan escaped his swollen lips. She gasped. "Do something!" she screamed at the nearby attendant. "Can't you see he's hurting?"

"You'd better leave now," the attendant said. "Time's up."

"But he's in pain. He—"

"We'll see to him. I'm sorry, but you'll have to leave now."

"But he needs me! I could…" She stopped, knowing she could do nothing. Not now.

Blindly she reached for the door and stumbled out.

She felt Scott's arms go around her. She clung to him, burying her face in his sweater, breathing in the nearness, the comfort of his presence. "I'm scared," she whispered. "Oh, God, if he dies…"

"Did anybody mention dying?" Scott's voice was gruff.

"No, but…" She tried to shut out the sight of raw flesh.

"Critical but holding his own is what the doctor said. Let's stick to that."

"But he's hurting! Really hurting. He—"

"Hurting's not dying, Jill. Healing, more likely."

She felt another flutter of hope.

"He's getting the best treatment. Now, let's—" He broke off. "Oh, there's your phone again."

"Phone?" She hadn't heard anything, and felt oddly abandoned as he released her to hand over the purse she'd left with him.

"You'd better answer. It's rung several times."

Mechanically she retrieved her phone and punched the Talk button. George Stewart's voice came through in a rush. "Sorry to disturb you, Jill. I got your message. How's your brother?"

"Not too good. He—" She couldn't speak past the lump in her throat.

Stewart voiced the concerns of the staff. "If there's anything we can do…"

"Pray," she managed. "And thanks."

"Wait. I need to— Jill, are you there?"

"I'm here."

"I hate to bother you with this now, but there are a few things I should run by you."

"All right." She tried to concentrate. Couldn't, and finally interrupted him. "You handle it, George. I trust your judgment."

"Okay. But wait, Jill! One more thing. Sim's been bugging me. He's trying to get in touch with Randall. Any idea where he is?"

"Oh. He…" She shot a questioning glance at Randall, pointed to him and then to the phone.

He took the phone. "Randall here."

Jill moved a little away. She'd been leaning on Randall who had his own concerns. George was in control at Chandler. Her concern was Jake, and she'd be here for a while. Thinking of hotel accommodations, she turned, and for the first time realized there were others in the room. A young couple holding hands, their expressions tense. On the sofa across from them, an older woman, sitting quietly, hands folded as if in prayer.

Looking at the folded hands, Jill's first thought was *cookies.* Crunchy, sweet-smelling, warm-from-the-oven cookies, which Rose Mason had handed out every Halloween, and sometimes when it wasn't Halloween. Rose had worked at the plant, too, for as long as Jill could remember. And her husband, Dan—

Oh, God! Dan. He managed the cooker.

God, forgive me. I hadn't thought… Only of Jake. But Dan… And others.

Guilt leaped through her. It was some time before she could cross to the sofa, take the woman's hand and look into her tear-stained face. Dan? Afraid to ask, Jill could only murmur, "I'm sorry, Rose. So sorry."

CHAPTER TWELVE

SCOTT HAD FINISHED the call with Stewart. His own cell phone had also been ringing all morning. It was at his ear now, but he was watching Jill, who was across the room, talking to that woman. He didn't like the way she looked. Was she going to fall apart again, as she had last night?

"Scott!"

The agitated voice on the phone got his attention. "Sorry. Didn't get that. You said—"

"I said that time's short. We need to review the Chamberlain deal before the board meeting," Al, his chief aide, repeated. "When will you be here?"

"Tomorrow. We've got plenty of time," he said and broke the connection. Jill was alone when he joined her, the other woman having left with an attendant.

Jill stared after her. "That's Rose Mason," she said. "Dan, her husband, was hurt, too. In the cannery fire. He…oh, God, he might lose his leg and she's… Well, I should wait and see to her."

"There's no one with her?"

"Oh, yes. Sally, her daughter. Buying coffee, she said. But—"

"Then we'll worry about you," he said. "We'll go to the hotel, have lunch and you'd better get some rest."

"Oh, that's right. I'll have to make reservations and—"

"That's done. Red took your luggage and checked you in at the Stanton. Is that okay with you?"

"Fine. Thank you." So much to thank him for. Simple things that she'd forgotten to do. Or didn't care about. Nothing mattered but Jake and what she'd done to him.

"Thank you," she said again when he opened the door of her hotel room and handed her the key.

"Will you be all right?" he asked.

"Sure."

He wasn't sure, though. He followed her into the room. "You haven't eaten," he said. "I'll call room service and—"

"No, don't. I…couldn't." The image of Jake's raw flesh swam before her and she felt sick. She sat on the bed. Held her breath.

She looked so forlorn that he wanted to take her in his arms, and tell her everything was going to be fine. Was it? "Don't let your mind play tricks, Jill. You're tearing yourself to pieces, imagining the worst."

She stared up at him, eyes flashing. "Third-degree burns. That's as bad as it gets, isn't it?"

"Hell, no. He's alive! Let's think positive. See him recovering instead of—"

"Easy for you to say. He's not your brother. You don't even know him."

"I know you're not doing a damn thing for him by torturing yourself. You need to—" He broke off. She had her hands over her ears.

She was hearing Jake. *Don't cry, Jill. It'll be okay.* That was the day she'd run down the block and got that long splinter in her foot. Jake ran all the way to the clinic carrying her. She rocked herself back and forth, remembering. Jake had been there for her. Not Pop or Mom, but Jake. And she hadn't been there for him.

Scott frowned. This wasn't like her. Not the efficient, alert, smiling Jill Ferrell who was always on top of everything.

The sight of her cringing and rocking like some empty-headed simpleton so enraged Scott that, before he could stop himself, he gripped her hard by the shoulders and shook her. "Stop it! Shit happens. A fire or a flood, nobody can predict it and nobody knows why."

"I didn't…oh, God, it's all my fault"

He saw the tears in her eyes and spoke more gently. "Don't be silly. It couldn't be your fault."

"But it is. I didn't send the money," she said.

She'd said something like this before, blaming herself for something she did or didn't do that surely couldn't have started the fire. But it was tearing her apart. He lifted her in his arms, sat in the big armchair and held her. "Tell me about it."

She buried her face against his chest. His protective warmth, the tender concern in his voice, released the tears. They rained down her cheeks and into his sweater. But tears could not dispel the grief and guilt banked in her heart, and for a long while she couldn't speak.

When her sobs subsided a bit, he urged her again. "Tell me. This money you didn't send…"

"The cooker. They needed a new one, and I didn't… didn't…" Her voice broke and she was suddenly silent.

"You didn't send the money. Why?"

"Because…because I was mad at him."

"Why were you mad?"

"Because Dad left the cannery to Jake, not to me, and I wanted it so much and I knew Jake wouldn't…couldn't…"

"Couldn't manage as well as you?"

"Well, he couldn't." She sat up, feeling defensive. "He kept running out of money. You can't bail a person out over and over again, can you?"

"Not a smart thing to do," he said.

"And this time when he asked me, I kept thinking about…" She stopped, not liking to mention women and gambling. She looked up at him. "It's funny how, when you get mad at somebody, all you remember are the things that make you mad. You forget everything else. Jake may not be that smart, but he cares about people. He wasn't even in the plant when the cooker…" She bit her lower lip and frowned up at him, eyes wide. "It was the cooker, you see. And…well, it just plain broke down, and the flames spread like crazy. Clem said Jake just rushed in as if the fire couldn't touch him, and started getting people out. Of course, Clem and practically everyone else was helping, too. They all had a friend or a relative in there. But Jake was the one taking huge risks. Rose said Dan was the first person he saved. She said Dan was fiddling with the cooker when it happened and part of it fell on his leg. But Jake got him out. Lots of other people, too." Now that her silence had ended, she couldn't seem to stop talking. "That's just the kind of stupid thing Jake would do!" she said, her eyes glittering with anger. "Like the time Sally Hendrix's four year old fell off the wharf. Jake jumped right in, boots, woolen jacket and all. Of course he got dragged under, and it's a miracle he saved himself as well as the child.

"But this time…Clem says Jake didn't stop until that beam fell from the ceiling and pinned him down. Clem managed to get him out, but…God! You didn't see him. There's hardly any skin…on his back, and…" Her voice caught, and she covered her face with her hands.

"They'll graft skin from other parts of his body."

"They say people don't recover from third—"

"*They* say," he interrupted. "Let's rely on what the doctor says, instead."

She tried to digest that. "Dan's holding on, too, Rose said, but…"

"Dan—the guy who got trapped?"

She nodded. "The man who handles the cooker. I talked to his wife at the hospital and she's afraid…he might lose his leg." Her lips trembled.

He took her hand in his. "Let's get one thing straight. None of this is your fault."

It was as if she didn't hear him. "The plant is virtually destroyed, Clem says. Others are hurt, too. Not as badly, but—"

"Hold it! I want to talk about *you*."

"Me?"

"You're smart." When she only stared in surprise, he smiled. "Okay, I know I've been giving you a hard time, but David said you were just what I needed."

"Who's David?"

"My smart-ass brother-in-law. He's always right, so I backed off. Good thing I did. You've saved me a bundle."

A wave of pleasure washed through her. He understood and appreciated what she'd done.

"Nobody told your dad, and I guess he didn't know."

"Didn't know what?"

"How smart you are. It's his fault, not yours, that he left the cannery in the wrong hands."

"Oh." She'd never thought of it in this light.

"How long has Jake been in charge?"

"Six…no, seven years. Since Dad died."

"And this Dan? How long has he handled the cooker?"

"Oh, my goodness. Forever. Since I was a child anyway."

"Strange that neither of them noticed that the cooker was a fire hazard."

"Oh, they did. Jake called me and—"

"Before appealing to you, I mean."

She was quiet, remembering. That had also occurred to her and made her so angry she hadn't sent the money. If she had…

"Their fault. Not yours."

She looked up at him, her expression doubtful.

"Time to let go, Jill." He saw that he had her full attention, and chuckled. "Past time. You're too intelligent to take the blame for faulty equipment three thousand miles away in a plant that's not and never has been yours. Nor is it," he added with emphasis, "your responsibility."

He was right. She'd left, but hadn't let go of the cannery that had never been hers. She'd never had control. So she couldn't be blamed.

This was a revelation to her, one she was beginning to accept.

He felt her relax against him. His words were sinking in. And some of the guilt was slipping away.

Not all of it. He realized it was difficult for the efficient Ms. Ferrell not to assume responsibility if she was even remotely connected. And when people she loved were hurt, her brother critically...

She felt so light in his arms, and looked so frail and helpless. Her eyes were closed, and he hoped she was falling asleep.

He was sure Jill hadn't yet grasped the full import of the crisis. The remains of the cannery in Petersburg would have to be dealt with; there was business to be handled. But she was not, at the moment, capable of handling it.

He'd let Al know he wouldn't make the Wilmington board meeting. The hell with the Chamberlain deal. *Deals, like death and taxes, are always with us.*

He'd stay with Jill until things got better for her.

He touched his lips lightly to hers, breathed in the faint elusive scent, and felt his heartbeat quicken. Strange having the tough, untouchable Jill Ferrell in his arms. As if that was where she belonged. Close to his comfort, protection and...love?

CANDY ATKINS GAVE a dismissive wave toward the corner table. She'd had enough of Lena's headache over the accounting system's switch. She ought to know by now that change was routine in this rat race.

Speaking of which... The scuttlebutt was that there'd be big-time personnel changes at Chandler. Which had her a bit worried. She'd felt pretty secure when old Wilcox was head honcho—held him in the palm of her hand. But now that there was a woman in charge...

Oh, the hell with that! *I'm tired of the rat race.* She'd rather laze on a beach, travel in a private jet, shop on Rodeo Drive. And when opportunity knocks…

More to the point, *when a Scott Randall comes within close range…*

She certainly wasn't wasting her mornings gossiping with the girls! Having discovered early on that Scott Randall wasn't to be found among the people exchanging hearty good-mornings in the executive dining room, she had planned well.

"And a Danish. That one," she said to the waitress who was arranging her take-out. That was the kind he liked.

"He's at his office early every morning," she'd told Shirley. "Working as if there weren't hundreds of people at his beck and call."

"Maybe he prefers to work alone," Shirley said.

"Well, he's too much of a gentleman to say so," she'd retorted with a sly smile. "Especially when you're bringing hot coffee." And, she'd added to herself, too male not to be intrigued by a sexy figure, coupled with a certain come-hither look in dazzling green eyes. Never mind that the glamorous green was from contacts and the inviting look from practice. It worked. She had the equipment and knew how to use it.

Plenty of men had fallen at her feet, but this was the first time so much old money had come so close. Imagine! Down the hall, only a few yards from her own office. If she handled things right, she'd be out of here for good!

Randall was part of a dying breed—the old-money, old-fashioned kind who wanted their women beautiful, decorative and without opinions of their own.

"I do hope you'll forgive me," she'd said that first morning. "I hate to disturb you, but I need some help. I did bring a bribe." She gave him a coy glance as she poured coffee.

"A delicious bribe." If he was annoyed, he masked it well.

"I'm glad." She flashed her prize-winning smile. "As I said,

I hate to disturb you, but I'm so excited about the new innovations, and promotion is such an important aspect of the business and… Well, I've run into a bit of a snag and I wondered if you could just give me a hint? I apologize. It's just that you were nearby and—"

"Of course. How can I help you?"

It had been that easy. He liked to advise and she was *so* appreciative. The morning-coffee routine was quickly established.

However, she was fast running out of troublesome snags to ask him about. And he hadn't made a move! No cozy after-work dinners, or any other invites, like a little getaway in his private plane. All she'd got out of him so far was one hurried lunch, during which he'd seemed more distracted than attracted.

Damn. She'd have to make the first move. Dinner at her apartment? She'd have something sent in, and when he arrived, she'd be wearing that sexy housecoat from Saks. "You must be tired of hotel fare," she'd say. "And I owe you. Why not join me for dinner one night?"

She was still practicing her approach when she reached his office.

And found it empty.

That was unusual. He was always in early, unless…

Unless he'd gone off in his private plane for one of his meetings back east.

His home base, come to think of it. He'd soon be leaving here for good, and if she didn't move fast…

She took the coffee to her own office, feeling so frustrated that she ate the Danish herself.

The morning went from bad to worse. A call from Stewart summoned her to his office to discuss "some reorganization." This had her feeling a little edgy.

Well, maybe George Stewart could tell her when Randall was due back.

It was in a disconsolate mood that she sauntered through the open door of Stewart's office at ten.

He acknowledged her presence with a nod and continued his phone conversation. "Certainly, Mr. Randall."

Candy's antenna shot up. Randall on the phone? Where was he? She studied her nails intently, and listened.

"Will do. Yeah, we'll hold the fort. Tell Jill not to worry. Yes, I'm glad you're with her."

With *Jill?* Interesting.

"Did I hear you mention Jill?" she asked when George replaced the phone. "Where is she? I'm supposed to check in with her this morning."

"You're to check in with me. She's gone to Seattle."

"Oh. Business?" Which, she presumed, needed Mr. Randall's input. At Jill's instigation, of course!

"Oh, you haven't heard." Stewart shook his head. "A sad business. Her brother got burned in a fire at his cannery, and he's in a hospital there."

"Oh, how terrible! Poor Jill. He's badly burned?"

"Touch and go, Randall says."

"Randall's with her?" But this was personal, not business! How the hell had *that* happened?

"Yes, and he says he'll stick around for a while. Says she's taking it pretty hard."

Naturally, Candy thought. With that handsome well-padded shoulder to cry on. "That's good," she said. "Someone should be with her." But…Randall?

Well, hell, why should that be a surprise? She got the top job in a New York minute, didn't she?

Oh, yes, the bitch is sly. All cool and official on the surface, but between the sheets… Now she's playing her deep distress to the hilt. Plenty of time to sleep her way into Scott Randall's pockets.

I knew it! She outflanked me. Cut me out while I'm still busting my butt trying to get in!

Candy didn't like to admit even to herself that she'd been bested. But she must've messed up somewhere. Playing the helpless woman while Jill played her own game.

Well, the game's not over yet, Jill Ferrell! He'll be back within reach soon and I know more between-the-sheets tricks than you've ever heard of!

If I can get him there....

"Now," George said. "You'll be glad to know we're making a change that considerably lightens your workload."

Candy jerked to attention. She didn't like the sound of that.

George, looking proud in his newfound authority, went on. "We're planning to add a few more high-powered sales staff to your group. They will, of course, continue to report to you. However, we're relieving you of the ad work altogether. That should be a good change, as your duties will be, shall we say, more...concentrated."

Diminished, she would say, like her prestige. And she didn't like it one bit. "Do you really think that's a good idea? The contracts with our clients are so critical."

"Oh, yes. We were lucky to get Al Goodman, the promotion expert, to head up contracts. He'll talk with the client and choose the team to do the desired work. He's bringing in a number of his own people, high-caliber artists in the creative field. Which should upgrade productivity and, happily for you, boost sales. This will entail some cutting of our present staff, of course. Making room for the new, so to speak. That should be done immediately, and I'll leave it to you, since you're familiar with the tenure and workmanship of the present personnel."

Candy left George's office, in a worse mood than when she'd entered.

Just as she'd expected, Ms. Jill Ferrell, in her officious role, was making big changes. And Candy's staff would be pared to the bone.

Downsizing or upgrading? They could give it all the fancy

names they pleased, but it still meant "You're fired," and no-body was going to take it lightly. They'd all be squealing like pigs at an empty trough.

No. They'll be squealing at me! While Jill Ferrell sits in her fancy office… No! Nestles in the arms of Scott Randall and sends out memos. I'm the one handing out pink slips and get-ting the why-me shit!

ON FRIDAY KRIS GOT her pink slip. When she returned to the condo that evening, Tom was in his office. She marched in and flung her purse on a chair. "I lost my job!"

"No!" Tom slid his chair back and looked up at her. "How could they let you go?"

"Cutting back. You know the policy. Last hired, first fired."

"Oh, honey, I'm sorry."

"I'm sorry, too." Kris perched on the desk and kicked off her sandals.

"Bad timing." Tom shook his head. "With Jill away and everything she's going through. Have you heard how her brother's doing?"

"Holding on, she says. I talked with her this afternoon and it's the first time she's sounded…well, up. Like she knows he's going to make it."

"Good. It's good for you, too. When she gets back—"

"That won't be for some time. She's staying there to look after Jake and the business. She says things are in a mess. I'm going to drop by her place every few days. Water her plants, feed the fish, stuff like that. Anyway, I don't want to worry her about me. She's got enough on her hands, and she'll have even more when she gets home. Chandler's in a whirlwind of reorganization. I'm not the only one getting a pink slip."

"But Jill's your friend and—"

"She's not my caretaker. I'll start job-hunting on Monday. The thing is," she mused, "I absolutely *loved* what I was doing. It's the first job I ever had that I really, really loved."

"And you were damn good at it. That must count for something."

"Ha!"

He paused. "I know someone else at Chandler who has a little clout."

"Who?"

"Candy Atkins. She heads one of the departments. Marketing, I think."

"You…" She studied him, slowly swinging her bare legs. "You know her?"

"Oh, sure. Candy and I go way back. Hit many a campaign trail together."

Kris's heart skipped a beat. Tom knew Candy Atkins? That stunning woman with the traffic-stopping red hair? He'd never said… Well, she'd never thought… Like he'd never had a past. Or any other woman. *Her* Tom.

He was laughing now in that hearty, happy way she loved, as he shared one of the campaign incidents with her. "That's Candy," he finished. "A real goofball. But a gorgeous one!"

She managed to laugh, but it was hard. The sharp painful stab of jealousy scared her.

"Yeah, Candy'll listen to me. I'll get in touch with her and—"

"No. Don't." She didn't want Tom in touch with any woman, especially the glamorous Ms. Atkins.

"Look, she probably has no idea how much you've contributed. Didn't you tell me they're going full-force with that soap ad of yours?"

Now she did laugh. "You're the only person who'd call it mine. You and maybe Jill."

"But it was your idea!"

"Oh, Tom, once an ad is developed, ideas change. They merge and grow, and—"

"And the creator might get lost," he said. "Well, you've got more than that going for you. You're a woman, a black woman, and in the corporate world today, minorities often have an advantage. You know, making up for lost time."

"Oh, please!" Her eyes rolled upward. "Don't go 'minority' on me!"

"Hey, if you've got it, use it. Everybody does— I know for a fact that Candy's used the woman ploy herself!"

"Well, I'm not using it. I'm not a category. I'm *me!*"

"Quite a delicious me, too," Tom said, tickling her foot.

"Stop it!" She giggled and kicked out at him. "I'm trying to think. I have to get a job."

"Oh, honey, you don't need to worry about that."

"I certainly do need to worry about that. I pay my own way."

"Well, I think we can work out an arrangement that might be—"

"I'm not a…a call girl!"

"Hey, it's the oldest profession going." He laughed. "I'll sign a contract. Top dollar for exclusive rights."

"Bastard!" She pounded at him with her fists. He pulled her into his lap.

No more talk of jobs or anything else that evening.

CHAPTER THIRTEEN

SITTING ON A DRIFTWOOD LOG at Honeycomb Beach, Jill was just out of reach of the gently swishing waves as the tide slowly receded. This was her favorite spot on Mitcof Island. Not very far from the little fishing and canning community of Petersburg, but far enough. She wasn't likely to be disturbed.

As a child, she'd often sat here to watch the whales that came to feed at Frederick Sound across the bay. It was a bit early in the year for whales and there was no sign of them yet, although she kept watching. Anyway, today she was here to think.

She didn't want to think. She watched the flock of gulls grubbing for food among the seaweed a few yards from her. She traced the flight of the bald eagles that rose from shadowy trees on Frederick Sound and soared across the sky. She breathed in the fresh misty air, reveling in a feeling of utter contentment.

How on earth could that be? Everything was a mess.

Jake was severely burned, still in intensive care.

But the doctor said the crisis was over, and maybe that was the reason for her contented mood. She was certainly happy that he was recovering, the intensive care only necessary during the early healing process.

She shuddered, thinking of the pain he must be undergoing. But, as Scott had said, hurting meant healing.

Scott. Lord, what would she have done without him? He'd been with her all through the nightmare of the past ten days.

Had held her in his arms like a child during the worst times, and talked away her fears. She smiled, remembering how warm and safe she'd felt in his embrace, soothed, even mesmerized by his soft intimate drawl.

But it was what he'd said that removed the heavy burden of guilt. The reasonable, honest words whispered in her ear had penetrated, made her understand that the fire wasn't her fault. Other words had lifted her spirits, made her believe that Jake would get well.

He was right. Jake had shown signs of improvement with each passing day. She could tell he was much better when he began to talk with her during the last couple of days she was at the hospital. She knew he was worried when he urged her to go to Petersburg, where she'd planned to go in any case. Jake was only repeating what Clem had said: somebody had to clean things up.

So she was here. With plenty to clear up. The cannery had crumbled to ashes. Thank God, people hadn't. There were only minor injuries, except for Jake and Dan who had, blessedly, both survived. But there was more than the physical damage to consider, like the livelihood of over one hundred and fifty employees, not to mention their children and other dependents.

She could strangle Jake! How could he let this happen? He'd just been going along on his merry way, letting the business go to blazes. And she did mean blazes. He'd let the fire insurance lapse. There was no money to rebuild the plant, and certainly no contingency fund to get going again.

Honestly, she could… Realizing she was set to light into her injured brother, she let her fists drop and almost laughed at herself. Almost. Funny how quickly compassion reverted to fury, once a loved one who'd made a fool of himself was out of danger.

Now she really did laugh. Better to laugh than to cry. No use being mad at Jake and mulling over what he didn't do. A waste of time.

She'd always wanted the cannery, hadn't she? Well, it was in her lap now, even if she did have to start from scratch. She'd have to sell most, probably all, of her stock, use her savings. Which still might not be enough.

Well, she didn't have a choice. Too many people depended on her.

Focus on the positive! That was what Scott kept saying those first awful days. He'd remind her that Jake was alive, then he'd talk about fresh starts and second chances.

Well, the positive was that she did have some money. Good solid capital. *Use it!* Hadn't she learned that the best way to build a business was on borrowed money? With collateral and her good credit, maybe some outside investors…

Right again, Scott! When you begin to think positive, you get good ideas.

And I've got plenty. From way back, when she'd wanted to get her hands on the cannery. And what a pleasure it would be to finally do things right. Shiny new equipment, a lounge for the workers, a baby-sitting area where workers could leave their children. The ideas flew through her mind and she could hardly wait for Scott to hear them.

Scott. Pure joy bubbled through her. He'd be here tomorrow. He'd called from Wilmington last night, saying he was leaving today. He planned to stop over in Seattle and check on Jake. That was thoughtful of him.

Then he'd join her, probably in the morning. She could hardly wait to tell him her plans.

The joyful sensations accelerated as she pictured him listening. Head tilted, brows lifted, his dark eyes brilliant with a patient intensity centered on her. Just as she'd had his full attention last week when she'd sat on his lap and poured her heart out. How wonderful to have a man you could really talk to, who made you feel safe and warm and…loved? In love?

That thought struck like a bolt of lightning.

It *couldn't* be. They weren't intimate at all, had never… Okay, she'd sat on his lap, but she'd never even kissed him, much less slept with him.

The only contact between them had been business. Until last week.

He wouldn't even have been with her if he hadn't happened to go to Tobey's that night.

He gave me a ride in his plane.

Probably because he saw you were a complete wreck, you idiot! And he said it was only a short detour, since he was going on to Wilmington

He didn't go. He stayed…talked, listened, consoled and supported. No friend could have been closer.

Good Lord! Am I turning plain friendship into something it isn't?

SCOTT RANDALL LOOKED down at the midnight-blue waters as the plane soared toward Mitcof Island. He was anxious to see the place where Jill had grown up. Anxious to be with Jill and learn more about her. More than he'd learned in the short space of one week when a crisis had torn down the barriers.

Oh, he'd known at first sight that she was a beautiful, desirable, sexy woman. But he respected her touch-me-not stand and backed off. Desirable sexy women came a dime a dozen.

Still, it had been intriguing to encounter a woman he didn't have to beat off with a slew of escape tactics. Jill was a refreshing change—independent, tough and as smart as she was sexy. A joy to spar with, not to mention the best business partner he'd ever had.

Red was circling now, preparing to land. Scott looked down at the little island that held Jill. The Jill he'd found at the hospital. Tough? Hell, no! Softhearted, caring, vulnerable. She'd snapped like a reed at the sight of her suffering brother. He was glad he'd been there to pick up the pieces.

There'd be pieces to pick up at Petersburg, too. Which was

why he'd rushed back from Wilmington. He didn't want her
to think he'd deserted her. She needed him.

Needed him like she needed a hole in the head, he thought,
as he stared at the tough little dynamo who met him at the airport. Had those rubber boots, worn jeans and oversize sweater
been stored away, waiting all those years for her return? Attired
like a fisherman, no makeup covering the smudge on her flushed
cheeks, the wind tossing her always-sleek hair in every direction, she was still utterly appealing, the loveliest, most irresistible
woman he'd ever known. He reached out to crush her in his arms,
run a hand through the tossing curls and kiss her until—

"Don't touch!" She laughed as she backed away. "I'm a
mess."

He didn't care that she was a mess. He wanted the closeness they'd shared a few days ago.

"I was at the cannery." She made a face. "At what was once
the cannery, I mean, and there's no way to keep from getting
messed up. But we're clearing the debris away and… But first
tell me how you found Jake."

"He's great, Jill. I mean, compared to a week ago. It's amazing how much he's improved."

"I'm glad to hear you say that. I thought so, too. I talk to
him every day, but on the phone you can't always tell—" She
broke off as his pilot approached.

Red gave her a friendly nod before turning to Scott. "Where
to, sir?"

Jill answered for him. "The Mitcof Inn. I made reservations
for all of you. And there's a jitney," she said, pointing. "It's far
more comfortable than my brother's truck," she said to Scott.

"I'll chance the truck." He wasn't about to let her out of his
sight. She was talking as fast as when she'd broken down about
her brother. Now she was probably anxious about the cannery.
"Just give me a minute," he said, and paused to give instruc-
tions to Red and Chuck, attendant as well as copilot. "They'll
check me in. I'm all yours," he said as he climbed into a rick-

ety truck that smelled of fish and was crammed with fishing tackle and other apparatus.

"I haven't cleaned up the truck yet," she apologized. "First I had to see to the cannery business, and straighten up the house, since that's where I'm staying. Sorry."

"No problem." If the truck was any indication, she must've had her hands full. Well, now he was here to help. "Shall we go by the cannery?" he asked.

"I told you. There *is* no cannery. Except in my head," she added, flashing a brilliant smile. "It's going to be… Wait. I'll tell you about it, but…"

She suddenly realized she didn't want to take him into the heart of town where people would rush over to her, just as they'd been doing all week, wanting to know what was going to happen. And when they saw her with a stranger… "Are you hungry? If you are, we could stop by the inn or rather, the house. I could fix something. Are you? Scott?"

"Huh?" He hadn't heard a word she'd said. He was still dealing with the smile—that radiant, confident smile. The old San Francisco smile before Jake's accident…

"I asked if you were hungry."

"Oh. Not at all. I had breakfast on the plane. Chuck fixed—"

"Good. Then we'll go out to Honeycomb Beach. It's lovely there now, and I want you to see it. Besides, we'll be undisturbed."

Undisturbed. He liked the sound of that.

She glanced at his smart slacks and Gucci loafers. "Better stop by the house anyway. I think you can fit into something of Jake's."

It wasn't exactly a fit, he quickly realized, but his belt would hold up the pants. And no way could his feet slip out of knee-high boots, he thought as he stumbled out of the house after Jill, who seemed to be in a hurry. He would've liked to linger in the spacious two-story house with large rooms and wide windows. Light, airy and as clean as the jeans and bulky sweater she'd handed him.

He stared at the colorful flowers in the window boxes as they drove away. "It looks like you still live here," he said. "You've been working hard."

"Not really. Jake keeps this house pretty much as Mom kept it. That's easy enough, since he lives mostly at the old house across from the cannery." She chuckled. "It's in the same state as his truck."

"The old house?"

"Where we lived until I was nine. That's when Dad built this house. He was making so much money that…" She paused. "Come to think of it, he always made money. It's a pity Jake didn't run the cannery like Dad did." She sighed. "Anyway, that's what I want to talk to you about. It can still make money." Her face became animated as she drove along the narrow gravel road and described her plans.

He couldn't take his eyes from the flushed, determined face, the lively sparkle in those hazel eyes, as he listened to the dreams he'd heard when she sat on his lap and poured out her heart. But more specific this time. Precise, delivered with the acumen of a well-trained, experienced and very clever business person.

He had forgotten. Would she ever need him again?

"What concerns me," she was saying, "is finding an architect. I want a design that's beautiful as well as practical, and finding an architect who understands the fishing as well as canning industries will be a problem."

A problem she'd handle, he mused as they descended from the truck, and Jake's boots sank into the sand of Honeycomb Beach.

"Isn't it gorgeous!" she exclaimed, her enthusiasm infectious as she talked of seagulls, bald eagles and the way water spouted from the whales who came to feed at the Sound across the bay.

He was fascinated by another Jill. The excited little girl who had roamed this island, dug along the shore for clams and swam in the murky waters of the bay. Before he could catch up with the child, she was again the expert businesswoman. What did he think the kind of plant she wanted would cost?

"Much more than the old one," he said, pleased by the thought. She *did* need him. "But that wouldn't be a problem if it became part of the Randall chain. I've been thinking that—"

"Oh, for goodness' sake, be serious, Scott," she said, laughing. "This isn't for Randall Enterprises. This is a tiny fish cannery, independently run by island people. Goodness, we've got less than two hundred employees and—"

"It still has to be financed, and you're talking about more than a few dollars."

"Oh, I've got that figured out," she said. Again she was the astute businesswoman as she spoke about collateral and the advantages of building on borrowed money.

"Collateral?" he asked.

He was stunned when she gave him some indication of her finances, particularly her stock portfolio. Yet, why should he be? No one knew better than he how fortunes could be made by shuffling paper. And, smart as Jill Ferrell was... Disheartened, he asked, "You'd stay here? To run the business?"

The question caught her off guard. And scared her!

To be stuck on this island. Away from Scott Randall? Not to hear his soft drawl and hearty laughter? Not to stride into the office every morning and see him, a lopsided smile on his face, ready to argue with her about another of his stupid giveaways? "I...hadn't thought that far ahead." But she was shaking her head. She didn't want to run the cannery? Wasn't that what she'd always wanted? When she couldn't, she'd run away and look what had happened!

Was she going to run away again? Jake's healing would be lengthy, and even when well he wasn't capable. Dan, too. It would take time for him to handle that leg. So many details. Lost records. Thank God unemployment insurance was a mandatory deduction from salaries. That meant the workers would have something to carry them until… How long would it take to rebuild?

The heavy burden of guilt returned.

"I may have to stay," she said, and had the curious feeling of a heavy trap door descending on her.

"Why?" Scott seated himself on a log and looked up.

"Because…." Why had he asked such a silly question? "Somebody has to be here to do it."

"Do what?"

"Oh, for goodness' sake! Everything. The plant has to be rebuilt."

"You're going to build it?"

Why was he angry?

"I…I'll certainly have to handle the business end."

"That can be done by phone or computer."

"Yes. I…suppose it could."

"And you don't have to be here at the site and watch bricks being laid."

She laughed. "Of course not. But I'm thinking about other things. Our workers will be without their salaries for some time."

"Unemployment insurance is between the worker and the state, isn't it? If you're thinking of supplementing their payments, I'd suggest you include that in the loan you're getting."

He was making more sense about her business, she reflected, than he ever did about his own.

"And," he added, "you don't have to be here to do that, either."

A spurt of joy bubbled inside her. Did that mean he *didn't* want her to stay? Because they were friends, she reminded herself. "You're right, of course. I guess I'm thinking more in terms of the long run. Who's going to run the business once it gets started."

"All you need is a good manager and a good accountant."

"Huh?"

"They'll report to and be responsible only to you. I'm surprised I have to tell you this. You run bigger companies from your desk at Chandler. The only difference is that you'd own the cannery—you and the bank."

No, the cannery owns me. It always had since the day she was born. Which was why she wasn't thinking straight now.

"Why do I get this outlandish notion that I have to handle every detail myself?"

"Because you know you'll do it better than anybody else."

She laughed. "Ego trouble, huh?"

"Oh, you just have to get used to being the boss. I did. I own a few companies myself, and I've learned to delegate, not direct."

She started to tell him he did a lot of directing at Chandler. Except he didn't. The Sims project was the only one that seemed to interest him. For all he cared, the corporation could go to pieces. Or into bankruptcy. Lucky that he did delegate. Preferably to people who were bent on making money, rather than spending it.

He stood and looked around. "So this is where you escaped. You must've been frustrated as hell."

"I guess so. I'd think about what I'd do if I ran the cannery."

"Because it was the only thing here that needed running," he said. "I'm glad you didn't get the chance."

"Why?" she asked, nettled. "I would certainly have done better than Jake."

"And been stuck on this island forever." He caught one of her wind-blown curls and twisted it around his finger. "You were destined for bigger things, sweetheart."

Again, she felt that spark of joy. Was it his touch? Or what he implied? That she was destined for San Francisco and bigger companies, broader knowledge, a wider world.

How could this man know her so well? With very few words he had released her yet again. Her happy heart soared, as free as the eagles who rose from the trees and soared across the sky.

"We'd better go," he said.

Only then did she realize the mist was rapidly becoming a heavy downpour, and they ran to the truck.

As she drove back along the winding road, the rickety vehicle rocked in the wind and rain that whistled through the nearby trees.

"Want me to drive?" he asked.

She shook her head. "I know the road," she shouted over the clatter of the windshield wipers. She should've noticed that a storm was brewing, but had thought only of Scott. Even now, the flashes of lightning and deep rumbles of thunder seemed to echo her joy that he was here. That she was safely secluded with him while the elements raged around them. She was almost sorry when they reached the house and raced through the rain, up the back stairs onto a small porch. "Leave your boots here," she said, and chuckled. "Guess old habits are hard to break." This particular habit was a sharp reminder of her mother; leaving no muddy tracks, they made their way to the living room. Julia Ferrell had kept the family house in perfect order, a sanctuary for her husband, Herb. No matter how long he'd stayed at the cannery. Or stayed at the old house with someone else.

A bitter mood was creeping in. Jill shook it off. "Let's have a fire."

Logs were already laid and were soon blazing in the big stone fireplace. Scott sat on the carpet before it, leaning against a bolster and stretching out his long legs. "Nothing like a nice hot fire," he said.

"How about some nice hot cider?" she asked, handing him a mug still steaming from the microwave.

He sipped. Coughed. "Hot in more ways than one," he said trying not to choke.

"Jeff Peters's special home-made brew." She grinned as she joined him on the floor, her back to the fire. "Potent and sneaky. Watch it."

"Lest I get lulled into erotic lunacy?"

"Into a drunken stupor, more likely. It has that effect." She laughed, but she was the one who felt lulled. Later she told herself it was that kind of night. Safely secluded from the wild storm outside, warmed by the fire and the cider…by him. By the firelight that danced on his face, spot-lighting the strength revealed in his lean handsome features. Lulled by the rain drumming on the windowpane, harmonizing with the same melodious drawl that had soothed and strengthened her through the bad days.

She had never told him what it meant to her. His being there had seemed so right, so natural.

"Did I ever thank you?" she asked.

He looked puzzled, then laughed. "Never mind. I can tell you weren't listening. And here I thought Red's reaction to Chuck's gourmet meal was so hilarious."

She still wasn't listening. She was feeling the pressure of a sensation she couldn't define. Not friendship or gratitude, but a gnawing hunger deep inside her.

She leaned forward and kissed him full on the mouth, whispering against his lips, "Thank you."

"For what?" he asked, his mouth gently caressing hers.

Reveling in the teasing tantalizing touch, she gave a little cry when he drew away.

He pulled her into his arms. "I'm not leaving you, sweetheart. Just setting the record straight. Why am I being thanked?"

"For…for… Oh, you know! For being there."

"And for being *here?*" he asked between slow sensual kisses that sent her heart soaring.

"Yes. Oh, yes!" she begged, hunger mounting with each kiss. "Please." She wrapped her arms around him and surrendered to the throbbing need. To stormy waves of passion roaring and thundering through her. To the ecstasy of fulfillment. To joy.

THE STORM WAS OVER. She woke to the sound of birds twittering a welcome to bright sunshine, and a fresh rain-washed breeze that stirred the curtains at her window. She lay cuddled in his arms, his long legs entwined with hers.

It occurred to her that this bed was too small for him. Sometime during their passionate union, he had carried her up to bed. Why had she directed him here instead of to—

No! Never to the master bed where her parents had coupled and quarreled. Where her mother had often slept alone, sobbing drunkenly. That bed was a curse that would taint their love—

Love? The word frightened her.

She wouldn't think about that. She was happy.

She lost herself in the happiness of the days that followed. Just being with Scott, walking on the beach, digging for clams, making love in her small bed.

To her delight, a few whales had begun to appear at Frederick Sound, a sight she didn't want Scott to miss. The day before they were to depart, they sat for a long time, field glasses trained on the gamboling beasts across the bay.

"Isn't it strange," she said, "how they know when and where to come for food and schedule it so precisely?"

"Yeah," he said. "Which reminds me. Shouldn't we be making plans?"

"Plans?" she repeated, her eyes on the whales.

"Marriage plans. When we'll do it, and where we'll live, and—" He broke off as her field glasses dropped and she jerked around to stare at him. "What's the matter?"

Her throat had gone dry and she could only shake her head.

"Oh, honey, I'm sorry. I'm a clumsy jerk, so crazy in love I'm going about it all wrong. Taking for granted that…" He stopped, looking anxious. "You—don't you love me?"

"Yes!" She wrapped her arms around him and held on, never wanting to let go.

He gave a satisfied chuckle and drew her even closer.

"That's all I need to know. Forgive me. I'll do it right when we get to San Francisco. Moonlight, roses and all the preliminaries. I'll even go down on my knees and—"

"Oh, shut up and kiss me." She didn't want to talk about marriage. The only marriage she'd known intimately had been one of great love and even greater misery. Was it possible to have the love without the grief? Did she want to risk finding out?

CHAPTER FOURTEEN

CANDY THREADED HER WAY through the throng of fashionably clad women in the hotel banquet room. She took a seat beside Shirley and cursed herself for being there. Women in Business dinner meetings weren't exactly a big interest of hers.

"Over here!" Shirley called to Sue Roberts and Lena Chambers, pointing to the two available chairs.

They hurried over, and Sue's eyes focused on Candy. "This is a surprise. Why are you here?"

"It's just for dinner and only because Shirley dragged me," Candy said. She'd seen the smirk in Sue's smile and knew what she was thinking. What they all thought.

Well, let them laugh! Maybe she was a throwback to the days when men were in charge. Lots of men were still in charge, and men were still men. Sex could be a productive strategy....

But this morning Shirley had kept harping on how "We women have to join together and fight."

On top of that, George Stewart couldn't stop talking about the excellence of the changes being made.

Changes that hadn't quite pushed her out. Just aside. But George had only one answer to any suggestion contrary to the big plan.

"As you know, we," he said, emphasizing the *we*, "are now under the jurisdiction of Randall Enterprises, and must adhere to Randall policy." He practically wallowed in importance as he spoke of other Randall successes, as if he was Mr. Randall Enterprises himself.

No point in buttering George up.

No point in being here, either, she thought as she surveyed the complacent women around her.

Most of them were high up in their companies, and a few were real movers and shakers. She had to admit that the fast-disappearing affirmative action had done some good. And these prosperous women were intent on other concerns—the latest designer fashions, the state of the stock market. And, as always, the men in their lives, current or ex.

Across the table Lena was telling Sue about her alimony problems.

"Got to stick to your guns," Sue said. "That's what I'm doing. Can you believe Hal wants me to quit my job? 'Because of taxes,' he said. We'd be in better shape if I quit my job.

"Quit yours, I told him. I enjoy my work. It's challenging. Just because he makes good money is no reason I should sit on my butt and play Mrs."

Better than the nine-to-five shift, Candy muttered to herself. *If the Mister's making good money, that is.* One personnel change could send a challenging job right down the tubes. *Like mine.* Anyway, she'd already decided to turn her considerable assets to a more lucrative pursuit.

"What's wrong with playing Mrs.?" she asked as she and Shirley stood on the parapet, waiting for their cars.

"Being subservient to and dependent on a man!" Shirley snapped. "That's what's wrong. Men haven't caught on. We're way past the barefoot and pregnant stage."

Candy had no intention of being either barefoot or pregnant. But dependent? Well, that depended on the man. "I could play Mrs.," she mused.

"Sure. *If* he's well off," Shirley said.

"What's wrong with having money?"

"The pickings are pretty slim." Shirley flashed a sly grin. "Looks like you missed out on the old money. Did you know Jill's in Wilmington with him?"

Candy did know, and her prospects there seemed slim indeed. But she played it cool. "There are more deep pockets in the city than his," she said.

"But not so close at hand." Shirley started toward an approaching car, but it wasn't hers. She turned back to Candy. "Looks like you missed out on some new money, too."

"What are you talking about?"

"Tom Harris. He's hot. And he just landed a big fat contract with SMS."

"Tom Harris?" Candy's eyes went wide. He was barely making it when she last saw him. "Isn't he still in that little office at TW?"

"Don't know about that. But I did hear he's living in a huge new condo at Ocean Heights. Too bad you let *him* slip through your fingers." The next car was Shirley's, and she waved goodbye as she sped away.

Candy stood there, trying to absorb this latest bulletin. Tom Harris? Good-looking. Sexy. And apparently rich. Not Randall rich, however.

But Randall's out of range, and Jill's playing hard. An iffy situation.

Ocean Heights. You didn't move into Ocean Heights. You *bought* in. And that took a lot of cash.

Maybe I made a mistake walking out on Tom.

Or was it Tom who walked?

Didn't matter.

Well, he always enjoyed a good lay. And it's never too late.

Or is it? She glanced at her watch. Not yet nine. Tom wasn't one to hang out at the bars. He might be relaxing in his fancy new condo. Alone?

Nothing to lose by checking. She reached into her purse, hoping he'd retained the same cell phone number.

THE CALL SURPRISED Tom no end. It was true that he and Candy went way back, but he hadn't seen her in— Had it been two years?

"Candy!" he said. "What's up?"

"Oh, Tom, I'm so glad I caught you. I was so afraid you'd changed your number. I've got a problem at work, Tom, and you know the promotion business better than anybody. Remember how I always used to get your advice? I miss that. But… Oh, I'm sorry. Am I interrupting anything?"

"No. Not at all."

"Are you sure?"

"It's okay, Candy. I'm just going over some paperwork that can wait."

"Well…then… Oh, I hate to bother you but I need your advice right now. Look, it'll only take a few minutes, and I'm not far from your apartment. Could I dash over and—"

"Hold on, Candy. I'm not at the old place."

"Got your own apartment, huh? All right, just tell me where."

"I'm pretty far out. Maybe…" He'd been about to suggest they meet somewhere, but remembered Kris had his car. She was at Bernstein's campaign headquarters tonight. They were sending out mailers.

"I don't care where you are," Candy broke in. "I really do need your help. Please. Just give me directions. I promise I won't take much of your time."

"That's not a good idea. Like I said, I'm pretty far out. But I'm glad you called. I'd like to see you—I need a favor. Why don't you come by the office tomorrow morning. Same place. Anytime. Just check to make sure I'm there."

"Whatever you need, Tom. If I can do it, it's done! But no. Not your office. Too many distractions. This is urgent and… Oh, Tom, I desperately need your advice. Now! I don't care how far out you are. Just tell me where."

As he gave her directions, he could hardly believe this was happening. Kris had told him not to bother, had been quite insistent that he not appeal to Candy. She'd said she didn't want to go over her own boss, especially to someone who didn't even know her.

But he knew how much Kris had loved that job. Now here was Candy, a big wheel at Chandler, about to appear on their doorstep. Out of the blue....

Maybe there was something to this "let go and let God" business.

That was Kris's way, not his. He wasn't that well acquainted with God. But who else could have staged it so well? It gave him an eerie feeling.

Even the timing was perfect, he thought as he replaced his file. Mostly he worked at his office but his was a people business and he kept his own people file, at home, out of danger of gossips—newspaper clippings, likes and dislikes, favors done and owed, people who might have some effect on his clients, pro or con. He'd been hard at work, perusing the background of a certain person who could influence a sticky situation at SMS, when Candy called, needing a favor.

One good turn deserves another, doesn't it? Too bad Kris wasn't here to promote herself. He wondered if she had some of the original sketches she'd done for Simply Soap. Probably not.

But she was damn clever, and had done a few things for him while she had time on her hands. Maybe he'd show Candy the sketches Kris had drawn for Bernstein and the campaign, which included some of the best political cartoons he'd ever seen....

CANDY THOUGHT HARD and fast as she drove toward Ocean Heights. What urgent problem could she present to Tom?

That old Haskins Hardware snafu?

No. Tom would know Haskins had been sold. Come to think of it, she wouldn't be surprised if he knew exactly what was happening at Chandler, too.

So what was wrong with the truth?

Plenty. It made her look bad. She certainly didn't intend to let him know she'd been...if not demoted, then pretty close.

But…if she stretched the truth a bit, turned it around…made it seem as if she'd negotiated the change.

"Such a heavy workload. I felt I'd been carrying it for too long. Without the compensation it deserves." She'd tell Tom she'd been thinking of starting her own little PR agency.

That might serve a double purpose. Tom had some big clients….

Too soon to suggest collaboration, but it actually was a good idea.

First things first. Get him between the sheets.

She was prompted to do just that when he opened the door. He wore an old T-shirt over a pair of ragged shorts, and looked absolutely delicious.

She threw her arms around him. "Tom, darling! It's been a long time."

"Sure has. Good to see you, Candy." She wasn't quite sure whether he'd pulled away from her or just pulled her in.

"Oh, my!" she exclaimed as she glanced around. "This is a surprise." Which she didn't have to fake. He'd moved way up. "I had no idea. Did Bob move with you?"

"Nope. Let me take your jacket. What are you drinking these days?"

"Same old."

"Good. I just started to mix martinis. Sit down. Won't take a minute," he said and disappeared into what she presumed was the kitchen.

She sat on the sofa, glad of the chance to study his place. She'd expected plush, but… Everything was uncharacteristically neat, and she'd never seen flowers in that stuffy apartment of his and Bob's. Signs of feminine occupancy?

She looked at the magazines on the table—news, sports, art. Not a single fashion magazine.

And no sign of another presence. Quiet. No television on anywhere.

Almost ten, a little late to be out. Well, there was no real indication of a live-in. *But I damn well intend to find out!*

"This is really a nice place, Tom," she said when he returned with a decanter and glasses on a tray. "Could I have a tour?"

"Later. Weren't you anxious to discuss your problem?"

"Oh, yes!" She put on her best hard-driven, trying-to-make-a-decision look. "I'm at a crossroad, Tom. And I'm afraid I—oh, you're going to think this is very naughty of me. But, well, you know there've been big changes going on at Chandler since Randall took over, and I thought this was the time to make a few changes in my own department. I suggested they split my load." She faltered a minute, a bit thrown off by his steady gaze. "It was… Well, you must know what a heavy load I've been carrying. Selling us—that is, Chandler—to the client. That's just the first step. Then you've gotta sell the client's ideas to the ad people or vice versa, which isn't always easy. So I suggested I handle only the business end, the sales people and contracts. Our ad work was sadly in need of upgrading. I knew Al Goodman was available and suggested we hire him, hoping he'd bring along some of his creative geniuses. They did get him and he's already brought in new blood. Things are looking up at Chandler," she said, hoping he'd infer that the improvements were due to her suggestions.

He merely nodded. "Which is what gave me the idea," she went on. "If I can do it for Chandler, why not for me? That is, start my own agency. I have contacts who'd follow me, and…" Switching to a plaintive expression, she peered up at him. "Is that sneaky of me, Tom?"

"A little self-serving, I'd say."

"Well, yes," she agreed, doubtful about his meaning. "Good business, huh? But now, you see, I'm…well, as I said, at a crossroad."

"I see." He did see. Candy had been downgraded. Was probably barely holding on herself. It seemed doubtful that she could do anything for Kris.

"I've gained quite a reputation, you know. I could stay put, of course. But I'd like to go out on my own, and I've got quite a list of established clients who'd go with me. That's why I was so anxious to see you tonight. I always depended on you for the right answer, Tom." She trailed caressing fingers along his bare thigh. "What do you think I should do?"

"I think you should slow down. Here, let me refresh your drink," he said and slipped from her clinging fingers.

"I wouldn't move too fast, Candy," he said as he returned, carrying the martini pitcher. He'd gone into the bathroom first, to turn on the Jacuzzi for Kris, who'd soon be home. "Stick with Chandler while you think it through."

"But…I *want* to start my own agency."

"It takes more than wanting."

"I know. Money."

He'd been thinking of brains and Candy's lack thereof, but all he said was, "A lot of money for the staff and office you'd need."

"Oh, Tom, isn't that just like you! I go dreaming big dreams and you plant my feet firmly on the ground. Are you suggesting I seek a partner?"

Nice work if you can get it, he thought. "Good idea," he murmured. "In the meantime, stay at Chandler. A bird in the hand…" He set down the pitcher without refilling her glass.

"If you say so. And I do appreciate you for lending an ear, Tom." She placed her hands on his shoulders and kissed him full on the mouth. "Thank you, thank you, thank you."

"You're quite welcome," he said and stood. She was after more than business, and he'd better get her the hell out of here before Kris got back. "I mustn't keep you. It's getting late."

"But you promised me a tour," Candy pouted.

"Sorry. It's pretty messy upstairs. And there's nothing much to see down here."

But Candy had already whirled away from him and was

starting her own tour. "Oh!" she squealed. "This is enchanting."

He knew she'd discovered the Jacuzzi, which had begun to fill. Kris was supposed to be home by about ten-thirty, and he'd promised to have her bath—*their* bath—ready. He followed Candy and saw her sitting on the side of the tub, gazing at the colorful flowers and comfortable pillows Kris had placed in the surrounding area. Maybe Kris had made it *too* damn enchanting!

Candy dipped her fingers in the water and peered at the skylight above. She held out her glass. "Don't throw me out yet, Tom. I've got to have that drink you offered me and a few minutes to relax in this beautiful place before I leave."

He took the glass and went to refill it. If she would just go!

When he returned, Candy's clothes were on one of the pillows and she was lying in the tub. "This is great, Tom. Come on in!"

"Candy, I'm sorry, but you have to go. I've got to—"

"Oh, don't be a party pooper. What've you got against a little skinny-dipping!" She got out of the tub and wrapped her arms around him.

He was trying to hold on to the glass while trying to push her off when he heard the front door slam. "Tom," Kris called. "Where are you?"

CHAPTER FIFTEEN

"OH, MY GOODNESS!" Candy shrieked. "Who's that?"

All he heard was the patter of footsteps and Kris's jubilant voice echoing from the den. "Guess what, Tom? We mailed over a hundred thousand—"

He tugged at Candy's arm. "Let go, damn it!"

But Candy retained her steel grip and was peering over his shoulder when Kris burst in. He heard her startled murmur. "Oh! Sorry."

The glass slipped from his fingers, a shove sent Candy stumbling backward, and he turned to race after Kris.

It was as if she had wings. He reached the front door just in time to hear the squeal of tires as his car sped away. His heart turned over and he felt a sudden cold fear. She could get herself killed.

"Oh, Tom, did we get into a little trouble? Who is she, anyway?"

He didn't hear her. In fact, was hardly aware of Candy's presence as he picked up the phone, dialed and listened to his car phone ring. And ring.

He felt a hand on his shoulder. "Oh, honey, I'm sorry. When we were just having a little fun…"

He shook off her hand and slammed down the phone, thinking of Kris's foot flat on the pedal of his high-speed sports car, racing around those curves.

God! If anything happened to Kris…

"Silly of her to fly off like that, wasn't it? Jealous possessive type, huh?"

The police? He picked up the phone again. Put it down.

At that speed in a car that wasn't hers? No. Not the police.

"Good Lord, does she think she's the only woman in your life?"

He could go after her. No, he couldn't. "She's got my car," he muttered.

"Took your car? That's a shame. We'd better go get it before she wrecks it!"

For the first time he came out of the nightmare to focus on Candy. "You'd better leave. Now."

"But I want to help. We'll take my car and—"

"You take your car and get out of here. I've got to—"

"Oh, honey, don't be mad. It's as much your fault as mine."

"Right. I forgot what a bitch you are."

"Oh, Tom! How can you say that? I just wanted to talk to you and—"

"You didn't come here to talk."

"Oh, but I did. I was desperate to get your advice."

"Advice? Like hell!"

"Now, Tom, you know as well as I do that what happened...well, it just happened. We always did send sparks flying when we got together, didn't we?" She moved closer, touched his cheek and looked up at him.

He felt her nude body press against him, caught the sly gleam in the green eyes. Turned away.

"Wait, Tom. If you want, I'll talk to her. It won't be hard to explain that we go way back."

Way back. How had he ever looked twice at this woman?

"I'll just tell her—"

"Better put your clothes on before you go," he said over his shoulder as he strode outside.

He drew in great gulps of fresh air. The guy next door.

Maybe he could borrow his car. But he wasn't there. The car wasn't in its accustomed parking spot.

How could he find Kris, anyway? He'd just have to wait.

Not inside with Candy. He walked rapidly toward the darkened golf course.

THE NEXT THREE HOURS WERE the most painful he had ever spent. He kept seeing Kris's broken bloody body tangled in the wreckage of the car smashed halfway down a steep hillside. Blocked out the image. Kris said you should always think positive and if you had faith…

Damn it, Kris! Where are you?

He paced the damp grass until he could stand it no longer. He had to do *something;* he wasn't sure what.

He returned to the condo, relieved to find Candy gone. He switched on the radio to check highway emergencies and police calls. Nothing about a black Jaguar.

He sat by the phone to think. If Kris made it safely down the hill, where would she go?

Jill's place. He called twice. If she was there, she wasn't answering. The only other place he could think of was the old apartment…. Mrs. Spinella. It was too late to call her, but he was beyond caring.

"Is Kris there?" he asked when Mrs. Spinella's sleepy voice answered.

"Kris? Here?" The surprise was evident.

"I, er, wondered…thought she might've stopped by."

"At this hour? She's out in the streets and you don't know where! Oh, the poor child!" The voice was alert now. And suspicious. "What did you do to her? If you so much as laid a hand on her…"

"It wasn't… I didn't… Nothing like that." He muttered something about being concerned because Kris wasn't back from a late meeting, but he could tell she didn't believe him.

He called the county hospital. No result.

He paced the floor. Waited.

By this time he wasn't scared so much as mad. Why the hell did she go tearing off like that? Damn fool stupid idiotic thing to do! Couldn't wait one minute to let me explain! His fist hit the table and several magazines tumbled to the floor.

Then he heard it. The soft purr of the motor as his car pulled to a stop under the portico.

Limp with overwhelming relief, he remained quite still for a moment. Then he was up, running to embrace her.

She brushed past him.

"Kris!"

"Oh." She turned back as if just noticing him. "Forgot," she said, throwing his car key at him before moving on.

He raced after her, upstairs and into her studio. Bumped into her easel. Cursed. "Kris, we need to talk."

She was reaching into the closet and didn't answer.

"Will you just settle down and let me explain?"

"Don't bother. I understand."

"Like hell you do. The only reason Candy was here was on your account. She called and… Watch it!" he cautioned, hit by the bulky suitcase she carried.

She took it to their bedroom, laid it open on the bed.

"What are you doing?" he asked.

"Packing."

"Oh, for God's sake, Kris! You're blowing this all out of proportion."

"Oh?" She snatched things from a drawer and threw them at the suitcase. "Guess it's me! Just a stupid country girl who can't be cool while the man she lo…lives with plays skinny-dipping hanky-panky with his old girlfriend and her fine body. Well, I'm *not* that cool, Tom Harris," she raved as she went on with her helter-skelter packing. "And if you think I am, you've got another think coming!"

He watched, fascinated. He'd never seen her that mad. Face flushed, hair a tangled mess, eyes bright and sharp as shooting stars. Her dimples dimpled and she seemed to be laughing instead of chewing him out. He almost chuckled as he reached to take her in his arms and—

"Don't touch me!"

It was only a flimsy piece of lingerie that brushed his face, but it was the third time she'd hit him, intentionally or not. He gripped her by both arms. "Will you stop trying to pick a fight and listen?"

She looked calmly up at him, her lips tight. He dropped his hands. "Please." When she didn't move, he took a deep breath. "It's not the way it looked, Kris. Candy phoned, saying she wanted to talk to me and I…well, I thought it was a good time to talk to her."

"Sorry I interrupted that deep conversation."

"All right!" he shouted. "She hadn't been here five minutes before I saw she was after more than talk and I—"

"Invited her for a little dip? That was nice."

"Oh, for God's sake! I didn't…" His mouth tightened. How to explain he was a fool who'd let a conniving bitch get him into one ridiculous unbelievable hell of an unexplainable mess?

Especially to a stubborn, suspicious, determined-not-to-listen woman, and he was tired of trying. The unpleasant encounter with Candy, his worry over Kris and getting hell from Mrs. Spinella was enough for one night! Not to mention that he hadn't finished the background work for the SMS meeting the next morning. He'd had it. "Think what you like," he told her.

"Thank you. I will." She snapped the case shut, picked it up and started out.

He wasn't angry enough to let her run off again. He stepped in front of her. "Where do you think you're going?"

The blank look told him she hadn't thought where. Only away.

"And how do you plan to get there?"

Clearly she hadn't thought of that, either, but she rallied. "I'll call a cab."

"It'll cost you a mint. If you're lucky to find one that'll come up here. Then you'll have to scrounge around in the middle of the night for some crummy place to bunk." He saw he had her attention and talked rapidly, using all his lobbying skills. "That seems pretty stupid when you could stay put, safe and sound, at a decent place in which you've invested a considerable amount of cash."

He saw light dawn in her eyes. "Right. *You* get out. You have a car and you can—"

"I'm not going anywhere. It's my place, too. Remember?"

"Then I'll leave. I certainly don't plan to stay here and watch you play little games with—"

"All right. All right! Have it your way!" He was shouting again, fear that she might really leave him battling with his fury over her insulting assumption that he was having a fling with Candy Atkins. "Just tell me this. Where and how are you going to live? You don't have a job, and you're flat broke."

"But I won't be broke. I'll be fine when you pay me my twenty thousand."

"Which won't be for quite a while. It hasn't occurred to you, I suppose, that I'm also flat broke?"

It hadn't occurred to her, and she wasn't sure she believed him. He was never short of cash, and never skimped on anything. Her birthday earrings must have cost… "You're not—"

"Broke?" He nodded. "I cleared out the stash I was saving for my own office to make my share of the down payment."

She swallowed. Money. It didn't matter that her world had fallen apart. A world that had centered on him.

She wasn't going to cry. She'd cried enough for one night. But if she didn't get out of here… "Move out of my way!"

He didn't budge. "Look, it doesn't matter to me if you cut off your nose to spite your face, but you ought to think about it. You spent a lot on that studio, didn't you? Gonna let it go to waste?"

"Certainly not! I'll move all my things out as soon as I—"

"Find another perfect place? Even if you should be so fortunate, how could you manage first and last months' rent, on the dim chance someone would rent to you when you don't even have a job—which may take you as long to find as it will take me to raise your equity in this house. Which, considering your suspicious and unpredictable nature, we should never have bought together!"

"My suspicious and— You *bastard!* You're blaming me for…for this…" She didn't want to cry now. She wanted to kick and scream.

"Sorry. I didn't mean that. But if you'd just get off your high horse and… Sorry! Look, just sit here and let's talk sense. Please."

His hands were so gentle and she was so tired. She sat on the bed.

He sat beside her. "Look, we've both made an investment in this condo. Why can't we live here and—"

"I'm not living with you another minute, Tom Harris."

"Not with. Together, at the same abode. But socially as separate as the fingers." He held up one hand, fingers wide apart. "Just as the great compromiser advised."

"I don't know what you're talking about and I don't think you do, either."

"Sure I do. Black History 201 when I was a sophomore. I learned about Booker T. Washington's famous speech at the Southeastern fair in the year… I forget the year, but it was on how to let black folks in and still keep them out."

She couldn't believe this. He had just split her heart into pieces and was sitting there talking about… "Black history! What were *you* doing there?"

He shrugged. "I just sat and listened to lectures about which famous black person did what. Like old Booker T., who said something like whites and blacks could work together as with the hands, and still remain as separate as the fingers. Didn't you know that?"

She didn't. Her major was literature. She hadn't taken one

course in black history and didn't appreciate a lesson now. Especially from an unreliable double-dealing cheating *white* man. "This has nothing to do with what's going on between you and me!"

"Sure it has. It shows how we can live together here. Separately, like the fingers. Don't even have to speak, much less touch."

She stared at him, too tired to argue.

"Sleep on it."

"I'm certainly not—"

"Oh, go to bed."

"I told you. I'm not—"

He gestured toward the bed. "It's all yours. I'm going to work."

SHE COULDN'T BELIEVE she'd slept.

And didn't want to wake up. She felt drugged, heavy, weighted under the deepest depression she'd ever known.

Alone. As alone as the bums and prostitutes who walked the streets she drove through last night. Drove over and over again, not wanting to return to what she'd left.

If she hadn't had Tom's car…

Tom! She sat up and listened. Not a sound.

She glanced at the clock. Not quite seven. Saturday morning. Of course—Tom had a breakfast meeting and then his regular golf session with Ted, his assistant, and maybe one of his clients.

Back to his usual fun and games.

Tom wasn't depressed or alone. What had been the end of the world for her was just a little spat to him. He'd come home to cajole her. Or maybe he'd prefer to cajole Candy!

She jumped out of bed fighting mad. More at herself than Tom. She'd known. Jill had warned her and she hadn't listened. Had let herself fall head over heels in love, thrown heart and soul into…

Her breath caught and she stood quite still. *Heart and soul.* Like Freda.

Well, I'm not Freda, Mr. Love 'Em And Leave 'Em! I'll do the leaving this time. I'll get out of here and...

No, she wouldn't! Leave this lovely place that was half hers for Tom and Candy or his next whoever to cuddle up in and enjoy?

Forget that!

Oh, she'd darn well clear out of this bedroom. But she'd stay right here in the condo, which was as much hers as his.

She flew into a fury of rearranging, glad she'd brought the bureau as well as her little bed from Freda's. Paints and brushes occupied only two of the drawers, and if she took those sketches out of the studio closet, she could make room for her clothes.

The beds were made and both rooms in perfect order before noon, when Tom usually returned, bringing his colleague Ted to share the delicious brunch she would have prepared.

They'll miss the brunch, she thought with some degree of satisfaction as she boarded the bus that rambled down the hill toward town. She was glad she had to look after Jill's plants and fish; it was good to have some place to go. She stared out at the beautiful landscape, trying to swallow the lump in her throat and ignore the numb sadness creeping over her. She didn't have time to be sorry. She had to think.

She wasn't exactly broke. She had enough in the bank at home to pay her half of the monthly mortgage payment and carry her for quite a while. But she didn't want to dip into that, and if she didn't have something to do, she'd go crazy. She needed a job.

She'd been without one for two weeks, had checked all the advertising companies, and knew that field was closed.

Oh, for goodness' sake, she'd find a job. She could read and write, couldn't she? She'd stay the night at Jill's and check the Sunday papers, always loaded with want ads.

It was lucky she did stay overnight. At the breakfast bar across the street Sunday morning, she was joined by Jill's neighbor, Pearl Sanders, a prominent lawyer. After confirm-

ing that Jill's brother was recovering and Jill would be returning in a few weeks, Pearl noticed Kris's load of Sunday papers
and smiled. "I see you plan to do a lot of reading."

"Job hunting," Kris replied.

"Oh?" Pearl looked surprised but politely inquired, "What's
your field?"

Kris laughed. "I'll take any field right now. Of course, all
I've ever done is teach, but—"

"Then why are you searching through the papers?" Pearl interrupted, clutching Kris's arm. "The school district is the
place to apply. They're badly in need of teachers, especially
at…certain schools."

Where angels fear to tread, Kris thought, noting Pearl's hes-
itation.

However, she hadn't known that Pearl was a member of the
city school board, or that she'd have breakfast with her that
very morning, or…

Well, never mind. As Papa was prone to say, "God moves
in a mysterious way his wonders to perform."

Which was why she was at the school district office the next
morning. Her credentials were found sufficient for substitute
teaching, and she was given her first assignment, an English
class on Wednesday at Tech High.

Where angels fear to tread, she thought again, as she
threaded her way through those halls and spotted three tough-
looking young men lounging against a wall.

One approached her. "Lookin' for me, honey?"

Kris smiled. This wasn't her first encounter with tough
youngsters. "Not really, but I'm delighted to meet you," she
said. "Would you please direct me to Dr. Gonzales's office?"

It worked. Papa's "do unto others as you would have them
do unto you" always worked. The boy grinned and muttered
a polite, "Sure," and was about to show her the way when a
distinguished gentleman rounded the corner, almost bumping
into them.

"Sorry," he said, but his eyes were on the boy whose companions had disappeared. "Pete! What are you doing in the hall? Shouldn't you be in class?"

"It's my fault," Kris said immediately. "I'm afraid I detained him. I asked him to direct me to Dr. Gonzales's office."

"Oh." The man's eyes focused on her...with interest. Then he turned to the boy. "I beg your pardon, Pete. Thank you. That was kind of you. You may be excused for class now. I'll take over."

He turned back to Kris. "I'm Gonzales, and I hope you've come to teach Mrs. Cooper's class, Ms.—?"

"Gilroy, Kris Gilroy. And yes, if it's an English class? I'm sorry I'm a bit late. It was short notice and my bus schedule didn't quite—"

"Never mind. You're here now. That's what counts. Come along. Let me introduce you to your charges."

She liked the way the man related to the students. As he introduced her to the class, he exuded a gracious dignity that accorded them as much respect as was expected of them. He also praised and thanked them for the help they'd give "Ms. Gilroy, who's new to us and in need of your capable assistance."

Evidently Gonzales liked her teaching methods and the way she handled the students, for she was called back to Tech High several times during the next few weeks. Substitute teachers must've been in demand, because her work schedule was pretty full. She realized she couldn't rely on the unpredictable bus system, and invested in a rental car. That also enabled her to remain in town for dinner and away from the condo as much as possible.

Tom had called her at Jill's, saying they needed to talk. She told him talking didn't fit with the separate living he'd suggested. She'd made adequate arrangements for that style of living, and thought they could manage until they reached a satisfactory financial settlement for a happy separation. Then she'd cut the connection.

It was hard though. Together like the hands and separate as

the fingers might do for those who'd never experienced togetherness. But when one glance at Tom made her want to fly
across the room and into his arms, no matter what he'd done...

Best to stay away.

CHAPTER SIXTEEN

"SO THAT'S THE WAY it is," Kris said to Jill when she'd returned a few weeks later. They had completed their trek on the beach, and sat at a table, their water bottles in front of them. "He's going his way and I'm going mine."

Jill listened, drowning in a flood of disappointment. She'd been so eager to tell Kris about her new relationship with Scott. He was still talking marriage, but wasn't rushing her. She was reveling in the same uncomplicated happy togetherness as Kris and Tom. But now...

"Oh, Kris, you can't mean it's all over."

"Over and out!" Kris gave a dismissive wave of one hand.

"Oh, Kris, I'm so sorry." More than sorry. Guilty. She knew Tom and his short-term stints. And she knew that Kris wasn't like Tom's usual bed partners. But she'd let Kris jump into bed with Tom—buy into a place with him, for heaven's sake! Without one word of warning when she knew...

Let her? Who could've stopped her? Kris might be the daughter of a straitlaced minister, but she had a mind of her own. "I read the Bible, too," she'd said. "Man, not God, put the sin in sex. God meant it to be a joy!"

She was right about that, Jill thought, remembering the hot pulsing waves of joy in each powerful union with Scott. At last she'd understood what Kris meant when she said she had never been so happy in her life.

But now, it was over and... "Out? Where are you living? Would you like to move in with me for a while?"

"Oh, no. Thanks, Jill, but I'm still at my place. Tom can't kick me out. It's as much mine as his."

"Right," Jill said, although she wondered about that. Tom must've put far more money than Kris into that expensive condo.

"'Course, I can't kick him out, either," Kris said. "I wish I could!"

"That must be awkward."

"Oh, not at all! I use the daybed in my studio, and we hardly speak, much less touch!"

After so much joy? Jill could hardly bear to listen. She could never be that close to Scott and not speak or touch. He'd left for Wilmington only a few hours ago, and she was already missing him. Longing to hear his soft drawl and throaty laughter, feel his touch, his kisses, his—

"The nerve of him!" Kris's bitter voice broke into her euphoria. "Can you believe that?"

Jill shook her head, although she wasn't sure at what. How could she be so immersed in her own joy when Kris was so miserable?

Kris didn't pause for an answer. "I told him no way! You can pick up your own dirty socks, wash your clothes and cook for yourself. I'm not a maid. I'm *me*. And I'll manage to pay my share of the mortgage!"

"Wait a minute. What are you talking about?"

"Oh, that's right. You don't know. I lost my job and Mr. Harris had the smug idea that I should do household chores in lieu of my half of the mortgage payments. I told him—"

"Lost your job? You were the moving force in that ad for Simply Soap. How could—"

"But I hadn't been there very long, so when they started cutting staff…"

"Oh." Jill sighed. "I forgot we'd planned to cut staff in certain areas." She'd been away for a month, back for only five days, and there'd been so many changes. "You should…" She paused, realizing she didn't yet know who was in charge of what. And there were other factors. Tenure and past performance usually prevailed. "Anyway, I can fix that. I'll find a spot for you in one of the other departments."

"I'm not asking for a favor, Jill! Besides, I'm okay. Thank goodness, I have the credentials for substitute teaching and I'm doing fine. To tell you the truth, I like just being on call. That way, I have days off to paint, which I can do at the condo, since Tom's at work. So far, I'm making enough to get by. I got a cheap rental car and I could get my own place if Tom would pay me even a part of my investment. He says he's flat broke, but I don't believe him."

Jill didn't believe him, either. She'd heard he was getting big clients. Big clients meant big bucks.

She'd have a talk with Tom Harris. He'd come on strong and fast with Kris, but it hadn't taken him long to break her heart. Jill could tell, even if Kris did have a high-spirited way of hiding it. Surely he could give Kris enough to get a place on her own, so she could forget the bastard. Oh, she'd tell him a thing or two!

Jill was still fuming when she got back to her apartment, but she didn't call Tom that night. Not at the condo. Kris would be there. She'd call him in the morning at his office and give him hell in private.

She sighed. So much had happened in the month she'd been away. Today had been her first chance for a run with Kris. All her time had been swallowed by the return to business routines.

No, that wasn't it. Scott. Every moment she could snatch had been with him and they'd talked and talked, just as they had on the island. In that one short week, she'd had begun to really know him. She'd had a glimpse of his rich-boy childhood, swimming and tennis at the country club, riding his horse, Trooper, at the fabulous family estate.

"He was some horse," Scott had said. "Won many a race."

"A race horse?"

"Oh, no. I'm talking about when some of the guys would get together and race each other just for fun. No, Trooper wasn't a race horse. Not a show horse like Shadow, either."

"Shadow? How many horses did you have?"

"Only one at a time," he said, laughing. "Shadow was Claire's, coal-black, and boy, did they make a picture!" He shook his head. "Can't count the trophies they won."

I'll bet, Jill thought. She'd begun to feel a bit jealous of Claire, even intimidated by this beautiful, elegant sister whom Scott obviously adored. She'd been surprised to learn that Claire lived right here in San Francisco, and Scott was anxious that they meet. Jill was almost glad the meeting had been delayed.

"Is Trooper still around?" she asked.

"They had to put him down a long time ago, soon after I left for college. I'm glad I wasn't there." His expression was sad for a moment, but then he suddenly brightened. "We'll have to visit the house soon. How would you like to live there?"

She looked so surprised that he chuckled.

"My headquarters are in Wilmington," he reminded her. "I have an apartment in town, but I stay at the house in Virginia quite often. It's an easy commute."

"What about your mother?" she prompted. He'd said very little about his mother. Only that she was married again and lived in New York.

"She prefers her New York social life. Except when they're traveling."

"And your sister…"

"Seems stuck on the West Coast. Her husband's a California Legislator. Dave Bernstein."

"Oh, yes. I voted for him."

"Good. Anyway, it seems I'm the only one addicted to the old home place. I go over just to check occasionally. I held the office Christmas party there. We keep a small staff and the house is well maintained." He leaned close to whisper in her ear. "The perfect place to rear children."

"Oh? Well, we'll think about it," she said, again skirting the marriage question.

The endless talk had continued back at the office, mostly on business this time. Not arguing as they used to, but a heart-to-heart sharing and understanding about the very things they'd once fought about. It was easy now that she really knew him. Scott had been reared on stocks and bonds, but he wasn't a businessman.

She smiled. Scott's problem was that he cared more about people than profit. The same compassion for people in general that he'd shown her. She'd had to fight hard to keep him from buying another HMO.

"Just because Jake and Dan aren't getting the after-hospital care they need?" she'd asked. "We can take care of them. You don't buy a whole HMO just because two people—"

"Sure you do. That's how you know whether members are getting the quality care they need. When Mom's cook told me her brother was getting kicked out of that nursing home because—"

"So *that's* why you bought HEALTH CARE!" she exclaimed. "I always wondered. And it's not breaking even yet. Listen, Scott…" He'd listened, and she'd been able to convince him that it was best to concentrate on HEALTH CARE, making it a paying proposition as well as improving the quality of care before taking on any others.

No, he wasn't a businessman, but he had a business vision of miracles to come in the wake of new technology. He'd already hired more technicians and scientists like that cocky Talbert Sims. She'd have to watch that, too.

She shook her head. Scott was such a generous, compassionate, easy-touch idiot!

But wasn't that exactly why she loved him?

God, how she loved him. Her sexual relationship with Scott grew more powerful, more meaningful, with each encounter. Because it was part and parcel of a much deeper union, one defined by compatibility, companionship and a tenderness she'd never before experienced.

As Kris had said, there was more to love than sex.

Kris. She'd call Tom as soon as she got to the office tomorrow.

AS IT TURNED OUT, she was so busy that it was quite late in the day before she had time to call Tom. And, just as she picked up her phone to do so, it rang.

"It's the switchboard," Nora said. "Somebody trying to get in touch with Mr. Randall. What should I tell them?"

"Let me take it," she said. There were too many people trying to get in touch with Mr. Randall—most of them for the wrong reasons.

It was a woman, a rather young woman, judging by the voice. "I'm trying to reach Mr. Randall, please. I need to talk to him."

"You are?"

"Brenda Young. I—I'm the baby-sitter."

"Baby-sitter?"

"For Mrs. Bernstein. She's Mr. Randall's sister, and—"

"Oh, yes!" The charming Claire. "Mr. Randall is unavailable just now. Could I take a message? Or…let me speak with Mrs. Bernstein."

"She's not—she can't come to the phone right now."

"Oh. Then I'll have Mr. Randall call her."

"Please, couldn't I speak to Mr. Randall? Mrs. Bernstein's not…well."

"Not well?" Jill felt a stab of anxiety. "What's wrong?"

"It's…well, she's just not feeling good. Mr. Bernstein's away, in Washington, and I don't know who else to call." The young voice sounded desperate. "I thought if Mr. Randall—"

"I'll get a message to him. But in the meantime, should I call a doctor? 911?"

"No, don't do that. I don't think… She's…well, mostly sleeping. But, you see, I just came to look after the kids while she went somewhere. But she wasn't dressed and didn't seem…well. I didn't want to leave the children while she's…sick. But I've been here all afternoon, and I…I have to go home."

"Stay. Please," Jill urged. "I…someone will be there shortly. Where are you?"

"I told you. At the Bernsteins'."

"Yes. But what's the address? I'll get in touch with Mr. Randall, but just in case…"

She didn't stop to call Scott. Clearly someone was needed to see about the children and Claire. It would take her some time to make her way through the evening traffic. She hoped that baby-sitter would just stay put until she got there. She looked again at the address she'd written down. Not the area she'd expected. And she'd assumed Scott's sister would have…well, maybe not a staff of servants, but someone—at least a housekeeper.

She drove through the streets, searching for the address. Worried. If Claire was seriously ill…

She finally found the house. The girl, Brenda, opened the door, but a woman clad in a bathrobe followed closely behind. Her hair was matted, eyes red and her bare feet stumbled as she came forward, awkwardly but in great haste, calling to the girl. "Scott? Brenda, I told you not to phone him." As she drew nearer, Jill noticed a strong whiff of alcohol. Seeing Jill, the other woman stopped abruptly, almost losing her balance.

This was Scott's elegant sister? Engulfed by a strange mixture of disbelief, pity and sadness, Jill struggled to find her voice.

Claire spoke first, standing very straight and in the voice of a cultured, condescending Vassar graduate. Her simple "Good afternoon" was clearly a question: Who are you and why are you here?

The ploy, like a knife, pierced Jill's heart. This was the per-

fectly-sober pose her mother had always assumed when caught
in a drunken stupor.

The memory hurt, but could serve her now. "Good afternoon, Mrs. Bernstein. I'm so glad I found you at home." Jill
spoke cheerfully and rapidly. "I promised Scott... Oh, excuse
me. I'm Jill Ferrell, a friend of Scott's. He's been wanting us
to meet and had planned to bring me over today. When he had
to rush off to Wilmington, he made me promise I'd stop by anyway. I hope I'm not intruding. Is this a bad time?"

Claire, trying hard, Jill knew, to maintain her poise, shook
her head.

"Good. Scott's told me so much about you." Taking Claire's
arm, she walked toward what she hoped was the living room.
It was. Very cluttered, very noisy and very lived-in. Two small
children squabbled over a pile of scattered Lego bricks. A
baby cried, and the evening news blasted from a blaring television. Claire motioned Jill toward a sofa, turned off the television and transferred the baby from his blanket to her
shoulder. This obviously took much effort, and she sank to the
sofa, trying to catch her breath.

"Hello." The little girl had abandoned the plastic bricks and
now stood, solemnly regarding Jill. "I'm Debbie."

"Hello, Debbie. I'm Jill, a friend of your Uncle Scott's."

The child's eyes brightened. "He's coming, too?"

"Not today. But soon. You're a very pretty little girl, Debbie."

"Thank you. This is Brandon, my brother. He's only three.
I'm five."

"Hello, Brandon, I'm glad to—" Jill faltered, caught by the
penetrating appraisal of wide dark eyes that stared at her from
a chocolate-stained face. Scott's eyes. "Glad to meet you," she
finished, unable to take her own eyes from the unruly jet-black
hair, the lift of the brow, even the curve of the tiny mouth. Her
heart turned over. This silent little boy with his thumb in his
mouth could be a replica of Scott at the age of three.

"Would you like a drink or something?" Debbie politely inquired.

The question alerted Claire and she spoke before Jill could answer. "Yes, Debbie. Ask Brenda to bring a glass of wine."

Brenda, who hadn't uttered a word, gave Jill an apprehensive glance.

Jill nodded. She knew she should suggest coffee, but thought it best to humor Claire, who was holding the baby with one hand, clinging desperately to a glass of wine with the other. She smiled at Jill, as if inviting conversation, but seemed unable to speak. Jill wasn't surprised when a moment later, the glass slipped from her fingers and her head lolled against the sofa. She'd passed out.

Jill knew she should have expected this, but it gave her a jolt. Did it happen often? Had Scott ever seen her like this? Had Brenda?

Jill looked at the girl, who'd returned with a glass of wine on a small tray and was staring at Claire. "Thank you. And thank you, Debbie," Jill said, taking the napkin from the child. "Could you help your brother pick up those toys while I talk to Brenda?"

Debbie nodded. "Come on, Brandon."

Giving Brenda a worried look, Jill sniffed at the wine and wrinkled her nose. "Is this the same wine Mrs. Bernstein was drinking?"

"Yes, it is."

"That's probably what made her sick. I think it's sour."

The girl's eyes widened. "Sick? Oh, my goodness. I thought she was— Well, that is, I've never seen her like this before and I didn't know what to do."

Jill heard this with some relief. If Brenda had never seen Claire drunk… "How long have you been baby-sitting for Mrs. Bernstein?"

"Two, almost three years," Brenda answered absently, gazing in horror at the quietly sleeping Claire. "Shouldn't we call 911 or… I've got the name of the children's doctor. I can—"

"No. We won't call anyone." No one, Jill decided, who could confirm that she was drunk. "The wine's probably just tainted enough to make her drowsy. I can take care of her. Mr. Randall's out of town, but I'm sure he'd want me to stay with her. I know you're anxious to get home."

"Yes but…"

"You needn't worry. I'll stay here until she's perfectly well. I'll call my doctor if needed, but I think she'll be fine. And I'd rather we didn't mention this to Scott or Mr. Bernstein. They'd only worry."

"That's what she said. But she was so… Well, I didn't want to leave the children and I figured I should call someone."

"You did exactly right." *And I'm glad you got me,* Jill thought as she opened her purse. "Now, you've been here since…?"

"One o'clock," Brenda said. "She was supposed to go to a meeting with Debbie's teacher, but she wasn't even dressed when I got here."

Before the girl left, Jill had elicited as much information as she could. It seemed that Brenda only came here when Claire was going out or needed to help at some political function. Anyway, it was quite definite that Brenda had never seen Claire in such a condition. If Brenda, here often during the past three years, had never seen her drunk, then neither had Scott. He lived clear across the country, and had said regretfully that he'd only visited his sister twice since he'd been in the city.

Maybe she wasn't a habitual drunk. Not yet. But she was getting there. Jill knew the signs.

Scott didn't know. To him his older sister was still the equestrian with trophies all over the place, the graceful dancer, the beautiful, elegant woman who had men falling at her feet.

To see her as she was now would hurt him.

But this woman needed help. Someone… Her husband?

Did he know? There was a possibility that he didn't. A Legislator. Away from home more often than not.

Or, like Dad, maybe he didn't care?

Stop it, she told herself. Kris was right. She shouldn't compare every man to her father. Or blame Dad for everything that had gone wrong. Dad was a heavy drinker himself. He would've taken Mom's drinking as a matter of course. He wouldn't have understood that his wandering eye was the cause, or—

Oh, for goodness' sake! This was a different time, a different woman! Deal with the here and now.

Tell Scott?

What could he do? It would only hurt him, she thought again.

Jill made a solemn vow. If she could prevent it, he'd never know.

CHAPTER SEVENTEEN

JILL, A PRACTICAL WOMAN, realized she'd just made a vow she might not be able to keep. She hadn't been able to help her own mother. How could she help a woman she didn't even know?

Well, she knew Dad's philandering had driven Mom to drink. Some trouble in Claire's life must be driving her.

And Claire will spill everything to you, and you'll know exactly what to do?

Fat chance!

Well, she knew what needed doing now. She gently removed the baby from his mother's arms and replaced him on the blanket. Thank goodness he continued to sleep. Next she settled Claire comfortably on the sofa and covered her with a lap robe.

That done, Jill smiled down at the two children and whispered, "I'm hungry. Let's go in the kitchen and find something to eat."

Debbie looked at her mother, then up at Jill. "What's the matter with Mommy?"

"She's just a little tired. I'm going to take care of you while she rests. Do you mind?"

Debbie shook her head. "No. We'll be quiet. Mommy gets tired lots."

That worried Jill. If Debbie had seen her in this condition... Both children followed her into the kitchen. They wanted pancakes, but settled for toasted cheese sandwiches and hot chocolate. The baby woke and Debbie found his cereal and told Jill how it should be prepared.

"You are such a help," Jill said.

"That's what Mommy says," Debbie replied. "I'll help you stack the dishes, too. Brandon can play with Joey."

The kitchen was soon spotless, and Jill suggested they go up for baths and bed.

Brandon stood mute, thumb in mouth, but Debbie glanced anxiously at Claire. "Is Mommy sick?"

"Just tired," Jill said a second time. "We'll let her rest. Later I'll come down and visit with her."

After a rollicking game in the tub with his sailboats, Brandon grinned up at her. "I like you."

Again Jill felt that tug at her heart. "And I love you." *Almost as much as I love your uncle,* she thought, kissing the little boy.

"You our baby-sitter?"

"She's not a baby-sitter, silly," Debbie said. "She's Uncle Scott's friend. Are you staying a long time?" she asked, looking hopeful. "You brought your things."

"My things? Oh!" Jill looked down at her running shorts and top, which she'd retrieved from the car and which were now stained and spattered. Better those than her Armani suit. She chuckled. "I'm staying awhile. And I promise to visit often." *As often as I'm needed. For Scott.*

No, not just for Scott. For these darling children, she told herself as they scrambled into bed and debated which story they wanted her to read.

"You can each choose one," she told them. Actually, she read four. By that time, the baby had finished his bottle and was happily settled in his crib.

Old habits come easy, she thought not for the first time. She closed the book on the last bedtime story and kissed the children good-night. She'd started baby-sitting when she was eleven, the first and only job her father had allowed her to do while on the island. She'd been well-trained for tonight.

Downstairs, she curled up in a big armchair and chose a magazine. It lay unopened on her lap. She wasn't well-trained for the next task, she thought, again reminded that she had not been able to help her mother.

She looked at Claire, who hadn't stirred. And very likely would have no recollection of anything that had happened before she passed out. No telling how she'd react to a perfect stranger who'd boldly walked in uninvited and taken charge of her household. *Well,* Jill decided, *I'll just have to wait and see.*

While she waited, she tried to analyze the situation.

There was so little to go on. She hardly knew Claire, and certainly had no idea what her problem was.

She did know Claire was a good mother, just from the way Claire had held on to the baby. The way Debbie had helped her, already responsible—and already a charming hostess like the mother Scott had described. Yes, anybody could tell the children were happy and well cared for. And there were signs that Claire was a good housekeeper. Not a perfectionist like Jill's mother. No, this house had the lived-in clutter of a happy family home. Considering that the house was big, the children small and active, Claire was keeping things in pretty good order. And she was doing it without help. Difficult for a woman reared in the lap of luxury.

That brought to mind something else that nagged at her.

Old money. There was plenty of that, Jill knew. Not that Scott bragged or was a show-off. Far from it. Horse shows, country clubs, and even the servants of his childhood were mentioned incidentally, taken as much for granted as his private jet, which had just whisked him across the country.

The money couldn't have disappeared; in fact, it must have been increased with the sale of the brokerage. And the way Scott was throwing money around…

A horrid thought flashed through her mind. Had it all gone into Randall Enterprises and Scott was gambling it away on his philanthropic ventures?

Only a flash. That wasn't how Scott did things. He would

look after his mother and sister before himself. Anyway, what was she thinking? Whatever happened with the money, it wouldn't have been Scott's decision. Rich people left wills and trusts, and made all kinds of strange provisions.

So…if Scott was rolling in wealth, why was his sister living in this….well, okay but definitely middle-class neighborhood?

A noise alerted her, and Jill glanced across the room to see Claire sitting up and staring at her. Before she could speak, Claire's gaze shifted, circling the room as if to determine where she was, then returned to center on Jill in confusion.

Jill spoke quickly. "I'm Jill Ferrell. Scott's friend. As I told you, I promised him I'd…" She broke off. Claire wasn't listening. She had staggered to her feet, looking scared and calling for Debbie.

Jill hastened to reassure her. "The children are fine. Fed, bathed and in their beds."

Claire's eyes scanned the room before focusing again on Jill. Jill saw the glint of distrust before she was brushed aside and Claire rushed to mount the stairs.

"They're all right," Jill said as she followed. "Don't wake them."

She needn't have worried. Claire's movements were as quiet as they were gentle. She touched Debbie's cheek, took Brandon's thumb from his mouth, straightened the baby's blanket. Only then could she be persuaded to return to the living room.

"Why don't you sit here for a moment while I make coffee," Jill said. She could tell that Claire still wasn't quite herself. Coffee and toast had always helped bring Mom around.

Claire stared at her once more, looking puzzled. "Brenda?" she quavered.

"She was here, but had to go home. I told her I'd stay."

"You… Who—who are you?"

"Jill Ferrell. I came earlier this evening. Scott had planned to bring me out today and then he had to leave for Wilmington. I came anyway. Remember?"

"No. I—"

"Oh, you must remember. I came out and we…well, we hit it off immediately, just like Scott said we would. And I…we decided I should stay the night." A bit of a lie, but it might make things easier.

Claire seemed dazed. "No. I…" She sank back onto the sofa. "Oh, God. I don't remember anything. I was not…I was rather…"

"You were drunk." Maybe it was best to be blunt.

Claire's head shot up and she glared at Jill. "That's not true. I've never been drunk in my life."

"I wouldn't know about that, but you were definitely drunk this evening."

"No. I couldn't have been." Claire sat up. The Vassar graduate was back. And indignant. "I remember now. Teachers' conferences were today and I was dressing to go. Brenda was coming to stay with the children."

"She came. You weren't dressed to go anywhere and appeared so unstable that she was afraid to leave you alone with the children."

"That's ridiculous!" Claire shook her head, vigorously denying what she refused to believe. "I certainly wasn't—well, I wasn't feeling too good and maybe I had a glass of wine, but…"

"More than one glass, obviously."

"No."

"Yes," Jill continued relentlessly. "In fact, you were still drinking when Brenda got here. She was concerned and called—"

"Oh, my God! She called Dave?"

"Dave?"

"My husband. He's in Washington and—"

"No. She didn't know how to reach him and called Scott, who's also out of town. She got me."

"Oh, my goodness. That girl! Calling everybody! And you. She talked to you? You don't even know me."

"Yes, I do. I know you very well. Scott's told me all about his beautiful charming sister."

"Scott?"

"Scott and I are…close."

"Oh?" For the first time, Claire's attention was fully on Jill. "He's never mentioned a…Jill?"

"Jill Ferrell."

"Not that he ever mentions any of his…friends to me," Claire said, and seemed to study Jill. "You're that close? So that you… You came all the way out here?"

"He'd do as much for me," Jill said. She thought of Jake.

"But to come and stay, and… Really, that was very kind of you but not at all necessary."

"I think it was. Soon after I arrived you passed out."

"No!"

"About six, I think." Jill gestured toward the sofa.

Claire looked at the rumpled blanket, then back at Jill's steady gaze.

Jill checked her watch. "It's after midnight now."

Claire seemed to shrink into herself. She pulled her robe closer. "All that time I was… Oh, God! Brenda. What must she think of me?"

"She thinks you drank some bad wine and it made you very drowsy."

"What?"

"I know. It was a stupid thing to say but it was all I could think of. Anyway, she believed me."

"She did?"

"Yep." Jill laughed. "After I poured what remained in that bottle down the drain, as well as two other bottles of the same brand, she was convinced."

"You…you…" Now Claire was also laughing. Or trying to. But she couldn't seem to stem the flow of tears rolling down her cheeks. They soon gave way to gulping sobs that shook her whole body.

Jill took her hand, feeling distressed and rather guilty. She had deliberately been blunt. "I'm sorry. I shouldn't have badgered you. I only wanted to make you realize what had happened."

Claire wasn't listening. She was bent double, her head in her hands. The convulsive sobs were punctuated by a stifled muttering, words of misery, shame and self-condemnation.

She looked so alone, so helpless. Jill couldn't stand it any longer.

"Stop it!" She took Claire by the shoulders and pulled her upright. "You're making a mountain out of a molehill. Get over it!"

"I can't. Debbie. Brenda. They saw me. Debbie will tell her dad and—"

Jill gave her a good shake. "You listen to me and you listen hard. Brenda thinks you got hold of some bad wine, Debbie thinks you were tired, Dave and Scott don't know anything and they won't!"

"I know."

"Right. So do I. And that's where this little episode is going to stay. Between you and me. Nobody else. Got it?"

Claire frowned at her. "Yes, but—"

"We'll discuss the buts in the morning. Right now, we're going to get you something to eat and then we'll go to bed. I need sleep even if you don't!"

THE BUZZ OF HER cell phone awakened her. Jill reached for it. Not there. The buzz came from the other side of the bed. In the guest room, where she'd slept.

She grabbed the phone. "Scott. Darling!" she cried, overwhelmed by longing. "I miss you."

"That's a likely story. The minute I leave town you disappear. Where have you been?"

"Right here. I've been right here," she said, reveling in the sound of his laughter and trying to think of a plausible reason. She couldn't tell him the real one.

"Right where? You're not at your place or at the office. I've been calling since five yesterday afternoon and all I get is 'leave a message.' Even on your cell phone."

"I know." She'd locked her cell phone, fearful that he would call and become aware of the crisis at Claire's house. She hadn't unlocked it until she was alone, long after midnight. She knew he'd call, knew she'd have to explain. How? "I meant to call you," she said. "But I've been closeted with…Kris!" There! That was a likely story, and a real one. "Remember my friend Kris? Yes, I know you've never met but I told you about her. She and Tom broke up and she's going through a really bad time and—"

"Enough. I know you, Miss Fix-it. I'm sure you fixed it for your friend, but I don't want to hear about it. Let's talk about us. Looks like I'm going to be here awhile and I don't like being without you. How do you plan to fix *that?*"

It was some time before she ended the call and became aware of the silence around her. Where were the children? Where was Claire?

Alarmed, she got into her shorts and shirt and raced toward the stairs. The minute her bare feet touched the steps, her ears caught the laughter and chatter of happy children, and her nose the wake-up scent of freshly brewed coffee.

The promise of coffee lured her to the kitchen, where she got her first glimpse of the beautiful, elegant sister Scott had described. Thick silky black hair pulled back and tied by a shoestring emphasized the milky smoothness of her skin; the perfection of delicate patrician features. Plain jeans and a shirt revealed a slender graceful figure. And yes, Jill thought in amazement, there was a graceful elegance even in the way she spooned warm cereal into the baby's mouth.

"Jill, you're up," Debbie called from her place at the table. "I was going to wake you, but—"

"Me, too," Brandon said.

"But Mommy wouldn't let us," Debbie continued. "I'm glad you got up before I have to go to school."

Alerted by the children, Claire looked up. "I made coffee. Why don't you pour yourself a cup and we'll have our breakfast after I get Debbie off."

"Sit by me," Debbie cried.

"Me," Brandon said.

"How about between you?" Jill said, and arranged her chair to do so. She engaged herself with the two of them while her mind grappled with the morning's miracle…after last night.

Ten minutes later, Debbie waved goodbye from the private-school van.

"I used to take her myself," Claire said. "But Dave felt that was too much for me after Joey came. It's pretty costly, tuition and transportation, but Dave never stints on the children." She sighed. "I just wonder how we'll manage when Brandon starts school."

Jill didn't comment, but again she wondered. Why did they have to stint at all?

A few minutes later, the children's mess was cleared away.

Brandon was sitting in front of the television watching *Sesame Street,* and the baby was cooing contendedly on his blanket.

"How do you like your eggs?" Claire asked.

Jill's eyes flew from the dainty place mats and delicate china to her hostess.

Claire grinned. "Stop acting so surprised. This is the real me."

At least the one with which you face your public, Jill reflected. *And maybe they've never seen that other one.* "Soft scrambled," she said. "I'll do the toast."

"It was really kind of you to come out last night, and to take over," Claire said when they were seated. "I'm really grateful. But I want you to know I've never been…well, what happened last night has never happened before. That's the truth."

Maybe, Jill thought. Maybe not. But… This wasn't the time for the *buts.* "I believe you," she said, not sure that she did. "Listen, I have to get to the office, but there's something we need to thrash out first. Scott called this morning."

"Oh?" Claire looked apprehensive. "What did you tell him?"

"Nothing about you. He didn't know where I was. But he'll call again and I'll have to tell him something. The children will know that I've been over here, and we'll have to explain how it happened. Perhaps," she suggested, "you called for him, got me, and we talked, and maybe you invited me out."

"Yes!" Claire cried, relieved. "And I'll say you came out and spent this weekend. While Dave was away. That'll explain your spending the night and the kids getting to know you. Could you come? This weekend? Tonight?"

"Perfect!" Jill said. "Scott's away, too. And thank God this is Friday. Of course I'll come." Excellent. That should give them a chance to at least start on the buts.

CHAPTER EIGHTEEN

I WONDER IF we'll ever become close enough to delve into the buts, Jill thought as she showered and dressed. Somehow she didn't see Claire welcoming her as a bosom buddy and confessing all.

Emerging crisp and smart in yesterday's office attire, she kissed the boys and hurried out, telling Claire she'd be back that afternoon.

"Good!" Claire, epitome of the perfect housewife, stood at the open door to see her off. "Do you like chili?"

"Love it!" Jill smiled at the facade that hid the real Claire. Could she get beyond the facade?

Well, she had this weekend, and meant to give it a good try.

She left the office early and stopped by her apartment to change and pack a few casual clothes. She threw in some old costume jewelry and a couple of fancy blouses slated for Goodwill. Little girls liked to play dress-up. Another stop to buy a jigsaw puzzle for a three year old and a Dr. Seuss book that hadn't been among the children's collection.

At a florist's shop, she found a small pot of violets for Claire. The real gift she planned to offer was friendship and a desire to help. Which might be misinterpreted as curiosity. She had to be careful not to bombard Claire with questions.

It was she who was bombarded.

The minute she entered the house, she was bombarded by the exuberant greetings of two children who'd been eagerly awaiting her return, the spicy pungent odor of something deli-

cious simmering in the kitchen, and a smile of delight from
Claire. It wasn't until after the kids were involved with their
gifts, and the violets placed in the perfect sunny spot in the window above the kitchen sink, that Claire started asking questions. They were casually tossed over her shoulder as she
moved about the kitchen, intent on dinner preparations. When
and where had Jill met Scott? Hmm, not very long ago—how
had they become close so quickly? Claire made no attempt to
hide *her* curiosity. Nor did she seem to notice the spark of fire
forming in Jill's eyes. With the smug confidence of an indulged southern belle, she continued the inquisition.

"Now, tell me about you," she said, sitting at the table
beside Jill. "Where are you from and what did you do
before—"

"That's enough!" Jill's hand hit the table so hard that Claire
jumped. "You don't have to be afraid," she said in a softer
voice.

Claire stared at her. "Afraid?"

"That I'm not good enough for your precious brother. You
needn't worry because, for your information, I haven't decided whether I'll marry him."

"But why not?" Claire's face fell. "Don't you love him? Oh,
you must. You came all the way out here when… Wait a minute!" She waved a hand as if to clear the air. "First, let's get
one thing straight. I'm *not* afraid you aren't good enough for
Scott." Jill's eyes must have registered her doubt, for Claire
added emphatically, "No! I'm thinking you're perfect for him
and I was hoping…" She reached across the table and took
Jill's hand. "Tell me. What did you think when you walked in
here last night?"

Jill, still trying to readjust her thinking, was caught off guard.

Claire persisted. "When you walked in and saw me, what
was your very first thought?"

Jill hesitated, not wanting to say. "I… Well, I—I was concerned for you."

"Oh, no, you weren't." Claire shook her head. "You were furious with me."

"No, I wasn't. I—"

"Oh, yes, you were. Mad as hell at me and concerned for Scott. I've had all day to think about it." She raised a hand to stop Jill from interrupting. "Let me finish. I'm eternally grateful to you. Not just for taking over like one of the family and doing it so beautifully that the kids fell in love with you. But for concealing it from, well, everybody. Oh, that stupid sour-wine lie!" Claire laughed so hard the tears rolled down her cheeks.

Jill found herself laughing, too. "Well, it worked."

"Yes, and that's when I found out," Claire choked. "You were as anxious as I am that Scott never know the worst about his terrible sister. Oh, I do wish you'd marry him."

She sounded so anxious that Jill sobered. "Why?"

"He's thirty-three years old. It's past time for him to settle down with a wife who'll give him a happy home and provided cousins for my little ones."

"But…why me?"

"Because you care about him. You're not one of those bimbos forever chasing him just because he's handsome, rich and a compulsive giver. He'd give away the moon if he could to anyone who asked. I'm always afraid some greedy socialite whose only concerns are money and status will get his ring on her finger and—" Claire sprang up to seize the phone.

Jill's gaze followed Claire, but her mind was envisioning the greedy socialite nestled in Scott's arms, the ring on her finger flashing a red warning signal.

A delighted scream from Claire captured her attention. "Oh, Dave, that's great! Really? Oh, I'm so proud of you."

More than proud, Jill thought, entranced by the pure adoration reflected in Claire's face.

Apparently Dave was being feted for something he'd done. There seemed to be lots of preliminary functions going on.

Shouldn't his wife be with him?

Last night. Maybe that was why Claire had drunk herself into such a state!

It was after Debbie and Brandon had both greeted their father that Jill zeroed in on something else. Thanks to a few last remarks by Claire… "Tell Meg hi. Is she enjoying it, too?"

Meg? There was another woman with Dave? That would drive any wife to drink.

"I gather your husband's being honored," she said as soon as Claire got off the phone.

"Yes, that's why he's in Washington. He's to receive the John Fitzgerald Kennedy Award," Claire said, glowing. "Tomorrow night, at a dinner hosted by the President and First Lady. The award's given once a year to someone who's made a significant humanitarian contribution. It'll be on the news for sure. We'll have to watch."

"Of course. That's quite an honor."

"And nobody deserves it more than Dave. He… Oh, I'll tell you later. Right now… Debbie, you and Brandon get your hands washed. Time for dinner."

So Jill had to wait through dinner, a short romp with the kids in the park, and the bedtime routine, before she could find out what she wanted to know. Who was Meg and why was she at Dave's special event, with Claire just watching it on the news? Was *that* the problem? If Claire could conduct an inquisition, so could she.

"All right if I make coffee?" she asked once the kids were settled.

"Sure. I'll do it. I thought you might be ready for bed, you were up so late last night. Won't coffee keep you awake?"

That was exactly why she needed it. Jill didn't plan to waste one minute of this weekend. "I'm a night person and a coffee addict," she lied. "Besides, I want to hear all about Dave's award. What did he do?"

"What he always does," Claire said, reaching for the coffee

beans. "Anything to help the poor and needy. Which isn't easy in this country where everything's designed to help the rich and powerful!"

"That's not true. Look at our welfare system."

"Look at tax deductions and the charity foundation loophole. Half the rich people here aren't paying any taxes at all." Claire dumped the beans in and waited for the grinder to cut off before continuing her tirade. "A poor man gets loaded with debt and he's had it! Let a big company get into the same fix, and Uncle Sam bails them out."

"But don't you see? That's because companies, investments, keep people working, keep the economy going."

"And keep the rich rich!"

"My goodness, you're hard on rich people. I thought you—" She broke off.

"You thought I was one of them."

"Well, yes. That is, I—"

"Oh, don't look so embarrassed. I am."

"Oh." Jill steeled herself not to say what she thought. "I...see."

"No, you don't." Claire laughed. "You're wondering why I'm not living like one."

"Well, yes. That had occurred to me."

"I fell in love." Again adoration glowed in Claire's eyes. "Do you know how different Dave Bernstein was from all the men I'd known? Suave, sophisticated silver-spoon braggarts who talked about the stock market and the state of the nation while they cruised on their yachts, played polo or— Oh, you know what I mean. Dave was down in the trenches, working to... No, he was more than a worker, he was a dreamer. Hoping to make a better nation, a better world. Just talking to him made me come alive."

"So you fell in love," Jill said. "You still had money."

"Which Dave was determined not to marry." Claire laughed. "I never worked so hard to get a man in my life. I had to convince him it was me he'd marry, not the money. It was only after I'd promised we'd live on what he earned that he capitulated."

"Oh." Jill finally understood. "That must've been hard." *Still is,* she guessed.

"Not at all. I'd had it with horse shows and Mother's charity balls and was ready for a change."

"Must've been quite a change."

"I loved it. For the first time in my life I was doing something worthwhile. I worked with Dave until we had the children. Even afterward, for a while. Dave's mother would come over and stay with Debbie."

"Oh, his parents live here?"

"They did. His father died shortly after we got married. A heart attack. And his mother's in a nursing home now." Claire drew a deep breath. "She seems happy and is as sweet and loving as ever, but she's… She doesn't even recognize us when we visit."

"I'm sorry." Claire looked so despondent that Jill hastened to change the subject. "So you worked with Dave when you first got married?"

"Yes, at his law office and for a while after he got elected. It's exciting just to watch him work." Claire pushed her cup aside and launched into her favorite subject. Dave Bernstein, how clever and witty he was, how many bills benefiting "ordinary people" he'd initiated and pushed through the legislature. "Dave doesn't need money, he has tenacity," she said. "This award he's getting. You wouldn't believe how long it took him to get the bill passed. It's for foster children who've reached the age of eighteen. That's when the State stops supporting them and they're dumped on their own, and they're not always ready. Dave's bill gives them two years of work and life-experience training that's— Oh, go to bed. I'll tell you about it tomorrow."

Jill's head jerked up. "Your Dave sounds exceptional. I'm looking forward to seeing the award ceremony."

Claire smiled. "Tomorrow. Right now we'd better get you upstairs before *you* pass out."

Jill knew she was right. Despite the coffee, she kept nodding off. But she climbed the stairs reluctantly. She'd been getting to know the real Claire. Like her brother, Claire Bernstein cared about others. She had a real concern for the people her husband championed, and regarded him as a hardworking, benevolent hero.

Still, there was something she hadn't learned. What, Jill wondered, was driving this loving, open and very delightful woman to drink?

She found out the next night. Or was pretty certain she had. Just by watching television.

That Meg woman! She was sure the minute Claire pointed her out, when Dave stood at his table to walk to the podium. "Oh, there's Meg. Next to Dave. In that green dress."

Jill's eyes flew to the woman in the green spaghetti-strap gown that flowed and yet molded to her perfect figure.

"Doesn't she look stunning?" Claire cried.

Too stunning, in Jill's opinion. Dave was the guest of honor, but the cameras lingered a mite too long on the woman beside him, clapping her hands and flashing a Julia Roberts smile brighter than the diamonds on her ears.

And standing where Claire should be!

Jill's own eyes were flashing as she turned to Claire. "Why didn't you—?"

"Shh." Claire's finger went to her lips. Her beaming face focused on Dave, her attention on his every word.

Why wasn't she furious? Jill was so furious she didn't want to listen to Dave's speech. If he thanked that woman for her assistance or even acknowledged her presence…

He didn't. His thanks was in appreciation of what had been done for the young people who were the future backbone of this wonderful country. He seemed oblivious to the part he'd played, and Jill wasn't sure he'd actually thanked anybody.

Of course, she'd missed most of his speech. She'd been too busy being mad at him and wondering why Claire wasn't.

She could hardly wait until she was alone with Claire to finish the question she'd started as soon as she saw that Meg woman. "Why didn't *you* go with Dave?"

"Oh, I couldn't. You see—"

"Don't tell me you couldn't afford it! You've got a pile stashed in some bank. Okay, you choose not to live on it. Surely you could use a bit for a special occasion!"

"That's exactly what Dave said I'd do! I had to swear I wouldn't, cross my heart and hope to die before he'd marry me."

"That was a stupid promise and this is more than a special occasion! Your husband should've insisted that you be there when he received such an important award."

"David?" Claire laughed. "You heard him. He's thinking about the kids, not himself. He couldn't care less about that award, and doesn't think the occasion's so special."

"Well, it *is* special and you should've been there. Dave must make some money. A trip to Washington doesn't cost that much."

"All right already, don't hit me!" Claire laughed again. "Money wasn't the problem. Accommodations for the two of us were included. But I couldn't leave the children."

"Not ever? There must be someone you could hire, or a friend."

Claire shook her head. "No one. Brenda's too young, even if she wasn't in school. I had a neighbor whom I could trust. We'd exchange baby-sitting, but she moved back east. I really miss her."

"Oh, for goodness' sake, there are agencies available."

"Not for my children. I grew up with nannies. You know something? I'm closer to Dave's mother right now, even though she doesn't recognize me, than I've ever been to my own mother. I want my children to know me."

"I don't think they'd forget you in one weekend."

Claire grinned in amusement. "I guess not, but I couldn't arrange it on such short notice. Besides, I've had dinner at the White House, more than once. My Dad was a high-roller Republican. I was glad to let Meg take my place. She deserved a treat. She's a good friend as well as a hard worker and has been such a help to Dave."

Jill stared at Claire. "You're not only stupid, you have bad eyesight."

"What?"

"Have you taken a good look at that Meg woman?"

"Oh, you're thinking— But Meg's not that kind of woman."

"Maybe so, maybe not. Anyway, if she's such a good friend, why didn't *she* stay with the children and you go with Dave?"

"Meg! I'd trust Brenda before her. Meg's a mover and a shaker at the legislature, but she's useless with kids."

"I'll bet. Kids are smarter than men when it comes to stunning women, and you should take a lesson from them."

"Just one minute!" Claire's eyes flashed. "I don't like this one bit. You're insinuating that my husband is a womanizing two-timer, which he certainly is not. You don't even *know* David and—"

"I know he's got a gorgeous babe right there beside him, sucking up all the glory, and you're here getting sloppy drunk."

"I wasn't... Okay, maybe I was a little woozy the other night, but it didn't have anything to do with Dave."

"Didn't it? Weren't you thinking about what was happening in Washington while you were here, stuck with the kids?"

"Stuck? I love my kids!"

"I know that, but—"

"Let's get something else straight. I love my husband. And I trust him. Absolutely."

"Oh, Claire, I'm not saying—"

"I know exactly what you're saying and I don't appreciate it. Dave is so open and honest he couldn't deceive anyone if he tried, and I won't have you calling him a lying, two timing son of a bitch. If you think that, you can just get the hell out of my house!"

The words hit like a physical blow. "I…didn't mean…" Dear God, what was she trying to do? Implant her own suspicious venom in a woman who loved and trusted her husband? Kris's words came back. *All men remind you of your father.*

Jill drew a deep breath and took Claire's hand. "Forgive me, Claire. I'm out of place in a situation like this. You're right. I don't know Dave. I have baggage of my own and was comparing him to…to someone else." She tried to laugh. "Evidently I'm as wrong about Dave as I was about you."

"You certainly are if you think I'm an habitual drunk."

"I mean before I even met you. I was sure you were a stuck-up, nose-in-the-air snob. I was actually surprised to find that you're a delightful down-to-earth person I'd like to have as a friend."

"Thank you. I think."

"Please just forget everything else."

"Forgotten. What's one little snit between future sisters?"

Jill tried to return Claire's smile, but her lips trembled. "About that night…" She paused. But she liked Claire and had to say it. "A one-time binge can be a beginning, Claire. I know. I watched my mother. She was a good mother, lots of fun, a bit like you, when I was little. But by the time I became a teenager she was a pitiful alcoholic."

"I'm sorry."

"So am I. Sorry that I was too young to help. Maybe I couldn't have, anyway. But I'd like to help you, Claire."

"Help me?"

"At least make you realize. You've got problems and you don't even know it."

"No, I—"

"Yes. In the first place, you're bored stiff. No, don't stop me. All right, maybe *stifled* is a better word. I've seen you glow with energy just talking about Dave and how much you enjoyed working with him and I know you miss the excitement. Okay, okay, just hold on a minute. And between the house and the kids, you're overworked."

"I am not. I love my kids."

"You can get pretty bored when you're listening to nothing but baby talk. Especially when you're missing the talk that made you come alive. And that's not an occasional thing. Dave's in Sacramento all week, every week, and sometimes on weekends."

"But we're constantly on the phone and—"

"That's not the same. And you're missing more than talk." Jill paused. Well, she didn't have much time. If she had to be blunt… "Listen to me, Claire. There are lots of beautiful, loving women out there, starving for what you have. And if your Dave is such a dynamo—"

"Stop it! That's an insult. Dave loves me, and…and we're happily married."

"Competition doesn't stop just because you're married. There are lots of beauties out there sucking up to David and you're missing out when you're at home looking like a bag lady!"

"Will you stop harping on one night? One incident! I don't look like a bag lady and I'm not a sloppy drunk."

"Okay, okay. But you're here when you ought to be with him."

"It's in Dave's interests that I'm here looking after his children."

"And it's in their interests that you hold on to their father. Men are vulnerable creatures, Claire."

"Not Dave! He wouldn't look at another woman."

"As far as you…" Jill checked herself abruptly. She was on dangerous ground again. "This isn't about Dave. I'm thinking of you. You're alone so much except for the children. Bored and—"

"Stop saying that! I'm not bored. I love and enjoy my children."

"Sure you do. Just as you love Dave and Scott and Meg and almost everybody more than you love yourself. You're becoming a workhorse, seeing that everybody else gets everything they need! And you're missing all the fun."

"I am not. I—"

"And that's stupid when you could do all that and still share the fun and excitement," Jill went on as if Claire hadn't spoken. "You've got money sitting in the bank doing nothing. You could hire a permanent housekeeper. That'll give you time to love Dave and the children and be with him at moments like this. Take the kids, too, for God's sake. Come and go as much as you like and… Oh, you know how rich people live. You've been rich. You *are* rich. Live like it!"

"I couldn't. That would demean Dave."

"Demean him? You've been married long enough for both of you to know he married *you,* not the money."

"Hold it, Jill." Claire laid a hand on her arm. "You're right about something. You don't know Dave. You saw him tonight on television. Saw the smart, witty, confident Dave, the guy who appears so secure. He isn't." Claire's eyes misted. "He's soft as a jellyfish under that defiant stance, still hurting from his struggling days, when he was 'the nerd.' Don't you see? He needs to be the caretaker, the giver."

"Don't *you* see? You could both have a fuller life! You'd have…well, my goodness…everything!"

"Dave means more to me than things. I'll never make him feel small."

CHAPTER NINETEEN

JILL DRAGGED HERSELF out of bed early Monday morning before Claire and the children stirred. She was dressed and on her way out when Claire called, "You're up already?"

"Early meeting at the office and I want to beat the traffic."

"All right. I'll have coffee in a jiffy."

"Not for me. I'm off." Jill hooked her overnight case over her shoulder and gave Claire a quick hug. "See you."

"You'd better. Remember your promise."

"Indeed I will," Jill called as she rushed out. She intended to see Claire soon and often. She liked her. She sped through almost empty streets, thinking about what she could do to help Claire solve her problem.

The trouble was, she hadn't convinced Claire that she had a problem. Having always been given whatever she wanted, she probably didn't miss material things. Not yet, anyway. Still, the washing, cooking and sole care of three active children must be a challenge to a person who'd never had to lift a finger except to stick a silver spoon to her mouth. According to Scott, Claire wasn't lazy. Maybe anybody who could sit astride a galloping horse could meet any challenge. Even enjoy it, judging from Claire's happy housewife facade.

But that first night… She had looked so lonely, so lost.

And she wouldn't even admit that she was missing the fun and excitement of the life she wasn't sharing with her husband! *She's so wrapped up in her sainted David that she can't see what she's doing to herself.*

Jill pulled into her parking slot and glanced at her watch. Plenty of time to stop for coffee. She walked toward the coffee shop, still thinking about Claire. Did her Dave deserve such complete trust and devotion? Whether he did or not, in comparison to Claire, he had it pretty good. He wasn't missing out on a darn thing!

The pungent scent of coffee and sweet crumpets greeted her as the door swung open. "Beauty before age," said a familiar voice. She looked up at the smiling face of Tom Harris.

"After you, Jill," he prompted.

Realizing she was blocking the doorway, she hurried in, at the same time shaking a finger at Tom. "We need to talk." *He* certainly hadn't deserved Kris's trust, she thought. "You wait in line and I'll hold that place." She pointed to an isolated corner table. "Bring me a latte, low fat and very hot, and a cinnamon twist."

"A twist doesn't go with low fat."

"Never mind that. Get going. I've got something to say to you and I don't have much time." She meant to take the time, meeting or not, and when he returned with their orders she was ready. "I don't like what you're doing to Kris, Tom Harris."

Tom yanked out a chair and slammed into it. "Stay out of this! You don't know anything about this."

"I know you're back to your old tricks."

"My…tricks?"

"Kris can't take that. She's not one of your bed-hopping fly-by-nighters."

"Jill, will you shut up and listen—"

"No. *You* listen. I'm not criticizing your lifestyle."

"Thank you. Just interfering with my life, huh?"

"Not at all. What I'm asking is that you let Kris go. And don't tell me you can't give back enough of her own money to get out on her own and forget about you. I know how many big clients you've picked up."

"You seem to know a great deal about me."

"Don't be mad, Tom." Jill reached over to touch his arm. "I'm just concerned about Kris."

"Who's doing just fine!"

"She may not show it, but she's hurting. She fell in love with you…. That old-fashioned hook-line-and-sinker kind of love. No questions, no reservations, no holding back."

"And you're suggesting I let that go?"

"Huh?"

"Okay, you're not concerned about *me*. But I'd like to tell you about a little scoop that might be of interest. I assume, my knowledgeable one, that you know Candy Atkins."

"Of course. She—"

"Works for you and she's in a bit of a jam, now that your company's falling apart."

"We're not falling apart! We're launching in a different direction and…" She stopped. She couldn't tell him that Scott's emphasis on product rather than paper profits was about to pay off. It was still hush-hush but it was true. They actually had a patent on the camera that would not only revolutionize medicine, but industry, as well. However, in order to be launched internationally, it first needed national accreditation, which meant obtaining authority from the FDA to even begin testing.

But this was about Kris… "What does Chandler have to do with your fooling around with Candy?"

"Everything. And let's get this straight. I am not and *was not* fooling around with anybody!"

"No?"

"No. It was Kris getting fired from your precious company and Candy seeking so-called advice concerning her role in your new direction that got her up to our condo in the first place."

"Nonsense. How could that have anything to do with—"

"How about you listen for a change!"

Jill did listen. As she listened and thought about it, she wasn't surprised by Candy's maneuvering. She also found

Tom's vain efforts to elude such persistence highly amusing. By the time he described Kris's entry with "Candy's nude body coiled around me like a snake," Jill almost laughed out loud.

"I'm glad you find it funny."

"It is funny." Jill wiped her eyes. "I didn't know you were such a gentleman. Why didn't you just tell Kris what happened?"

"Do you think I didn't try? I did—I tried to tell her, just like I told you."

"She didn't believe you?"

"Didn't listen. Go ahead. Laugh your head off!"

"Oh, I can't…help it," she stuttered. "Sorry, but I keep thinking about that old joke. Who was Kris gonna believe, you or her lying eyes?"

"Ha, ha! So I was stupid enough to let a sleazy bimbo like Candy maneuver me into a situation that made Kris think I was having an affair—and that's what makes me so damn mad! How *could* she think it? How could she let that Candy bitch destroy in one night everything we had!"

"Now, Tom, be fair. Kris didn't—"

"Didn't she? Where's all that hook-line-and-sinker stuff? No questions, no reservations, you said? What about a little pure, unadulterated trust?"

"Oh, Tom, I'm sorry." She looked at his tense face and got a glimmer of the hurt and frustration he was trying to hide. Now it was Tom she wanted to comfort and reassure. "Don't for one instant think that Kris doesn't love you. She was hurt and she's still in shock. You must admit that what she saw— All right, all right," she said quickly. "I just want to point out that you're both victims of Candy's dirty tricks, and if you let this pull you apart—"

"I'm not stupid. Why do you think I'm holding her money? It's the only way I can hold on to the best thing that's ever come into my life and I'm not about to let her get away. So you can tell her… No, don't tell her anything. If she believed you and not me, I'd—"

"Still be there. With all the tender love and kisses you're hoarding just for her." Jill got up and leaned over to hug his shoulder. "Hang in there, Tom. It'll work itself out. I have a feeling Kris isn't about to let you get away, either. Did you know I offered her a bed at my place?"

"You did?" He looked up at her, surprised and a little wary.

"She refused. I wonder why." She kissed him on the cheek and hurried away.

Outside, her heels clicked hard on the sidewalk. She knew what Candy was. She should have told Kris.

Oh, no! You were too busy telling her about Tom and comparing him to your father!

Jill shut her eyes, thoroughly ashamed. She had done just that.

Well, If Kris had one smattering of Claire's trust…

What about you? You're aching with so much love for Scott that you can't stand it when he's away. But you don't have enough trust to marry him!

That's not true. It's not Scott. She tried to reason it out. *Maybe it's marriage I can't trust.*

Too bad for you. There are women who aren't afraid to risk it, her unruly mind cautioned.

Again she saw the socialites Claire had told her about; women whose focus was on money and status without a thought for Scott nor his needs. Again the red-light warning signal blinked.

Lord, how could she conduct a meeting now? She had to call Scott and make arrangements to join him. This was a good time to check out the Virginia homestead. Maybe that would be the best home for their children.

LEFT ALONE, Tom reached for his coffee. Pushed it aside.

Drinking coffee from a paper cup with a roomful of strangers and casual acquaintances wasn't what he wanted to do. Not anymore. Not after coffee with Jill. An early-morning frosting on the intimacies of the night before. Laughter, light morning kisses, promises and plans.

He missed her.

Jill said Kris was hurting. She didn't look it. There was still the jaunty walk and dimples deepening with a bubbly smile. The smile cooled every time she skirted past him. On her way to some school or wherever she went. Or to shut herself in her room to paint or mark papers or whatever she did. He couldn't even tell when or where she ate, or when she washed her clothes, or…anything.

She was gone even when she was there!

He got up to place another order. Eat, drink and be merry. Places to go, people to influence.

WHEN HE GOT BACK to the condo about eight that night, Tom was surprised to see Kris's rattletrap rental pull in beside him.

"Hi. You're here early," he said.

He got the cool smile. But the jaunty walk was missing, and she looked a little… Could brown skin turn pale?

By the time he got in, she was closeted in her room.

What was wrong with exchanging a few courteous how-was-your-day remarks?

"Not good," he'd tell her. Then they'd talk it over. Laugh about it.

He was pretty fed up with this isolation. Better give Kris her money and let her get the hell out of his life.

He jerked off his tie, drew a deep breath. No use taking his frustration out on Kris. It wasn't her fault that money was tight in the Bernstein campaign and there were no TV funds to capitalize on Dave's Kennedy award. They were having a hell of a time getting sponsors for fund-raisers, too.

He threw aside his jacket, loosened his tie and reached for the Scotch. Drink in hand, he slowly climbed the stairs.

As he passed Kris's door, he heard her coughing. It sounded like she was in trouble, and he peered in to check.

She was lying on her bed, fully clothed, retching as if she might choke. Putting his drink on her dresser, he rushed over to lift her in his arms and hold her erect. She tried to push him away, but he kept a firm grip. "Easy now. Just lean on me and let it go."

Exhausted, she did lean and let it go—over both of them.

"Sorry," she whispered when she finally could.

"It's okay," he said. But it wasn't. She was hot as blazes and he was scared. If anything happened to Kris...

"You'll be all right. A tepid bath will cool you down," he said as he tore off their clothes and lifted her into the shower. Holding her close, he let the cleansing water pour over them both, ran his fingers through her hair, kissed her.

She protested. "You'll catch what I've got."

"Not me. I'm commune immune," he said, and chuckled.

Good thing he'd spent half his life in communes. He was immune to anything. Good thing he'd learned to cope without a doctor, too, now that you couldn't call a doctor, even if you knew one to call. Kris was connected to an HMO, and he knew there'd be an advice nurse on duty—who'd probably recommend he bring her to the hospital. But he wasn't about to haul Kris off to some crowded emergency room.

"Feeling better?" he asked as he gave her a last pat with the towel and helped her between clean sheets.

She wanted to nod. Couldn't. She did manage to sip a little water and swallow the aspirin. When his fingers lightly touched her cheek she buried her face in his hand, clinging to the cool comfort.

FIVE MORNINGS LATER Kris awoke, wondering if it was over. Her head didn't ache and she wasn't dizzy. She was afraid to lift her head and check. Afraid she might arouse the chills, fever, nausea and pain again. Tom said it was a virus that was going around and had poured gallons of juice and ginger ale down her, along with some pills the doctor had suggested.

Lord, she'd never been so sick in her life. If it hadn't been for Tom...

A warm feeling enveloped her. He'd been with her every minute, day or night, doing what she was too weak to do for herself. Just as if they hadn't been mad, hardly speaking for weeks. Not as if it was a duty, either. After all, they'd never promised all that forever-after, in-sickness-and-health stuff.

She turned her head on the pillow. Testing. She was feeling all right now. More than all right. How could she feel so good when she'd been so sick for...how many days?

"Oh, you are awake. Good."

The warm glow deep inside her sparkled and spun. *Tom.* She watched him place the tray he carried on the bedside table, and smiled. He looked so handsome, fully dressed today in jacket and tie.

"Feel like sitting up? Let's try it." He threw back the sheet and lifted her out of bed.

She leaned against his chest, loving the familiar scent of his refreshing aftershave, loving being in his arms, wanting to—She was disappointed to find herself quickly seated, her legs dangling against the side of the high bed.

"Are you okay?" he asked.

She nodded, relieved to find her head didn't swim. He was regarding her so intently that she looked down at herself. She saw that her legs dangled from the sexiest gown she owned—the short lavender one with matching ruffled panties. Tom had put it on her. Was he thinking—

"Better drink this," he said, handing her a full glass from the tray. "It'll build up your strength."

He was thinking sick, not sex. Well, maybe once you spilled your guts all over a guy, he didn't think—

"Drink it," he repeated.

Dutifully she drew several swallows through the straw.

"Will you be all right?" he asked, looking a little anxious. "You're on your own today."

"You're going to work?" She didn't want him to leave.

"Yep. There's sandwich stuff and yogurt in the fridge. And this smoothie should hold you for a while. It's pretty nourishing."

"And delicious," she said, feeling very selfish. Her throat didn't hurt, she wasn't even dizzy or anything, but she didn't want him to leave her. "You mustn't worry about me, Tom. I'm fine now. You shouldn't miss any more days from the office."

"That's no big deal. I can work from here. But today's not a work day. Big Saturday seminar by big-pocket client I can't afford to lose. Gotta be there. Sure you'll be all right?"

"Of course. I'm all right now. But…oh, Tom, I'm sorry I was such a mess. I was so sick." She caught his hand. "If you hadn't—"

"Enough already! You're welcome."

She laughed. "Well, may I at least thank you for the flowers? They're beautiful."

He followed her gaze to the extravagant arrangement on the bureau. "Oh, those." He walked over, extracted the small envelope, and handed it to her. "Sorry, I can't take the credit."

She read the enclosed card. *Get well soon. We need you here.* "It's from R. Gonzales and staff at Tech High," she said. "That was nice of them. I wonder how they knew."

"Tech High?"

"Yes. I've been substituting for an English teacher, and boy, did those kids need to learn English."

"You must've created quite an impression. They made a special request for your services. You were out like a light. Whoever called from the school district probably passed along the news." He frowned. "I once knew an R. Gonzales. Who is he?"

"The principal. Stately, well-informed, dignified and very dedicated."

"Then he's not the R. Gonzales I knew. Gotta run." He started out, then turned back. "I'll get home as soon as I can," he said, and kissed her full on the mouth.

Her fingers flew to her lips, held the kiss long after he was gone, his last words ringing in her ears. She wanted him to hurry back.

Lord, how she'd missed him. She shouldn't have made such a big deal of his cavorting with that Candy woman, she thought, trying to squelch the painful memory. They hadn't promised to forsake all others, had they?

Anyway, if all those macho Bible heroes had played around as much as they pleased, what could you expect of an ordinary man in this free-wheeling city of San Francisco?

And she'd known what Tom was the first time she'd met him. Jill had told her.

The trouble was, she'd fallen in love with him.

And you thought he would change because you loved him?

It came to her then. The Shakespearean sonnet she'd had to learn in high school. *Love is not love that alters when it alteration finds. Nor bends with the remover to remove.*

She couldn't remember all the words, but she got the message. Love isn't love if it seeks to change a person. She loved Tom, loved what he was and would always be. Okay, an attractive man, a little free with his favors. But also smart, witty, fun-loving, kind, tender, warm-hearted, caring...

To everyone! Who *wouldn't* love him?

Well, darn it, a smart woman wouldn't pull out of the game and leave the field wide open. No, indeed.

And...if he'd stuck by her when she was sick and messy, surely he would if she was...alluring?

Like those Biblical Bathshebas with their womanly wiles, oil baths and exotic scents.

Which reminded her of that Arresting Aroma stuff she'd bought and never used. Pointless after the fight with Tom.

But now...

Kris slid to the floor, stumbled a bit, but held on to the bed, regaining her balance.

In a moment, as soon as she caught her breath, she'd ready herself to outplay any other woman. For Tom.

It took some time, considering all the sitting and lying down between the doing. But her energy was returning, and soon all signs of a sick room had vanished, and she could begin on herself.

It was almost four when Kris emerged from a long, relaxing, enticingly scented bubble bath, swathed herself in lotion and powder of the same enticing scent, and searched for something equally enticing to wear. She settled on shorts and a halter top, casual but even more provocative than the lavender gown.

She splashed on a bit of perfume. Maybe if she sprayed it around the room…

"What the hell is that?"

Kris whirled around to face a furious Tom. "W-what?"

"That obnoxious smell?" He rushed to open the window. "What the hell is it?"

"It…it's supposed to entice you." Kris blinked, holding back the tears.

He turned from the window and looked at her, a strange expression on his face. Surprise? Anger? She couldn't tell. Everything was beginning to blur….

"You…wanted to *entice* me?"

"I'm sorry you find it ob…obnoxious."

"No. Not bad. Not bad at all really." He walked toward her, his eyes alight with laughter. "In fact, it's getting more enticing by the minute."

"Oh, Tom!" She flew into his arms. "I'm sorry. I was trying to make up, I've been such an idiot. I forgive you. No. I don't mean that. There's nothing to forgive. You're free to do whatever you like and I was stupid to make such a big deal about Candy and—"

"Hey, hey, wait a second." He held her a little away and

looked down at her. "We need to talk and get a few things straight. First of all, who should forgive whom—and I'm not sure I can forgive you for thinking me such a creep. Even if I wanted to fool around, how could you believe I'd do it in our own place practically in front of your face?"

"I'm sorry. I shouldn't have—"

"And what about trust? What's wrong with believing a guy when he tries to tell you what he's *not* doing?"

"I'm sorry," she said again, somewhat taken aback that she was the one apologizing.

"High time you were sorry. Do you know what I've been going through?"

"Me, too," she said, all at once not caring who apologized— Or who did or didn't do what. "Oh, Tom, don't be mad." She wrapped her arms around his neck and rained kisses across his face. "I'll never doubt you again."

"Promise?"

"I promise. No matter what."

That *no matter what* bothered him. What had she said about being free to do whatever? They'd have to talk about that.

But not now. An exhilarating warmth was stealing through him, and he realized he had on too many clothes. He lifted her in his arms, and carried her to the bed.

He had discarded his jacket and she was removing his tie when he heard the loud peal of the doorbell. Damn.

He wanted to ignore it, but a caller at their door was so unusual. "I'd better see who that is," he told her. "Don't move." Downstairs, he opened the door to a tall man, backing up as if to check the number.

A man tall enough to look down at him and stare.

Tom stared back, unable to believe his eyes. Was this the guy he'd never forget? Head man of the Mexican Mafia at Bell High?

The other man also seemed perplexed. "Are you...Tom Harris?"

"The same," Tom said.

A wide grin spread across the man's face. "The gringo my friends and I were going to wipe off the map way back when?"

"If any of you sorry dudes could catch me," Tom said, holding out a hand. "Ray Gonzales. Long time no see."

"Almost twenty years, and you look the same." Gonzales took Tom's hand in a firm grip. "Good to see you, Tom. How are you?"

"Fine. And I understand you're the principal of Tech High."

"Yep, I've done a little running myself."

"Well, you've taken on quite a job. How're things going?"

"So far, so good. But…" Gonzales glanced again at the number. "I certainly didn't expect to see you. I'm looking for 1027 Oceanside."

"This is 1027."

"Kris Gilroy's place?"

"Our place," Tom corrected, to make clear how things stood. He smiled. Gonzales didn't look nearly so intimidating in horn-rimmed glasses. "Come in. I'll tell Kris you're here."

CHAPTER TWENTY

WHEN TOM CALLED out that she had a visitor, Kris hurried down, sure that it was Jill. Jill would be glad to see that she and Tom were back together. Well, at least on the way back.

At the sight of Gonzales, Kris stopped short. "Dr. Gonzales. What a...a surprise."

"And not a pleasant one?"

"No, I'm delighted to see you. I just..." She looked down at her bare feet and laughed. "Well, I should've put on my shoes."

More than shoes, Tom thought, not liking the inspection Gonzales was giving that scanty halter.

"Don't mind me," Gonzales said. "I'm glad to see you so relaxed. And well, I take it?"

"Yes. Now. But the last few days..." She winced. "Oh, I must thank you. The flowers are lovely. That was so thoughtful of you."

"It was the least we could do, since you probably caught the virus from us. We've had quite a few absentees. Sorry."

"Nonsense. You're not responsible for bugs. Let me introduce you to my...friend. Tom, this is—"

"We've met," Tom said, nettled. When did he get to be just a *friend*?

"Oh." Kris looked from one to the other, wondering what was wrong with Tom. "This is the R. Gonzales you said you knew?"

Tom nodded. "More than a decade ago. Sit down, Ray. We should drink a toast to old Bell High. What'll it be?"

"Do you have a root beer? Coke?"

"Pardon?"

"You're obviously surprised." Gonzales assumed a sedate pose as he settled on the sofa and stretched out his long legs. "I'm a shining example for my students."

"And quite a revelation to me." Tom chuckled. "But a cold root beer sounds great. I'll be right back." In a few minutes he returned with a tray of assorted cheeses, crackers and three tall frosted glasses of root beer. If Ray thought he was going to be left alone for a private tête à tête, he had another think coming.

Kris was on the sofa beside Ray, deep in conversation. She broke off to make room on the coffee table for his tray and helped pass out the refreshments. "Guess what, Tom," she said as she sat back on the sofa. "Mr. Gonzales thinks he may be able to arrange a permanent position for me at Tech High."

"Oh?" Tom said. *I'll bet.*

"Yes," Gonzales added. "We're not exactly a continuation school, but with our emphasis on trades, we seem to inherit quite a few…" He put his glass down, scratched his chin. "Guess there's no other way to put it. Kids like me at that age. You know what I was, Tom. More interested in raising hell than opening a book."

"Well…"

"Oh, don't dodge the issue. I know you're wondering how I got from there to here. Well, I'll tell you. Lucky for me, the do-gooders were in control, and affirmative action got to the schools—special classes, special teachers, even tutors and study sessions for losers like me."

"Yeah," Tom said. "I remember that time. Lots of new guidelines. A black man was the State Superintendent of Education."

"Wilson Riles." Gonzales smiled. "That man might have saved me from prison. I got introduced to a whole new world, and I joined it."

Funny what one man could do, Tom thought. Bob saved me. I was too chicken to get in much trouble, but it was Bob's direction…

"But I digress," Gonzales said. "This isn't about me. Except that I'm trying to do for my students what was done for me, and I'm not getting much help. Affirmative action is out and high achievers are in. Most teachers don't take to the so-called losers and we have quite a placement problem. Kris is not only an excellent teacher, she's good with the students. They seem to like her. I could make a special appeal to the school board, tell them that while she's working on her credentials, she could—"

"Hold on a minute," Tom, a bit alarmed, broke in. Kris was too much a do-gooder herself to spend eight hours a day in the company of another do-gooder, especially a good-looking one who obviously had the hots for her. "I sympathize with your teacher problem and that sounds like an excellent recruitment plan. But not for Kris. We can't spare her."

"We?" Gonzales looked puzzled.

"The business, I mean. Kris and I are partners." Tom shot a quick glance at Kris. She was staring at him, her mouth open. But she didn't deny it. Not yet.

She was actually too stunned to refute him. Anyway, she couldn't call Tom a liar in front of a man she was anxious to impress. Okay, so she didn't like teaching. But any job was better than no job at all, and if Mr. Gonzales could get her a permanent position… *Partners?* What was Tom trying to prove? Again her eyes flew from one man to the other as she tried to focus in on the rapid-fire dialogue.

"Lobbyists," Tom was saying. "We've gained several new clients. I don't think Kris will be available even as a substitute teacher."

"I guess not." Gonzales's tone was bitter. "Why be a teacher when you can get big bucks peddling influence so big corporations can get even bigger bucks?"

"We like to think of ourselves as negotiators for better government and the public good."

"Bull!" Gonzales scoffed. "Who negotiated for Chevrolet to get a zillion bucks to pull out of a slump that might very well have been caused by the flood of foreign cars imported into this country? Mercedes and Toyota have the bucks to hire lobbyists, too."

Tom shrugged. "Competition is the name of the game, buddy. And it's all for the public good. Whatever the source, foreign or domestic, what's wrong with more dealers, mechanics and paychecks for the people of America?"

"Something's wrong." Gonzales glared at Tom. "Kids are people, too. How is it these big companies can get bailed out of bankruptcy and my kids can't get a decent gym or even parking space for the leftover junk heaps they buy from said companies?"

Tom laughed. "I gather you have more than teacher problems?"

"You can say that again. The parking lot's so small the kids are parking all over the neighborhood, and you can't imagine the scraps they get into or the hell I'm catching from our neighbors. And the gym's leaking so badly it's dangerous."

"Sounds like you need a lobbyist."

"Ha!"

"What do you mean…ha?"

"I mean, no way can we compete with your rich clients."

"I think a couple of us were involved in getting that school bond bill through last month."

"Thank you very much. But it was a drop in the bucket. And for academics, not for building or maintenance. We may get a few computers, but not a new gym."

"Oh, for goodness' sake," Kris muttered. "Maintenance is a regular expense, which should include a leaky roof."

"Of course," Gonzales said, "but the whole building's so dilapidated, a new roof would only be a waste."

Tom was so silent Kris looked at him. He was staring at the ceiling as if he was thinking of something else and had lost interest in the conversation.

Gonzales apparently got the same impression. "It's been good to see you again, Tom. I enjoyed the visit." He turned to Kris. "I'm certainly glad to see you in good health, Kris. And deeply sorry my plans to capture you for our school didn't work out. Guess I was moving too fast, but I had no idea you were otherwise engaged."

"Of course you didn't." She didn't say she didn't know it, either. "It was kind of you to think of me. Perhaps later..." She floundered, trying to think of something that would leave that door open. She needed the job. What had made Tom say they were *partners?*

"I should be on my way." Gonzales stood. "I'm enjoying your company, but I've imposed on you long enough with problems you can't do anything about."

"I don't know about that," Tom said. "You did say the emphasis is now on academics and high achievers?"

Gonzales nodded, gazing at Tom as if surprised to see him back with them.

"Then it's quite possible you could use our services." Tom sprang up and held out a hand. "Give me your card, Ray. I'm not quite sure of your location."

Gonzales, still looking puzzled, gave him a card.

"Thank you. Kris and I will look in on you on...Monday, if that's convenient."

Kris, equally puzzled, was gracious and polite as they showed Gonzales out. As soon as the door closed behind him, she turned to Tom. "Why did you say we were partners?"

"A step up from friends, wouldn't you say?"

"Oh." She smiled. "*Meet my lover* didn't seem quite the right terminology."

"*Meet Tom Harris* sounds pretty good. Let him wonder." Tom sounded angry. "We *are* more than friends, aren't we?"

"But not partners. Certainly not business partners."

"We could be," he said, lightly touching his lips to hers.

"That's ridiculous! I need a job, Tom, and I can teach. I know nothing about politics or corporations or…any of that lobbyist stuff."

"Are you unaware of the amazing talents you possess?"

"Be serious, Tom. Even if you wanted a partner, I—"

"I want you." His hand slipped beneath her halter, gently caressing, teasing, sending urgent tremors of a primitive hunger spiraling through her. "Are we lovers, my sweet?"

"Yes, oh…yes," she said, lost in the hot pulsating waves of desire.

"Lovers and partners." He lifted her in his arms and carried her back to bed.

"Wake up, sweetheart," Tom said.

Kris returned his kiss, ran her fingers through his hair, still damp from the shower, but didn't open her eyes. "I'm sleeping in," she said, burying her face in the pillow to return to the most restful sleep she'd had in a long time.

"Not today, partner." Tom had moved away from her and was reaching in the bureau for a clean shirt. "I want to stop by the office before we meet with Gonzales."

Her eyes flew open and she sat up. "We?"

"You heard me tell him we'd be out this morning."

"Yes, but…" He'd also told Ray Gonzales they were partners, which they certainly were not. After Gonzales left, she'd tried to get that straight. She'd been distracted—for the rest of the weekend, in fact. "Tom, we need to talk."

"We'll talk on the way. Hurry up. Don't make me late."

She did hurry. He sounded serious and she thought she knew what he was trying to do. It was another way of saying she didn't need a job, that he would take care of her, just as he'd said when she lost that great job at Chandler.

Today was an opportunity. He wouldn't be able to distract

her while he was driving. She'd make him understand that she had no intention of being a kept woman.

She broached the subject as soon as they were in the car. "Tom, I don't know anything about lobbying."

"Sure you do. You undervalue yourself, Kris."

"Look, I know what I can do and what I can't. And anyway—"

"I want you to hear this CD. Tony Bennett doing Duke Ellington. I bought it last week, especially for you. If you ever started speaking to me again, that is." He laughed as he switched it on. "It's an old song, one you probably remember. It applies to us, and I'd like you to get the message. Listen."

She loved Tony Bennett and did recall the song, which referred to a spat between two lovers because the woman had heard her man had another love.

"Get it?" he asked as the music died away.

"Oh, I get it. And it does *not* apply to us. I don't listen to gossip. I got mad because of what I saw with my own eyes."

"And didn't listen to a word I said. It does apply. Didn't you hear the title and the refrain?" he asked, quoting, "'Do nothing 'til you hear from me.'"

She laughed and tenderly stroked his leg. "All right, all right. I promise to trust you and I'll never make another move until I hear from you. Anyway, we won't have that problem. Didn't we agree that we're both free to do whatever we please?"

"That's another thing. You agreed. I didn't. This do-as-you-please, screw-who-you-like business doesn't appeal to me, and if you think—"

"Oh, for goodness' sake! I didn't mean—"

"Well, let's get this straight. I won't have you—"

"Watch it!" She caught her breath as Tom swerved just in time to prevent a collision with a speeding convertible. "You'd better be more careful, hon."

"You upset me."

"You're upset over nothing. If it's commitment you want, you've got it. Okay?"

"Okay, but…"

"No buts. We're together again and happy, and I don't know why you're determined to pick a fight," she said. "Relax. We need to talk about this partners thing."

"That's settled."

"No, it isn't. It's sweet of you to offer, but what on earth could I do for you? No! Don't interrupt. Let me finish. I do need a job and it seems Gonzales can get me a permanent position and—"

"No."

"Why not?"

"I don't like the way he looks at you."

"You don't like—" She burst out laughing. "Oh, don't be ridiculous. I'm not interested in that man. Besides, what about trust?"

"I trust you. I don't trust him. And I don't want you closeted with him for eight hours, five days a week."

"That's crazy! We're not closeted—"

"Come on." Tom pulled into his parking slot. "I've got things to do before we leave for Tech High."

Kris followed Tom to his suite, surprised at herself. She ought to be angry, but what she felt was a kind of amused delight. Tom was jealous!

His office was another surprise. More spacious than she'd expected. And more people. Ted, of course, and two women, whom Tom casually introduced as Katie and Pam. He spoke a few words to the older woman, and took some papers from the younger one. "I'll only be a minute, Kris," he said, before disappearing into another room with the man, calling over his shoulder, "Coffee? Pam'll get it, won't you, Pam?"

"Oh, sure." The younger woman turned to her. "Cream? Sugar? Danish?"

"Just coffee, please. Black." Kris wasn't about to regain the couple of pounds she'd lost during the virus siege. This Pam was as slim as Jill and cute as a button and right here in Tom's office. *I'd be here, too,* Kris thought, *if I worked with him.*

Lord! She was the jealous one.

During the drive to the high school, Tom was occupied with his constantly ringing cell phone. She was impressed by how easily he could switch from one client, one problem to another.

She was also impressed by how quickly those problems were dismissed and he focused total concentration on the problems at the high school. It was evident he already had a plan in mind before they inspected the gym and visited some of the trade classes.

"You say the emphasis is on academics and high achievers," he said when they retreated to Gonzales's office. "Rebuilding the gym would fit into that category if the students were involved." They listened openmouthed as he explained that funds for the experiment could be provided by the academics achievement bonds bill, as well as the new Bernstein Bill providing work experience for teenagers. "Combine that with a construction company eager for a goodwill project, and you might have a new gym." He laughed. "I'd thought of high-rise parking over the gym, but… Well, one step at a time."

"Anything's possible!" Kris cried, really excited. She knew students who'd be eager for such a chance, and who would later be qualified as construction workers.

Gonzales was equally excited, but hesitant. "It's a great plan, but there's a lot of negotiating to be done. I'm just not sure who or how—"

"I thought I mentioned that we're negotiators for the public good. Also that you might be in need of our services."

Gonzales grinned. "Yeah. And I think I mentioned that your fees come pretty high."

"Don't worry about it," Tom said. "Now and then we also do a bit of pro bono."

When they reached the car, Kris could contain herself no

longer. She threw her arms around Tom right there in the parking lot and kissed him hard. "You're absolutely wonderful! And so clever. You just sat there and in less than a minute pulled together a scheme that will do so much for so many."

"I'm liking this." Tom pulled her closer and returned her kiss with enthusiasm. "Even if we're ahead of the game," he added, grinning, "we haven't pulled anything off yet."

"But we will. I'm going to help you. I'd like to talk to the students. Do you know how many of them are busting their guts to participate? Not just to sit down and scribble answers on paper or make an ashtray for their mom or... Oh, you know what I mean. This project will be their opportunity to participate in the real world where they expect to earn their living. They'll be doing something practical that'll benefit them all in their lives. Oh, I'm going to enjoy working with you!"

CHAPTER TWENTY-ONE

WHEN THE PLANE DESCENDED at Dulles Airport a little before noon, Jill was in a jubilant mood. Scott had said he'd meet her there.

"It's near our place," he'd added. "We'll go out and build a fire and..." His voice had softened. "Get reacquainted."

She basked in the promise. She would be wrapped in the loving warmth of his arms before a cozy fire, isolated in the quiet Virginia countryside. What could be more romantic?

His arms enclosed her immediately, but he looked anything but romantic.

Anxiety quickened her heart. She touched his cheek, wanting to smooth the tired lines from his face, kiss away the troubled tightness of his mouth. "What's wrong?" she asked.

He smiled as if to reassure her. "Nothing wrong, really. It's just...well, everything's going so slowly."

"Bogged down, in fact," came another harsh voice. One she recognized.

She looked over Scott's shoulder and froze. Of course Talbert Sims was here in D.C. for the hearings, but... Why on earth had Scott brought him to the airport?

"Talbert's getting antsy," Scott said, answering the question she hadn't asked. "He came along to see if we could figure out a new approach with the FDA. I keep telling him it's not up to us. They have their procedures and we just have to get in line."

Typical of Talbert's get-out-of-the-way-and-make-room-for-me attitude, she thought, but didn't say it. She wasn't going to let him rain on their parade. As soon as they got rid of him...

It was not to be soon. She was dismayed when she found they not only weren't dumping Sims, but were accompanying him to the Food and Drug Administration offices.

"We're meeting with an official from one of the health committees," Scott explained. "Talbert thinks he can speed things up."

Actually they met with two officials from two different committees, and, since Scott wanted her by his side, she accompanied them. As she listened to the discussions, a line from a poem of Wordsworth's came to her. *The world is too much with us.* It certainly was, here in Washington.

Well, the world was with her in California, wasn't it? Along with her daily problems. Keeping Chandler afloat while pouring millions into the Talbert Sims experiment. Constant consultations with the Alaskan cannery and Jake, almost back on his feet. She hadn't contacted Kris because she was afraid she'd tell her what Tom had said she must not. She wondered if an e-mail just saying "Be patient" would be too much. She could counsel trust, like Claire's? A prickle of fear lingered at the thought of Claire. A loving, caring woman skating on thin ice.

Something in the voice of the official caught her attention. Dear God, had she been so deep in worries at home that she'd forgotten where she was?

"This is certainly an excellent and worthwhile project, Dr. Sims," the woman official said. "It's destined to save many lives, and should definitely be moved ahead."

Jill looked at Sims, feeling a sudden rush of pride. *Go ahead, be a peacock,* she silently intoned. *You're doing a good thing.* And Scott was paying for it, while she helped keep his finances in condition to do so. She gestured a thumbs-up to Scott.

"I'll check the schedules again in the morning." The official glanced at the clock. "My husband will be circling around to pick me up and I don't want him stalled in traffic," she explained, reaching for her purse.

Jill was strangely cheered by the bustle as the halls filled with five o'clock leave-takers. Putting work aside to hurry home, fix dinner, spend time with the kids. Or, like the beaming couple hurrying past, meet for a date? The normal routine of living.

And the joy of living, she thought once they'd deposited Sims at his hotel and headed for that cozy fire. Again she basked in the promise as traffic thinned and they drove through the rolling hills of the beautiful Virginia countryside. So much greenery. There was a touch of fall colors on some trees, but most leaves were still green. And the grass in the pastures where she spotted horses grazing, was the greenest she'd ever seen. The same luscious green covered the spacious well-kept lawns that swept back to stately mansions.

Why did she feel she'd come home? Nothing about the orderly beauty or the obvious wealth of this place remotely resembled the disorderly rustic beauty of her Alaskan village. She smiled. Maybe she was so wrapped up in Scott, she'd adopted everything that went with him.

"I see that smile," Scott said. "What are you thinking?"

"That I'm beginning to like stately mansions and private jets. I think I'll marry you," she teased, knowing she'd marry this man if he didn't have a dime.

"Better make it quick. I'm up for grabs and there's a long line." He chuckled, but gripped her hand. Hard. "Shall we pick up the license in the morning?"

"Yes! While I'm still first in line. I… Scott, what…?" He had pulled to a stop, his hands now on her shoulders, and he was kissing her so fervently she could hardly breathe.

"You promised," he whispered between kisses. "First thing in the morning. And we'll get married right away. Unless… Do you want all those fixings or…"

"No." She smiled against his lips. "I don't want all those fixings. We'll make it quiet, simple and quick."

Scott's family home was set farther back than most, but they saw the smoke rising from the chimney when they turned into the drive. Scott wondered about the fire. "I didn't tell Murray I'd be here."

She had forgotten. There was a couple who maintained the house. They weren't going to be isolated, after all.

As usual, Scott read her thoughts. "Sarah and Murray have their own place. We'll be alone in ours." But he frowned when he saw the jazzy sports car parked in front of the house. "That doesn't look like Murray's. I wonder…"

Jill was absorbed in the house. The two-story structure of wood and stone had a look of strength and permanence. Something about the careful arrangement of surrounding shrubbery, the stillness and quiet serenity, added to the feeling that she'd come home.

Scott slipped his key in the lock, opened the door and led her into a wide hall. She saw a small marble-topped table against one wall, an antique mirror above it and in a far corner, a large plant. Or was it a small tree? Somewhere in the distance, she heard soft feminine laughter, and Scott drew her toward the sound.

The first thing Jill noticed through the open double doors were the logs burning in the big stone fireplace at the end of the room. *Here's the cozy fire at last,* she thought, feeling a warm welcome in its radiant glow. She didn't even see the two women until one stood, looking pleasantly surprised. "Scott, darling! I was just going to call you. But, of course, that's why you're here. Whitney must have called you, and…" Her voice trailed off as her eyes focused on Jill. "Oh! Sorry. I didn't realize…"

"Hello, Mother. A surprise all around," Scott said, laughing. "I didn't realize you'd be here, but I'm glad. I've wanted you to meet." He put an arm around Jill and drew her forward. "Jill, this is my mother, Alicia Sandusky. Jill Ferrell, Mother. I've told you about her."

"Oh, yes." Alicia Sandusky's fingers touched Jill's outstretched hand. "I'm delighted to meet you, Ms. Ferrell."

Anything but delighted, Jill thought, judging by the tone of her voice. But she smiled. "I'm happy to meet you at last, Mrs. Sandusky. Scott's also told me about you."

"Oh? And just what did my boy say about his mother?"

"Everything good, I can assure you. Only he forgot to tell me you look more like his sister than his mother," Jill said, and was rewarded by a twinkle in Alicia's eyes. She'd guessed right. The slender woman in the silk lounging pajamas reveled in flattery. But it wasn't flattery. Alicia's dark eyes and classic features were much like those of her daughter, Claire, her skin as smooth and youthful. Jill wondered if she'd had a face-lift.

"Oh, and here's Whitney," Scott said, turning toward the younger woman. "Looking good as usual, Whit!"

That was certainly true, Jill observed as he drew her toward the beautiful blond woman wearing casually elegant designer jeans and soft, leather five-hundred-dollar loafers.

"Jill, Whitney Caruthers."

Mentally scolding herself for thinking of price brackets, she cordially extended her hand in response to Scott's introduction. "How do you do, Ms. Caruthers?"

The woman clasped it warmly. "I'm Whitney, for heaven's sake. And you're…Jill? I'm thrilled to meet anyone who could put up with this guy for five seconds. He was a pain in *my* neck for…gracious, how many years has it been, Scott?"

"Too many to count. And I think you've got it wrong about who was whose pain in the neck! Sit here, sweetheart," he said to Jill, pulling her to the sofa with him. "Let me tell you about this obnoxious braggart. Whit really thought she could outride any of us."

"I could. Still can."

"Oh, ho! Sounds like you're itching for a race!"

Whitney's excellently arched brows shot up in contemplation. "No, I don't think so. I'd hate to embarrass you. Tell me, Scott, when was the last time you got on a horse?"

Scott shook his head. "You've got me there. Unlike you, my lady of leisure, I'm a working man. So...how's Kevin? Or have you already dumped him?"

The teasing banter continued, with Alicia gleefully throwing in a comment now and then. Even Murray, who brought in more sandwiches, cakes and hot tea, joined the fray. He was detained to judge the debate on who was the best equestrian. And did it quite diplomatically, in Jill's opinion. "Well now, there's no denying Miss Whitney could sit a horse and take them jumps more gracefully than anybody at a horse show," he said. "But I gotta admit nobody could gentle a rambunctious horse like my boy here. Remember that frisky stallion old man Hunter brought over for you to ride, Scott? You tamed him right down."

Jill was seated between Whitney and Scott, his arm close around her. But she felt as alone as she had years ago, standing on a San Francisco sidewalk, her bare feet in sneakers, watching plush people enter plush places. Whitney might be one of the socialites Claire had mentioned, she thought.

Was it only a few minutes ago that she'd felt as if she'd come home? Now she felt as out of place as an alien from another planet.

What was wrong with her? Was she resentful that Scott had another life before he met her? Or just plain mad about missing the privacy they'd been looking forward to? She couldn't dislike Scott's mother. She was family, or soon would be.

Get over it, she told herself sternly. She could participate by listening, couldn't she?

She did so and learned that Whitney, who also had a home in New York, had been recently married to her third husband, Lord Kevin Caruthers. As they planned to reside at his estate in England, she'd decided to sell her family home in Virginia. Alicia had flown down with Whitney to help her decide about personal possessions before arranging for the sale.

"But I'm glad you've decided to hold on to the place for a while," Alicia said, and it sounded as if she was repeating herself. Jill suspected she'd come here hoping to change Whitney's mind. She was sure of it when Alicia added, "I'd hate to have some stranger living there. I've always envisioned the joining of our neighboring properties."

Through marriage, Jill presumed, and wondered if Alicia envisioned Scott as Whitney's fourth husband. At the thought, a tremor of fear rippled through her. Something about this elegantly polite woman gave the impression that she invariably got her own way.

Jill was glad to hear that both women were leaving the next day to get back to New York for some charity ball or other. She was just as glad to see Whitney drive off in the sleek sports car a few minutes later.

"Mother," Scott said as soon as the three were alone. "I have good news for you. Jill has consented to be my wife."

Jill held her breath, waiting for Alicia's response.

Because Scott's mother seemed a bigger threat than all the beautiful socialites in the world.

CHAPTER TWENTY-TWO

"THAT'S A RELIEF," Tom said as he opened the car door for Kris. "I'm glad we got this partner business settled."

"But I won't be your partner," she said as he slid into the seat beside her. She knew how little she had to offer and didn't intend to take advantage of their relationship. "I'll be a paid employee, like the other people in your office."

"I'll take what I can get. We'll work it out," Tom said and clicked on his ringing phone.

They did work it out, and settled on a salary, too large by Kris's standards and too low by Tom's. But they were working together. Kris was astonished to find that she really was of service to Tom—following bills in the Legislature and noting the pros and cons in the various committees; lunching or meeting clients with or sometimes for Tom. She quickly caught on to the goals of each client and how Tom could assist in achieving them. More importantly, how *she* could assist Tom in that endeavor. She grinned as she typed an e-mail to Jill, describing her reunion with Tom. "We're partners in business as well as in bed, and I'm loving every minute of it all!"

She hoped she'd get an answer. There'd been no word from Jill for some time, and she wasn't at work or at her apartment. That was worrisome. Problems with her brother in Alaska?

Kris was relieved and delighted when she finally got an e-mail from Jill.

Hi Kris,

I'm so glad to know you and Tom are back together. He's quite a guy and we had him pegged wrong. He had me laughing like crazy when he told me the real facts about the Candy episode.

Here Kris paused, wondering. The Candy episode was nothing to laugh at. The real facts? She hadn't listened to him that horrible night, and once she was back in his arms, had blanked the whole episode from her mind. She'd just decided to take Tom as he was, happy for every precious minute she spent with the man who made her life a heaven.

No matter how brief that happiness was? She wouldn't think about that. She lifted her shoulders and read on.

Surprise! I'm with Scott and I want you to know that's where I always plan to be, although I'm not sure where. Right now, we're dashing between his Wilmington office and piles of Randall Enterprise business, to Washington for FDA testing authority of the special camera.

It should interest you to hear that a certain gorgeous redhead has latched on to Talbert Sims, the scientist who's accumulated quite a sum from his inventions, including that "magic" camera, as Scott calls it. I think she's having a bit of luck. Good for both of them. She craves money and he craves praise, which she can certainly dish out.

Now for the big news. We're going to get married—if we ever have time to get the license and do the deed. We did have a few days at his fabulous Virginia home, where I met his mother. I'm not sure she'd choose me as a daughter-in-law, and held my breath when Scott told her we're getting married. I was bowled over when she immediately began to plan the wedding. A big social event, which I certainly don't want, at her Episcopal church in

New York, followed by a reception at her country club. She thumbed through her social calendar and settled on a suitable date, over a year from now. Maybe she thinks I'll disappear before then.

Oh, I must tell you about my brother, Jake. He's recovering rapidly. Other good news is that he's also getting married. To Clem's daughter, Clara. Clem is Jake's right-hand man. He was the one who called me about the fire and has been a strong shoulder during all the adjustments with Jake, as well as the new building, which is rapidly taking shape. Clara and Jake have been an off-and-on pair for ages, and I'm glad they're on for good. She's perfect for him.

Oh, here's Scott. Gotta run.

Kris switched off the computer, trying to imagine Jill in an old-fashioned wedding gown. Scott's mother might not know it, but she had a battle on her hands. Once Jill made up her mind to do something, she did it, and in her own way. Kris was glad she'd decided to marry Scott.

She wished...

No. She wouldn't spend her time wishing. She had accepted that Tom was not the marrying kind. She loved him, whatever he was. As long as they were together, nothing else really mattered.

She also loved working with Tom, and was especially pleased when she could help him solve a problem.

Like funds for the Bernstein campaign. "I could organize a fund-raiser," she said the next morning.

"I thought about that," he said. "But it wouldn't be worth the trouble."

"Why not? Sit down. I'll get it," she said, reaching for the coffeepot. "Why not?" she persisted as she refilled his cup.

"We need big money."

"And?"

"Big donors are looking for bargains, and Dave's not for sale."

"Oh." She considered that for a moment. "So we'll have to sell them something else."

He grinned. "Your bran muffins, perhaps?"

She ignored that. "How about 'A Flea Market Fling'? Strictly invitational because people like these things to be exclusive and, to make it even *more* exclusive, a stiff admittance fee, all proceeds going to the Bernstein campaign."

"And what will draw moneyed people to this very exclusive event?"

"Forgotten treasures. Just like poor people, they get to haunt the flea market looking for some priceless gem buried among the junk. I've seen them. Oh, we'd have the usual dancing, food and drinks, but more. Booths from the real flea market set up for a private search. We'd get a cut from all sales."

"I see. These booth merchants—they'd be interested in offering their wares and sharing the profits?"

"Sure. They always have to pay for space and they're glad to set up anywhere at any time. And I know just the ones to approach. There's this girl who sells antique jewelry. I don't know where she gets it, but some of the pieces are real. And there's a guy who does personalized T-shirts, and there are others. I could do sketches and donate whatever they brought in. What do you think?"

"I think I love morning coffee with you. I love the way you sit on the edge of your chair and the way your eyes sparkle when you get an idea—"

"You don't like it?"

"Well…"

"You figure it won't make money. You'd be surprised." She looked at him earnestly. "I was. At how many people liked having their images done…just in charcoal. And by a rank amateur. In one day I could sell—" She broke off, exasperated. She'd lost him. She snapped her fingers in front of him. "Come out of that trance, and tell me what you really think."

"I think we're lucky we have you."

"Then you *do* like it. I'll go down to the flea market today and talk to Rose and—"

"No. I don't plan to get bogged down with jewelry, T-shirts and such."

"But for a flea market we'd have to—"

"Hush. I'm thinking." He pushed his cup aside, tapped a finger on the table. "One priceless gem is worth a dozen maybes."

"Huh?"

"How about a raffle for a painting from the famous Kris Gilroy collection?"

"What?"

"You heard me."

"I couldn't believe my ears. I'm not famous."

"Haven't you heard about publicity and promotion?"

"I don't deal in lies. Anyway, I don't have a collection."

"Now *that's* a lie. You have stacks of paintings all over the place. What are they if not collectibles?"

"Junk."

"Let's take a look." Tom sprang to his feet and raced upstairs. When she caught up with him, he was already spreading her paintings around and giving them a critical appraisal.

She was actually embarrassed. "See? Like I told you, junk. Practice pieces." She wondered why she'd kept them.

Tom, completely absorbed in the paintings, said nothing. He would pick one up, hold it to the light, inspect it carefully. Put it down and select another.

"Tom," she said, growing increasingly uncomfortable. "These are all unfinished or no good."

"They look damn good to me."

She felt a glow of delight at his praise, and smiled. But… "You're prejudiced," she said. "And you're no more an art critic than I'm an artist."

"Who gets to say who's a critic?" He turned to look at her. "That's always been a puzzle to me. And more of a puzzle when some so-called critic lauds a tangle of colors signifying nothing, and appraises it at a zillion bucks."

She chuckled, having puzzled over certain pieces of modern art herself. As much a farce as the emperor's new clothes? "I don't know about critics, but I do know I'm not an artist. I've never had an art lesson in my life."

"Maybe you're another Ella Fitzgerald."

"Ella… Now how did she get into this?"

"No training. I've heard that her voice was so pure, her pitch so perfect, no trainer would touch it. The band could tune their instruments by her pitch. 'Give us an A, Ella.'"

She laughed. "Is that true?"

He shrugged. "I don't know. What I would like to know is whether you're willing to give your considerable talent and possibly some of your paintings to a worthy cause."

"I don't see how—"

"Just answer the question."

"If you mean Dave, I'd do whatever I could for him. Since I've been working on his campaign I've really come to admire—"

He held up his hand. "That's all I wanted to know."

"Well, know this. I'm me. I'm not a famous artist, and I will not be touted as something I'm not."

"Agreed, agreed."

"And even if I were, or had what you term considerable talent, what use could that be to Dave Bernstein?"

"I'm thinking. I'm thinking."

THE HOUSE WAS SPOTLESS. And quiet.

Too quiet. Claire hated it when the kids were asleep and she was alone with time on her hands and nothing to do.

She opened the fridge. Hesitated. Too early. She turned away, not touching the bottle of chilled wine.

She'd been careful to pace herself for more than two months now. Since the horrible night Jill Ferrell, a perfect stranger, had found her…well, not herself.

Jill hadn't acted like a stranger, Claire thought. As if to remind her, the violets Jill had brought glowed, a shimmering lavender in the afternoon sun.

All right, I owe you, Jill. You caught me in a jam, got me out and stayed here the whole weekend to help me. They'd covered a lot of territory that weekend, and would have become even closer if Jill hadn't immediately left to join Scott.

I'm glad about you and Scott. At least I think I am. You're inclined to be bossy, and some of what you more than hinted at our knock-down, drag-out discussions really ticked me off! My husband's not a philandering jerk and I'm not an alcoholic.

I'm not overworked, either. I'm organized and efficient, and my house is in perfect order. No reason I shouldn't relax with one glass of cold zin on such a hot afternoon.

To prove it she poured a glass, sipped.

Retreating to the living room, she turned on the television and idly switched to Tip Taylor's *Town Talk.*

"So I take it this interest in your work is a surprise to you," Tip Taylor was saying.

"Well, yes," the woman interviewee said, explaining that painting was just a hobby.

Hobby or not, she must be good, Claire thought. She was sure getting lots of attention. This was the same black woman who'd been featured on the morning show a couple of weeks ago. And there'd been a long article about her in the scene section of the *Chronicle* last Sunday. Owen Lafrey, a renowned local art dealer, had compared her ability to perceive and portray the inner person to that of portrait painters like Augustus John and, in a different sense, the American impressionist Mary Cassatt. That was after studying some of her sketches done in the flea market for almost nothing. Those now hanging in Lafrey's gallery cost considerably more.

"Good for you, Kris Gilroy!" Claire cried, raising her glass in a toast to the screen. "I'll bet the people who met you at the flea market are holding on to their sketches. I'll bet—" Claire broke off, staring openmouthed at the enlarged painting displayed on the screen.

That was Jill. Jill Ferrell. She knew it.

"Done in oil from one of her charcoal sketches," Tip Taylor explained, and turned to the artist. "How long have you been experimenting with oils and acrylics?"

But Claire had lost interest in the discussion. Jill wasn't the type. She wouldn't be caught dead in a flea market. Would she?

But it *was* her. In a beautiful portrait that captured the exact color of her hair and the golden flecks in her hazel eyes. *I'm sure she doesn't know about the oil. I'll call and tell her. No, I'll buy it and surprise Scott. It must be for sale. I'll go to the Lafrey gallery and I don't care what it costs.* Surely Dave wouldn't object to a present for her brother. She reached for the phone, but was forestalled by a cry from upstairs.

Joey. First things first. She put her empty glass down and rushed upstairs. She'd take the boys to the park before Debbie got home. Then dinner and Debbie's homework. *That bossy Jill was wrong about something else. I'm much too busy to be bored.*

IN TOM'S OFFICE, Kris and Tom also watched the Tip Taylor interview, which had been taped the day before.

"You were great, Kris. Fantastic," Tom said as the show ended and he switched off the television.

"What's fantastic is the story you've created about me."

"No, sweetheart, it's you. Don't you see how your big eyes and dancing dimples come across on the screen? Maybe I should've billed you as an actress."

"You keep your hands off me, Tom Harris. I'm beginning to feel like Eliza Doolittle in the hands of Henry Higgins. In just a couple of months you've turned me into—well, I don't know what."

"Come on. You were already an artist with plenty of paintings to prove it."

"I wasn't the famous portrait artist you claim."

"Not famous. But highly acclaimed. And not just by me." He spread his hands. "I told no lies, I take no credit. I just showed a few of your paintings to Owen who, I might remind you, is a prestigious gallery owner and well-known critic." Tom grinned. "Even I, your greatest fan, was astounded by his praise. Honest."

"And of course you had nothing to do with all the propaganda that's floating around."

"Well, I may have to plead guilty there. I thought you deserved the publicity. Owen thought so, too, since he had some of your works hanging in his gallery."

"And the value of said works will be increased by said publicity! Not entirely altruistic on Owen's part."

"That might be." Tom shrugged expansively. "But I only spoke of you to one person."

"I don't believe that."

"Honest. One person."

"Who was that?"

"Don Fields. He's an excellent media consultant. Always knows which newscaster or show host needs a good story to fill an empty slot."

She stared at him, feeling a little dizzy. "You hired…paid a media consultant. Just to promote me. You're crazy." Suddenly she was laughing. Or crying. Actually a bit of both as she flung her arms around him. "Oh, Tom! You really are a Henry Higgins. I'm not…not worth all this." She reached up to touch his cheek. "But I'm loving it. For the first time in my life, I feel as if…well, as if it's all right to do what I like. Just paint. Thank you."

"You're welcome. And you did say you'd do whatever you could for Dave Bernstein."

"Yes, I would. But…this is promoting *me*. Not Dave."

"What's wrong with killing two birds with one stone?"

"What? I don't see how on earth this could be of any help to Dave."

"Then you'll be surprised, my sweet."

CHAPTER TWENTY-THREE

DAVE BERNSTEIN MADE a point of leaving Sacramento early on Fridays. He looked forward to playtime with the children and the later quiet time with Claire. But this Friday was different. With all the wrangling about the budget, today's session had been unusually long, and he hadn't been able to leave until after five. Traffic was heavy, and to top that, Tom had insisted Dave stop by his office as soon as he reached the city. The kids would be asleep by the time he got home. Damn!

But he knew he'd make that stop. If Tom said "jump," he'd say "how high?" Things had changed since Dave was the big politician and Tom a volunteer college student, later Dave's right-hand man. Dave had hated to lose him, but he'd urged Tom to leave when he was solicited by Baker. Tom was a natural lobbyist, and not only because of his likable personality. He was a born negotiator, knowing who needed what and what he could trade with whom to get it. Yes, Tom had come a long way, and was doing him a favor. And Dave knew that the amount he was paying him was peanuts compared to the amount Tom charged other clients. *I'm damned lucky to have him.*

Still, he glared at Tom when he entered his office. "This better be good, buddy. It's Friday night, which I prefer to spend with my loved ones. And it's about time you found someone to…to…" Dave floundered, realizing Tom was not alone.

"Oh, I am with my loved one," Tom said. "Meet Kris Gilroy. Be nice to her, Dave. She's about to do you a huge favor."

"She already has." Dave smiled at the pretty woman with the dimples. "I've seen you stuffing envelopes at the campaign office, Ms. Gilroy. I'm extremely grateful."

"She does more than stuff envelopes," Tom said. "Sit down and listen to this."

When Dave left the office, he was beaming. He could hardly wait to tell Claire.

She met him at the door, and he lifted her in his arms. "I've got some great news," he said, joyfully swinging her around.

"That sounds nice," she said when she caught her breath. "Come in the kitchen and tell me all about it. You haven't eaten, have you?"

"Of course not." Never, if he could avoid it, would he miss his Friday-evening dinner with Claire. "Just let me kiss the kids good-night and wash up. I'll be right down."

It was just an at-home dinner in the kitchen, but with Claire's elegant touch. Dainty place mats, fine china and a fat candle burning in the center of the table. Dave kissed her on one ear, breathing in the appetizing aroma of the casserole she was dishing onto their plates. "I love you," he said. "You make me feel special."

"You are special." She added a couple of spiced peaches to each plate and set them on the table. "Pour the wine while I get the rolls, okay?"

"Now tell me the good news," she said when she was seated across from him.

"Well, I *think* it's good." He took a hot buttered roll from the basket and frowned. His enthusiasm had waned. "Can't count on how many will show up."

"At what?"

"At a black-tie dinner this woman is sponsoring for me. I don't even know her, Claire. I've only seen her once or twice when I dropped in at campaign headquarters. Tom says she's a big fan of mine, but I think she's mostly there for him. They seemed pretty chummy."

Claire chuckled. "Women will do anything for Tom. What's this one's name?"

"A Ms. Gilbert. No, Gilroy, I think."

Claire dropped her fork. "Kris Gilroy? The artist?"

"You know her?"

"You would, too, if you watched television. She's been on every show in town this past month. Oh, Dave, that's wonderful! She'll draw a crowd."

"At a thousand dollars a plate? I doubt it."

"You forget, Dave Bernstein. You're a celebrity yourself. And now there's the added drawing card of this artist. People will come just to see her in person. They showed some of her work on television, and—"

"Oh, that's another thing. She'll be doing charcoal sketches during the cocktail hour. For those who want them. One hundred dollars each, all proceeds to the campaign."

"Really?" Claire's eyes grew wide. "They'd better expand the cocktail hour. People will be standing in line."

"Maybe," Dave said uncertainly. "How did the interview with Debbie's teacher go?"

"Very well. She's says Debbie's work is always good and on time, and she's a great help with the other students." Claire gave him a detailed account, and they moved on to other topics.

AS THE DAYS PASSED, Claire grew even more enthusiastic about the dinner. More than three hundred people had sent their checks and the cocktail hour had been expanded. Claire knew she'd willingly stand in line to be sketched. A pity it would be black tie and she couldn't bring the kids. That woman really did seem to bring out the inner person in her portraits. At least she did in Jill's, which Claire had seen when she went to La-frey's to purchase it. The portrait wasn't for sale, but it hung in the gallery. It revealed Jill's personality, not just her beautiful face, catching that eager I'll-fix-it sparkle in the gold-flecked eyes.

I'd like to have each of the children done by Kris Gilroy. To show them just as they are now—Brandon's stubborn streak, Debbie's ladylike way of taking charge. And not in charcoal. In oil. Kris Gilroy had a way with colors; absolutely spectacular in that beach painting, also hanging in the gallery. Claire wondered if that one was for sale. She'd like to buy it.

But first the kids.

My goodness, what am I thinking? The price of Gilroy's pieces must be skyrocketing every minute now. And where was she getting this urge to spend, spend, spend?

She knew. She was getting it from Jill Ferrell.

Jill Randall now. Claire smiled. She'd had two phone calls and an e-mail from Jill, and hadn't been the least bit surprised when they called to say they were getting married. Just a quick civil ceremony at Wilmington's city hall before rushing back to California. A honeymoon business trip was the way Jill put it.

No, Claire wasn't surprised. She'd seen how Jill had looked whenever Scott was mentioned, and Jill wasn't one to waste time.

What did surprise her was the letter she'd received from Jill.

Dear Claire,

Sorry to be so slow getting this to you, but snail mail seems to be the only means of private communication in this electronic age. Remember, we're two sisters who started out with secrets between us. Let's keep it that way. This is for your eyes alone.

I'm writing to thank you for giving me the guts to marry Scott. If he knew, Scott would thank you, too. It's because of you that he's not married to a scared, suspicious, jealous woman, which I certainly was until I came to blows with you. It amazes me now that I could ever have harbored ugly doubts about my honest, kind, thoughtful, gentle, loving Scott, who's making me the happiest woman in the entire world.

Sorry we sneaked off to City Hall, but we didn't have time for the extravaganza your mother was planning to host. I was in a hurry. I want children and my clock's ticking away.

Anyway, I was so happy that it felt as if City Hall was a beautiful cathedral with most of the people I love around me. And Scott seemed pleased to have Sarah and Murray as our only attendants. He tells me they've served your family for years, and they certainly treat him like their son. The four of us celebrated at the Four Seasons before Scott and I rushed back to his office. I haven't told Scott yet, but I plan to get pregnant as soon as I can. So we're doing lots of loving between our business meetings. And, yes, I did say *our* meetings. I'm right there to see that my benevolent husband doesn't give everything away and yet reserves enough to continue his good works. It's a wonderful feeling to be partner as well as lover with my own darling husband!

I may be more involved in Randall Enterprises these days, but I still have a soft spot for Chandler—George Stewart is now CEO, although I'm keeping an eye on things. And Scott was right about KLICK *and* Talbert Sims (who's getting married to Candy Atkins—no surprise.) The camera software is coming along well, and KLICK is showing an upsurge in profits as a result.

All I can say is that I'm happy in my work life and in my home life, because Scott and I are partners in both.

Isn't it ironic that I'm now practicing what I preached to you? Not that you listened. But I'm doing it, and I plan to keep on doing it forever. We'll bring along a nanny when the children come, maybe even a tutor when they reach school age. We'll make Virginia our peaceful home base, but we won't always be there. There's too much going on in this crazy world that needs fixing, and my family will be out there helping to fix it.

I'm still preaching as you can see. So I'm reminding you that you could be as happy as I am if you weren't so compliant and a little stupid. (I mean that in the nicest possible way, of course!) It would be easy. All you have to do is convince St. David that it's all right to spend his wife's money. Marriage is a partnership. Make it a joyful one. Share *everything*.

Gotta go. I want to mail this off and be ready when Scott gets back from the hotel gym. You should see the sexy nightgown I bought.

Kiss the kids for me. See you soon. Well, not that soon. Scott says he didn't want a grand wedding, but he doesn't plan to skimp on a honeymoon. So we'll miss the grand fund-raising dinner. But we're sending a check and plan to be there later to help with Dave's campaign.

Love you, Jill

Claire refolded the letter, feeling an overwhelming rush of envy. She wished... Oh, she would *not* let Jill make her feel depressed!

Our situations are different. Men are men, and despite the advances of feminism, it still made a difference when the woman had the money and the man didn't.

She started to put the letter away. But she wasn't in the habit of hiding things from Dave, and with the reference to secrets and the snide remark about St. David... She burned the letter.

She was happy, darn it, and she was a partner to Dave, no matter what Jill thought. They were doing just fine. She must tell Jill about seeing her portrait.

Meanwhile, she'd better decide what she was going to wear

for her own little sketch. She smiled. As if more than her face would be showing!

Still, this was a big event for Dave, and she did want to look her best. It was with this thought in mind that she went through her closet.

Claire's wardrobe had always been full of the latest and smartest fashions money could buy. When she got married, she'd brought along a bounty that had served her well.

Until now, she decided as she tried on each garment suitable for a black-tie dinner. Too tight, too shabby or too out of date. Eight years and three pregnancies had taken their toll.

Anyway, shouldn't she have something fresh and new for such a special event? For the first time since her wedding, she'd have to do some serious shopping for herself. Perhaps she could find something on sale.

At a little shop in the mall, she found the perfect dress. A simple, sleeveless black silk, cut on the bias so the skirt flared gracefully at the knee. The low-cut back was a bit provocative, but not too much so. Anyway, it was a perfect fit and looked just right on her. But...

"Even the sale price is scandalous," she said to the clerk.

"Not for a Suzanne," the clerk replied.

No wonder, Claire thought. She hadn't looked at the label, but Suzanne was her favorite designer. Anyway, one thing was for sure: David never looked at a label and wouldn't know one from another if he did. She plunked down the eight hundred dollars from her own private account without a second thought.

Of course, the dress demanded black suede pumps, but they only cost four hundred dollars.

Later, she was to think that if it hadn't been for that purse...

But not now. Now she only felt happy, strangely free and very frivolous.

Still, if she hadn't seen that purse...

Claire didn't care about fine jewelry. Hers was securely locked in a bank vault, out of sight and out of mind. She loved the tiny emerald earrings Dave had given her on their wedding night. They'd be perfect, the only jewelry needed for the black dress.

If she hadn't seen that purse… A tiny oblong box, only two by six inches, safely enclosed but clearly visible in its glass case. The multitude of tiny emeralds studding the golden box sparkled and beckoned to her.

She knew it was a Judith Lieber, and she never knew which inspired her more—the purse itself or its creator. She'd always been touched by the story of Judith Lieber, a Jewish girl who, at sixteen, had been caught in the trauma and desolation of the Holocaust when the Nazis invaded her native Hungary. Many friends and co-workers were herded off to concentration camps. Only through the actions of kind and very brave friends were Judith and her family able to narrowly escape the Nazi death camps.

After the war, Judith Lieber had resumed her work with handbags and was now famous for the evening bags she designed, often in the shape of an animal and always encrusted with jewels. "Slung over your shoulder to leave your hands free for cocktails," Judith was prone to say, "and tiny because all you need is a lipstick and a hundred-dollar bill." Now in her seventies, she had an almost iconic stature among designers.

Claire purchased the bag, writing the five-thousand-dollar check with a flourish.

"A tribute to you," she silently whispered to the woman who, after living through unbelievable horror, could resume normal life with a sense of humor and create such beauty.

Like this purse. Slung over her shoulder by its slender gold chain, the emeralds would enhance the sparkle of her matching earrings. The right and final touch.

CHAPTER TWENTY-FOUR

THE BOOTH IN THE center of the Ritz Carlton's plush ballroom was much fancier than Kris's little stand at the flea market. She wore a serviceable cotton smock over the gold-threaded jumpsuit that had replaced her frayed jeans. Instead of the flea market crowd with their bundles and shopping bags, she was surrounded by a bejeweled throng in fancy evening attire.

She sat at her easel thinking that only the sketching was the same. And just as much fun.

The TV camera focused on her and the reporter continued his interview. "You seem to enjoy your work."

"Yes," Kris said, her eyes on the woman seated before her.

"You're never bored?"

"Never. It's always a challenge. No two people on earth are exactly alike."

"What about identical twins?"

"Personality makes a difference."

"That's right. It's said you bring out the inner person in your portraits. How do you manage to do that?"

Kris shrugged, wishing the reporter would go away. She didn't know how she managed. She just talked, listened and studied the face before her while her fingers flew, delving beneath the physical to automatically portray what her mind read—the kind heart behind the forbidding set of the mouth, or the glint of calculation in the bewitching smile. She couldn't explain.

She was glad when the reporter moved away. How could

she talk like an artist? She was just beginning to feel like one. She smiled at the young woman who expressed pleasure over her portrait and at the distinguished older man who took her place. The chair in front of Kris hadn't been vacant since she began sketching.

"You're crazy," she'd told Tom. "Nobody will pay a hundred dollars for a charcoal sketch by me!"

"You'll be surprised," he said.

She *was* surprised. At Tom. He could come up with the most incredible idea, and before you could grasp it, the inevitable was happening. Like at Tech High. The new gym was going up with parking space above it. The media acclaimed the innovative venture that so skillfully combined academia, government and commerce. Everybody was taking credit—the contractor, the City Council, the School District, even some of the enthusiastic participating students. But it was Tom who'd orchestrated the whole thing. For neither pay nor credit, and he didn't seem worried about either.

For a moment, she was overwhelmed by a wave of pure love for him.

It was hard to blot out Tom and concentrate on the man she was sketching. As soon as he stood, the hostess in charge of scheduling drew her next sitter forward.

"Kris, I'd like you to meet Claire Bernstein, Dave's wife. She's anxious to be sketched. We shouldn't take her check, should we?"

"No indeed. It would be an honor to sketch you, Mrs. Bernstein."

"Claire, please. I'm the one being honored. And how can I ever thank you for what you're doing for Dave?"

"Thank Tom Harris. He put it together."

"He couldn't have without you and—" A wave of her hand encompassed the little booth "—the gift of your talent. You're a wonderful artist."

Kris laughed and whispered, "I'll let you in on a secret. I'm

Tom's Pygmalion. Before he took me over, I was an ex-school-teacher with a desire to paint. Certainly no artist."

"But you are. I've seen your work. And I've heard the critics. I've watched you on television."

"What you saw was Tom Harris at work. He has a magic way of putting people and things together." She touched Claire's chin and tilted her head. "That's it. Hold still and look directly at me. Do you know how beautiful you are?" She'd love to do her in color, catch the violet in those deep-blue eyes, the unmistakable quality of pure goodness. "Would you... That is, would you have the time to sit for me? I'd love to do you in oil." She'd give the portrait to Dave. He'd be delighted to have it.

"Oh, I..." Claire almost turned her head in surprise. It'd been a long time since anyone had called her beautiful. Anyway, she didn't care about herself. If she could have the children done in oil, she'd pay from her own bank account, the way she had for the purse and all. Dave would love portraits of the children, and if he didn't know how much they cost... "I'd be happy to sit for you," she said. "Where? And when?"

"It'd have to be in the den at my condo," Kris said. "I don't have an actual studio." She smiled. "That's another of Tom's plans, but I'm not sure we'll carry through with it. All this build-up was for Dave."

"For Dave? The focus on you was for Dave?"

"A drawing card to raise campaign funds. Killing two birds with one stone was the way Tom put it. We may have enough now for a few TV spots for Dave."

"I see," Claire said. All this trouble for funds that wouldn't have made a dent in her bank account. But Dave had to be his own man, and she'd promised. Anyway, she would never have met this wonderful artist and... Well, she might arrange to have the children done. "I wouldn't call it killing. I think Tom has sent two birds soaring high," she said.

Claire had felt as if he'd sent her soaring, too. As she left the booth, she felt as light as a feather on a cloud of pure happiness. She loved being where things were happening, loved being part of the crowd that had come to support her Dave, loved feeling attractive and a part of it all.

"Oh, there you are!" Dave called to her. She looked over and saw him only a few yards from her, standing beside a woman with a soft cloud of gray hair. "Sweetheart," he said, "I'd like you to meet Mrs. Davenport. She's one of my greatest supporters."

An extremely wealthy one, Claire thought, judging by the fashionable crepe evening gown, diamond earrings and heavy gold chains around her neck. She took the woman's hand in a warm grasp. "I'm delighted, Mrs. Davenport. It's always a pleasure to meet someone who appreciates what Dave is doing."

They were soon joined by others who were eager to speak with the guest of honor. Claire stood among them, silently listening. Exhilarated by their wholehearted admiration of Dave, his statesmanship, accomplishments and good prospects in the coming election, she soared high on her happy cloud.

She was knocked off the cloud and almost off her feet when a young woman seized the purse hanging from her shoulder.

"This is a Judith Lieber! Oh, my God!" the woman exclaimed. "Isn't it absolutely gorgeous?" she asked, displaying it to all, but hardly listening as the others enthusiastically agreed. "I *love* it. I want one so badly. There was one in the shape of a bear studded with diamonds.... But, God! My husband would kill me if I paid five thousand dollars for a purse. You're a lucky woman, Mrs. Bernstein."

Claire just stood there, her tongue stuck to the roof of her mouth. She couldn't look at David. They weren't touching, but she felt his start of surprise. His embarrassment. His...anger?

Never in all their years of marriage had Dave been angry with her or expressed any disapproval.

Dear Lord, what had she done?

People were now moving toward the dining room. She felt Dave's hand on her arm and moved with them. He pulled out her chair and she sank into it, grateful that they weren't on the platform.

David hated platform seating. He liked being with the crowd, one of the people, a participant in all the talk and laughter.

She stole a look at him, and reeled from the shock. It was as if he'd shrunk into himself. Oh, there was a smile or nod in response to some comment, but he was no longer a lively participant.

He hadn't uttered one word since that woman had grabbed her bag and opened her big fat mouth! If only she hadn't mentioned labels and waved a price tag in front of David—and everybody else. Including that Davenport woman, who probably put a bundle into Dave's campaign while his wife plumped down five thousand dollars for a dinky little bag.

She wanted to smash it against the wall.

She wanted her confident, witty, wisecracking husband back.

She wanted to...to cry. She managed to whisper, "Ladies' room," and hurried away.

IN THE LADIES' ROOM, Kris had washed her hands and discarded the smock. She ran a comb through her hair and was applying a touch of lipstick when she heard the door open. She turned to see Claire Bernstein looking as if she didn't know where she was or why she was here.

"Hi," Kris said. Feeling an urge to calm her, she added, "Do you need something? Can I help you?"

"No, nothing, thank you. I..." Claire's words came in a rush. "I was hoping to find you. You're doing so much for David. We're so grateful. I want you to have this."

Before she could speak, Kris found herself alone, holding an emerald-studded gold purse. It wasn't empty, and she opened it to find a handkerchief, a lipstick and a hundred-dollar bill.

She didn't mean to give this away, Kris thought and hurried after her. The hall was empty, except for Tom who came toward her. "Did you see Mrs. Bernstein?" she asked.

"No. I was looking for you. Come on," he said. "Dinner's being served."

"Tom, something's wrong with Mrs. Bernstein."

"Claire?"

Kris nodded. "She gave me this and just left. She seemed very upset."

"I'll find her. You go on in."

"Hurry. She may be leaving. And return this to her."

Tom tucked the little purse in his pocket and strode toward the lobby, hoping Claire would be delayed there, if she was indeed leaving. Before Dave's speech? What could have happened? A few minutes ago, she was in great spirits. Surely it wasn't one of the children, he thought, feeling his heartbeat quicken.

He found her outside with the doorman who was signaling a cab. She seemed relieved to see him. "Oh, Tom, thank goodness. Could you lend me a ten? I forgot I'll need cab fare."

"I'll come with you. What's wrong?"

"Headache," she floundered, putting a hand to her brow. "I'd…better go home."

"Nonsense. We'll fix it." He put a firm arm around her and dismissed the cab. Claire wasn't sick. She was agitated and he wanted to know why. "Dave know you were planning to leave?"

"Oh, God, no!" she said in alarm. "He'll be wondering. Would you tell him that—"

"I'll take care of it," he said, leading her back into the hotel. "But you're not leaving. A couple of aspirins and some food and you'll be fine." When she balked at returning to the banquet hall, he drew her into the coffee shop and scribbled a note to Dave. *Claire's with me, getting away from the noise. She's fine, just a slight headache.* He didn't want Dave upset. Tonight was important, and he sure didn't want it spoiled.

But whatever was wrong with Claire was bigger than a headache.

As he scribbled, he scanned possibilities. Kids okay? Marriage trouble? Another woman?

He couldn't fathom that. Dave was as straight as an arrow.

Still, the straighter they are, the harder they fall. And nobody knew better than Tom how tenacious some women can be.

"Be right back," he told Claire and went out to dispatch the note. He was beginning to feel a smoldering anger. Claire was the kindest person he knew. If someone had said something to hurt her…

Well, he'd find out. He and Claire were close, going way back to when they both worked for Dave. He hadn't seen much of her since the children, but the kind of friends they'd become… She'd tell him what was wrong.

When he returned, the waiter was placing a glass of wine in front of Claire, and Tom remembered that he was hungry. "Did you order?" he asked.

Claire touched her glass. "Just this. I'm not hungry."

"I am." He ordered a pastrami sandwich and coffee, then turned to her. "What's the matter?"

"Nothing. I—I…just needed to get away from the turmoil."

He didn't believe that but he went along with it. "Pretty good turmoil for Dave," he said, and, for a moment, launched into money, TV coverage and election possibilities. The waiter brought his order and another glass of wine for Claire. Claire's voice was beginning to slur and he wondered how much she'd indulged during the cocktail hour. Surprising. She'd never been much of a drinker. She was trying to shut out whatever was agitating her, he supposed, and began to probe. "Something's wrong, Claire. What is it?"

She shook her head.

"Come on. You can tell your old buddy. Who are you upset with?"

"Nobody. I...I... Oh, God, I did it."

Claire? Who couldn't hurt anybody? His voice gentled. "What did you do?"

"I...I...bought something."

His mind flew to the purse Kris had thrust at him. He took it from his pocket. "This?"

She stared at the purse. "It cost five thousand dollars."

Tom swallowed. A bundle. Very unlike Claire. But he was relieved. This was only a domestic altercation that—

"I hate it," she cried, covering her eyes. "Throw it away!"

Dave must have blown his top, Tom thought. But that was easily fixed. "Don't be silly," he said. "Return it. Get the money back. That way—"

"It's not the money! It's... It's..." Her eyes were wide open now and seemed to stare through him. "Oh, it *is* the money! I promised..."

She seemed to have lost control. She was beginning to cry.

Tom glanced around the coffee shop. There was only one couple some distance away and totally absorbed in themselves, thank goodness. He bent toward Claire. "You're overreacting, honey. Don't you know Dave would forgive you anything?"

She wasn't listening. "I'm not a sneaky person, Tom. What came over me? How could I sneak and lie and hurt David? I only wanted to be with him and love him, so I promised not to touch the money."

He tried to stop the flow, but couldn't. He could only sit and listen, too astounded to believe what he heard as the past ten years unfolded from her lips.

It finally got through to him that she was a Randall with a hell of a lot of money. She dwelt on Dave and the promise she'd made and broken, and how that broken promise had hurt Dave this very night. But all Tom could see was Claire as Dave's secretary, accountant and gopher, in his little office on Market Street ten years ago. She was a dynamo and always a delight.

Even after Debbie's birth, she often worked with the baby on her shoulder. Then when Dave was able to hire a staff…

Hell! The dumb son of a bitch was *always* able to hire a staff! All that money. A well-kept secret.

Tom could hardly restrain himself. Once he got hold of Dave and shook him until his teeth rattled, he was going to tell him a thing or two.

Meanwhile, Claire… Somehow he managed to calm her down. "Don't you worry about Dave," he told her. "I'll bet he's glad you finally decided to spend something on yourself." *I mean to make damn sure of that,* he told himself as he tucked her into a cab and sent her home. When he got hold of Dave…

Dave was just as anxious to get hold of Tom. Despite Tom's note, he was worried about Claire. She didn't have headaches. That woman had said the purse cost…

He shook his head. He'd never hidden his financial standing, and Claire didn't do that kind of spending.

But then she shows up sporting a five-thousand-dollar matchbox purse right in front of Mamie Davenport who just plunked down a bundle to boost my campaign funds. Mamie must think I'm a master con artist!

That purse. It wasn't like Claire. A present from her mother? A copy?

No. He recalled the guilty look on Claire's face. The way she'd left the table.

What had come over Claire? Was it Scott?

Scott's one of my best friends, but having him so close has been bugging me.

It could get out that Claire was a wealthy Randall. That bothered Dave; he supported his family and wanted people to know it.

But now… Either his supporters—and detractors—were going to think he was a con artist or a gigolo living off his wife.

And he was concerned about Claire. This erratic behavior wasn't typical.

As soon as he could get clear of the disbanding crowd, he rushed over to Tom. "Where's Claire? What's wrong with her?"

"She's gone home," Tom said. He moved closer to quietly hiss, "And what's wrong with her is *you,* you pompous self-centered son of a bitch."

Dave's head jerked. "Me? What did I—"

"Oh, here you are, Dave!" Mamie Davenport pressed forward to give him a hug. "Great speech. You've got this crowd in the palm of your hand."

He returned her hug, but was too stunned to speak. Everything was going wrong tonight. Why was Tom so riled up?

He tried to regain his composure as others joined them. Like Tom, he smiled and responded heartily to congratulations on his speech, wishes for a successful campaign and admiring comments on the charming artist who'd hosted this affair. But, as soon as they were alone, he turned to Tom. "I want to know what you're talking about."

"And I intend to tell you! Hold on." Tom paused to ask Kris to help Pam take care of the bill, adding, "Pick me up at the office. Dave and I are going for a conference."

"Sounds like we're going for a boxing match," Dave muttered.

"You got it."

Dave waited, but Tom said no more.

"All right, spill it," Dave prompted as they drove from the hotel. "What's bothering you?"

"Quite a lot, pal! I'm trying to run a campaign on peanuts for a pompous fool who's got his zillionaire wife hiding in the closet!"

Dave sighed. "So she told you?"

"It took her ten years but she finally broke down and confessed her guilt. Crying like crazy 'cause you'd never forgive her for breaking her promise."

"Stop right there! I never said one word. I—"

"You didn't have to. She reads you like a book. And when she shows up with a little trinket she's splurged on—"

"All right. I was…well, surprised. Listen. Let me explain." Dave was still trying to explain when they reached Tom's office. He talked about his frustration at being confronted by the wealth of the only woman he could ever love. "You don't understand. I didn't have a dime and I sure didn't want to be pegged a fortune-hunter. It was Claire who… Well, we made an agreement that we'd live on what I earned."

"I see. An arrangement satisfactory to a chauvinist pig."

"I may be a chauvinist, but I'm no freeloader. I've never touched a cent of Claire's money. I've kept to our agreement and—"

"Stupid agreement." Tom unlocked the door and switched on the light.

"Not so stupid," David said as he followed Tom in. "Actually we've done fine. The folks turned the house over to us, I started my practice and—".

"*You've* done fine. How about Claire? No, wait a minute. Sit down and let's talk about you." Tom leaned against his desk and pointed a finger at Dave. "You might've managed okay in your little law office, but then you decided to go into politics. Politics is an expensive career, pal. And the higher you go, the harder it gets. Take that crummy apartment you share when you're in Sacramento."

"That's just temporary. I'm home most of—"

"It can get worse. Do you know that some House members in DC are sleeping in their offices, bathing at the gym and eating in cafeterias? It takes a hell of a lot to maintain two homes on one salary. And that's not taking into account the kind of money you need to get there."

Dave sighed. "Yeah. I guess it goes with the territory."

"You don't have to have those problems, Dave. With Claire's money—"

"No. I don't think it's right to use my wife's money on me."

"You get to decide where she should spend it?"

"No! I only object to her shouldering my responsibilities.

She contributes to many charities and good causes. She has one that—"

"Speaking of good causes…what about you?"

"Huh?"

"Why do you think I work for you for practically nothing?"

Dave stirred in his chair, embarrassed. "Well, we go back a long way and—"

"The hell with that! The fact is, you're a statesman, committed to the public good. And there are damn few of you left! You're the best cause your wife could promote."

Dave stared at him. A minute ago, Tom was giving him hell. Now…he felt a little daunted by this kind of praise. Still… "I've never thought of myself as a cause," he said. "And, well, I never liked the idea of being dependent on—"

"Shut up and listen! Take a look at your wife. Smart, good looking and clearly in your corner. On stage, she'd double your votes and her money would finance your career in style. What's wrong with being partners with your own wife?"

"Guess I never thought of it that way. I just didn't like taking her money to—"

"You took everything else, didn't you?"

"What…what do you mean?"

"She's been working like a dog ever since she married you, first in your office and then at your home with your kids, alone most of the time. Missing you and missing out on lots of good things you should be sharing. Shut up and let me finish! Dammit, Dave, you've even made her feel ashamed that she's rich. Sitting there crying like a baby and lapping up four glasses of wine because she might've dropped a hint of her awful secret. I had to send her home in a cab before she fell flat on her face."

That hurt. Had he done that to Claire? He knew she sometimes went a little heavy on the wine. But he'd never seen her drunk. Tom's "alone most of the time" rang in his ears. A lump formed in his throat, and he tried to swallow, thinking… She never seemed unhappy or stifled. Always happy and upbeat, eager to talk about him and what he was doing.

But never about herself or what she did or wanted.

God! Had he been that selfish? Dave reeled, trying to recover from the blistering lecture. Had he been a stupid, self-centered fool? "I love Claire. I never wanted to hurt her. I'd do anything to—"

"Okay, let me tell you what to do. Go home and tell Claire that the sight of that purse made you come to your senses. You're glad she's spending her money on herself and that sharing it might be a good idea. You're missing out, too, being away from her and the kids so much of the time. You need her, and the money would make it easier for both of you—or something. I don't care how you do it. Just lay it on thick and make her come out of that closet, and live the life you should both have."

"I'll try. I want her happy. I—"

"Keep it down. That's Kris," Tom said as light footsteps sounded in the hall. "Just one more thing. We never had this conversation. I never said a damn word to you and this new perspective is entirely yours."

CHAPTER TWENTY-FIVE

"DING DONG!" Tom shouted, and kissed the check. He *had* rung a bell.

Pam, his faithful secretary, grinned. "Just came in the morning's mail. I figured you'd like it."

"Like it?" He waved the check at her. "This is going to put the Bernstein campaign in TV heaven!" Going to do more than that, he thought. It was signed by Claire Bernstein, but he had a feeling the account would soon bear a Randall/Bernstein caption. His lecture must have done some good.

He was sure of this when he got a call from Kris. "I'll be in later, Tom. I'm going out to talk with Mrs. Bernstein."

"Oh?"

"Guess what! She wants me to do her three children in oil. Individually or as a group. Probably both, she said. And she asked if I'd do them at the house if she paid me extra. I told her of course I'd do them at the house and I wouldn't charge her anything at all, and she said—"

"Wait a minute. Let's get this straight about not charging anything. I was just talking to Lafrey about that. He's had several calls from people who want to commission you to do their portraits. He says your price should be pretty steep. Commensurate with the value of your work."

"Value of my... Good Lord! I've barely started practicing with oil!"

"No, my sweet. You're not practicing with anything. You are an extremely talented, well-renowned art—"

"I'm a multimedia scam and you know it. You did the scamming!"

"Not me. I only…" No use. He couldn't stop laughing.

"Anyway, I'm not sure I want to paint just anybody."

"Like you did at the flea market?"

She laughed, too. "All right. I needed the money then. Not now. I'm in business, remember? With you."

"Look, Kris, I don't like you giving away your talent."

"This is Dave's wife, Tom. You know how hard up he is."

"Yeah. I sure do."

She didn't seem to notice the sarcasm. "Well, you shouldn't mind my doing him a favor. Besides, I *want* to do it. I really want to do her. She's absolutely beautiful, and not just on the outside. D'you know what I mean? She wants me to paint the children and I'll start with them. Then I'll ask her—"

"Shut up a minute, will you? Do what you like, but stop here first. It's not out of your way, and there's something I want you to take a look at."

When she stopped by an hour later, she took one look at the gleaming silver convertible and squealed. "Tom! It's beautiful. I love it." She walked around the car, opened it, peered inside, ran a hand over the smooth cushions. Smiled. Sighed. "But I love your Jag, too. What'll you do with it?"

"I'll keep it. This one's yours."

"*What!* You don't mean…" Her eyes went wide. "Oh, Tom, you're so sweet and I love you dearly. But you know I can't let you buy this for me. It's too—"

"For me, then. The rattletrap doesn't go with the Harris Company image." It took some time to persuade her, but she finally drove off in the new convertible. He sighed with relief, and sent her rental back to the agency.

Still exuberant about the check for the Bernstein campaign, he called Calvin who did his TV spots.

Calvin was as enthusiastic as he was. "Great! We'd better get started right away. Be right over."

"No. Another appointment. Make it in the morning." It was actually Kris who had the other appointment, of course. He wanted her there when they started work. He liked her quips and ideas.

Nothing urgent at the moment. Might as well get in a round of golf.

SAN FRANCISCO'S STEEP HILLS were a bit much for him, Allen Gilroy thought as he drove up the winding road. He could've had Christina meet him at the hotel, but he wanted to surprise her.

Now that wasn't quite true, he admitted. He wanted to take her by surprise. He wanted to see for himself that she was happy. And safe.

She sounded as if she was on top of the world, but you couldn't judge by that. Even when she was burdened with the care of Freda, Christina's voice had held that happy ring. Her naturally cheerful attitude must have boosted poor Freda's spirits. He was pleased that Freda had left what little she had to Christina.

Smart of Christina to use that pittance to buy a place. She said rents here were so high. Still… His hand tightened on the wheel. He didn't understand why she'd stayed. He'd expected her to come home where she belonged, near him and… He sloughed off the thought of Ed Simmons. He wasn't a matchmaker. But Ed was like a son to him, and he and Christina had always been close. And that boy was going places. He was elected a county supervisor two years ago, and was about to make a bid for the U.S. House of Representatives. *Don't think he'll make it, but…* Well, nothing wrong with trying.

A sudden turn in the road afforded a beautiful glimpse of the ocean. He was reminded that Christina had said something about an oil painting she'd done, which seemed to be generating a bit of success in that field. She was always drawing or dabbling with paints. He smiled, remembering the sketch she'd done of Huckleberry Finn with a corncob pipe dangling from his mouth. She'd added it to a report she'd turned in on that book. Was she in ninth grade then? He only remembered how proud he was of his baby.

Well, she was still his baby girl, and San Francisco was a long way from Piney Woods, Georgia. In more ways than one. He wanted to know how she was faring in the big city among all those artsy folk with their artsy ways. He needed more details than her address and cell phone number.

He wasn't prying. But his attendance at an ecumenical conference in the same big city afforded him an excellent opportunity to visit his girl.

Ah! *Here we are…1027 Oceanside.* He pulled to the curb and parked, already feeling relieved and pleasantly surprised. Who would've thought she could buy in this kind of neighborhood with the stipend Freda left her!

Tom had just slung the golf bag over his shoulder and started out when the doorbell sounded.

Who the hell could this be? he wondered as he opened the door.

He knew as soon as he saw the smartly dressed black man in the well-cut business suit. Another smart-ass professor after Kris? It looked like he had a few years on Gonzales and he reeked of that officious dignity Gonzales was still trying to acquire. He greeted the man with a curt, "Yes?"

"I was looking for… This is 1027 Oceanside?"

"Right."

"Miss Gilroy's residence?"

Tom nodded.

"Is she in?"

"She's not in. And not available."

"Pardon?" The sharp question and shocked look gave Tom a glow of satisfaction. Out of your clutches, buddy!

"She is no longer on the register," he said.

"Register?"

"School District. I'm surprised they didn't inform you." Gilroy exhaled. "I am not employed by the school district!

I am—" He broke off. *Who I am isn't any concern of this impudent SOB,* he thought, surprising himself. That was a vulgar expletive he never used. This brash so-and-so was unnerving him. He tried to regain his composure and spoke calmly. "I'm from Piney Woods and would like to—"

"Piney Woods?" The young man's eyes widened. "Oh, I beg your pardon. I assumed... Oh, never mind." He swung the door wider and gave him a warm smile. "Come in, come in. I know Kris will want to see you. She had a business appointment, but should be back shortly."

Gilroy stepped in, not liking the look of this. *Who's the loafer wearing a golf bag? She's working and he's—*

"Sit down and make yourself comfortable." The loafer set the golf bag aside. "You shouldn't have a long wait, and I'm sure Kris will be glad to see you," he said again.

"I certainly want to see her."

"Let me get you... What would you like? Coffee? Something cold or—"

"Nothing, thank you." *Whoever he is, he's devilish at home in her place.*

As if sensing his antagonism, the man made an apologetic gesture. "Look, I know I was...well, rather rude out there. I thought you were someone else. Sorry."

"You're...the keeper of the gate?"

"Kind of, I guess. I like to watch out for Kris. She's so...vulnerable. Trusts anybody."

Even you, apparently. Gilroy nodded. "And you feel the need to protect her?"

"In a way I do. She's very attractive, you know, besides being so warm and open. People are drawn to her, and she's...well, so innocent and trusting and not quite wise to the big city." Tom grinned. "I try to tell her she can't always leave it to God, gotta look after herself sometimes. But do you think she—"

"Papa!" Kris stared openmouthed at her father, her mind whirling in several directions at once. Papa, right here in her living room, so engrossed with Tom that neither of them had heard her come in. That was good, wasn't it? She knew he'd like Tom if he ever got to know him. She hadn't thought he ever would because how could she tell him they were living together? But now…

Overwhelming joy rippled through her. Her strong, steady, always-supportive and loving papa was here, and she had so many wonderful things to tell him. She flew into his arms, inhaling the familiar fragrance of tobacco that filled the pipe Mom couldn't stop him from smoking. "Oh, Papa, I'm so glad you're here! Why didn't you tell me you were coming? And—" she looked around. "You didn't bring Mom? How is she? Oh, you should've told me. I could have picked you up at the airport."

"That's my girl," he said, still holding her so close she could hardly breathe as he answered her questions. "I didn't tell you because I wanted to surprise you, and I didn't bring your mom because she had another commitment, and I'm only going to be here a couple of days anyway."

"Oh, no!" She broke away and stared up at him. "Well, never mind. We'll enjoy the two days. Where's your luggage?" He could have their bedroom and they could— Her face grew hot.

"Oh, I'm at the Embassy for an ecumenical conference. It's more convenient to stay there."

"Oh." That problem was solved. But the awkwardness of the situation had reared its ugly head. She braced herself to face it. "I'm just glad you're here and you've met Tom."

"No, we didn't quite get around to that," was her father's stiff reply.

She whirled to face Tom. He was standing well apart, giving Dr. Gilroy an amazed examination. "Your father? I wondered when he said he was from Piney Woods. But at first I thought… Well, I could tell he was older than Gonzales, but—"

Kris's peal of nervous laughter rang out. "Oh, Papa, he thought you were a gentleman come a-courting!" she sang. "This is my father, Allen Gilroy. Tom Harris, Papa."

Tom held out his hand. "Guess I owe you another apology. Certainly a warmer reception. Happy to meet you, sir."

Kris watched her father take Tom's hand and her heart sank. The handshake was without his usual firm grip, accompanied only by a curt silent nod. It wasn't his nature to be silent and she knew the what's-going-on-here outburst wouldn't be long in coming.

Her first instinct was to protect Tom, and it was with some relief that she spotted the golf bag. "You were on your way to the club?"

"Yes—almost forgot." Tom glanced at his watch. "I'd better call Ted and cancel."

"No, don't. Go on over. Papa and I will have a chance to catch up while I fix dinner, and you'll be back to join us by the time I have it ready."

"Need anything?" he asked.

She shook her head.

"Then I'll see you later, sir," he said, and picked up his golf bag.

Kris, wishing she could be just as nonchalant, watched him leave, then turned to her father. "Let me take your coat, Papa. You can sit in the kitchen while I make dinner, and tell me what's happening at home."

"I'd rather you told me what's going on here." Dr. Gilroy threw his coat on the sofa and loosened his tie as if readying for a fight.

"Here? Something so absolutely wonderful has happened here that… Oh, I can't wait to tell you. Come on back. I think I wrote you about the art fiasco. Well, it wasn't really a fiasco, but…" She'd forced herself not to run, but had finally reached the kitchen. She opened the fridge. "Oh, good. Ginger ale. Just what you like, Papa. Let me get a glass and—"

"Sit down, Christina."

"I'll just get ice. I know you like it cold," she said as the crushed ice tumbled out. "There. Would you like a straw or—"

He snatched the glass and slammed it onto the table. "Sit down!"

She sank into a chair, staring at the glass. It hadn't broken, but… "Goodness, Papa, there's no need to—"

"Stop babbling and look at me!"

She looked up at him, as anxious as when she'd been a child confronted by him for some small misdeed.

"Who's the bum?"

"B—bum?"

"The lazy good-for-nothing who's loaded himself on you?"

"You mean…Tom?" Her face burned with indignation. *He's talking about Tom.* "He's not a bum and he hasn't loaded himself on me!"

"He seems quite at home at *your* place or lazing around on the golf course while you're off earning a living."

She drew a deep breath. She'd expected this for herself. But Tom? "Oh, Papa, you've got things all wrong."

"This *is* your place?"

"Yes, but—"

"He obviously lives here, too."

"Yes, we both do. We bought it together."

This disclosure seemed to shake him. He sank into the chair across from her, and for the moment he was speechless.

"It's like I told you, Papa. Rentals are outrageous, and no way could I buy into a decent place with what Aunt Freda left. So I…well, I joined with Tom and—"

"Kept the details from us." He sat up. "An evasion is still a lie, Christina."

She sighed. "I'm sorry. I…knew you'd worry."

"You knew we'd disapprove."

"You wouldn't if you knew Tom!"

"I thought I knew you, Christina." His smile was rueful and a little sad. "I was all set to defend my innocent girl from a free-loading bum who was taking advantage of her kind, loving nature to—"

"Papa, it's not like that!"

"I know." He shook his head. "When I sent you to Freda it never occurred to me that you might adopt her foolish ways."

Foolish? No, joyful! *That* was Freda's way. "I…don't think her ways were foolish."

He lifted his hand. Let it fall. "Then I'm helpless. How can I defend you against yourself? If you've lost the self-respect, the Christian conduct and moral codes I believed we'd instilled in you—"

"Oh, please!" She found herself growing angry. "This has nothing to do with moral codes."

"Do you deny that you're sleeping with this man?"

"No, I don't. Nor do I deny that I'm happier than I've ever been in my entire life."

"As Freda was for a minute. Until he left her high and dry, and she was like a broken reed for the rest of her life."

That wasn't true, Kris thought. Even Freda's memories of the man who'd left her had been joyful. She kept us laughing about Gus and his Basin Blues Boys, the hard times as well as the good ones.

"And Freda's just one of many. People bring me their burdens, Christina. I've seen it happen over and over again. Many a woman goes into this kind of relationship—like Freda did—thinking marriage will come. It doesn't, Christina. It's an old adage, but it still holds true—no man buys a cow when he's getting the milk for free."

That did it! Kris stood and looked down at her father, breathing hard, talking fast. "I'm not a cow and I'm not for sale." She took a deep breath. "This is a give-and-take situation, Papa. For your information, I'm getting more than I'm giving. And it's not about sex. It…it's like Tom has set me free. I love children, but I hated teaching, hated being trapped in a classroom. I love working with Tom, love meeting all kinds of people, dealing with all kinds of problems. It's exciting to watch Tom show people how to bargain with what they have for something they want. Often he has to point out what they actually have." She slowed a bit, let a smile touch her lips.

"He did that for me, Papa. My painting. I'd been dabbling all my life. But it was Tom who made me feel like a real artist, Tom who made me know I had something of value to offer. It's...well, it's like he showed me I could do and be whatever I want." She caught her breath, jolted by the fierce pounding of her heart as it flooded with love. "He...he does that for people, my Tom. He's a wonderful human being, Papa."

CHAPTER TWENTY-SIX

ALLEN GILROY TRIED to swallow the lump in his throat. Watching his daughter, listening to her, face flushed, eyes bright… She'd never looked like this, talked like this, about Ed Simmons who adored her.

But this man… For God's sake, how could she get so involved with this— *Who is he?* "How long have you known this man, Christina?"

"Forever, it seems." Her voice was dreamy, her eyes misty.

"I mean how, where and when did you meet him?"

"Actually, it was soon after I got here," she said, returning to her chair. "At a coffee shop. Jill introduced us."

"Jill?"

"My friend. I told you about her. We met in the flea market and she got me my first job here. I like Jill. We clicked right away. Tom and Jill and I would get together with Aunt Freda, who was doing pretty well for a while. She'd play the piano and we'd sing and dance and have a ball. Aunt Freda loved Tom. He'd bring her the egg rolls she liked from a Chinese place near his office, and—"

"Freda," Allen snorted. That was just like her. Rabble-rousers picked up at flea markets and bars. What on earth had possessed him to turn his daughter loose with his loony aunt! He should've gone himself and brought poor Freda home. And why in God's name hadn't he checked on Christina before now!

Better late than never. He cleared his throat.

"I…ran into John Meadows just before I left. He's Assistant Superintendent now. He asked about you, wanted to know when you'd be coming back, said there'd always be a place for you. But you shouldn't stay away too long, Christina."

Her smile was rueful and a little sad. "You didn't hear a word I said, did you, Papa?"

"Indeed I did. You…" He tried to remember. Between raving about that man, hadn't she said something about teaching? About not wanting to do it anymore? "You wouldn't have to teach," he assured her. "You'd be at home, free to do whatever you pleased. And it would be so good to have you with us. Your mother would be so happy and I—"

"I don't *want* to come home! I… Oh, Papa, don't look like that." She rushed around the table and cupped his face in her hands. "I love you and Mom, and I'll come home to visit… often. But I want to stay here."

He stood and put his arms around her. "Your place, baby, is in Piney Woods where we can look after you."

She put both her hands on his chest, and looked up at him. "I'm not a baby, Papa. I'm twenty-six years old, and you prepared me to look after myself. This is an exciting city and I'm happy here. I'm earning my way and I love my work."

"Your work?" he sneered, unable to keep the fury from his voice. "Or that man you're working with?"

She stepped back. "All right. Perhaps I do love the man, as well. And his name is Tom, Papa."

"Does he love you?"

"I…don't know. I think he's fond of me."

"Fond enough to marry you?"

"I doubt that. Marriage isn't his style."

"It's the Gilroy style. Perhaps I should inform him."

"Don't you—" She broke off and he saw her throat tighten as if in restraint. Her voice was low and quite calm as she said, "I'd rather you didn't, Papa."

"Somebody needs to tell him. Somebody needs to take care of you."

"I told you. I'm quite capable of taking care of myself."

"Doesn't look like it. Living in this unstable, not to mention immoral, situation."

Again the rueful smile touched her lips. "I know it seems that way to you. And…to be truthful, Tom and I have been through some rough times and I'm sure there'll be others. Nothing is perfect. But at this moment, in this situation, I'm happier than I've ever been in my life." She hesitated, swallowed. "I don't think I could forgive you if you ruined that."

"Christina—"

"Please, Papa. Let's not talk about me anymore." Her arms were around him, her head on his shoulder. "I'm sorry this makes you unhappy, but I'm glad you know. I hated deceiving you."

"Still… Nothing's resolved. We need to thrash—"

She put a finger to his lips. "Not now. Tom will be here soon and I need to start making the lasagna. Tell me about Mom and Miss Lizzie and… Oh, Mom wrote that Ed is planning to run for Congress. Is that true?"

"Yes, he is. And he may have a good chance. That boy's going places, Christina." The mention of Ed Simmons brought him to his senses. He didn't want to alienate his daughter. "Get on with your cooking and I'll tell you about Ed," he said, releasing her. If she knew how big a man Ed had become in Woods County… Allen realized he should be dealing with *her*, not the bum whose style wasn't marriage.

Come to think of it, that was a relief. He didn't want her, married or not, living with this bum in San Francisco. He watched her pulling out pots and pans, and saw her in Piney Woods, fixing dinner for Ed Simmons and a passel of his grandchildren. If he could persuade her to come home for a while, Ed could easily outshine this upstart.

The rest of the evening went well. In fact there was no

chance for things to get awkward. The bum brought his golf buddy back with him, a cheerful freckled redhead named Ted who declared, "I heard Kris was making lasagna and I wasn't about to miss that."

It turned out that Ted worked with Tom, and most of the table talk focused on business. Gilroy was glad to sit back and listen. Christina hadn't put a name to the bum's business, and he'd wondered what it was.

He almost choked on his wine when he heard. Lobbyist! That was the shadiest business going. And Christina was participating? Dammit! He'd get her home, come hell or high water.

It was in the hotel the next morning as he sat listening to the public relations lady from the ecumenical council that it came to him.

How did that saying go? Something about if all you had were lemons, make lemonade.

He smiled. Remembered the conversation about a campaign the bum was handling—Greenstone, Brownstone, or...

Not important.

The point is I have a lemon. Lord, he prayed, *forgive Christina for working with a lobbyist. But...if she has campaign experience, she's just what Ed Simmons needs.*

He had to pitch it right—an old friend in need, and what it would mean to have a black representing Woods County in Washington....

He left the meeting and went directly to the telephone.

"PAPA IS LEAVING tomorrow, and has meetings all day," Kris said. "He wants me to join him at the hotel for a late dinner tonight."

Tom turned to look at her. Papa didn't mean *us,* but... "Sounds good. We'll be working late anyway and can go directly from the office."

Kris's eyes brightened. "You'll go with me? Great. This'll be a good chance for the two of you to get to know each other. Last night was... Well, Ted was there."

Ted wasn't the problem, Tom realized. *I know a cold shoulder when I get it. I can ignore it. But I'm not sure how much Kris can ignore, and if she's left alone with Papa for too long...*

His smile was warm as he greeted Dr. Gilroy that evening. "Good of you to have us, sir. We didn't get a chance to really talk last night." He knew the reverend was too much of a gentleman not to respond in kind.

He was right. Dr. Gilroy's reply was cordial. "Glad you could come. I'm missing the conference banquet, but my daughter is more important."

"How's the conference going?" Tom asked. He really wanted to know. Much of his own work dealt with finding common ground between adversaries. If common ground could be found for the world's various religious adversaries, it would eliminate most of today's battlefields. He wondered if they were making any progress.

"It went very well, very well indeed," Dr. Gilroy said, rather absently. Clearly his mind was on something else. He sounded distracted as he politely inquired, "And you? Get in any golf today?"

Tom said he hadn't had time, and the talk drifted to the weather, entrées on the menu and other pleasantries.

"I can't understand why Mom didn't come with you," Kris said. "What on earth was so important that she couldn't put it aside to visit me?"

"You know she's president of the Women's Auxiliary," her father replied. "And they were hosting a regency conference this weekend. An important one," he said, and suddenly seemed to warm up. He was no longer distracted and his eyes were bright as he went on. "Everybody's gearing up for Ed's campaign, and all the auxiliaries are joining together to raise funds. The main purpose of this weekend meeting is to coordinate their efforts. Need I say more?" he added, laughing. "You know how your mother feels about Ed."

"Indeed I do." Kris joined in the laughter. "He was always

telling me he wished…" She darted a quick glance at Tom and trailed off.

He probably wished Kris loved him as much as her mom did, Tom thought. Seems that goes for Papa too.

"How's the campaign going?" Kris asked.

"It hasn't really taken off yet. And, to tell you the truth, I'm a little worried."

"Why? Yesterday you said he had a good chance."

Dr. Gilroy brushed his fist against his chin and frowned. "Maybe I was quoting Ed. You know how he is once he throws his heart and soul into something. He can only focus on the right outcome. I'm thinking more realistically. We can't base things on the landslide he got when he ran for supervisor. There's lots of blacks in Woods County, and he had the support of many whites, too. But the Congressional seat covers much more territory, and…well, I'm afraid Ed needs more support than he has. Hank Cooper, his opponent, may be an upstart but he's also a wealthy farmer, as are many of his friends. And money is just one of Ed's problems. He's made his mark in the county, but…well, let's face it, Ed's really new at the political game. He just goes along, his head in the clouds, intent on what he feels should be done and how he could make it happen. No idea about how he's going to get there to do it."

Papa's on a roll now, Tom thought, as Dr. Gilroy talked at length about this Ed guy, his diligence and persistence in working through unbelievable difficulties to accomplish miracles, like the Welby Dam for the farmers, and on and on and on.

Tom, bored and hungry, stopped listening and concentrated on his steak. Medium rare and tender. Just the way he liked it. The potato was baked just right, too. He and Kris ought to stop here for dinner more often, he decided as he picked up his glass of wine.

He halted it halfway to his mouth when he heard Dr. Gilroy's hearty "You know Ed's wild about you, Christina. Always has been."

Tom jerked to attention. This put a new slant on things. He wasn't sure he liked it.

"For goodness' sake, Papa. Ed and I were never more than friends."

"Didn't look that way to me. I couldn't make a move in my own house without stumbling over him."

"Well, we did study together quite often. We were classmates. Classmates and friends, that's all. Ages ago, at that," Kris said, and changed the subject. "Listen, Papa, we got a new client today. Well, not exactly a client. She's a representative for the deaf and really just wanted some advice. What's her name, Tom?"

"Dorry Sanders," he answered, knowing Kris was desperately trying to bring him into the conversation, but he couldn't think of another thing to say. Couldn't get his mind off this Ed guy. What was Papa up to?

Kris was still trying. She talked rapidly, turning first to one man, then the other. "Somebody directed her to Tom because, of course, everybody knows Tom's the expert," she said. "You must've helped her, Tom. She was sure grinning when she left. What did you say to her?"

"Just routine stuff. She's new at this and just needed some pointers."

"Which is what Ed Simmons needs," Dr. Gilroy broke in as if this was the break he was waiting for. "And that reminds me. Weren't you talking about some political campaign last night? One that you're handling?" For the first time that night, he spoke directly to Tom.

Tom only nodded, but he was alert. Papa had found an opening for whatever he was up to.

Kris, looking pleased, answered for him. "Oh, yes. We're working with Dave Bernstein, who's running for the California Senate. Tom doesn't usually handle campaigns, but he's had a lot of experience in that area and Dave's a good friend."

Gilroy turned to her. "And you're involved?"

"My goodness, yes! I like Dave and I've spent a lot of time on his campaign."

"Now that is interesting," her father said. "I've always placed you in the classroom, Christina. Never in a thousand years could I have pictured you in politics, and certainly not in this…this lobbying business, but…" He drew a deep breath. "The Lord moves in mysterious ways, his wonders to perform. He plants his footsteps on the sea, and rides upon the storm!"

Kris seemed puzzled, but she smiled. "I don't think God's the one who got me into this. It was Tom. He thinks I can do anything I put my mind to. I was sure I'd be lost in the lobbying business, but all I had to do was watch Tom. And learn."

"And just in the nick of time," Dr. Gilroy said. "Nothing could be more opportune."

"Opportune?"

Kris might have been puzzled, but Tom wasn't. He caught the drift, and wasn't surprised by Dr. Gilroy's reply. "God has prepared you for Ed's campaign."

"But how… What are you saying, Papa?"

"That this is your opportunity to pass on the things you've learned, Christina. This is just one example of His Divine Order. God always has a plan, and if you follow His guidance…"

He might as well be in the pulpit, Tom mused. Although what he was preaching now wasn't God's will, but his own. He wanted Kris right there in Piney Woods in close proximity to this Ed guy, and he was preaching up a storm to get her there. Tom's mouth tightened as he listened.

When it came to sermons, the Reverend was no piker. With the eloquence and down-to-earth style of a Martin Luther King, he held them both spellbound as he cleverly mixed the Divine with the mundane, turning ordinary happenings into God's plans. Somehow, in the midst of this, he made a point of how Ed had always been there for Christina. When she was in third grade and afraid of the neighbor's bulldog, he'd hauled her on his bike, taking her to and from the schoolhouse every day. He'd taught her to swim. Was a reliable and faithful escort. "Your mother would always let you go, even to a function in Macon, if Ed was with you."

Typical behavior for any guy who had the hots for Kris. How the hell was the Reverend turning it into the heroic actions of a friend who was there for you when you were in desperate need?

"And now it's Ed who needs your expertise," Dr. Gilroy finished.

"Papa, I'm no expert."

"You're the closest we have. We don't have the money to hire a real pro."

"But…"

"And think what it would mean to the folks back home to have a black representative in Congress. Not only that, but a man of Ed's caliber, an honest man who's in it for the good of the people, and has a way of making good things happen. You know what a dynamo Ed is, Christina."

"That's true," Kris said, looking a bit dreamy. "He's a darn good speaker and he's very smart."

"You're right about that. Got you through algebra, didn't he?"

Kris chuckled. "He sure did. I guess I do owe him. If I could help…"

Holy cow! *She's buying it.* Tom stirred in his seat.

Kris turned to him. "What do you think, Tom? Could I really be of any help?"

"Well, you know the ropes."

"Do you think I should go? It might take some time."

"It's up to you."

She turned back to her father. "I'll think about it."

"It's past time for thinking. We need you now."

She sighed. "All right. I want to see Mom anyway. But I can't promise how long I'll stay. And there are a few things I have to complete here. Maybe in a week or so."

"We'll take what we can get. But make it as soon as you can," Dr. Gilroy said. He was beaming. His mission was off to an excellent start.

"DO YOU REALLY THINK I could make a difference, Tom?" Kris asked when they were in the car heading home.

"Of course, honey. You're smarter than you think."

"But there's so much to do here. I'd like to get started on the painting of the Bernstein children. And…you wouldn't miss me?"

"Of course not. I'm going with you."

For a moment she stared, eyes and mouth wide open. "You are?"

"Sure."

"Oh, Tom that's wonderful! But…your business?"

"I have business in Georgia."

"That's right! The power company in Atlanta."

"Exactly. And with this energy crisis at its peak, all the power companies are getting flack. I should take a close look at what's going on." He knew the Georgia company was on the up and up, but that was as good an excuse as any.

"And you can also take a close look at the campaign and what I should be doing. Hallelujah!" she cried, giving him a spontaneous hug.

"Watch it! And fasten your seat belt."

"I can't help it. I feel so much better. I wasn't sure I could handle it."

"Oh, you could handle it, but I'm glad to help out. Ted'll cover the home front. And what with e-mail, telephones and only one day's travel, it's no big deal."

"That's absolutely fantastic! With you there… A real expert. Papa will be so pleased."

Tom doubted Papa would be pleased. *But if he thinks I'm going to leave my girl alone in Piney Woods at the beck and call of him and his wonderful Mr. Ed, Papa had better think again!*

CHAPTER TWENTY-SEVEN

Piney Woods, Georgia
Two weeks later

LIZZIE MCMASTER LEFT the Gilroy house early Friday afternoon. "Didn't get the roast you wanted," she told her sister when she reached the house they shared.

Sadie looked up from the pot she was stirring on the stove. "You didn't stop at the market?"

"Scooted right past it when I seen Luella Jenkins."

Sadie grinned. "With her ears wide open for what's what at the Gilroys', huh?"

"You got it. Like I'd tell her." Lizzie settled her plump form in a chair at the table and grunted. "Telephone, telegraph, tell Luella."

"Now, ain't that the God's truth! She a talking piece of plunder."

"And she's still hot after Ed Simmons. She's glad to put it out that Christina's got somebody else, even if she don't know anything about it."

"Well, you can't put it all on Luella. Christina set the whole town talking when she brung that man here with her. Folks say she was living with him in California."

"Folks say. How do folks here know what they're doing way out there?"

"By how they look, Josie Lee says. She's got something

there. I seen them in town and— Oh, tell me this. Is he—
what's his name? Is he white or just a light-skinned one of us?"

"His name's Tom Harris. I told you that. And I don't know
what color he is.'"'

"Gotta be white with them blue eyes."

"Half them Winstons up on the hill got blue eyes, and they's
as black as us. Sadie, that soup sure smells good. Ain't it time
for a snack?"

"Guess it is." Sadie assembled spoons, napkins and a plate
of corn bread on the table, but she stuck to the subject. "The
way folks are mixing it up these days, guess it don't matter
what color he is."

"Don't matter to me," Lizzie said. "I like him. He ain't a bit
uppity. The other day when I was getting ready to hose off the
porch, he come right out and help me move every one of them
chairs."

"I see why you like him." Sadie chuckled as she filled two
bowls with the savory soup and joined Lizzie at the table. "But
you ain't got no say. What's her pa think?"

"Oh, he never seen nobody but Ed Simmons for Christina.
And you know the Reverend. What he want gets to be the will
of God."

"What about the missus?"

"She just want everybody happy. And she see stars in her
daughter's eyes. She a little anxious, though. I can tell. But
she's nice to him like she is to everybody, and she's just waiting and watching."

"Everybody's watching. I feel kinda sorry for the poor fellow."

"Him? He don't even know they're watching. Or don't care.
He just goes along doing what he came here to do."

"Which is?"

"The campaign. I told you the Reverend went out west and
got Christina to come home and help Ed. Tell you the truth, I
think he got the surprise of his life when this Harris guy showed
up with her. He some kinda specialist in politics."

"So how come he ain't staying at Ed's house? Or at the inn near Ed's office?"

Lizzie laughed. "Guess that was Christina's doing. Just breezed in, taking it for granted that Mr. Harris would occupy the guest room. So that's where he is. It'd be kinda awkward if they said he's got to go someplace else."

"Yeh." Sadie shook her head. That Christina! She always were a flighty one."

"She ain't flighty!" Lizzie sat up. Nobody, not even Sadie, was gonna badmouth Christina to her. "And it's good she got some gumption. Else she'd never take a step that pa of hers didn't tell her to take."

"Guess you're right 'bout that. And maybe her pa likes them under his nose so he can see what goes on."

"Nothin' goin' on at the Gilroy house." Lizzie's throaty laugh rang out. "Not with two bedrooms between them. And the Reverend's a light sleeper."

"I see what you mean."

"Yeh. They musta been glad for that overnight in Atlanta."

"Atlanta?"

"Like I told you. He got some business there and she went with him. And then she took off from there for San Francisco. To finish some painting. She's doing portraits."

"Lord, that Christina! Don't tell me all that doodling she used to do is paying off."

"Paying pretty good from what I hear."

"So good she gone off and left that man here by his self?"

"Oh, he ain't by his self. He's closeted with her pa and Ed Simmons, doing what he come here to do. You know the Reverend's the power behind Ed's campaign. What he calls the strategy is goin' on at the Gilroy house. The missus keeps me running to his office with coffee and snacks and I hear them talking—mostly this Harris guy telling them what to do. And they listen."

"That don't sound like the Reverend," Sadie said. "He's the one does the talking. Don't never listen."

"He listens to Tom Harris. Maybe 'cause that boy got a easy smooth way, not arguing or nothing, and he always start out like he agrees. The Reverend says something, and he comes back like 'That's a good point, sir. How do you think it would affect this or that?' And before you know it, he comes up with a lotta reasons why they ought to do it his way 'stead of what the Reverend said. And he turns it around like it's what the Reverend wanted in the first place."

"Guess the Reverend's beginning to like him now."

"Can't tell about that." Lizzie shrugged. "Just 'cause he's buying what the man say don't say he buy the man. Not for his precious daughter."

TOM CLICKED OFF his cell phone reluctantly. Talking with Kris wasn't enough, but it was better than nothing. How the hell had this happened anyway? He'd come here to hold on to her. And now... He was here and she was back in California.

Still, he was glad she was doing the portraits. Claire wanted them finished in time for Dave's birthday. He smiled. Nothing would please Dave more than portraits of Claire and the children.

Kris sounded as if she were having fun doing them. He'd known she and Claire would hit it off, but he hadn't realized Kris liked kids so much. When she talked about them, what Debbie did or Brandon said, he could almost see her dimples and her bubbly smile. She was having a ball with them. And Jill was back with her new husband.

Everybody's there except me.

But it looked as if Simmons had a chance, and he wanted to stick around a bit longer, tighten up a few things. Also there was that new contract he'd just picked up in Atlanta.

But...well, hell, he didn't like being without Kris.

Anyway, it would only be two more days. He supposed he could stand it that long.

He stepped off the porch into the yard and took a deep

breath. It was about an hour's drive to Macon, Ed had told him, and they were due there at noon. He glanced at his watch. Ten, maybe twenty minutes before Simmons would show.

He didn't mind the wait. The recent summer rain, unheard of in San Francisco, had cleared the air and it smelled so good. He could just stand here and breathe.

He breathed in the sweet fragrance of Annie Gilroy's nearby flower bed, the pungent odor of ripening grapes from the distant vineyard and a variety of other odors, including manure from the pasture across the road.

He was almost sorry to see Ed's Lincoln roll up the drive. The air would be different on the busy highway. He scanned his surroundings and wondered—how long before this abundant good earth would also be covered in concrete?

"Sorry I'm a bit late," Ed said when Tom slid into the passenger seat. "Been waiting long?"

"Not long enough."

"Oh?" Ed looked puzzled.

"I was enjoying your fresh country air," Tom said, and smiled. He hadn't expected to enjoy being here.

"Refreshing, isn't it?" Ed nodded toward the house. "Reverend Gilroy's not coming?"

"Nope. Something at the church, and Mrs. Gilroy's off to a women's function. I'm all you have today."

"All I need. Still can't believe I'm getting your know-how for free, thank you very much!"

"Don't thank me. Thank Kris."

"Oh, I do. Every day. Don't know where she found you, but I'm glad she did."

"Glad somebody's glad," Tom grunted.

Ed shot him a quick glance. "Problems?"

"Yeah. Papa."

Ed laughed. "Oh, I wouldn't worry about Papa. Christina's in charge of her own heart and mind," Ed murmured, dismissing her and launching into what was on his own mind. "Now, before we get there, I'd better give you a rundown on the Rotary membership."

Tom was still thinking about Kris. What exactly was in her heart and mind? He knew she loved her papa. Was she really not influenced by—

"So what would you consider the best approach?" Ed asked.

Damn! He'd forgotten all about Ed. "Let me think. Run that by me again."

This time he listened. He was in Ed's corner. Another surprise. He hadn't expected to like the guy. But he did. The man was smart, straightforward and much like Dave in his thinking. More important, he had no romantic feelings for Kris, seeing her more as a troublesome sister.

Yep, Ed would be a bonus in Congress and Tom planned to make every effort to get him there.

At the meeting, he was pleased to find Ed a well-liked and well-respected Rotary member. "These are the local movers and shakers, and I think they're in your camp," he told Ed when they left the meeting. "Regardless of party affiliation, almost everyone, in one way or another, is tied to commercial farming. If you stick to your issues, you've got 'em."

"That's encouraging, coming from you. Let's hope you're right," Ed said. "Now, do you have errands in the city or are you ready for the backwoods?"

"More than ready. Let's go."

Ed grinned. "Getting addicted to our little town, are you?"

"Guess so," Tom mused. "Something restful about being there. Like moving back in time."

Ed smiled. "No such luck! Just a momentary retreat from the big-city bustle. Which is why I still live in Piney Woods although the bulk of my business is in Macon."

"And why I envy you," Tom said.

When Ed turned off the freeway onto the old Piney River Road, Tom looked at the so-called river. "Looks more like a puddle to me."

"Watch your mouth! It's deep enough to swim in. And there're fish and— Holy cow! That's the Major." He brought the car to a screeching halt. "How the hell did he get way out here?" he muttered as he sprang from the car.

Tom had also spotted the man on the riverbank. Walking… No, by God, stumbling like he didn't know where he was going. One slip and…the puddle was deep enough to drown in. Tom got out of the car and raced behind Ed.

The man fell to his knees, and Tom reached down to help Ed lift him up. This was no river bum, he thought, noting the fine leather of the boots that had slipped on the riverbank. He was an old man, but, once up, stood quite erect. He pushed back his baseball cap, fingered strands of thinning gray hair and focused glazed blue eyes on Ed in puzzled speculation. "Sam? Sam?"

"I'm Ed, Major. Sam's boy. Good to see you, sir," Ed said as if they'd met in the middle of town instead of on a remote and rather deserted riverbank. "I'm going out your way," he added, taking his arm. "Let me give you a lift home."

The man held back. "Hank," he muttered. "Can't find…"

"Hank's not here. Come along. We'll find him," Ed said.

The man lapsed into silence and didn't seem to notice Tom, who took his other arm. They propelled him forward and settled him in the backseat of the car.

"Alzheimer's," Ed explained as he once again took the wheel. "That's Hank's grandpa. Been looking after Hank since his father died in Korea and his mother soon after. Now Hank's looking after him and having one hell of a time. The Major wanders."

"Major?"

"World War Two. Don't know why the title stuck, but he's been Major Cooper all my life."

Tom pondered the name. Cooper. Hank Cooper, Ed's opponent? He started to comment when Ed touched the horn and brought the car to a stop. A sleek sports car about to speed past also stopped.

Ed rolled down his window and called to the driver. "Right here, Hank. I've got him."

A tall robust man in tennis shorts jumped from the other car. "Can't turn my back for one minute. Just ran over to the club for a short match," he said as he started to open the door to the backseat.

"Hold it a minute, Hank," Ed said. "I'd like you to meet my friend, Tom Harris."

"Friend, my eye!" Hank gave Tom an appraising look and grinned. "So you're the high-powered consultant from California!"

"I've been called worse," Tom said, returning the grin. "Good afternoon, Mr. Cooper, glad to meet you."

"Mighty glad to meet you, too. But if you've come all the way out here to give Ed a boost, I'm sorry to tell you you're wasting your time. When this dude outruns me they'll be serving ice water in hell."

"Not a bad idea," Tom said. "Might start a new trend."

More good-natured wisecracks flew between them as Hank tried to coax his grandfather out of the car. The Major had settled back comfortably and seemed about to take a nap.

"He sleeps most of the time. Beats me how he knows whenever I'm gone," Hank muttered. "Got a guy on the watch, too. Come on, Gramps. Ida's got dinner ready. Peach cobbler."

That seemed to tempt the old man and he allowed Hank to help him out.

"Thanks, Ed," Hank said. "I owe you one."

"I'll collect at the polls," Ed responded, and both men laughed.

Politics were different in Piney Woods, Tom thought. Friendlier.

At the house, Miss Lizzie opened the door. "Come on in, boy. You're just in time. I just took the dasher out."

Tom smiled, liking the "boy" better than Tom, which he'd asked her to call him. It was spoken with affection, and anything was better than the cumbersome Mister Harris. Had he ever been addressed as Mr. Harris in his entire life? But… "What's a dasher?" he asked.

"That thingamajig in the middle. It…" She stopped and looked at him. "Ain't you never had homemade ice cream?"

"Never."

"Bless my soul." Lizzie shook her head. Well, you're in for a big surprise. I'll dish you up a bowl 'fore I pack it. You need some meat on them skinny bones."

He smiled. Nobody had ever cared whether he had meat on his bones. "You're a very special woman, Miss Lizzie."

"Oh, go 'long with you! Come on back here with the Reverend. He's having a sample, too."

He followed her into the big old-fashioned kitchen that in two short weeks had become so familiar—the nickel-plated range, the cuckoo clock, the late-afternoon sun glowing against the geraniums spilling across the windowsill. Comforting. As if the room reached out to enclose him in a warm embrace.

That warmth wasn't diminished by the presence of Dr. Gilroy. In fact he looked up with a welcoming smile. "So you're back? How did the afternoon go with Ed and the Rotary?"

"Very well indeed," he said and began a detailed account of Ed's positive reception. "Ed has a way of drawing people to him, and when he talked about the issues…" He paused. He had dipped his spoon into the bowl Lizzie set before him and could think of nothing but the taste—cool, creamy and delicious; melting on his tongue, the soft crunch of fresh fruit, the pungent fragrance of ripe peaches tickling his nostrils. "I've had peach ice cream," he exclaimed. "But it never tasted like this."

"Elbertas." Gilroy actually grinned as he pushed back his empty bowl. "Our best peaches, and my favorite. I schedule my out-of-town meetings so I'm here during Elberta season."

Here, Tom thought…for peaches, for peace and quiet, and summertime smells. "You're lucky to have a place to come back to," Tom mused, not realizing he'd spoken aloud.

Gilroy gave him a keen look. "Don't you?"

"What?"

"Have a place to come back to."

"Oh." Tom's mouth twisted. "Not really. Seems I was always moving on."

"Your…parents?"

"Never knew my father. He died before I was born. But yes, I had a very loving mother." Too loving, he thought, toward her many lovers, as well as him. "She was young. More like a child herself." He managed a rueful smile. "A Haight Ashbury flower child."

"You mean that San Francisco district where—"

"Guess you've heard of it," Tom said, seeing the shock on the older man's face. "Yes. That's where we lived most of the time. But never in the same place."

"Your mother… Where—what happened to her?"

"Died when I was fifteen."

"There was no other relative?"

"Oh, yes. An uncle. You might've seen him. Bob Harris, the sports commentator. Bob provided the stability in my life. His apartment did, anyway." Bare. Lonely. "He was away most of the time."

Dr. Gilroy's eyes fastened on the man before him.

Oh, he'd studied him before. Had seen a bum, sponging on his daughter. A dashing lecher who'd lured his innocent Christina into immorality.

Be fair! he told himself. He had to admit he'd also seen a hardworking, astute, knowledgeable young man. A man who gave…Was giving of his talents.

Now… Strange. It was as if he'd looked into the eyes of a lost and lonely boy.

Tom felt uncomfortable under the penetrating gaze. He already knew how he rated with Papa. He stood and pushed back his chair. "Better get going. I told Ed I'd be over," he said and moved quickly toward the door.

Once there, he hesitated. Turned back. He ought to… There'd be some kind of protocol here. He should ask her father's permission.

Hell, he hadn't even asked Kris's permission yet. And, face it, no way was he gonna get Papa's blessing.

Only right to warn him.

He drew a deep breath. "There's something you should know," he said. "I'm going to marry your daughter—if she'll have me."

Gilroy opened his mouth to speak, but Tom had disappeared. Just as well. He wasn't sure what he meant to say. He looked at Lizzie, an interested witness to the whole discussion.

Lizzie smiled. "She'll have him."

EPILOGUE

KRIS, ENGULFED IN the billowing clouds of tulle and lace that comprised her mother's old wedding gown, looked up and smiled.

I know you're here, Aunt Freda, waiting to see the holy matrimony stamp on what you started. You and Jill.

Don't you wonder how she still manages to look sleek and not at all four months pregnant in that deep-rose, matron-of-honor gown? She'll probably be an efficient mother, too. See how she's keeping those frisky flower girls under control?

Those two? Don't they make a beautiful contrast? Debbie's blond hair and dancing blue eyes next to Leelee's serious dark eyes and beautiful black skin that seems to glow against the pale pink dress. I'm going to sketch them together as soon as we get back from the honeymoon. Tom chose Leelee, Miss Lizzie's granddaughter, because he absolutely loves Miss Lizzie, and said he had to have something of hers in his wedding. I fell in love with Debbie, the Bernsteins' daughter, when I sketched the family for their portrait. Evidently she loves me, too, because she insisted on being in my wedding, just as she fetched and carried for me and yes, dabbled with my paints. I think we may have a budding artist.

Like me? Not quite famous, but in demand nonetheless. Maybe because I choose whose portrait I'll do and I don't do many.

Painting's important to me, but I feel as if my real work is with Tom. I love to watch him out there getting people together and getting things done.

I got a little nervous when he suggested we buy the old Winston farm near Papa's place and build our house on the hill beside that cedar tree. For space and for closeness, he said. It took me some time to figure out that he meant space for our children to romp and climb trees, and a closeness of family and friends he'd never before experienced.

Back to the glass cage of Piney Woods, Georgia, I thought! But, thank goodness, he's still an international lobbyist as well as the gentleman farmer he's now trying to be. I'm glad we're keeping the office and condo in California. But I must confess I'm beginning to enjoy the comfort of this tight circle of family and friends almost as much as the excitement of a wider, more complex world.

Doesn't Papa look suave in that white tuxedo? And quite calm as he prepares to take me down the aisle to the altar, where Tom will be waiting, then turn around and marry us. A mystery how he'll manage everything, but he insisted he'd do the whole thing.

And that's a turnabout since the day he first met Tom.

A real turnabout altogether since last June.

Kris smiled...wondering. "It was Mom who insisted on a June wedding, Aunt Freda, but you must've had a hand in it. Did you plan that this June I'd be—"

"Christina, honey, take your eyes off the ceiling and turn this way." Annie Gilroy made a last adjustment to the short wedding veil and kissed her daughter. "Be happy. I love you."

"I love you, too." Kris returned the kiss and watched her mother take Ed's arm to be escorted down the aisle. Ed had a hand in it, too, she told her Aunt Freda.

If he hadn't been running for Congress, then Tom and I wouldn't have come to help out. And Tom wouldn't have found that he loved Piney Woods almost, he said, as much as he loves me. And Ed and Dave Bernstein would never have banded together as they have. Or maybe they would have— both being, as Tom says, good statesmen. They're real buddies in Congress. And Dave's invited Ed to bunk at their place when the House is in session. The Bernsteins bought a place right next to Scott's family home, where he and Jill have settled. Scott says his mother always wanted to have the two estates joined and he likes being right next to his sister's family. I'm glad Tom has clients in Washington so we often have an excuse to visit both families.

Oh, it's time. It's beginning.

Josie Lee Turner's soprano echoed from the chapel. "Ah, sweet mystery of life, at last I've found you. At last I know the secret of it all."

It really is a mystery how we all got together. All from different places, all seeking something different....

She, however, was only thinking of Tom, and didn't even hear the lilting pronouncement that rang out loud and clear. "'Tis love and love alone the world is seeking...."

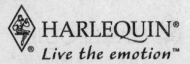

Into Thin Air
by Elizabeth Ashtree
(Superromance #1264)

Late one night Captain Kelsey Dixon watches in horror as a man falls thirty feet to the concrete floor of the supply warehouse at Fort Belvoir. She sees the blood pooling under his skull just before she's hit from behind, but when she awakens there's no body, no blood, no evidence. Now she has to convince Major Julian Fordham of the Criminal Investigations Division that she's telling the truth. He's her only hope of uncovering the facts. The trouble is he's also the one man she can't afford to get close to—again.

Available in March 2005 wherever Harlequin books are sold.

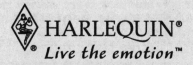

HARLEQUIN®
Live the emotion™

HARLEQUIN *Super*ROMANCE®

Receive a FREE hardcover book from HARLEQUIN SUPERROMANCE in February!

Harlequin Superromance invites you to celebrate
Black History Month with this exclusive offer
valid only in this Harlequin Superromance.

To receive your FREE HARDCOVER BOOK
No Crystal Stair, written by Eva Rutland,
send us the proof of purchase and the
completed order form below. Mail with
$2.00 for postage and handling to:

In the U.S.:	In Canada:
Harlequin Books	Harlequin Books
P.O. Box 9057	P.O. Box 622
Buffalo, NY	Fort Erie, Ontario
14269-9057	L2A 5X3

Name (PLEASE PRINT)

Address   Apt. #

City   State/Prov.   Zip/Postal Code

098 KKC DXJA

To receive your FREE HARDCOVER book (retail value $12.95 U.S./$15.95 CAN.)
complete the above form. Mail it to us with the proof of purchase (found only in
this Superromance book) in the right-hand corner of this page. Requests must be
postmarked no later than April 30, 2005. Please enclose **$2.00** (make check payable
to Harlequin Books) for shipping and handling, and allow 4–6 weeks for delivery.
New York State residents must add applicable sales tax on shipping and handling
charge, and Canadian residents please add
7% GST. Offer valid in Canada and the U.S.
only, while quantities last. Offer limited to one
per household.
© 2004 Harlequin Enterprises Limited

HARLEQUIN *Super*ROMANCE®

FREE HARDCOVER BOOK
One Proof of Purchase

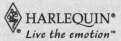

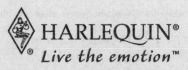